HALLOWEEN SLAUGHTER

SERGIO GOMEZ

Copyright © 2022 Sergio Gomez

All rights reserved. No part of this publication may be reproduced, distributed, or transmitted in any form or by any means, including photocopying, recording, or other electronic or mechanical methods, without the prior written permission of the publisher, except in the case of brief quotations embodied in critical reviews and certain other noncommercial uses permitted by copyright law.

This is a work of fiction. Names, characters, places, and incidents either are the product of the author's imagination or are used fictitiously. Any resemblance to actual persons, living or dead, events, or locales is entirely coincidental.

Cover Design: Teddi Black
Interior Design: Megan McCullough

ISBN:

For Iskender

You always wanted to read one of my books but never got the chance. So, this one is for you. Rest in peace, brother.

*"Lookin' at the devil and the angel on my shoulder
Will I die tonight?
I don't know, is it over?"*

—Juice Wrld

CONTENTS

PART I: NECK OF THE WOODS	1
PART II: HILLTOWN	43
PART III: A NEW BEGINNING	67
PART IV: WATCHING	85
PART V: STALKING	133
PART VI: THE SHERIFF	151
PART VII: FROSTY HOLLOW MANOR	177
PART VIII: HALLOWEEN	227
PART IX: SLAUGHTER	269
PART X: AFTERMATH	343
EPILOGUE	409

Neck of the Woods

THE MUSIC PLAYING through the speakers of the gold-metallic Hyundai cut off, replaced by the recognizable ringtone of an iPhone. Diana Santos glanced over at the hands-free holder centered in the middle of the dashboard. Incoming call from Mom, the screen read.

She reached over and tapped the green button to pick up the call.

"Hey, Mom."

"Hey, about time you answer." Her mom teased. "Been calling and texting you all morning."

Diana could hear pots and pans clattering around on the other side of the line. Further in the background, she could hear one of her brothers shouting over a video game. Gunfire and explosions were amplified by the car speakers, making them more jarring to listen to.

"Eduardo! Will you turn that down?" her mom hollered. "I'm on the phone with Diana."

"I saw your calls and texts, Mom. I was just busy getting ready for the interview and forgot to get back to you. Sorry."

"You had me a little worried."

"Yeah, I figured." Diana said, shaking her head, glad they weren't Facetiming.

"You know how I am, always worrying. What is it you call me?" Miriam Santos let out a small chuckle. "A worry-head?"

"Yup. That's you."

"Sure is. Anyway, how long until you get to the town?"

Diana glanced over at the clock on the radio. "About forty-minutes."

Thank God. She thought. She'd been driving for almost two hours and the muscles in her legs were starting to cramp.

"Did you have breakfast this morning?"

"I did," Diana said, trying her hardest to not sound pestered by her mother's questions.

"More than just a smoothie?"

"More than just a smoothie," she said, trying to hide a sigh.

"Well, what did you have?"

No matter how old she got, her mother would always worry about her diet. "Two pieces of toast with peanut butter and honey. Oh—*and* a smoothie."

"You're not lying to me, are you Diana?"

"No," Diana said, rolling her eyes again.

But she was. And Diana was positive her mother knew she was, too. She actually hadn't had anything to eat. She'd been too nervous about today to have much of an appetite. Butterflies were taking up all the available space in her stomach.

She was driving the three hours north from where she lived for a job interview. It was her first since graduating college—at least, the first that wasn't a thinly veiled pyramid scheme or a door-to-door sales job, anyway.

For the last year, Diana had been working at a local pub in the college town where she lived to pay her bills, the whole time waiting for a call back from one of the many applications she'd sent out.

Two weeks ago, she finally heard back from the Hilltown Wildlife Clinic. She'd never heard of this place before, but a quick Google search told her that Hilltown was a small town, easy to get to but still well off the beaten track.

There wasn't much to do in the area from what she'd seen. There were some lakes in the surrounding area, a few parks, and some farms. Mostly, though, it was woods up there. It would be quite the change of pace from the town she lived in now, where the big college campus was within walking distance and nightlife was aplenty.

But she would make do with it, because getting this job would put her closer to her dream of one day running her own wildlife clinic.

Even knowing all that, her mother's biggest concern as she headed up to this life-altering job interview, was what her daughter had for breakfast.

Typical, Diana thought.

An explosion in the background of the phone call snapped her out of her thoughts.

"Ed! What did I tell you? Turn that down! I'm on the phone!" her mother yelled.

"What's he doing home, anyway?" Diana asked as she negotiated a curve in the road. "Is he faking sick again?"

"I don't think he's faking," her mother said.

"Did you just get him a new video game?" The question prompted a pause in the conversation, making Diana laugh. "You did, didn't you?"

Her youngest brother had been pulling this on their mother for years. A few days after he convinced her to get him a new video game, he would conveniently get sick.

"Yeah, but it's not that," her mother sighed. "I mean, I don't think."

"Yeah, sure," Diana replied.

"What's with your attitude?" her mother asked, a tinge of agitation in her tone.

"What attitude? What are you talking about?"

"All this sighing and now 'yeah, sure.' What? Do you not want to talk to me?"

"I do, Mom. Of course I do. It's just…" Diana felt herself getting defensive. "You know. It's just annoying when you treat me like a child."

"Treat you like a child? I'm just asking if you had breakfast."

"Yeah, and I've got other things on my mind besides your nosy questions."

"Nosy?" Her mother laughed, except there was no humor in it. "I'm your mother, I'm supposed to worry about you. Ugh. You know, what? Forget it. Just call me when you're not busy, then."

Diana felt a wave of guilt go through her. Maybe she was being unfair.

"I will," she responded in a small voice.

"I gotta go anyway. I need to get Johnny's clothes from the drycleaners for his dance tonight."

"Wait, what? Johnny's going to a dance tonight?"

"Yeah, the Pumpkin Patch Dance. You know the one?"

"Yeah, of course I do."

Diana knew it very well. She'd attended it many times when she was in junior high. It was the dance hosted in the middle school gymnasium. The place would be decorated with pumpkins and bales of hay and autumnal wreaths. All the chaperones dressed up like farmers, and there was a station to get warm apple-cider. At the end of the night there was even a pie-eating contest where the winner got a gift card to Applebee's.

"He's going with his little girlfriend," her mother said, excitedly.

"Johnny has a girlfriend?" Diana was so surprised by that she nearly drifted the car off the edge of the road.

"Yes, he does. He's been seeing her since the end of summer." Diana heard her mother going into the living room, the sounds from the television getting louder momentarily until she started climbing up the stairs. "Anyway, I'll let you go, *mija*. I just wanted to call to wish you luck on your interview."

The conversation felt more natural now. Talking about her other brother, instead of her, had soothed their tempers.

"Okay, Mom. Thanks," Diana said. She had about a million questions she wanted to ask about this girlfriend of Johnny's, but she decided to save them for another time. She had other things on her mind as she got closer and closer to Hilltown.

"I'm going to say one more thing, and you better not get mad at me."

Diana heard the playfulness in her mother's voice and grinned. Being that Diana was the oldest of the siblings, she and her mother had always argued the most. The little disagreement they'd just had was nothing in comparison to the fights in her teen years. Those had been vicious, with both of them raising their voices and either one or both slamming a door.

She knew her mother's playfulness coming out didn't always absolve Diana of the guilt she had after one of their fights, but it made her feel better when she heard it, even now.

"Be safe, okay? I know you're strong and can handle things, but I just need to say it." A pause. "Also, you better not be lying to me about what you had for breakfast."

"I'm not," Diana laughed. "And I will be safe. I promise."

"Okay, honey. Call me when you get the chance. I love you. *Ciao.*"

"Bye, Mom. I love you too."

The call ended. In just a few seconds the iPhone switched back to playing music, but in that small stretch of silence, Diana felt an inexplicable loneliness set in. It stayed with her as she drove deeper and deeper into the isolated regions of Northern Pennsylvania.

2

TIM SQUEEZED THE trigger on the rifle. The gunshot thundered through the woods, scaring some birds from the treetops overhead. Several yards out, the bullet pierced the side of a buck's head, right below one of his antlers. The deer collapsed, legs still twitching, but it was as good as dead.

"Woo! That's how you do it, Chuck!" Tim cheered for himself, relaxing out of his shooting stance.

Next to him, his brother nodded while sipping on a Monster energy drink. Chuck wiped at some of the yellow liquid that dribbled down his long beard and then downed the rest of it. Crushing the can, he threw it behind him into the trees.

The woods were so quiet that the sound of the can hitting a rock on the ground echoed.

Chuck bent down to the backpack by his feet and pulled out a rolled-up tarp.

"Come on," Tim said, slinging the rifle over his shoulder.

The brothers made their way toward the dead buck.

Blood was steadily draining out from the side of the buck's head, but Tim gave it a small kick with the toe of his boot just to make sure the damn thing was dead.

He'd gotten into the habit of doing this after he'd heard a freak story from a someone at the local bar. The guy claimed he'd once shot a deer in the neck and thought it was dead as a doornail, but when he got close to it, the animal got up and gored him before running out into the woods.

The guy had even shown Tim a scar on the side of his body to prove it. It looked a lot like the scar his brother Chuck had where his appendix had been removed, but Tim wasn't a doctor and didn't bother questioning it.

"This is a big son of a gun, huh Chuckie?" Tim said, bending down in front of the buck now that he was sure it was dead. "We gonna be eating good, boy!"

"What's it look like? One eighty or so?" Chuck asked as he finished spreading out the tarp behind the deer.

"Just about," Tim said, grinning as he grabbed the animal by the hindlegs. "On three."

Chuck grabbed the buck's front legs, and then on the count of three they hauled it up and placed it on the tarp. Judging by how heavy it was, he thought his guess on its weight was pretty good.

"Suckers gonna make a whole lotta jerky," Tim idled by as Chuck tied the tarp tight with a tweed rope. "Come on. If we hurry up, we might make it back in time to catch Family Feud."

With that, they headed back through the woods to where their truck was parked.

Twenty minutes later, Diana was still reeling from the revelation of her brother going to a school dance. She hadn't lived at home in five years, and she hadn't been back to visit since last winter. Things changed, of course, but whenever she thought of Johnny, he was still that scrawny kid with glasses that she'd grown up protecting from bullies.

The thought of her brother growing up made her realize how fast time could move when you weren't paying attention to it.

Diana glanced out of the driver's side window and looked at the trees racing by on the side of the highway. Their leaves had changed from the vibrant greens of summer to the warm reds and yellows of autumn. Some of the trees were already mostly bare.

For a second, Diana wondered when exactly *that* change had started.

"*In one mile, stay in the left lane to exit off the highway.*" The GPS's voice brought her out of her reverie.

Diana glanced at the side mirror before merging onto the lane, even though she hadn't seen another car on the highway for a while. The last car, an Outback Subaru with an orange canoe tied to its roof, had gotten off several miles ago.

Up ahead, she saw her exit. The midday sun glinted off the guardrails that would stop someone from running off the sides of the ramp and plummeting into the dense woods below.

Diana had grown up in Quakertown, which most city folk would consider the boonies, but out here was a whole other level of remoteness. The woods seemed to stretch out as far as her eyes could see.

Diana guided the car off the highway, descending the ramp. As the road leveled out and the Hyundai dipped under the shade from the surrounding trees, she couldn't shake the sensation of driving straight into the maws of a gigantic monster.

"*REROUTING... REROUTING...*" The dreaded words played through the car speakers over and over.

The GPS had been guiding her down a series of winding roads through the woods. The roads were bumpy, unpaved, and looked like they were hardly traveled. It'd been a miracle that she only lost service about ten minutes ago.

"*Rerouting... rerouting...*" the mechanical voice continued, seemingly taunting her.

Shit. Diana slammed her fist into the side of the steering wheel in frustration, wondering how things could possibly get worse.

Without warning the Hyundai's engine stuttered. On the dashboard, the needles on all the gauges went to the right, then the left, all in unison. The radio turned off. The light on the Bluetooth device in the cigarette burner winked out.

What the hell?

Diana felt the car losing speed. She hit the brakes and steered the car onto the grass separating the road and the woods. The Hyundai came to a rolling stop.

Grayish white smoke began billowing out from underneath the hood.

Diana took in a deep breath. *Okay. It's just car trouble. Cars can be fixed. This is fine.*

She exhaled, thinking of the time her and her friend got stuck in a strange town during a terrible snowstorm after a party. It had taken them a whole night of shoveling her Hyundai out of the poorly plowed roads and a whole lot of cursing to finally get back home that night. In comparison, this should be easy. All she had to do was call a tow truck to take her to the nearest repair shop.

She glanced over at her phone. There was only one bar of reception, and the letters "LTE" kept blinking off and turning into a spinning wheel. She had service, but it would be spotty at best.

It was better than nothing. And besides, if she walked a bit, she might be able to find a spot with better reception.

But before doing that, she wanted to see the damage. She knew the basics of how a car worked, and she'd done several things herself with the aid of YouTube videos. If she could fix whatever was going on underneath there, it'd save her a whole lot of trouble.

Diana pulled the lever to pop the hood, then got out of the car and propped it up, taking a step back as she got a face full of acrid smoke. Through the haze, she could see the gash in the water pump's hose. It was about two inches long.

The rubber had probably been on the verge of rupturing for a while now—her car was a 2001, after all—but driving down the uneven dirt roads had been the last straw.

If she had duct tape and water, she might've been able to seal it up and get herself to the nearest repair shop. Unfortunately, she was without either.

She let the hood drop, groaning in frustration, and went back into the car to grab her phone from the holder. It only had one bar of service.

Better than nothing.

Diana tapped the Safari icon and entered "nearest towing company" into the search button. She watched the blue bar at the top of the browser fill up ever so slowly, hoping not to get the "connection lost" message.

It felt like a miracle, but Google finally opened. The first result was a place called Harvey's Towing & Junk with an advertised price of eighty dollars for the first tow.

She'd spent more than that on textbooks she never once opened while in college. Eighty dollars to get her out of this was a no-brainer.

Diana hit the call button and waited for the call to connect, keeping her fingers crossed in her other hand.

The phone rang three times before the line was picked up. Diana breathed a sigh of relief when she heard the old man's voice.

"He—llo. Harvey's Towing & Junk—help you?"

The connection was breaking up, threatening to disconnect at any moment.

"Yes, hello? I broke down on the side of the road," Diana said with a sense of urgency. "Could you send someone to tow me to the nearest repair shop?"

"Hello! Are you there?" the old man said, coming in clearer now.

"Hi. Can you hear me?"

"I can hear you better now, yup."

"Okay, great," Diana said, trying to stay composed. "I broke down on the side of the road and need someone to tow me to the nearest repair shop."

"You're breaking—again, but I think you said you need—repair shop?"

"Yes, yes," Diana said in a rush, glad the man could piece together what she was saying. It dawned on her that he was likely used to communicating with people on lines that were breaking up, considering the location.

"Do you know where you are?" he asked.

"No, I don't. I'm not from around here and I haven't seen any street signs. I got off the highway about thirty minutes ago? I was heading toward Hilltown if that helps any?"

"You said—illtown?"

"Hilltown, yes."

"Okay—sorry, I'm—osing you again." The line went silent for a minute. Diana felt her stomach sink. Then, the old man's voice came back. "—what car—are—driving?"

"A 2001 gold Hyundai Elantra," Diana said, speaking fast to get as much information out to the man as possible.

"Is the road you're—paved?"

"Yes." Diana said, looking out into the road, as if she might've seen it wrong before. "It's a paved road. Lots of trees around, if that helps?"

"Okay, little lady, hang tight—send my best guy—find you—"

Then, the beep she'd been dreading started as the call dropped. The line went silent.

Diana moved the phone off her ear and saw there were zero bars of service.

"Fuck."

She took the car keys out of the ignition and slipped them into a different pocket in her jacket as she looked down the stretch of road in both directions.

To her right, about a quarter mile from where she was, the road forked. Both directions led into more woods. She wasn't sure she'd be able to navigate her way to town or back onto the highway without the GPS.

Maybe her car breaking down was a blessing in disguise. At least now someone who knew where they were going would take her to the nearest town.

Feeling a little better about her situation, Diana walked along the grass, keeping her eyes on the phone screen, waiting to see if the reception bar would start to fill up. Once she had at least two bars, she would call the towing company back and ask her how long the wait would be.

After that, she would call her mom to let her know what happened. The Hilltown Wildlife Clinic could wait. There was no way she wouldn't be late for her interview now. And besides, right now what she really wanted was the comfort of her mother.

The irony in that, after her outburst earlier, almost brought out a smile as she continued down the side of the road.

"Slow down, Chuck."

"What?" Chuck said, not understanding his brother's concern.

"I said slow down," Tim repeated. He pointed his thumb to the side of the road, where a young girl was walking by her lonesome up ahead.

"For what—" Chuck stopped when he saw the girl. Behind her was a gold Hyundai

"I wanna take that home with us, too." Tim said, licking his lips. "For a different kind of meal, know what I mean?"

"Aw, no. Come on," Chuck pleaded. "Let's just head home. Watch Family Feud like you said—"

"Shut up," Tim commanded, slapping his brother on the gut. "Shut up and slow down. We're just gonna make sure she don't need help with her car."

Chuck sighed, knowing Tim was lying. Reluctantly, he stepped on the brakes. He outweighed his older brother by at least thirty pounds, but he was scared of Tim. Tim was reckless. Violent. Chuck wasn't a saint himself. He'd slapped around women before and beaten people within an inch of their life, but Tim's brand of recklessness was…different.

Tim was more like their father. He acted on impulses without any regard for consequences. He might get pissed at Chuck for not slowing down and punch Chuck in the face, even if it risked sending them both careening off the road and crashing into a tree.

"Stop next to her car," Tim ordered.

Chuck looked over at him. Tim's brows were furrowed the way they got when he was focused on a goal. He had his sights set on getting this girl. They were way too close to town for Chuck's liking, if she got away from them, she might run to the police station, but there was no way he was going to defy Tim when he was in this kind of mood.

Chuck stopped the truck in the middle of the road, only a few feet away from the Hyundai sitting on the grass. The tires rasping against the pavement alerted the girl of their arrival. She turned around and looked at them with a wary expression.

Chuck glanced over at his brother, and saw his mouth spread into a big smile.

Diana watched the two men climb out of the mud-streaked truck. The passenger, a slim man wearing a full camo outfit, a gaiter around his neck, and a TAPOUT hat on his head was smiling at her, showing off browned teeth.

She couldn't see the driver that well from her angle until he came around to the front of the truck. He had his hands in the pockets of a dirty hoodie and kept his head low.

The two men were the same height, but their builds were almost polar opposites. The passenger was slim and swimming underneath his clothes, while the driver was burly.

"Looks like you got some car troubles here, young lady," the passenger said, walking over to her Hyundai.

Diana judged the distance between herself and her car, realizing she'd walked several yards while trying to get reception. She hadn't noticed it because her focus had been on the phone screen.

"What's the matter? Cat got your tongue?" the passenger said, leaning against her car.

"Sorry," Diana muttered, hoping that being polite would be enough to keep her safe. "Just startled to see someone out here. I haven't seen a car in a while."

"Yeah, we know," the man said, grinning, and looking over at the driver. "People don't really travel up here to this neck of the woods very often."

"Yeah," she responded, kicking herself for saying too much to these assholes.

"Why don't you go ahead and come over here and pop the hood?" the slim man said, standing up straight. "Me and my brother here know a thing or two about cars. We might be able to fix ya up and have you on your way."

"That's okay," Diana said, gulping. "I, uh, called a tow truck to come get me already. I'll just wait for them."

The man glanced over at his brother, standing by the truck with his hands in his pockets.

"You hear that? She called a tow truck." The passenger chuckled. "How long you think till they come out here? An hour, maybe two?"

The driver shrugged.

Diana looked at the burly man. For a second, she thought she saw a flash of discomfort across his face. Things were getting stranger by the minute.

"I called a while ago," Diana said. And then, because the lie sounded weak even to her own ears, she added, "Been waiting for about two hours now."

The slim guy laid his hand flat against the hood of the car, then rapped his knuckles against it. "Really now? Cuz this feels pretty darn hot to me. And there's still smoke comin' out."

Shit. Diana thought. She hadn't thought that one through.

"I understand why yer scared. Really, I do," the slim man said, taking two steps toward her. There was still quite a bit of distance between them, but just the same, it made Diana take a few steps backward. "Two strange guys. A road in the middle of the woods with no cars passing through it? Pretty little thing like you, all alone out here? I get it."

Pretty little thing... The phrase hit Diana's ears like a worm trying to slither into them.

A thought passed through Diana's head. Maybe *they* were lying about how long she'd be out here. The old man hadn't gotten a chance to tell her how long her wait would be before the call had dropped. Shit, for all she knew, the tow truck could be here any second now.

"I'm alright with waiting," Diana said, then decided to drop the nice girl act. "So, you two can kindly fuck off now."

Diana was no stranger to batting away creeps. Being that she was the eldest of her siblings, whenever a weirdo had approached them at the grocery store or parking lot or at the county fair, it had always been her responsibility to fend them off.

This situation was a bit different, though. The stakes were higher.

She gulped, trying not to think about what could happen if things went wrong for her.

"Tell ya what," the slim guy said, laughing. "I'll step away from the car so you can get inside, but then pop the hood open for us and we'll—"

"I said fuck off," she said, trying to sound forceful, but she felt her lip quiver.

The man spat. "Okay, fine."

The slim man smacked his brother on the shoulder and said something to him that was inaudible to Diana. Then, the two of them climbed back into their truck. Much to her chagrin, they didn't drive off. They just sat there, the passenger staring at her through the window. Next to him, the burly man was looking down at his lap like he'd just spotted a new stain on his pants and was trying to figure out what it was.

Diana counted off a few heartbeats, trying to will the two assholes to drive off, but it was no use. They stayed put. Intent on whatever it was they had planned for her.

The worst part was that Diana was prepared for these types of situations. She had a can of pepper spray and a switchblade in her purse, but in her haste to find service she'd left it on the passenger seat.

So close, yet so far away. There was about a ten-yard gap between her and the car. She would have to sprint as hard as she could to get to the door, open it, and close it behind her before either of the two guys could grab her.

That didn't seem possible, even though she'd have an extra second or two with them being inside their truck.

Her only other option would be to run into the woods and hope to run into another car that could help her. Or find her way to Hilltown. Considering she'd been lost before her car crapped out on her, she didn't think that was likely.

There was really only one option, and she couldn't waste any more time.

Diana sprinted toward the car, opting to go for the passenger door. She kept her eyes on the brothers.

They didn't move—at least, not yet.

Using the remote key in her pocket, Diana unlocked the car door as she closed in on the Hyundai. The alarm chirped.

She threw the door open, grabbed her purse, and then jumped inside. In one fluid motion she closed the door and mashed the lock button. She sighed, feeling at least a little better.

Misguided perhaps, but at least she had the purse. She rummaged through it, feeling for the weapons while at the same time keeping her eyes on the truck. She found the can of pepper spray first, then the switchblade, and put them into her pocket.

Then, as she feared would happen, the brothers started getting out of their truck again.

This wasn't over.

No, not even close. If anything, it was just beginning.

Diana watched the slim man head to the back of the pickup. She heard him rummaging through the stuff back there, but the only thing she could see back there was a pair of antlers. They stuck up several inches over the edge of the truck bed. They looked like claws, reaching out for the sky.

The burly man had walked around the vehicle and was standing by the passenger door. Diana wasn't sure if it was how the sunlight was hitting him or what, but the color seemed to have drained out of his face. He stood there, hands in the pockets of his jeans, shoulders hunched.

"So, this is how you wanna play it, then? Huh?" the slim man hollered, pulling a crowbar out from the bed of the truck. The sunlight hit certain parts of it in a way that made it glint as he tucked it under his arm.

Diana scanned the road, hoping the tow truck was coming. Or at least another vehicle. People *had* to drive down this road—no matter that it was in the middle of nowhere. *It's fucking paved for God's sake*, she thought.

But there were no signs of vehicles. The only form of life she could see was a small animal several feet down the road. A gopher or a woodchuck, maybe, she couldn't tell because it was obscured by the shade of the surrounding trees. Diana watched the animal skitter across the road, as if sensing the danger in the vicinity, before disappearing into the woods.

She shifted her focus back to the brothers.

The burly one was approaching her car now, coming toward the driver's door.

The other one was walking around the back of her vehicle, brandishing the crowbar like a major league player about to step up to bat.

"Hey, we wuz trying to be nice about this," he said, slapping the crowbar against his palm.

He made it around the back bumper and was on the passenger side of the vehicle, coming up to the front door now.

It was time to move.

The two of them effectively had both the driver and passenger doors blocked off, but her car had four doors. She lowered the seat she was in as far as it would go, then climbed over it to get into the back. Diana unlocked the passenger door behind the driver's seat, deciding that the burly man would be easier to outrun and deal with than the armed slim man.

Seeing what she was doing, the burly man moved down to the door, intending to block it off. Diana threw it open as hard as she could.

The metal smashed into his knees, sending him stumbling backward with a loud groan. Diana took the opportunity and jumped out of the car. The second her feet touched the ground, she started running.

While all this had been happening, the slim man had started swinging his crowbar. It went through the passenger window at the same time Diana had jumped out of the car, sending hundreds of shards of glass flying through the interior of the Hyundai.

"Grab 'er!" the slim man hollered at his brother.

Diana felt the burly man grab her by the arm. She twisted away from him but couldn't break his hold. His grip on her coat was too strong. Diana reached into her pocket for the pepper spray, popped its safety off, and sprayed it in his direction.

The man screamed as an orange film covered his face. His grip loosened, and Diana pulled away from him.

He put one hand to his face, trying to wipe the liquid away. But despite the pain and blindness, he was still on her. He lunged at her with one hand and grabbed a fistful of her jacket, then threw her back as hard as he could.

Diana hit the car door, her body slamming it shut. Her back exploded in pain, but worse than that was the feeling of losing her grasp on the pepper spray. The can went flying out of her hands, then hit the ground, clinking as it bounced underneath the car.

A full can of pepper spray—her only defense at this second—gone, just like that.

Before Diana could move, she felt the burly man's weight on her, pinning her against the car.

She'd been hoping to get out of this without having to resort to this, but she had no choice now. Diana reached into her pocket for the switchblade, her hands trembling. In one quick motion that was more graceful than she thought she would have been capable of under the circumstances, she hit the release button and took the knife out.

She stabbed it into the side of her assailant's body as hard as she could. The burly man shrieked in pain. His face was so close to hers she caught a whiff of his morning breath before he fell backward.

Diana stepped over him and tore across the street on shaking legs. She went past their truck and headed for the woods on the other side of the road. The thought of looking both ways to make sure she wasn't going to get ran over and turned to roadkill didn't even enter her mind. Her only thought was getting the hell away from these two.

She dared one peek over her shoulder.

Everything had happened so fast. The slim man was just passing his brother as he chased after her. The burly man was sitting on the ground, bleeding, and holding onto his eyes, but still very much alive.

The slim man, showing no sympathy for his brother's condition, yelled something at him. Diana couldn't make it out over the sound her heart thumping in her ears, but she got the sense of some angry insult.

Up ahead, the woods were only a few paces away. She prayed to God she'd be able to lose them in there.

Maybe that would mean losing herself in there, too.

Better lost than, dead, she thought, charging into the trees.

Glass shattering. Screams. Feet stamping.

He was close.

The Boss had told him he was looking for a girl. She might be by herself. She might be in trouble.

He needed to get to her before something bad happened.

He stepped on the gas pedal. The tow truck sped up, heading to where all the commotion was coming from…

Chuck was on the ground still, despite his brother's command to get up and help him chase the girl down. The switchblade was still lodged into the side of his body. He grabbed it by the handle, feeling his blood slicked onto it, and yanked it out of the wound.

He grunted in pain, but he knew he couldn't sit here much longer. If he didn't hurry and help Tim chase the girl down, his older brother would give him hell when this was all said and done.

Fighting through the pain from the knife stab and the pepper spray, he started getting up. He used the side of the car for leverage, pressing his back to it, until he was up on his feet.

He rubbed at his eyes and blinked. They felt like they were on fire, and all he could see were blobs of color in his vision.

Mostly oranges and yellows from the trees, but he knew the white object out on the street was their truck.

Chuck hobbled over to it. He stopped at the back of it, and blindly searched for one of the jugs of water they always took hunting with them. He needed to get as much as this burning crap out of his eyes if he was going to be any good at helping Tim.

He found the water jug in the back corner of the bed. He picked it up, the water inside was cool from sitting out in the October air. Chuck popped the lid off it. Then tilted his head back and poured water onto his face.

"Oh yeah, that's the stuff," he muttered, feeling the crisp water wash the pepper oil out of his eyes.

He stopped to rub at his eyes for a few seconds, then went back to pouring water on his face. He kept repeating those actions until the jug was nearly empty. Too distracted the whole time to notice the tow truck coming down the street.

The driver stopped the tow truck several yards away from the two vehicles.

The gold car the Boss had sent him out to get was sitting on the grass. From this angle, he could see the passenger window had been broken. The shards of glass were scattered all over the dry grass, shimmering under the sunlight.

Parked next to the car was a white pickup truck with its doors open. There was a man standing next to it, pouring water into his face and rubbing at his eyes.

He scanned the surrounding area. It seemed this man was the only person on the road.

The driver shut the engine off and focused his hearing. In the woods nearby, he could hear people running. He listened to the rhythm for a second.

It sounded like only two sets of feet. One of them had to be the girl who spoke to the Boss.

He reached across to the passenger seat to where a duffle bag was sitting. From a side pocket, he pulled out a tattered mask. The mask had big stitches crisscrossing roughly in the middle of it. There were white blotches all over from where he'd tried to scrub bloodstains out.

The driver pulled the mask over his head and slipped his ponytail through a hole in the back. Then, he tugged on the laces in the back to secure it against his face.

Out in the street, he saw the man was leaning into the bed of the pickup truck, trying to find something.

This was going to be easy.

The driver reached underneath his seat and grabbed a hunting knife. Then he climbed out of the truck.

Varias Caras was awake. It was killing time.

CHUCK RUBBED AT his eyes. They still burned like fucking hell and his vision was still blurry, but he could see much better now. Shit, he could even see the individual tines on the deer's head.

He put the jug back in the bed of the truck where he'd found it and started looking for the medical kit that had the gauze. Over the sound of him moving around fishing poles, tools, and half-empty bottles of car liquids, he heard the footsteps of someone approaching him.

"Whoa, that was fast. You got the girl already—" Chuck said, turning around slowly. The rest of his question got stuck behind his teeth.

His vision was still fucked, but he didn't need to see right to know that the blob of colors—the shape, if you will—standing in front of him wasn't his brother. Whoever this was, they were much, much bigger than Tim.

Chuck blinked three times. Maybe it was just the adrenaline of the situation, but his vision snapped back into place, and he could see the person was wearing coveralls.

The tow truck driver. Oh, we fucked up big time, Chuck thought.

And then, as he watched the man pull a knife from his back pocket, he realized how much of an understatement that was.

Ignacio watched the man jump at him, both arms out. The look on his face was one he'd seen many times, the look of someone hoping their attack would be enough to fend him off.

It never was.

Ignacio reached out with one hand and grabbed the man by the throat. The sudden pressure against his jugular made him stop, his eyes getting big.

The expression of determination was replaced by fear.

With his other hand, Ignacio stabbed the knife into the side of the man's torso. He felt the blade puncture into his kidney and felt the organ burst.

The man's agonized screams filled Ignacio's ears like music.

Still clutching onto his throat, Ignacio threw him backward, slamming him against the side of the truck.

Chuck brought his arms up to try to claw at this masked maniac's face, but before he knew it, he was turned around. The buck's antlers were only a few inches from his face. Knowing what was about to happen, and knowing he was too powerless to do anything about it, Chuck screamed again.

Varias Caras grabbed the back of his head and forced his face into one of the tines. There was a loud sound, like cloth being torn, as the tip of the antler ripped through his throat and came out of the back of his neck.

Blood gushed out of Chuck's mouth, raining down to mix with the deer's own blood on its blood-stained head.

Ignacio stepped back, admiring the beauty of the kill for a second. He would have to clean this mess up, but that would be later.

Right now, he had other tasks.

He pulled the hunting knife out of the corpse, then shifted his focus to the woods across the street. Almost as if on cue, a scream rang through the air. It sounded like the girl was in trouble.

Ignacio hurried into the trees.

7

DIANA'S SHIRT WAS torn at the right shoulder, and she was bleeding from running into a crooked branch she hadn't seen but she continued running. Behind her, she could hear her assailant's huffed breathing. Diana looked over her shoulder.

His mouth was wide open, his face as red as a cherry. The hat he'd been wearing had flown off his head at some point. He'd stripped the gaiter off and she was close enough to see bulging veins in his neck.

He was gaining on her. Diana put her focus back on the woods ahead of her, and pumped her legs harder, kicking it into the next gear. The muscles in her thighs and calves felt like they were about to explode, but she thought she could outrun him.

She *had* to outrun him.

Tim watched the girl start to get away from him. He'd been almost within arm's length, but now the gap between them was widening and his lungs were running out of gas. He wasn't sure how much longer he could chase her down like this.

He had to change strategy.

Cocking back the arm holding the crowbar he threw it as hard as he could. The tool spun through the air with a rhythmic whumping sound before striking Diana on the side of the head.

She heard a metallic cling against the side of her skull, and the next thing she knew, she was falling over, tumbling down a hill. She screamed and thrashed her hands to grab onto something to slow down her momentum. Her left hand snatched a young sapling, but only for a second because it broke under her weight.

Diana continued to fall.

The few seconds it took to reach the bottom felt like an eternity. Stomach down, face planted in the cold dirt, she turned her head wearily.

The world spun around her. Her ears were ringing. Her arms and legs felt weak.

Fuck.

Past the buzzing in her ears, she heard her assailant hollering from the top of the hill.

"You run like a damn rabbit, y'know that?"

She heard twigs snapping and leaves crunching underneath his boots as he made his way down to the hill. She was much too dizzy and disoriented to know which way he was coming from, but she knew he wasn't far.

Noticing how hurt she was, Tim wasn't in any hurry. He strode down the hill like he was out for a nature walk.

"To tell ya the truth, I don't really like huntin' all that much." He stopped halfway to Diana and crouched down to pick up the crowbar from where it had landed. "I really only do it because it's good eating. The rest of it…the animal runnin' for its life. Shooting at it. Blood everywhere."

His boots came into her view, so close to her nose she could smell the crusted mud on them. He crouched down, putting his lips close to her ear. "It really ain't for me."

He knelt down and put a knee in her back. He wasn't gonna let her get up and run again. No, sir. He'd had enough of that. The girl let out a small grunt. He was disappointed. He wanted a scream.

"But you, pretty little thing?" he told her. "I'm going to enjoy this."

He dropped his weight down on top of her and started undoing his belt.

Now, she found the breath to scream.

IGNACIO WATCHED, CROUCHED behind a bush at the top of the hill. There was a skinny man sitting on top of a girl. He couldn't see the man's face because his back was to him. The girl underneath him was kicking her legs and screaming, but she couldn't get him off.

Her screams excited Ignacio.

Not yet, Varias Caras said, reining him in.

"Not yet," Ignacio repeated under his breath.

Out here, hunting wasn't like back at the camp where the woods stretched for miles and miles without anyone around. No, out here, if the prey got away, they might find a town or someone on the road to help them.

That would be bad. Varias Caras said Ignacio would be in trouble if that happened. Big trouble.

So, out in these woods, he had to be more calculated. Patient.

Ignacio licked his lips, and continued to wait…

The man shifted his weight forward and started undoing his belt, and he heard the man zip his pants down.

Ignacio wasn't sure what the man was doing. *Maybe he needs to pee?*

Whatever the reason, it made the girl scream louder. She screamed and screamed and tried to get him off, but she wasn't strong enough. The man leaned forward some more and cupped a hand over her mouth, muffling her screams.

Ignacio stretched his hearing sensitivity up. He could hear both of their hearts beating in their chests. The beats were fast.

The man's from excitement.

Hers from fear.

Ignacio licked his lips again.

The skinny man started to pull his pants and underwear down until his pale butt cheeks were exposed. His heartbeat sped up even more. Even more excited now. His focus was totally on whatever he was about to do.

Ignacio raised his knife again, still slicked with blood from his first victim. He made his way down the hill, crouching and stepping lightly while avoiding the crunchy leaves on the ground so as to not be detected.

Diana could feel his hard dick dragging across her back as he squirmed down her body, trying to reposition himself. The disgust she felt gave her a sudden surge of energy, and she writhed underneath him hard enough to free one of her hands.

She threw her hand back, fingers curled to rake at his eyes, but she felt her hand swipe at nothing but air.

The next second, his weight left her, like the man had just floated off into the air.

What the—?

She rolled over on her back, and saw what was happening, although it took her a moment for her brain to accept the scene.

A massive hand was wrapped around her assailant's neck, pulling him back like he was a ragdoll. For a split-second, she entertained the crazy thought that it was the hand of God or a guardian angel.

She watched this new stranger, a man in coveralls and built like a brick house, force her attacker's chin upward with the same hand he'd been choking him with. Then, with the other hand, he pressed a knife against the slim man's throat. The slim man reached up to try to pry his way free, but it was futile. The disparity in strength was too much.

The gigantic man slashed the knife across her assailant's throat. Blood sprayed out into the air. Her attacker's extremities went limp. His arms fell to his sides, his legs buckled backward.

The gigantic man shoved his victim to the side. The deadweight of the corpse crashed onto the ground with a heavy thud.

He'd been staring at her this whole time, never taking his eyes off her even when he was dispatching her attacker.

She looked at him closer now. His coveralls and arms were splashed with fresh blood. Too much to be just from this one kill. But the most alarming thing was the grotesque mask on his face. It had white blotches all over it, and three long lines of stitches weaved in uneven lines like grotesque millipedes trying to coalesce into one being.

Diana met his gaze, and any lingering thoughts that this might have been a divine intervention evaporated.

The dark eyes staring back at her from behind the mask told her everything.

He wasn't here to protect her. No, not at all. She had gone from one bad situation to one that was seemingly worse.

Diana looked at the knife in his right hand. It was red with blood. And hers would be on there soon if she didn't act fast.

9

DIANA SAW THE crowbar laying a few inches from her left hand.

The masked man's eyes flickered over to it.

Shit. He knows. But she couldn't waste any more time. Diana lunged and grabbed it and swung it at his leg.

The crowbar smashed right below his knee. He let out a grunt, but it didn't take him off balance the way Diana hoped. He grunted. That was all. It didn't have much more effect on him than that.

Diana kicked her legs to get up, swinging the crowbar through the air again. This time it was a wild swing with no aim. She was just hoping it would keep him at bay.

But he was prepared for it. He caught it in one of his massive hands and pulled on it. Diana felt herself losing balance and opted to let go of the crowbar.

The gigantic man chucked it into the woods.

Diana watched it fly through the air like it was a leaf in the wind, exemplifying the man's strength.

She turned to run, took two steps, and then felt him grab her by the arm. He pulled her back, but it didn't feel anything like when the burly man had done something similar earlier. No, this man's strength was something else. Something inhuman.

Diana was thrown to the ground, the wind knocked out of her. She opened her mouth to take in a gulp of air, but one of his massive hands wrapped around her throat. With that single hand, and with seemingly no effort, he picked her up off the ground.

She kicked her legs and dug her nails into his forearm, trying to fight him off, but it was as fruitless as the skinny man's attempts to fight him off. His forearms felt like fucking concrete, and he was holding her up too high to hit him in the groin. The toes of her shoes just slammed into his belly. And even though it was round, there was nothing soft about it.

He slammed her against a tree, causing some of the lower branches to shake off a few dying leaves. The orange and yellow leaves flittered around them in a swirl while he continued to choke her.

Diana stared into the dark, expressionless eyes behind the mask. With each passing second, she could feel her body getting weaker and weaker, the will to live smaller and smaller…

Ignacio watched her eyes close. Felt her legs stop kicking. Her hands fell away from him as her arms fell to her sides.

She was asleep. Not dead. He didn't want her dead.

"Sleepy Barbie," Ignacio said, relaxing his hand around her throat.

He put the girl over his shoulder, and turned around to look at the corpse of the second guy he'd killed. The slash across his throat was still spilling blood, turning the leaf-covered ground red.

Varias Caras made a mental note of where this body was located to come back to clean it up.

He would take care of that later, though, after securing his new doll.

Ignacio started out of the woods. Behind him, the orange sun glowed bright against his back. Its light shone off the top of Diana Santos' head, making her dark hair shine like obsidian.

10

"YOU'RE FINALLY AWAKE," someone off to Diana's side said.

Diana lifted her head up. Her throat felt raw and itchy, as if she'd swallowed a wad of sandpaper and then regurgitated it. Parts of her neck were sore like someone had been squeezing it—no, no. Not "like." Someone *had* been squeezing it. She remembered now, and she froze with fear all over again.

The masked man. The one who slit her assailant's throat.

Diana felt like a fog was lifting from her mind as her senses came back to her.

Underneath her, she felt a cold and hard surface. It was too smooth to be dirt or grass, meaning the masked man had brought her elsewhere. Diana shuddered.

"Okay, never mind. Maybe you're not awake after all," the same person muttered.

Diana pressed her palms flat against the ground, feeling grainy sediment bite into her flesh. And now that she was aware of it on her hands, she realized she was covered in it.

She pushed herself up to her knees, blinking against the pale light. The source of it was a single, naked bulb hanging from the ceiling of the room.

"Oh," the other person—a girl, she realized now, was only a few feet away from her. "You *are* awake."

"Wh-where am I?" Diana asked, looking around. She sucked in a breath when her eyes focused enough to realize she was trapped inside a cage made of steel wire mesh. It was like something livestock would be kept in.

"I guess you can call it his playroom," the girl said and shrugged.

The girl was kneeling in the middle of her own cage, surrounded by a ring of dirty plushies that had stuffing coming out of rips in their fabric. She wore a filthy t-shirt that once upon a time had probably been white and a pair of cargo shorts. Makeup was smeared all over her face, applied in sloppy swathes. Days-old mascara encircled her eyes, giving her a disheveled, clown-like appearance.

"We were playing zoo this morning. Before he left for work," she said, as if that explained everything.

Diana's head was swimming. "Wh-who are you? What the hell is going on?"

"Me? They used to call me Madison." The girl put a finger up to her chin and looked up at the ceiling, as if the answer was written somewhere in the shadows looming above them. "Madison Charleston. Yeah, that was my name before. In here, though, I'm Barbie."

"B-Barbie…?"

"That's what he calls me." Madison shrugged. "I found out a long time ago I'm not getting out of here alive, so I figured this is who I am now. You know?"

Not getting out of here alive…? The question popped into Diana's head, but she couldn't bring herself to ask it.

"How long have you been here?" She asked, instead.

"Oh, boy. That's hard to answer." She shrugged again. "You lose track of time when you're here."

"You have to have some idea," Diana said, desperation seeping into her voice.

"You would think. But you'll see. After you're here long enough, you'll understand."

Diana didn't say anything, she just looked away from the girl.

"I bet you're thinking you can find a way out of this, huh?" Madison asked, smirking.

Once again, Diana didn't answer her.

"If it makes you feel any better, I was like you when he first brought me here. Scared, but hopeful. Thinking I would find a way out… but eventually, this place will take that out of you, and you'll accept your—"

Out of nowhere, Madison threw her head back and cackled. Her laughter bounced off the walls, making the room feel even more confined. Just as quickly as she'd started, she stopped. She walked over to one of her cage walls and smacked it. Again, and again. The steel rattled.

Before Diana could react, they heard heavy footsteps on the other side of the door. Someone was climbing a staircase, heading for this room from the sound of it.

"He's coming," Madison's eyes shifted over to the door. "He's probably going to kill me. He doesn't need me anymore. He has you now, he doesn't need me, doesn't need me, doesn't need me!"

The footfalls stopped, replaced by the sounds of locks being undone. Then the door was flung open.

The masked man from the woods stood in the doorway. He'd changed out of his coveralls and was instead wearing camo pants and a gray tank top, but there was no mistaking that behemoth.

His eyes slid around behind the bleach-stained mask, alternating between Madison and Diana in their cages, like a curious zoologist.

Diana felt her heart thumping in her chest. Her palms started to sweat. Madison had asked her if she was going to try to find a way out. Of course she was. She needed to get out of this nightmare…but now, all of that confidence seemed to disappear as she stared at her captor in all of his enormity.

His eyes settled on Madison. With his gaze locked in on her, he trudged over to her cage.

Diana watched the calmness melt away from Madison's face, replaced by panic

"NO, PLEASE!" Madison screamed, backing away into a corner. "Please, no, no."

The masked man stepped into the cage and grabbed Madison by the back of the neck. Madison screamed louder. She kicked and thrashed her arms. The masked man forced her arms to the side in a bearhug. Then, like she weighed nothing at all, he lifted her into the air and carried her out of the cage.

"HELP ME, PLEASE!" Madison screamed, pleading with Diana with her eyes as the masked man carried her away. "DON'T LET HIM KILL ME! PLEASE"

He took her over to a wooden table in the corner of the room. Diana couldn't see what was happening, because the huge man's enormous back blocked most of her view. But she could see Madison still kicking her legs as he pinned her down with one arm.

The other arm reached behind him for a knife sticking out from his back pocket.

"PLEASE!" Madison screamed, her voice hoarse. "PLEASE DON'T KILL ME…*Please…!*"

Her screams turned into sobs as the masked man held the knife above her.

Then he drove it down.

Diana heard Madison's cries turn into gurgling gasps and watched her kicks turn to twitches, before she finally went still.

The masked man moved away from the table, going over to some cabinets built into a wall. Diana didn't know what he was looking for, but she didn't care.

She turned her attention to Madison's corpse. The hunting knife was sticking out of her chest. Her face was twisted in agony and fear. Her eyes, as lifeless as they were, still pleaded for mercy. Blood pumped out from the wound in her chest and from her mouth, running down the side of her body and cheeks in crimson rivulets.

The masked man returned to the table, blocking Diana's view again, but she could still tell what he was doing. He pulled the knife out of Madison before he started wrapping her up in a dark green tarp. Once the corpse was secured, he draped it over his shoulder.

He turned to Diana. He stared at her from across the room, standing as still as a statue as he did this. It felt like he was trying to burn a hole through her with his dark eyes.

After a few seconds he walked over to the door. He put his hand on the knob, staining it red with blood.

"We will play soon," he said to Diana, turning the knob and pulling the door open.

She watched him leave, close the door behind him, then heard the locks being secured again. Diana listened to him clamber down the staircase, his heavy footfall fading with every step until his movement was nothing but a murmur.

The light bulb in the center of the room went out. Darkness shrouded Diana. But in her mind, the sight of Madison's corpse burned bright.

And deep down inside, she began to believe she would suffer a similar fate.

HILLTOWN

1

Hudson Crosley woke up with the October sun shining in his face. He sat up in bed, and before his eyes were even fully open, he swiped the marker off the nightstand next to him. As he rolled over to the opposite side of the bed, where a DragonForce calendar was tacked onto a wall, he took the marker's cap off.

Hudson yawned as he drew a big "X" over the current date, October 29th, same as he had done with all the days leading up to today.

Two days until Halloween. Two days until the best day of the year, he thought, a wave of excitement jolting through him.

Maybe some people would think it was odd that a twenty-two-year-old was this excited over Halloween, but Hudson had loved it since he first heard of the holiday. The idea of being able to go to parties dressed up as his favorite characters was something that would likely appeal to him for the rest of his life.

He jumped out of bed. As he did, his phone buzzed on the nightstand. He put the marker down and grabbed the phone. *Your package has been delivered!*, the notification from the email read.

"Oh, hell yes!" he said, pumping his hand in the air.

Hudson raced out of his bedroom and climbed down the stairs two steps at a time. In the kitchen, he heard his dad tinkering around with the toaster oven he'd been attempting to repair for the last two days.

"Morning, pal!" his father said, twisting in the chair as Hudson blurred past the kitchen.

"Morning, Dad!" Hudson called back, not bothering to stop to talk to him.

He had his mind on one thing, and one thing only.

Bursting through the front door he leapt out into the crisp morning air. Despite the fact the sun was shining bright over the neighborhood, turning all of the perfectly raked and mowed lawns in the neighborhood vibrant, it was in the low sixties.

The package was sitting at the top of the porch steps. It was a brown parcel with the addresses written on it in sloppy handwriting. Across the flap were several crudely applied strips of tape. If Hudson hadn't recognized the seller's Idaho address, he would've assumed this was a bomb.

He crouched down and picked up the package.

The next-door neighbor's front door opened and out came Mrs. Bigley holding a big mug of coffee in one hand. Her tiny wiener dog, Nacho, came yipping out behind her. He darted between her feet, and then tore across the lawn to find a corner to pee in.

"Good morning, Mrs. Bigley," Hudson called to her, tucking the package under his arm.

Mrs. Bigley hadn't looked at him until now. She'd been too busy watching her dog. She turned to look at him and opened her mouth to respond to his greeting...but then realized he wasn't wearing any pants. She stopped, her face twisting into a horrified expression.

Hudson forced the smile on his face bigger and waved with his free arm.

Mrs. Bigley shook her head and then headed back inside.

What was that about? Hudson thought, heading back inside.

Maybe she hadn't put enough cream and sugar in her coffee.

Hudson rushed back into his room, happier than a kid in a candy store—or on Halloween night, if you will. He threw the package on the bed, then grabbed a pair of scissors from his computer desk.

As he started cutting the tape off the flap, his phone rang on the nightstand. He looked over and saw the name "Tucker" on the screen. Hudson put the package and scissors down on the bed and went over to answer the phone.

"Hello?"

"Yo, Hud," his friend said. "What are you up to?"

"Nothing much. Just about to try on my costume." Hudson couldn't help the smile on his face. He'd been waiting all month for it to arrive.

"Wait, what? You're at the Halloween Store already? Isn't it like, nine o'clock?"

"No, I had it delivered."

"Oh, right," Tucker said, sounding like he didn't care. "Are you working today?"

"Yeah, second shift. Why?"

Hudson walked over to the full-length mirror hanging from his closet door as they talked. He checked himself out, trying to figure out why Mrs. Bigley had looked so distraught. Sure, he was chubby and had a fading farmer's tan he'd gotten over the summer, but her reaction had been over the top. Maybe she wasn't a fan of Batman underwear.

"Because I wanted to hang out," Tucker said in response to his question.

"Sure. I got a few hours," Hudson told him, looking over at the alarm clock at his bedside. "What time were you thinking?"

"Now."

"What?"

"I'm pulling up to your window right now." Tucker said, ending the call.

Hudson stood there for a second, perplexed. Then he heard the engine of a quad outside his bedroom window and looked out into his backyard.

Tucker came riding out of the woods behind Hudson's house, the wind blowing his shaggy hair all over the place as he made his way across the backyard. A few seconds later, he was pulling up in front of the bedroom window. Hudson crossed the room to meet him there.

"Open up!" he hollered, lifting his riding goggles up on his forehead, then he noticed Hudson was in his underwear and said, "Wait, never mind. Get some damn pants on first."

"Fine." Hudson huffed, putting his cellphone on the windowsill and going over to his closet.

He slipped into a pair of sweatpants, then went back to let Tucker in.

This was the way Tucker usually came into his house, ever since they were in middle school, because Hudson's parents weren't Tucker's biggest fan ever since they caught them drinking on the porch one night.

Hudson's parents were supposed to have been at Hickory Run for a weekend camping trip but had come home early after Hudson's father got food poisoning from some clams they'd undercooked on the grill. They'd come home without warning and found them on the porch swing, passing a forty-ounce bottle of Colt 45 between each other.

Hudson had gotten grounded for three weeks, and Tucker had been all but banished from the Crosley household. Of course, Tucker kept coming over after Hudson's punishment was done, and his parents never said anything or kicked him out when they saw him in the house. But just to play it safe, more often than not, Tucker would sneak in through the window when they wanted to hang out here.

Tucker came in through the window now, his red and white riding jacket rustling as he made his way into the bedroom. He had a greasy takeout bag tucked under his arm that he tossed onto Hudson's computer desk.

"I brought breakfast." Tucker said, plopping down on the computer chair.

"Sweet. What'd you get?"

Tucker took out a sandwich and a hashbrown, then threw the bag at Hudson. Hudson caught it in the air, trying to secure it without smooshing whatever was inside.

"Bacon, egg, and cheese on a bagel." Tucker said, taking a bite out of his hashbrown.

"Tuck, I'm lactose intolerant." Hudson frowned.

"Oh. Well, shit, my bad." Tucker shrugged.

Hudson went over and sat down on the edge of the bed. He took the sandwich out, unwrapped it, and started scraping the cheese off with a fingernail. It was going to be a greasy ordeal, but no way was he going to let this sandwich go to waste.

"So," Hudson said, continuing to modify the sandwich to make it more bearable on his stomach. "What's up?"

He knew Tucker hadn't come just to deliver him breakfast. If anything, the sandwich was a tipoff that he wanted something from him. It was like a preemptive payment, or a way to soften him up to agree on doing whatever he wanted. Either way, he knew the food wasn't free.

"I got this crazy idea," Tucker said.

Uh-oh, Hudson thought. Tucker and ideas were never a good thing. And him admitting it was "crazy" made it doubly bad.

"Don't look at me like that," Tucker snickered. "It's not *actually* crazy."

"What is it?" Hudson said, putting the top of the bagel back onto his sandwich.

"Do you remember that manor we found a few months ago?"

Hudson nodded and took a bite of his sandwich. He knew exactly what Tucker was talking about. Over the summer, both had been in a volunteer search party to try to find a girl that went missing around Hilltown. Hudson and Tucker had ridden their quads through the woods, going into the most isolated parts where they knew cars couldn't go, and they had stumbled upon an abandoned house in the middle of nowhere.

"Do you remember what that place was called?" Tucker continued.

"Frosty Hollow Manor," Hudson said, swallowing. "What about it?"

"I've been thinking we could throw a sick ass Halloween party there," Tucker said, his eyes shimmering with excitement. "Think about it. It's far enough away from town that the cops wouldn't show up, but close enough that people wouldn't mind making the drive."

"Do you remember where it was?"

"Yeah. I dropped a pin on my GPS when we were there."

"Really?"

"Yeah. Before we left." Tucker took a bite of his hashbrown. "I was planning to go back to break inside some other day. That's when I got this genius idea."

Hudson had talked him out of going into the building to explore. Whenever Tucker wanted to do something dangerous and/or stupid, he usually did it even if Hudson protested. Stopping him from going into Frosty Hollow Manor had been one of the rare moments he'd won. It'd been getting dark at the time they arrived at the manor, and they had no idea what they would find in that place. After arguing for a few minutes, Tucker had admitted he didn't have his tetanus shot up to date anyway and just agreed to head home.

"Would you be down for it, though?" Tucker went on. "I can borrow my dad's work truck to take heavy stuff there. I can probably even get a portable shitter from him, too."

"What if it's uninhabitable?"

"Then my idea is shot." Tucker laughed. "Come on, though. I need you on board for this."

"Why?"

"Because, if you agree to it, then the other guys'll be more likely to be in." Tucker paused, thinking about how to better word what he meant. "They won't think it's as stupid."

"Other guys? Who are you talking about?"

"Dan and Baxter."

"Wait, Baxter? Isn't he at Bloomsburg?"

"Not anymore." Tucker chuckled. "His dumbass got kicked out. He's been back in Hilltown since the summer working at the junkyard. He just didn't tell anyone except Dan."

"Then how do you know about it?"

"Oh, Dan told me last night."

Hudson nodded, thinking it through.

"Come on, man. You know it would be cool," Tucker said, bringing the subject back to Frosty Hollow Manor. "A costume party in a real abandoned house on Halloween night—I know how much you love Halloween."

"I do love Halloween," Hudson agreed.

"Yeah, exactly. And every Halloween in Hilltown is the same shit. We drink in the woods like high schoolers, or we drink at the bars like old people. We could shake things up this year."

Hudson couldn't deny that it would be cool. "Do you think people would actually go?"

"Yeah, I do." Tucker said. "Baxter could invite people he knows from college. And you know word gets around quick in Hilltown. I'm sure we could get a good turnout."

"Everyone has to wear a costume, though. That's gotta be a thing."

"Yeah, sure," Tucker said, not caring about that detail.

"If someone shows up without a costume, they... uh, they don't get to drink," Hudson grinned.

"Sure, buddy." Tucker said, shaking his head. "You have fun enforcing that one."

"I mean, come on. If we're going to have a sweet Halloween party, everyone has to be in costume, right?" Hudson wasn't willing to give up the idea that easily.

"Yeah, yeah. I get it. I'll make sure to tell everyone to come in costume," Tucker said.

"Okay, good." Hudson nodded, satisfied. "Good."

"So, I take it that means you're down?"

"Yeah." Hudson took a bite of his sandwich. "I'm in."

"What time are you off work?"

"Ten."

"Let's go to Annie's tonight."

"Okay." Hudson said, not really wanting to go. He was planning to stay in tonight and watch corny horror movies with a big bag of fun-size candy. But if it meant that much to Tucker, then fine.

"Cool. I'll text the other guys and tell them to meet up around ten-thirty."

They finished eating their sandwiches while chatting about other stuff. Once they were done breakfast, they powered on Hudson's Xbox to spend a few hours just hanging out and playing video games.

2

Officer Rick Gordon was hanging a ghost doll to the front awning of the Hilltown Police Station. He'd made the decoration himself by tying a rag around one of the many rubber band balls on his desk. Using a Sharpie, he'd drawn two big eyes and a zig-zagging mouth, giving the ghost a cutesy, nervous expression.

He was just putting the tweed rope onto the hook, and giving it a few tugs, when he heard the phone ringing inside. No one was in the station. The sheriff and the lieutenant were out patrolling the town along with the two other officers on duty.

Officer Gordon hurried down the ladder he was on and went into the police station. He swooped the phone's receiver up from its cradle.

"Hilltown Police Department. Officer Gordon speaking, how can I help you?"

"H-hello. I'd like to report a missing person," the woman on the other line said in a meek voice.

"Okay, what's the name of the person?" he asked, grabbing a pen and a police report form.

"Her name is Diana Santos. She…she's my daughter." The woman sniffled. "Last time anyone heard from her was yesterday… I was the last person she spoke to."

"Does she live here in Hilltown?"

"No." She sniffled again. "She was driving up there for an interview at the Hilltown Wildlife Clinic. I called them this morning, and the woman there—I think her name was Erica?—told me she never showed up for her interview."

"I see." Rick wrote this all down. "Give me a description of her, please."

"She's about five-six. Maybe a hundred-and-twenty pounds? She has light-brown skin and long dark hair."

"Eye color?"

"Dark brown. They look black most of the time, though."

"Age?"

"She's twenty-three. Just turned twenty-three in June."

"Okay. And what time exactly did you last speak to her yesterday?"

"Around ten in the morning. No one has heard from her since. Not her brothers or any of the friends I was able to contact."

Officer Gordon looked down at the digital clock on the phone. It was almost one p.m. now, which meant Diana Santos had been missing more than a full day.

"Okay, ma'am, and what is your name?"

"My name is Miriam Santos."

"And you're not a resident of Hilltown, correct?"

"No. I never even heard of this place until my daughter had her job interview."

Rick Gordon nodded. Most people hadn't heard of Hilltown. It was a small town tucked away in the wilderness of Northern PA. People driving up to New York might see the signs on the highway pointing toward the town, but other than that, it was a place people's eyes would gloss over if they were looking at a map.

"No offense," Miriam Santos added.

"None taken," Officer Gordon said. "Where was your daughter driving in from?"

Miriam told her the college town.

"What kind of car does she drive?"

"A gold 2001 Hyundai Elantra."

Officer Gordon wrote this down as well, then gave her the email address to the Hilltown Police Department so she could send pictures of both her daughter and the car.

"Ma'am, the Hilltown Police Department is going to do all they can to try to find your daughter. We'll go around town and ask if they've seen her and post all these details on our social media pages."

"Thank you." Miriam Santos started bawling on the phone.

Officer Rick Gordon gave her a few seconds to compose herself before continuing. "We'll send this information to surrounding departments and the County Police Station as well."

"Do you think…do you think my daughter is still alive?"

Officer Gordon hit the mute button on the phone and let out a loud whistle. Then unmuted the phone, and said, "I don't think I can answer that. But, like I said, ma'am, we'll do our best to make sure your daughter is found."

"Okay… Okay, thanks again—what did you say your name was?"

"Officer Rick Gordon."

"Thank you, Officer Rick Gordon."

"Is this the best number to reach you at if we find anything out?"

"It is. This is my cell number."

"Okay, Miss Santos. I'll make sure the sheriff and everyone else who needs to get this information receives it. You try to take it easy, now."

"Uh-huh. Yeah. Okay, bye." Miriam Santos let out a small sob, then the line went dead.

Officer Gordon put the phone back on the receiver and stared down at the information he'd jotted down. As he stood there, going over the report, the police station door opened. The sheriff and Officer Dan Sigler came in, carrying on an upbeat conversation.

"Sheriff," Officer Gordon said, catching his attention. "We've got another missing person, sir."

"Twenty-three years old…" Sheriff Olmos muttered, skimming over the info on the sheet Rick handed him. "Not from around here. This just come in?"

"Yes. Think this is the Bakers' doing?" Officer Gordon asked.

"I don't know. But I don't think it would hurt to pay them a little visit," Sheriff Olmos said, handing the report back to Officer Gordon. "Radio us if Diana Santos is found within the next thirty-minutes or so."

"Got it, sir," Officer Gordon said, going back behind the main desk and sitting down in front of the computer.

"Come on," Sheriff Olmos said, waving for Officer Sigler to follow him. "Let's go see what Hilltown's favorite duo is up to."

3

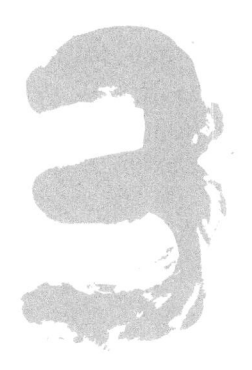

DIANA WOKE UP to the discomfort of growling hunger. She sat up on the thin mattress inside the cage where she'd fallen asleep crying for what felt like hours.

She wasn't sure how long she'd been asleep, but the room looked different now. It wasn't just that the cage next to her was empty. No, it was something else. The light coming into the room from the window was different now.

The only window in this place was boarded up with two pieces of lumber that formed an "X" over it. Between the gaps in the planks, rays of sunlight seeped into the room. Partially lighting the room and illuminating dust particles floating in the air.

Mostly, though, the room was dark.

The light coming in through the window had been brighter before she fell asleep. It had that certain white harshness to it that could only mean it was from an artificial source. A light fixture that was hanging outside near the window, probably. Now it was more like natural sunlight.

If she was correct about this, that would mean she'd been here at least one night already.

Diana thought of Madison telling her she would lose track of time and gulped, realizing how easy it would be to do so.

Before Diana could do anything else, the lightbulb hanging from the ceiling came on, flooding the room with light. Diana shielded her face with one of her arms against the sudden brightness.

On the other side of the door, she heard heavy footfalls. The masked man was coming to pay her a visit, no doubt.

The attic door swung open. Diana let one of her eyes peek out over her arm and saw the enormous man standing in the doorway. He was wearing dark gray coveralls, clean ones, without any bloodstains on them.

The mask on his face was different, too. This one was a series of leather lattices crossing over his face. The spaces between the straps were too small for Diana to discern much of his features, but she could see enough to tell he was clean-shaven underneath it.

He stared at Diana from the doorway with his dark, expressionless eyes.

A minute or so passed, and then he came into the room.

First, he went to a wooden shelf near the table where he'd killed Madison. The shelf was lined with various canned goods—vegetables, diced tomatoes, beans, and so on. He grabbed one of these, set it on the wooden table, then headed over to the cabinets.

Diana couldn't see inside them because his back blocked her view, but she could hear him rummaging through the cabinets. Once he grabbed what he was looking for, he returned to the table.

The sound of a can opener grinding through metal filled the otherwise silent attic, followed by the contents of the can plopping against the container they were being poured into.

The masked man turned around, holding a bowl with a plastic spoon sticking out of it, and carried it over to her cage.

Diana couldn't help but notice how much the floor underneath them vibrated with each of his footsteps. She hoped the damn wood underneath him would splinter and drop him dead to the bowels of the house below. Her wish didn't come true.

He stopped in front of the cage, and her worries went elsewhere.

The masked man crouched down, reaching into his back pocket with his free hand. From it, he pulled out a keyring with several keys dangling on it. He inserted one of the smaller ones into a padlock at the bottom of the cage.

Diana only now noticed the feed door built into the cage as he took the padlock off and set it on the floor before opening the small mesh square and sliding the bowl through it.

"Food. If Barbie wants to eat," he said, getting up and moving away.

While he went back to the cabinets, Diana stared down at the bowl. It was filled with kidney beans floating in their juices.

The masked man returned with two water bottles. He placed these on Diana's side of the cage next to the beans.

"I have to go," he said, his hands working to put the lock back on the feed door. "Playtime next time."

Diana watched him get up and then cross back to the attic door. The keyring bulged out from one of his back pockets. In the other, she saw the handle of that huge knife. The same one he'd used to kill both Madison and the skinny man in the woods.

If I could get it from him…maybe during "playtime"…

Fantasies of using the knife on him raced through her mind.

Maybe slashing his throat. Maybe stabbing him in the stomach several times. Maybe putting it through one of his fucking eyes for staring at her.

The attic door clicked closed behind the masked man, bringing her back to reality.

She heard the locks being thrown, followed by the wooden steps creaking underneath his weight as he descended the staircase.

Then there was a second of silence before the light was flicked off.

Darkness enveloped Diana. But she would come to find out, that in this place, that was preferable to the light.

4

The Baker brothers' cabin was located fifteen miles outside the heart of Hilltown, in an isolated wooded area that people stayed away from because of the family's reputation. The grandfather, Thomas Baker, had purportedly built the cabin himself. No one knew if this was true or not because Thomas Baker was a known liar.

Not only that, but he'd been a notorious criminal. In his heyday, he'd been arrested by the Hilltown Police for a litany of crimes including fighting, sexual assault, burglary, and breaking and entering into people's homes.

His final run-in with trouble—so to speak—was the night he drunkenly crashed his Ford Taurus into a power pole. The impact had caused the post to crash down on top of the vehicle, crushing Thomas Baker while he was still inside. The rumor around town was that when the first responders showed up, he'd been nothing but a pile of goo from his ass up.

A crowd had gathered at the sight of the scene within minutes, mostly made up of the people who'd lost power due to the outage the accident caused. One group came from a nearby bowling alley, still wearing their bowling shoes and respective team polos. Whispers of concern and gasps murmured through the crowd as people laid their eyes on the mess of metal, human remains, and smoke. But when someone recognized the vehicle as belonging to Thomas Baker, they all knew that the only real loss was the electrical power.

Sheriff Olmos could remember pulling up to the scene as clearly as if it'd happened yesterday. He'd just joined the Hilltown Police Department a few months prior and had been sent out with two other officers to help with crowd control. Henry Smoke, the sheriff at the time, told him he wanted Greg to see it, so he could be prepared for what he'd be dealing with for the rest of his career.

At the time, being that he was only in his mid-twenties, it'd been the worst thing Sheriff Olmos had ever seen. After thirty-six years of being in the police force, he knew it got worse, but he always thought of Thomas Baker's bloodied, splattered remains trapped inside of that wreckage when he was paying the man's grandkids a visit.

The night Thomas Baker had died, it had felt very much like a victory. One of the big bads of Hilltown was gone for good, and although Sheriff Smoke didn't come outright and say they were celebrating his death, he'd ordered Mexican for the entire station that night.

As it turned out, though, the seeds Thomas Baker left behind were just as bad. His son, Maron, had been the tamest of them all. He'd been a punk kid in high school who'd been caught smoking marijuana on school property and underage drinking in the woods a few times, but he never did anything more than that. He'd married his high school sweetheart, a woman named Sheila Meyers whom he knocked up twice.

But working long hours at the local automobile factory left him no time to properly raise the two boys.

Without any real parental guidance, and perhaps because they carried their grandfather's genes, Timothy and Charles Baker took to criminal activity. They were known as hoodlums by their teen years, and outright violent criminals by their twenties. Their reputations preceded them so much that any unsolved mystery would come to be known as a "Baker crime" around town.

Many people said it was all the older brother, Tim Baker, who was the mastermind behind everything, and Charles just went along with it.

But that was a bunch of bullshit to Sheriff Olmos. He didn't care who the so-called mastermind was. They were both filth as far as he was concerned.

There'd been a rumor going around town that they grabbed women off the side of the road, women whose cars had broken down, and brought them back to the cabin to do God knows what to them.

They hadn't been caught yet, but maybe Diana Santos was their big mess up.

Sheriff Olmos glanced over at the rookie cop, Officer Dan Sigler. He was staring out the window, watching the trees rush past the cruiser as they sped down the narrow roads.

"One thing you should keep in mind whenever you stroll up to someone's property," Sheriff Olmos explained, "badge or no badge, uniform or no uniform, you're just a person coming to someone's doorstep with a gun on your hip."

Officer Sigler turned to him, nodding. "Understood, sir."

"I don't mean to make you nervous," Sheriff Olmos said, clapping him on the shoulder to bring his morale up. "We're only gonna ask them a couple of quick questions and then we'll be on our way."

Up ahead, past some trees and shrubbery, the cabin came into view. A confederate flag on a pole bolted to the outside wall was flapping in the wind. The shell of an old VW Golf sat on the small, wispy patch of grass that could barely be considered a lawn. Old, dirty tools were laying discarded all around. A few feet away, a stack of tires caked with mud sat on the side of the gravel driveway.

"They're not here," Sheriff Olmos said, stopping the cruiser in front of the cabin.

"How do you know?" Officer Sigler asked.

"Truck's gone."

"Oh. What do we do? Come back later?"

"No," Sheriff Olmos said, unbuckling his belt.

Next to him, Officer Sigler did the same. They both climbed out of the cruiser.

The sun was beaming down at full force this morning, turning the leaves on the trees vibrant. The oranges, reds, and yellows came together in a way that made the scene look like a miasma of warm colors.

They both turned their attention to the cabin. Despite the beautiful nature it was surrounded by, the cabin itself was hideous. It was made of old, worn logs that badly needed to be replaced. Its roof slanted to the side, giving the impression that it was ready to topple over at any moment.

Sheriff Olmos and Dan Sigler started toward it, meeting at the front of the cruiser. Then, with the sheriff leading the way, they went up the front steps. At the porch, they split up and went to two different windows. The curtains were drawn open, so they could see through the glass, but it was dark inside.

Sheriff Olmos unclipped the flashlight from his waist and shined it into the middle of the cabin.

There was a couch in the living area with a box of Cheez-Its and a TV remote sitting on it. The coffee table and the floor in front of the couch was riddled with empty cans of cheap beer.

Sheriff Olmos swept his beam to the right, meeting with Officer Sigler's light, hovering over a half-open closet with a shoe rack containing old sneakers and boots. Besides that, they could see a pair of fishing rods in the back, a tacklebox, and a few boxes of ammo up on a shelf.

Almost in unison, they both moved their beams to the other end of the cabin, shining it into a kitchenette. The small sink was full to the brim with dishware. The top plate on the stack was smeared with dried-up egg yolk and bacon grease.

But what caught the sheriff's attention most were the raw steaks sitting on the counter. They'd been left out to thaw, as evidenced by the puddle of water that had formed underneath them. The pinkish water was dripping off the edges of the counter like drool.

The cabin was as still as a portrait—yet, somehow animated.

"Well, they're *definitely* not here," Sheriff Olmos said, trying to make it sound like a joke, but it didn't quite come out right.

"What do we do, Sheriff?"

Sheriff Olmos put a hand on his hip and took a step back. "I think... I think we should probably wait."

"Until they come back?"

"Yeah," Sheriff Olmos said.

A breeze blew by, making the branches on the trees clatter against one another like a cacophony of chattering teeth.

The hairs on the back of the sheriff's neck stood up. He knew it wasn't just from the chilly wind. No, something was telling him—police instinct, if you will—that Diana Santos wasn't the only one who'd gone missing yesterday.

They waited almost thirty minutes at the cabin, but the Baker brothers never showed up. Sheriff Olmos locked himself in his office when they returned. He had the names, pictures, and ages of all the people who'd gone missing around Hilltown in the last year pinned to the corkboard on the wall:

Giana Smith. Age 19. Missing since January 2nd
Last seen: the Wawa on Ridge Street

Harley Evans Burch. Age 30. Missing since March 5th
Last seen: by her mother at home

Marissa Jones. Age 23. Missing since May 15th
Last seen: Tough Annie's

Bryan Emerson. Age 34. Missing since June 12th
Last seen: The Golden Pub

Madison Charleston. Age 22. Missing since July 25th
Last seen: The 24/7 Laundromat

Darren Wilkins. Age 37. Missing since August 9th
Last seen: Wawa on Ridge Street

Natalie Collins. Age 23. Missing since August 30th
Last seen: Tough Annie's

Anastasia Hilton. Age 26. Missing Since September 13th
Last seen: The Golden Pub

Gordon Stevenson. Age 40. Missing Since September 20th
Last seen: Leaving the grocery store

Diana Santos. Age 23. Missing since October 28th
Last seen: By her coworkers at work

The first thing that jumped out at him was that it was only women who went missing in the beginning of the year. Then, once summer hit, it was indiscriminate, men and women both. So, in the literal meaning of the word, there was no pattern.

The second thing was how more people started going missing in the summer. If this was all the Bakers' doing, they'd certainly picked up the pace once May hit.

Sheriff Olmos turned over to his desk. He picked up the two strips of paper where he'd written down the Baker Brother's names and tacked them under Diana Santos' name.

The brothers weren't officially missing, but for the sake of being thorough, he was going to assume they were.

Before he could really get his brain geared up, though, a knock on his office door broke his concentration.

The sheriff crossed the room and opened it.

Lieutenant James Rooney stood on the other side, holding two cups of coffee in his hands. Sheriff Olmos made space to let him in.

"Well, Sheriff, I just called around town," Lieutenant Rooney said, setting one of the cups on the desk. "Only person who's seen the Baker Brothers was Luke over at the Wawa. He said they stopped by to fill up their truck before going hunting."

His eyes fell on the list of names tacked to the corkboard. "What's this?"

"Everyone who's gone missing this year within twenty-miles of town," the sheriff explained.

"You think they're really missing?" the lieutenant asked. "It's possible they kidnapped Diana Santos but decided to take their sick shit elsewhere."

"Yeah, definitely possible," Sheriff Olmos said, picking up the coffee cup without taking his eyes off the list. "But something's not adding up."

"What do you mean?"

"Look at how the numbers pick up after summer." The sheriff pointed to the latter part of the list. "Men and women both. As far as the rumors go, the Baker brothers only kidnap women."

"More people come up here in the summer, though. For fishing and camping and all that."

"Yeah, I know that, James," Sheriff Olmos said. "I'm just turning over every possibility I can."

"Gotcha." Lieutenant Rooney took a sip of his coffee. While he did, he glanced over at the sheriff, who was suddenly in deep concentration. "I know that look, Sheriff. What're you thinking?"

"I'm wondering if maybe… Hmm. Well, if maybe, just maybe there's some other threat we're unaware of here."

"Huh…" James Rooney took another sip of his coffee, considering things. "Who the hell would come to this place? Usually, it's the opposite. People want to leave Hilltown."

"Yeah," Sheriff Olmos said, looking over at his lieutenant. "Also makes you wonder what they would be doing here, doesn't it?"

A NEW BEGINNING

6 MONTHS EARLIER

1

Camp Slaughter, PA

IGNACIO LOOKED IN the Toyota's rearview mirror. Behind him, the farmhouse was on fire. The flames rapidly spreading throughout the interior, roaring as they fed off the gasoline Varias Caras had poured all over the place.

Soon, it would burn down, and the place Ignacio had called home for years would be reduced to a pile of ash.

Without warning, one of the windows in the farmhouse burst, sending shards of glass flying at the back of the Toyota. The sound of the glass shattering hit Ignacio's ears like a javelin.

He winced against the pain, then put the car in drive. Ignacio was told he was dumb his whole life, but he wasn't dumb enough to ignore a sign from God when it came.

Ignacio hit the gas and headed into the campgrounds.

The *fantasmas* were out in full force, staring at him. It was like they knew what he'd done. Like they knew what would become of this place. Ignacio recognized the ones he'd put here himself, but there were others he'd never seen before. The ones from before.

The ghosts were everywhere. Inside the cabins, looking at him through dirty and broken windows. Some were on the porches. An old man was on a rocking chair out front of the dining hall, the glare on his face reminding Ignacio of when his schoolteachers would yell at the class for doing bad on a test.

A couple sat on the stairs out front of the rec building, holding each other close. The woman cried on the man's shoulders. Her tears were shiny streaks against her glowing cheeks. The man's face was full of confusion and anger, but Ignacio could feel that he wanted to cry, too.

Ignacio remembered them. He'd killed them while they'd been tent camping the other day. He'd broken the woman's neck and chopped the man's head off with the machete. They hadn't been dead for too long, which was why they were so scared.

Ignacio licked his lips as he passed them, remembering the tostadas he'd topped with their shredded meat.

Near the exit, there was a kid sitting under a tree, his knees drawn up close to his chest. Ignacio felt a similar energy from him as he had from the couple, the feeling of trying to figure out where he was. Or *what* he even was anymore.

Ignacio met the boy's gaze. He could see the pain and sadness in his eyes underneath the shaggy hair. The boy was waiting for something to happen… No, no, he was waiting for someone. Waiting for someone to come save him and bring him back to the living world.

Not just anyone, though. The boy was waiting for a specific person. Someone he'd trusted more than anyone in the world but was unsure if they would ever come.

The sadness from him was too much. Ignacio looked away and focused on driving into the woods.

2

IGNACIO DROVE AND drove across Northern Pennsylvania with no direction. He needed to get away from the camp. As far away as possible before someone saw the smoke from the fire.

He'd been driving nonstop for the last hour. The back of his head hurt. The bullet wound in his shoulder and rib did, too. But it was the ax wound in his chest that concerned him the most.

Back at the camp, at least two people had gotten away from him. The muscled-up dummy, who'd hit him with a rock in the back of the head, and the silver-blond girl who'd hacked his chest with the ax. And that was after that old man and that other woman had shot him.

After he'd woken up, he returned to the farmhouse, took the bullet out of his shoulder, and then bandaged himself the way he'd seen Mamá bandage people. He found a clean shirt to wear, too. One without a big slash in it.

But he could feel himself getting weaker and weaker with each passing minute. He needed to rest.

As he was thinking this, his stomach growled. He needed to eat, too.

Up ahead, off the side of the highway, he saw a small wooden booth. There was a large handwritten sign in front of it that read: FRESH CORN SOLD HERE.

Ignacio traced the road passing in front of the stand, and saw it connected with an offramp about a quarter of a mile away. He switched into the left lane.

Dale Henderson heard a car pulling up in front of his stand. He looked up from his phone where he'd been surfing the internet, trying to find a cheap canoe on Craigslist for the last few hours. He moved his feet off the crate he was using as a footrest and stood up, setting the phone down on the chair behind him.

"Well, well," he said, watching the green Toyota parking in front of the booth.

The only customers he'd had all day had been a couple that got lost on their way to a nearby lake. Dale had given them directions to the spot they were looking for, and in exchange they'd bought two ears of corn from him.

That'd been a few hours ago, but here was a potential third customer. Or maybe this person was just lost, too.

Dale went over to the booth window. The sun glared off the Toyota's windshield, obstructing his view, but he could see enough to tell that the driver was enormous.

Sonofagun looks like he could eat a season's worth of harvest, Dale thought, seeing money signs. *Maybe that canoe for the kids won't have to be used.*

He smiled, but the look on his face quickly changed as the driver came out of the vehicle. The man was built like a bull and had a wild mane of curly hair on his head that somehow made him look bigger. His hair was tied back in a loose ponytail, giving Dale a view of the bloody bandage over his right eyebrow.

Without taking his eyes off this enormous man, he reached for a Bluetooth speaker on a shelf next to him. He turned the knob on it until the classic rock coming from it was inaudible.

Dale watched the driver make his way toward the booth, a slight trace of a limp in his gait. He noticed there was a second bloody bandage on his cheek. Dale was a man of God, and he tried not to judge people, but this poor fellah looked like he'd been put through the ringer at least twice.

"Hey there," Dale said, his voice feeling small. He cleared his throat. "How can I help you?"

"Corn," the driver said. He stopped in front of the window, his enormity almost blocking out any light from coming into the booth.

"Sure, bud," Dale said, trying not to sound put off by the sight of him. "How many you want?"

The big man held up one of his hands, showing three thick fingers.

"Three it is," Dale said, feeling more chipper now that it seemed to be turning into a normal transaction. "Want 'em grilled?"

The man nodded.

"No problem," Dale said, stepping back into the booth.

He grabbed three ears from a wooden bin, then a skewer hanging off one of the walls and headed to the back of the booth.

Dale stopped in front of the back door. The sudden eerie feeling that his every move was being watched made him pause and turn around.

Sure enough, the driver's gaze was riveted to him. His eyes as dark and blank as a shark's. They moved from Dale's face to the skewer in his hand, and then flicked up again.

"I'll be right back, pal," Dale said, giving him a friendly nod, trying to break the awkward tension in the air.

The man returned the nod with a subtle one of his own.

Dale had no idea what the guy's deal was, but one thing he was sure of was that the sooner this man was out of here, the better he'd feel.

Ignacio could smell the charcoal grill. Could see the tendrils of smoke rising in the air through the windows at the back of the booth. He could see one of the man's arms from this angle, could see it moving as he turned the corn on the grill, could smell the corn.

His stomach grumbled at the scent. *Tengo hambre, Ignacio.* Varias Caras wanted to eat, too.

Ignacio knew corn wouldn't be enough.

No, not for El Monstro. El Monstro needed something more…

Ignacio climbed over the counter, crawled through the window. He dropped down into the booth, making as little noise as possible. He went over to the wall with the utensil rack the man had gotten the skewer from and took a moment to appreciate all of the sharp, shiny objects hanging from it. In particular, he was impressed by how nice and filed the knives were. But Ignacio didn't take one of them. Instead, he grabbed another of the metal skewers. They were the long kind meant for safer grilling.

Skewer tight in his hands, and crouching low, Ignacio made his way through the booth to the back door.

He poked his head out of the booth and saw the man was standing only a few feet away. He was in the middle of rolling the ears of corn around, his back to Ignacio.

This was going to be even easier than he thought.

He lowered his stance some more, then slowly walked over to him. The closer he got, the lighter he stepped.

Once he was within arm's length of the man, he stood up straight.

Dale was reaching for a spatula when he noticed the shadow. Before he could react, though, he was being grabbed by the back of the neck.

Ignacio pulled him backward, off his feet, making him lose his grip on the spatula. The utensil went flying over their heads and hit the booth with a metallic clink.

Dale tried to twist out of his grip, but even as hurt as he was, Ignacio was still strong enough to hold on. He aimed the skewer and drove it into the man's ear. The point ripped through everything in its way through the ear canal. Blood gushed.

Ignacio felt the skewer get stuck about halfway through the man's head. In his other hand, he felt the man's body go limp, the familiar feeling of a person being turned into a corpse.

Ignacio took his hand off the skewer, and then using both hands, propped the dead body up by the armpits. Holding it like this, he dragged it over to the booth.

He set the corpse down on the grass, leaning it against the back wall. If it wasn't for the expression of sheer terror, the blood flowing out of his ear, and the metal rod sticking out of his head, it would've looked like the Dale Henderson was simply resting against the booth, waiting for the food to finish cooking on the grill.

Ignacio found the spatula laying on the grass a few feet from where he left the dead body. He picked it up, and then went over to check on the corn.

The husks were blackened in several spots. He'd seen Mamá and Papa grill corn before, and he knew that meant they were done. He took them off the grill and wrapped them in tinfoil to keep them warm.

Then, he went inside the booth to retrieve one of those shiny knives he'd been admiring a few minutes ago.

Thirty minutes later, Ignacio took several chunks of meat off the grill. He put them on a paper plate alongside the two grilled ears of corn.

He carried the plate over to a dark blue Chevy truck that was parked behind the booth. The vehicle's windows were down and its radio was on. Ignacio had found the keys in the ignition, which allowed him to start the engine and tune to a local news station with the volume cranked while he grilled. Even though he'd listened, he'd heard nothing about the burning campground he'd left behind. Maybe he was too far away from where it happened. He wasn't sure.

He sat down on the hood of the truck, looking down the stretch of field behind the booth. On the horizon, the sun was beginning to set, daytime lackadaisically giving way to twilight. Ignacio watched fireflies shimmering on and off in the purple swath of the sky for a few seconds, then picked up a piece of meat and stuck it in his mouth.

The meat was charred on the outside, but juicy and tender on the inside. *Delicioso*, he thought, as he savored the bite.

Behind Ignacio, Dale Henderson's corpse still leaned against the booth. From the shoulders down to the biceps both arms were stripped bare to the bone. The meat from them sat on Ignacio's plate, seasoned with salt and pepper and paprika, and would soon fill his stomach.

3

IT WAS FULL dark now. Ignacio carried a lantern in one hand. The other hand was holding onto Dale Henderson's tank top straps like the handles of a luggage bag as he dragged the corpse through the woods.

Ignacio counted thirty steps from where he'd left the truck parked and dumped the body down in front of him. This was a good spot. It was in a clearing of trees, but far enough away from the road that it would take a while for anyone to find the body. If they ever found it at all.

Ignacio crouched over the corpse's head. He set the lantern on the ground nearby, so that his hands and Dale Henderson's face were still bathed by its pale glow.

From his back pocket, he took out a scalpel and pressed it under the corpse's chin. The point stabbed into the spot where a beard would stop growing and the "neck skin" began.

Then, he curved the scalpel upward toward the left ear. The little bit of blood that was left in the capillaries oozed out like a thick syrup as the blade sliced the skin open. Ignacio stopped short of the ear and continued tracing along the circumference of the face, staying close to the hairline until he came back to the point where he started.

He'd been focused on making the cut as clean and straight as possible, but now that he was done with it, he heard twigs snapping behind him.

His head shot up, worrying that someone had followed him. Another snap.

Ignacio looked over his shoulder. In the distance, beyond the trees, a pair of bright eyes glowing in the dark stared at him. It was just an animal, though. A fox or raccoon or some other animal.

"Shoo!" Ignacio hollered.

The animal sprinted away, rustling leaves and snapping more twigs as it went.

Ignacio waited a few beats before turning back to the corpse.

Now that the incision around the face was complete, he stuck his fingers underneath the skin, and pulled. The face tore away from the muscles and tissues with wet sounds. A few ambitious chunks and bits stayed on the body, but for the most part the face came off in a single sheet.

Ignacio would have to patch those holes to use the face as a mask, but he wasn't worried about that right now. Right now, he wanted to get back to the truck and listen to the radio. To make sure no one was out looking for him.

He stuffed the scalpel and face skin in his pockets, then grabbed the lantern and jogged back to where he'd parked.

Ignacio left his Toyota back at the corn stand. He'd unloaded everything from his car and put it in the back of the Chevy truck and now he was off again. Ignacio had been told he was dumb his whole life, but he was smart enough to know that switching vehicles would make it harder for someone to find him.

He sat inside the truck with the owner's face safely stashed inside the glove compartment. The radio was tuned to the same local news station he'd been listening to while he'd been eating. There was still nothing about the campsite, nothing about him. Not even anything about a forest fire.

But he still didn't think it would be a good idea to ride around at night. There would be even less cars out on the road during these hours. Less cars meant a higher chance the cops would notice him and stop him. He parked instead, finding an area to rest off the side of the highway.

Ignacio turned the key, killing the electrical power on the truck. The radio shut off. The interior lights on the ceiling winked out. He leaned the driver seat back and closed his eyes and tried to fall asleep. Morning would come faster if he fell asleep.

Ignacio laid there, motionless. Now that he was relaxing, he felt his wounds throbbing with pain.

The sounds of the woods became deafening. Cicadas hissing. Owls hooting. The wind stirring with a mournful, soft susurration.

He sat up and turned the electrical power on. A digital face on the radio smiled at him as it came back to life. The screen changed to the preset color Dale Henderson had picked, flooding the interior of the vehicle with blue light.

Ignacio thought about putting the headlights on, but then decided that would be too risky. Someone might see the beams through the trees, even though the truck was facing away from where the highway was, it was possible he'd be shining the light toward a backroad he didn't know about.

No, it was better to keep them off.

Ignacio sat there, staring out into the woods. Wishing he was elsewhere. But he couldn't go anywhere.

He had to wait…wait until he was sure they weren't coming after him.

Somewhere in the distance, an animal—maybe the same one that had been watching him earlier—let out a shrill scream.

4

IGNACIO WOKE UP slumped against the window. The glass had a circle of sweat where his head had been resting. He didn't remember falling asleep, but it must've been for hours because it was daytime now.

He looked out the windshield as a cardinal landed on the hood of the truck. The bird took two hops toward the windshield, its tiny little claws rapping against the metal. The bird cocked its head with curiosity, then took off flying, as if put off by what it found inside the vehicle.

Ignacio sat up and turned the key in the ignition. He didn't remember doing it, but he must've powered the car off sometime before falling asleep. Ignacio turned the radio on and listened.

The newscaster was talking about a bear sighting at a nearby town. Then the broadcast cut to a series of commercials. A few car dealership and political advertisements later, the newscaster was back on-air reporting about a dog who saved a kid from a lake.

Still nothing about the campgrounds or a forest fire.

That was good.

We can't be too sure, Varias Caras warned.

Ignacio looked out of the vehicle. The woods were different now. Sunlight beamed in through the treetops, turning the plants and grass bright green. The hooting of the owls had been replaced by birds twittering morning songs.

But Ignacio still didn't want to be here. He didn't want to be surrounded by trees. Not now. Maybe not ever after what happened yesterday back at the camp.

As if to remind him, the wound in his chest throbbed. A wave of pain flashed through his chest. Ignacio let out a small groan. He reached under his shirt and felt the bandage. It was dry and hard from the crusting blood, but when he pressed on it, he felt some new blood squirting out.

"Not good… not good," Ignacio whispered, shaking his head.

The way he'd slept must've caused it to tear open again. Ignacio slid out of the car and took his shirt off in front of the sideview mirror, then undid the bandages around his chest.

The girl had gotten a good hit on him with the ax, but she'd missed anything vital. A few more inches lower or higher and she would've either hacked through his heart or his throat. What he had now was nothing more than a deep flesh wound a few centimeters below his collarbone.

The major concern now was that it was getting infected. The area around the slash was purple. A thick, yellow liquid was dribbling out of it along with some fresh blood.

"Bad, bad…" Ignacio whispered.

Ignacio went to the back of the truck and grabbed some alcohol wipes and bandages from the medical kit that was in there.

He started cleaning up the wound the best he could. The alcohol was cold and stung, but the whole time he kept repeating Mamá's words as he endured the pain: *Es para que sane, Ignacio.*

She'd always said that to him when treating his cuts and scrapes as a kid.

Mamá.

He really wished she were here right now.

Ignacio finished cleaning himself up, then using the side mirror he redid the bandages. He'd seen Mamá treat Papa's wounds. Ignacio was just copying the way Mamá did it.

Done with bandaging himself up, an idea popped into his head. He went back to the truck bed and rummaged through his belongings until he found the stake with Mamá's head. He'd buried it underneath the other belongings so no one would see a severed head in the bed of the truck and call the cops while he'd been on the road.

Ignacio grabbed the sides of Mamá's head and pulled on it. There was a deep slurping sound, like a shoe stepping out of mud, as Mamá's head popped off the wooden stake.

He took the head into the truck with him, settling into the driver seat. As he continued to listen to the radio for any reports of his doings, he hugged Mamá close to his belly and brushed his fingers through her hair.

Before he knew it, the sun was going down. The news station had switched over to coverage of a local baseball game.

Outside, the woods were growing still yet again as the diurnal animals settled in for the night, clearing the area for the ones that roamed by night.

Ignacio opened the door and slid out of the truck. He took his shirt off in front of the rearview mirror and undid his bandages again. Pus and blood oozed out from it. The skin was a deep purple now, like someone had punched him in the chest several times.

"It hurts. It hurts!" he complained.

He looked over at Mamá's head resting on the passenger seat. She would know what to do. Mamá had been a nurse. She would have used things from the hospital to make it all better.

But Mamá wasn't here.

Ignacio balled his hands into fists and punched the side of the truck. He hit it so hard the sidemirror vibrated.

"What do I do? What do I do?"

Ignacio smacked himself on the side of the head a few times. *Think, think, Ignacio!* It was Papa's voice speaking to him. It was what he always said when he was trying to teach him a lesson.

Ignacio hit himself on the head a few more times, until it finally came to him.

He could find a town. A town with a hospital. Someone there would fix him up the way Mamá would.

"Yes!" Ignacio squealed in excitement.

No one was coming to look for him. At least, no one around here, miles away from the campgrounds. He was sure of that. Because if they were, he would've heard something by now.

He opened the truck door and reached inside for Mamá's head. He carried it to the back of the truck, moved things around to make space, and then nestled the decapitated head between the first-aid kit and some bags with clothes in them.

Ignacio bent over and kissed the top of Mamá's head, not caring about the stench of death coming from it. He brushed a flake of dead skin from her scalp before hiding the head underneath a blanket.

Excited, and moving faster than he probably should've, he climbed back into the truck. As he did so, on the radio, there was a series of cheers as the home team's pitcher struck out the rival batter to win the game.

About thirty-minutes later, Ignacio was driving past a big wooden sign. It was the first thing in miles he'd seen that was more than a stretch of woods, a field of grass, or a farm. The sign read:

EMERGENCY STOP
HILLTOWN HOSPITAL
3 MILES

In the distance, he saw a gray building with a red cross on it. Further away, true to its name, he saw a town sitting atop a hill.

Later, he would realize that was the heart of the town, and that there were more neighborhoods scattered in all directions.

For now, though, his focus was on getting his wounds treated the right way. He followed the arrows on the small, metallic signs posted along the road pointing to the Hilltown Hospital.

He didn't realize it then, but he was heading into the place that would become his hunting grounds for the next few months.

WATCHING

PRESENT DAY

1

IGNACIO WATCHED HER from the rooftop of a shop called Vape8. The name of the shop was spelled out in big, neon letters across the roof allowing Ignacio to crouch below the curve at the bottom of the "8," looking through the hole. The rest of the number cast a massive, dark shadow over him.

He watched her jog down the sidewalk. She was on the opposite side of the shop, so Ignacio had a good view of her. She wore a pink track suit and a pair of Nikes that had a matching pink checkmark. Her hair was up in a messy bun. Sweat rolled down her forehead and neck, making her skin glisten in the sunlight.

Ignacio itched to touch her. She was the reason he was still here in Hilltown. He'd first met her at the hospital, on his first night ever in this town. She'd been his nurse. She'd tended to his wounds and asked him if he was feeling better every time she came in to check on him.

Ignacio longed to feel her small, soft hands touching his arm again the way she had when taking his blood pressure. She was careful with him. Delicate. In that way, she was a lot like Mamá.

Except, she looked nothing like Mamá. She was the opposite. White skinned. Pinkish cheeks. Blond hair. Eyes the color of an ocean. A perfect Barbie.

But better than a Barbie. She was Judy.

That was what she'd said her name was. Judy.

Ignacio forgot names all the time, but hers he didn't. He couldn't. "Judy..." he muttered, as he watched her run past the shop.

Ignacio had a wide view of her path. She came to a corner and turned down another street, giving her back to him.

She was at the end of her loop. She would be home soon. At home, she would drink a smoothie. Either a mix of berries or a mango and pineapple smoothie. It was always one or the other.

Ignacio knew this because he knew her patterns and habits very well. He'd been following her for the last few months. Tracking her. Waiting for the perfect moment to take her back with him...

But he had to have patience. Had to wait... The rules in this town were different than back at the camp.

Ignacio clutched his hands into fists, the itch to touch her growing.

Paciencia, Ignacio, Varias Caras said to him. *En tiempo, serra tuya.*

2

Judy Olmos came into her apartment and went into the kitchen. From the freezer, she took out a bag of mixed berries, set them in a bowl to let them thaw for a few seconds, and then sat down at the kitchen table to look at her text messages.

The most recent one was from her mother, telling her to come over for dinner tonight. Judy checked the schedule app in her phone and saw she had nothing scheduled for tonight.

> **Judy:** Yes, I can go over for dinner tonight. What time should I be there?
>
> **Mom:** Can you make it at 7?
>
> **Judy:** Yes
>
> **Mom:** Ok, great. Your dad's been bugging me for lasagna
>
> **Judy:** Haha, every time I see him he mentions it
>
> **Mom:** Poor guy. Okay, see you tonight Judy. Love you
>
> **Judy:** Love you too, Mom

Judy tapped out of the thread and checked her other messages.

The second most recent message was from her roommate. She'd sent pictures of Halloween decorations. There was a ghost holding onto a tombstone like they were best friends, a black cat with an orange witch hat, and a plastic raven skeleton. A text message was attached to the last picture, asking which one she liked better. Judy texted back, "the ghost and tombstone".

Next, Judy checked her social medias. People were talking about a girl who'd gone missing yesterday. She skimmed through the posts and looked at the picture of the Hispanic girl, committing it to memory.

Her roommate's cat came trudging into the kitchen. He stopped by her legs, let out a short mew, and then sniffed at her sweaty pantleg.

"Hey, Nos," Judy said to the black cat, putting her phone on the table. She pet him on the head, and he let out a few chirps of excitement and started purring. "You hungry, boy?"

Judy got up and went over to the pantry and grabbed the bag of kibble from the bottom most shelf. She filled his food bowl, checked his water, and then went over to the sink to wash her hands.

The window behind the kitchen sink looked out into a twelve-foot stretch of grass that ended in a hedgerow. The bushes were tall and spire-like and planted close together to provide privacy between the apartment building and the houses behind it, but there were spaces between the branches that let you see some of what was going on beyond them.

An abrupt movement out there made Judy pause for a second, her hands dripping soap into the sink as she watched the October wind swaying the bushes. The ones directly in front of her seemed to move unrhythmically with the others, as if disturbed by a different force.

Every once in a while, there would be movement from them that caught her off guard in this way. It usually turned out to be a bird hopping around or some rabbits jumping into them. But still, the erratic movements always got her attention.

Judy watched the bushes for a minute, waiting to see if any critter came out from them. Nothing.

The passing breeze died down. The branches started to settle.

Judy shook her head. It was probably the lightheadedness from the jog tricking her eyes into seeing things. She'd feel better after refueling.

Judy finished washing her hands, then went over to the counter where the bag of fruit was. She threw the berries into the blender with some ice and water. Then she poured the smoothie into a glass and stuck a rubber straw in it, then went back to the table to drink her smoothie.

As she sat there, enjoying the cold sweetness, she scrolled through recipes to figure out what to take over her mom's for dinner tonight.

Outside, only twelve feet of grass and some bushes separated her from the cannibal watching her through her kitchen window.

3

IGNACIO COULDN'T WATCH Judy as long as he would have liked to. He had to go to work. He drove the Saturn Ion through the gates and into the junkyard.

Harvey Moon, the man Ignacio knew as "the Boss," was sitting on the bench outside the office building, munching on a TastyKake cinnamon roll and reading the newspaper. He looked up when he heard Ignacio's vehicle pulling up to the curb and waved to him with the half-eaten roll.

Ignacio parked the car in front of the office building, next to the Boss' red truck and got out of the vehicle.

"Hey there, Iggy," Harvey said, putting the cinnamon bun on his lap so he could fold the newspaper and put it aside. He stood up with his snack in hand. "How you doin', boy?"

"Good." Ignacio nodded.

"We got a bit of work to do today," Harvey said, taking a big bite of his cinnamon roll. "Baxter and I just came back from picking up a buncha tires from a mechanic out near Reading. They'd been sitting in the back of his lot for almost three years taking up space. Three years!"

Ignacio nodded again, but he didn't know what the Boss was talking about.

Harvey stepped off the curb in front of the office building.

"But anyway," Harvey said, waving for Ignacio to follow him. "Let's get to the good stuff. I'll show ya how to use the tire shredder."

Piles of demolished cars, tires, scrap metal, and other miscellaneous discarded detritus laid about the junkyard, stacked high and long enough to be considered walls. Between these junk walls, the spaces—or "aisles" as employees of the junkyard thought of them—were wide enough to drive a car through. The whole layout was maze-like, with no real rhyme or reason to where the piles began or ended.

Harvey liked it that way, though. The confusing paths discouraged people from just wandering around the property. The height of the piles of junk made it almost impossible for anyone to see how far the yard stretched out. For all they knew, if they came in here and got lost, they might never find their way back.

Most people who Harvey had hired got lost within the first week or so, but this new guy he'd hired over the summer was different. He'd learned the layout of the junkyard on his first day.

The man was as quiet as a mouse, the size of an elephant, and had the work ethic of a darn mule.

They navigated through the piles of junk until they came to a large clearing where the shredder was located. The shredder was a blue machine that looked like a shipping container with another smaller container—the hopper—that resembled a bathtub hanging over it. An enclosed chute connected the two parts of the machine.

Harvey led them to the back of the machine. He stopped at the foot of a set of metal stairs that led up to a platform hovering over the massive device.

"You ever use a machine like this before?" Harvey asked Ignacio.

Ignacio shook his head.

"It's a bitch because you gotta carry stuff up there." Harvey pointed to the platform. "But it does wonders. Come on, grab one of 'em and I'll show you."

Harvey pointed to the stack of tires about a foot away from the machine. The tires were bloated and deformed or were deflated from large gashes, all useless in their own way.

Ignacio grabbed one from the top, and then Harvey took him up the stairs. The metal grating echoed and rattled underneath their weight.

"Alright, well, there ain't really much to this," Harvey said as they reached the platform, a six-by-six-foot area surrounded by a guardrail. To their right was a control box with a silver switch, a red button, and a red and green light on top of it.

"You put whatever junk you're tryin' to shred into the feed port over here," Harvey said, walking across the platform to the side that overlooked the hopper.

The bottom of the feed port was lined with eight sets of metallic "teeth" that resembled large gears. They were idle at the moment, but even in this state, they looked like something you wouldn't want to get caught in.

"First, though, you want to make sure the machine is on." Harvey took them over to the control box. He flipped the silver switch from "OFF" to "ON."

The machine whined as it started, vibrating the metal grating they stood on. The teeth at the bottom of the feed port started to turn, each row turning into the one behind it. They didn't move particularly fast, but it was like watching the mouth of a giant mechanical beast chewing, waiting to be fed.

"You want to make sure the machine's going first, so you don't choke it up with whatever you're trying to shred."

Ignacio nodded.

"If you need to stop it for whatever reason, this big red button does the trick." Harvey mashed the button with an index finger.

The machine made a guttural, mechanical complaint as the teeth came to a sudden halt.

"To get it going again, you gotta turn it off and on." Harvey flipped the switch twice. The teeth began turning again. "All the junk gets ground up in the port, then gets spit out through that chute and collected at the bottom of the machine. It's that simple."

"Simple," Ignacio repeated.

"Go ahead, throw that tire in there, big man," Harvey said, clapping him on the shoulder. "And step back quickly over here when you do. We don't need someone gettin' hurt up here, you know?"

Ignacio did as he was told and dropped the tire over the guard rail into the feed port.

The teeth got their first bite into it, pulling it down as it shredded pieces off. Rubber flew through the air, but most of it was being sent down the chute and into the container below. The metallic teeth didn't slow or whine or stutter for even a second as they munched through the tire, reducing it to nothing but tiny pieces.

Ignacio watched without blinking. He watched intently, until five minutes later, the tire was gone. A few pieces of rubber were stuck between the teeth here and there, but that was the only evidence left.

The metal teeth continued spinning like they were begging to be fed more.

Harvey went over to the control box and flipped the switch off.

"What do ya think?" he asked Ignacio, watching the metal teeth come to a halt. "Pretty impressive machine, huh?"

Ignacio nodded.

But he couldn't tell the Boss what he was thinking. Couldn't tell him how inside of him, the monster was wondering things, making him picture things…

No, the Boss wouldn't like that. It was best he kept these thoughts to himself.

Harvey Moon took a second to admire his star employee going to work. He watched Ignacio take several tires from the stack at a time, go up the grating staircase, and drop them into the feed port. The man was doing this with the focus and movements of a worker ant.

Tireless and efficient.

This mysterious man who appeared in his office back in May was a specimen, to be sure. But more than that, he was a godsend to Harvey. Harvey's knee and hip had been bothering him for years, so he needed all the help he could get around the junkyard.

He'd put up "help wanted" signs around Hilltown years ago, but not a whole lot of people jumped at the opportunity to work for him.

Most people figured it'd be grueling work to have to lift heavy scrap metals and operate machinery in both the scorching hot months and the blistering cold months—and they were right to make those assumption. Working at the junkyard was not light work.

In fact, most people who came in through his office were knuckleheads or rednecks that caused more problems for him. Harvey would fire them within months, long before he would ever even start to think about letting them operate something as dangerous as the shredder.

Ignacio had been a special case. He'd come into the office, carrying one of the "help wanted" signs in his hand. He'd put it on Harvey's desk and said just one word, "Work."

After a few short questions, Harvey realized he wasn't a man of many words, but he hired him on the spot because of his size and build. Harvey had been so impressed by his diligence that by the end of the day he'd opened his home to him. Ignacio needed a place to stay, and he had room in his old home, a rancher about half a mile away from the junkyard.

Ignacio had agreed. Harvey drove him there, gave him his spare key, and told him they'd go to Walmart in the morning to get him some basic stuff.

It'd been a gamble, but it paid off because Iggy was the best worker he'd ever had.

Harvey took a few more seconds to appreciate him, watching him pick up another five tires in one go without so much as straining.

"Sheesh," Harvey muttered to himself. Not even in his prime would Harvey have attempted something like that.

He took the newsboy hat off his head and wiped his brow with it before heading back into the office to do the paperwork he was more suited for nowadays.

4

Hours later, Ignacio finished shredding all of the tires. The Boss had been impressed. That was good.

Papa always told him to get in the good graces with the Boss at work.

He was coming home now. Ignacio pulled into the driveway in front of the old rancher. The house the Boss was letting him stay in was a lot smaller than the farmhouse he'd been living in back at the camp. But that was okay. Ignacio didn't need a big space.

He only needed a place to sleep, make his masks, and keep his Barbies in. Once he got Judy, he might leave this place. Maybe not. He wasn't sure.

He liked this house.

Like the junkyard, it was located outside the heart of Hilltown. The nearest neighborhood or establishment was about two miles away, which meant there wasn't ever anyone around this place. Ignacio could do what he wanted without worrying about it.

He could hang pieces of leather on clotheslines out in the backyard, bring lumber and reinforced steel mesh into the house, board up the attic windows, and no one was around to question it.

The Boss hadn't come here even once since showing it to Ignacio. Ignacio thought it had something to do with the locked room the Boss had told him to stay out of. He wasn't sure.

Ignacio was just grateful for the privacy.

He went inside the house to make dinner.

The bag of meat made a wet plop as Ignacio set it down on the counter. He went over to the windows behind the kitchen sink and peered out of them, holding onto the yellow curtains on either side.

He looked out into the narrow road that led from the junkyard to the house. It was covered with autumn leaves, most of which were intact because no one came this way. The few leaves that were broken up had been damaged by the rain, walked on by animals, or driven over by Ignacio's vehicle as he came home from work.

Ignacio watched the road for a good minute or so, but the road remained as lonesome as it always was.

Still, he had to make sure no one was coming.

Things are different out here, Varias Caras reminded him.

"*Si,*" Ignacio said, closing the curtains and returning to the counter.

He grabbed a knife from a butcher's block and a cutting board from a nail on the wall. Then, from the brown paper bag, he pulled out two large chunks of meat that had come from the back of Charles Baker's thighs. Ignacio placed them on the cutting board and started cutting off the layer of skin and fat.

While Ignacio butchered away, he listened to some birds twittering outside the kitchen window. They were perched on a nearby tree, singing their songs full blast into the radiant October afternoon.

About twenty-minutes later, Ignacio had the thighs cut up into bite-sized pieces and cooked. He dumped the meat into a pot filled with a red broth, diced onions, garlic, and chopped up peppers. With the meat added, the soup was done.

Using a wooden spoon, Ignacio mixed everything in the pot. Then, he filled two bowls with the soup, placed them on trays, and headed up into the attic.

5

DIANA WAS LAYING back on the mattress, staring up at the ceiling. In the dim lighting of the room, she could just make out parts of the wooden beams above her.

Her stomach growled.

Even though the smell of the beans wasn't exactly pleasant, it was still food. And it was touching a primal part of her. A primal part that was telling her she needed to eat something. Anything.

But she refused. If she ate his food, she would be stripping herself of her humanity.

Her stomach grumbled again. Harder this time. It felt like a tremor had gone off in her stomach.

Before she could react, the attic was flooded with light. The masked man climbed up the stairs, undid the locks, and then burst through the door.

Diana turned her head and saw he was carrying a plastic tray with two bowls and a small bottle of hot sauce on it. The bowls were identical to the one inside the cage, except there was steam rising out of these.

As he neared the cage, the smell of soup hit Diana's nostrils. The scent so strong it overtook the acrid smell of the attic—for the time being, anyway.

She sat up on the mattress, watching him work the lock off the feed door.

"Did not like beans. Maybe you will like this." He slid one of the bowls into her side of the door, then the bottle of hot sauce. "If you like spicy."

"Fuck you," Diana spat. "I'm not eating your food."

He looked down at the bowls, then up at her. His head cocked to the side like a confused dog. "Why?"

"Why? Why are you doing this to me, you sick fuck?"

"You are afraid. That's OK," he said, standing up.

"My family's looking for me. They probably already told the cops I'm missing."

"Cops won't find you," he said, walking over to the other cage, the one he'd kept Madison in. He reached inside of it and gathered some plushies in his hand and returned to Diana's cage.

"They will," Diana protested, trying to keep the confidence in her voice.

"No," he said, shaking his head like a little kid that didn't want to believe something. "They didn't find the other Barbie. They won't find you."

Her heart sank as she realized he was right. According to Madison, she'd been in here long enough to lose track of time, and no one had ever found her. Diana shrunk back in the cage, her morale taking a hit.

"When I was a little boy, Mamá would give me animal toys…when I was scared. Made me feel better." He put two plushies—a white tiger that had a purple button replacing one of its eyes and a bean-filled monkey—inside her cage. "Maybe they will help you."

"How many girls did you do this to before me? How many have you killed?"

"Not girls. Barbies," he said, shaking his head. "You are my Barbie. I will take care of you. Comb your hair. Play with you."

"I'm not your Barbie. And neither were the others, you sick fuck. They were people. People with friends and family who loved them." Diana thought of her mom, thought about how she wished she could have one more phone call with her, no matter how annoying she might be.

"No!" he roared, stomping around now. The floor shook underneath them. "No! No! You are being a bad Barbie! Bad Barbie! Bad Barbie!"

"Let me out of here!" Diana broke down crying. She grabbed onto the cage and rattled it as hard as she could, the steel mesh almost cutting into her fingers. "Let me out, you crazy fuck!"

"No, no, no. Stop!" he said, shaking his head. He hit himself on the side of the head multiple times. "You must…stop…or he will hurt you…There are times when I cannot control him."

"Who?" Diana felt a shiver go up her spine at the possibility of a second person being involved in this demented shit.

"*El Monstro*. The monster…who lives inside of me." The masked man was speaking in a low voice now. He had his eyes closed and his head hanging low, trying to calm himself.

"When he takes control…he does things I do not want him to," he continued. "So…stop being bad, and he will leave us alone…and not make me break you."

The last two words hit Diana differently. *Break you.* Like he was talking about a toy. That's all she was to him, a Barbie doll.

"Eat," he ordered, opening his eyes. "I will play with you some other time."

He picked up the tray with the other bowl of soup still on it and left the attic. Diana waited until his footfalls were near the bottom of the staircase, then buried her head in the crook of her arm and wept.

6

JUDY FOUND HER mom sitting out on the porch swing next to a brunette girl drinking an iced coffee. Both of them noticed her and waved as she parked her car in the driveway, behind her mother's SUV.

Judy waved back, trying to figure out who the brunette girl was. She looked familiar despite the fact her outfit was the exact polar opposite of what anyone in Hilltown would wear. She looked like she'd just gotten off a runway. She wore a faux-fur jacket, gold bracelets on both her wrists, designer jeans, and a pair of Louie Vuitton boots. Definitely not from around here.

Judy got out of her car, taking the jug of apple cider on the passenger seat with her. As she came up the walkway toward the porch, the brunette gave her a big smile.

A smile that was just a little too big to be genuine—and Judy recognized her instantly.

Brie Berk. She'd been Judy's next-door neighbor growing up, and one of the "popular" girls at Hilltown High. Brie had gone off to a college in New York City after she graduated, and Judy hadn't seen her since. As far as she knew, Brie Berk never came back to Hilltown.

Until now.

"Judy, you remember Brie Berk, don't you?" her mother said, greeting her at the top of the porch.

Brie stood up, her faux mink coat draped down behind her like a queen's cape.

For a second, Judy felt like a vagabond, considering she was wearing an oversized cat sweater and a pair of canvas shoes she'd thrifted downtown.

"I do." Judy said, looking over at her former neighbor.

"Long time no see, Neighbor." Brie said cheerfully, coming over and giving her a quick hug.

"Yeah. How long's it been?"

"I think like six years," Brie said, doing the math in her head. "Yeah, six years is right."

"So. How've you been?" Judy asked, trying to force politeness into her tone.

Brie Berk hadn't exactly been nice to her in high school. She never flat-out bullied Judy or anything, but they were parts of different crowds. Brie had hung out with the crowd that averted Judy's friends, labelling them "nerds" or "dorks."

"The city-life is amazing, Jude. Something everyone should experience once in their life." Brie said, then she frowned. "As for how I've been, well, I've had better days. I'm back in Hilltown to help my dad around the house while my mom is in the hospital."

"Wait, what? What happened to your mom?" Judy asked, astonished. She'd just left the hospital this morning and didn't remember seeing Mrs. Berk there.

"Her appendix ruptured this morning," Brie said. She noticed Judy's mother looking over at her and frowned more. "My dad rushed her into the ER this morning and I drove all the way out here ASAP."

"That's awful," Judy said. "I'm sorry to hear that."

Brie shrugged. "*C'est la vie.* I'm sure she will be OK."

"Judy's a nurse at Hilltown Hospital," her mom said.

"Oh?" Brie said in a tone full of honest surprise. "Is that a fact. Who would've thought?"

"Yeah, I am," Judy said, a little defensively. "I actually got off an overnight."

"Ah, guess you just missed my mom, then."

"I'll be back in tomorrow morning, and I'll make sure I stop by to pay her a visit."

"I would love that," Brie Berk said, beaming with excitement.

"Yeah," Judy said, nodding, but feeling that Brie was kind of putting on an act now.

"I need to go check on the lasagna," Judy's mom interjected. "Brie, are you sure you don't want to stay for dinner?"

Brie shook her head. "No thank you, Mrs. Olmos. I'm in charge of making dinner for dad tonight. Can't leave him to fend for himself. He's not that kind of guy, you know?"

"Oh, I understand. Most men aren't, sweetheart."

Brie let out a forced, phony laugh. "Oh, Mrs. Olmos, you're too much."

"Jude, you want me to take that?"

She'd almost forgotten the jug in her hand. "Oh, yeah. I bought some cider from the Amish market last week. Figured I'd bring it over."

Her mother took it, nodding in approval. Then to Brie she said, "Anyway, I hope you and your father will stop by for dinner sometime before you head back to New York."

"We definitely will. Thank you, Mrs. Olmos."

"It was nice seeing you."

"Nice seeing you, too, Mrs. Olmos."

Her mother opened the screen door and disappeared inside the house.

Brie waited until her footsteps recessed deep into the house, and then plopped down onto the porch swing. She stretched out across the seat, all but putting her boots on the cushions, leaving no space for Judy to sit.

Judy leaned against the porch railing, and without realizing she was doing it, crossed her arms in front of her.

"I see you haven't changed much," Brie said, looking her up and down.

Judy paused, unsure how to respond to that. She wasn't even sure if it was meant to be a compliment or an insult.

"Thanks," she finally said, settling on keeping this cordial.

"Be honest, did you miss me, Neighbor?" Brie asked, grinning. She shook her head and laughed. "You don't actually have to answer that."

Now that Judy's mother was gone, Brie's entire demeanor had changed, including the tone of her voice.

"So you work overnights at the hospital?" Brie continued.

"Yeah. Sometimes I do first and second shift. Just depends on what they need."

"Jeez." Brie shook her head. "I have to ask, what the hell makes someone want to stay in a place like Hilltown?"

Judy shrugged.

"I mean, no offense if you like it here, but this place smells like horse manure."

Judy let out a courtesy chuckle and shrugged. She was hoping if she made this conversation as boring as possible, Brie would head home sooner rather than later.

"Anyway, what's there to do around here? Everyone I know has left this place except for like two people, and they have kids! Can you believe that?"

"It's how things go for some folks around here." Judy shrugged again.

"Such a shame. If they saw NYC in person instead of just on the TV, they'd know how much more there is to life than this small town."

"I bet."

"Anyway. You didn't give me an answer. What's there to do around here? I'm here all week. You know of any Halloween parties going on?"

"Not really. We usually just go downtown for Halloween."

"Aren't there like, three bars in town?"

"Two, actually," Judy corrected her. "The Loft closed two years back."

"Oh, great," Brie scoffed. "Who're you going with? A boyfriend?"

Judy shook her head. "No. It'll probably just be me and Daphne."

"Daphne?"

"Daphne Woodson. She was in my grade."

"Ohhh, that name rings a bell. She was that emo-goth chick, right?"

Judy bristled, but the description was kind of accurate. "Yeah."

"Oh my god," Brie threw her head back and cackled. "I remember her. I remember seeing you two walk down the hallway together; you in your sweaters and pencil skirts, and her in her black jeans and shirts she got from Hot Topic. Such a funny sight."

"I guess that would look funny to some," Judy said, trying to hide her annoyance.

"No offense. I'm just talking about kid's stuff." Brie took a sip of her iced coffee. "That was then, this is now, you know?"

"Right," Judy said, wishing this conversation was "then" instead of "now."

"Anyway, if you don't mind, could I tag along with you two?" Brie said. "I brought my Halloween costume with me and everything."

"Yeah, that's fine." Judy said, regretting the words as soon as they escaped her mouth.

"Great!" Brie jumped up to give her a quick, loose hug. It was the kind of hug you would give to a distant relative at a family reunion.

Judy fought the instinct to push her away.

Brie stepped back and took her cellphone out from a pocket in her jacket. She shoved it in Judy's direction. "Here, put your number in my phone. I think I lost it way back in the day."

Judy was pretty sure they never had each other's numbers to begin with. But still she took the phone from her, put her cell number into it, and then gave it back to her.

"Okay, great," Brie said. "I'll text you later and we'll figure it out. I gotta head out now."

"Alright," Judy said, holding back a smile at the thought of getting out of this conversation.

Brie grabbed her iced coffee off the table next to the swing and started down the porch steps. Halfway down, she stopped and turned back.

"Hey, where's a good spot to get sushi around here?"

"There's only one place. And it's downtown." Judy told her.

"Oh… well, shit." Brie shook her head. "Guess I'll have to order pizza then."

"Didn't you say you were cooking dinner? Or did I just hear you wrong?"

"You heard right, but I just said that to your mom because I know old ladies love hearing stuff like that. I don't *actually* waste my time with cooking."

Figures, Judy thought. Same old Brie.

"Okay, ciao, Neighbor," Brie told her, continuing down the steps. "I'll see you on Halloween."

"See ya later."

She stayed on the porch for a few seconds, listening to the click clack of Brie's designer boots heading up the sidewalk.

Judy wondered how any of that just happened. The last person she'd ever thought she'd be inviting to hang out with her was Brie Berk. Coincidentally, Brie was also the last person she ever thought would *want* to hang out with her.

Life is strange, she told herself, a trace of a smirk forming across her face.

She leaned off the railing and headed inside to see what her mother needed help with.

7

AFTER DINNER, THEY went into the living room to watch TV. Judy's dad had put on a channel playing the original *Creature from the Black Lagoon* while they drank warm apple cider and ate homemade peanut butter cookies. The only lighting was provided by the fireplace, a few candles here and there, and a small tableside lamp Judy's mom was knitting a scarf by.

They hadn't talked much or paid much attention to the television, but there was a certain closeness between them as they sat together.

In the hall between the dining and living room, the grandfather clock chimed, the sound loud enough to be heard over the TV speakers. Judy checked the time on her phone. It was ten o'clock.

"Alrighty, I think it's time for me to head out," Judy said to the room.

"Already?" her father said, sitting up on the couch.

"You wanna take some lasagna with you, Jude?" her mother asked, setting the scarf and knitting material on the armrest of the couch.

Judy looked over at her dad, who was giving her a small shake of his head and a mischievous smile.

"Greg," her mom said, looking over at him and rolling her eyes at him.

They laughed, then her mom started for the kitchen without waiting for an answer to her question. They all knew it had been rhetorical, and she was going to send Judy home with leftovers no matter what.

"I'll pack some cookies up for you, too," her mom called from the hallway.

"Cookies, lasagna. You really need to come over for dinner more often," her dad said, picking up the TV remote and flicking through the channels.

Judy grinned, knowing the lasagna had nothing to do with why her father wanted her to come over more often. Ever since she'd moved out and started nursing school two years ago, she only saw her parents every other week or so. Now it was even less than that, what with taking every shift she could grab at Hilltown Hospital.

"I might be able to come next weekend," she half-promised.

"You better," her dad chuckled. "I miss you already."

Judy got out of the Lay-Z-Boy and walked over to her father, pinky out. "I pinky promise."

He hooked his finger around hers, then got up and hugged her tight to him.

"You know…if you ever wanted to relocate and come live here again, I wouldn't mind a bit."

Judy laughed with her head still pressed against his chest. "You'd have to take Daph in, too. I have a pinky promise going with her that we'd be roomies wherever we move to."

"As long as she smokes her dope outside the house, sure."

Judy let go of him and laughed. "She's never once touched the stuff."

"You've never been a good liar, Jude," he chuckled.

"I put in some extra for Daphne as well," her mother said, coming back into the room carrying a plastic bag heavy with food.

"Thanks." Judy said, grabbing it from her mom.

They walked her to the front door. Judy grabbed her jacket from the coatrack. Judy hugged and kissed her parents, then they said their goodbyes and she started out of the house.

"Oh, Judy," her mother called before closing the door, "would you mind blowing out the Jack-O-Lanterns?"

"I got 'em, Mom!" she replied, descending the porch.

The carved pumpkins were sitting on the ledge past the porch railing. Judy went over to them and tipped one over. Feeling the warmth of the candle inside of it before blowing out the flame.

She took a second to watch the black smoke rising out of the hole at the top disappear into the night.

8

THE LIVING ROOM furniture was rearranged when Judy came home.

The apartment was dark, except for the flames from a circle of candles. Her roommate, Daphne, sat cross-legged in the middle of the circle and behind her, on the coffee table she'd pushed up against the couch to make room, sage was burning in a ceramic holder. Smoke hazed through the apartment in lackadaisical wisps.

"What the…" Judy whispered.

"Shhh," Daphne said, keeping her eyes closed. "You don't want to disrupt the spirits."

"Oh, brother," Judy giggled, crossing the living room past her roommate's séance setup.

"The spirits say…you should have a drink with me." Daphne opened her eyes. She reached behind her for a glass of wine on the coffee table and sipped some of it. "I bought some of that wine you like—the junk that tastes like fruit punch."

"Appreciate it," Judy said, yawning. "But I'm sleepy. I feel like my mom's lasagna put me in a food coma. I brought some for you, too, by the way."

"Oh, come on." Daphne said, getting up off the floor. She crossed the living room and hit the light switch. Witching hour was over. "Just one drink, please?"

Judy eyed the wine glass Daphne was holding. It was enticing.

"Okay, fine," Judy said. "Let me just put this in the kitchen and go get changed into something comfier."

Daphne beamed and went to pour a second glass before she could change her mind.

The living room was somewhat back to normal when Judy returned from changing. The cat tree and TV stand were still smooshed into a corner, but everything else was back in place.

Daphne was lying back on the couch, letting a cloud of smoke drift out of her mouth. The bong she'd taken a rip from was on the coffee table, along with a bottle of wine, two glasses, and the candles she'd been using for her séance.

"Sorry to interrupt," Judy teased as she sat down on the couch across from her.

Daphne held out her index finger, holding her breath before exhaling the double lungful of smoke. She watched the smoke drift out of her mouth as she exhaled.

"Whew. New guy at the store has some really good weed."

Judy laughed and picked up her wineglass. She took a sip of it, savoring it. It was sweet and chilled, just how she liked it.

"How was dinner?" Daphne asked, sitting up. She grabbed a throw blanket that had a pattern of spiders and candy corn on it from the back of the couch and wrapped herself up in it like a burrito.

"Dinner was good," Judy said. "The leftover lasagna is in the fridge. Don't feel like you have to eat any of it. But she gave us cookies too."

She hefted the plastic container of goodies that she'd left out for this exact moment.

"Oh, yum," Daphne said, holding her hand out and wiggling her fingers. "Gimme one."

"They're peanut butter," Judy warned, handing her the bunch.

Daphne undid the plastic lid and stared at them with a gleam in her eyes. "You're mom's the best. I don't know why you don't go over there more often."

"Yeah, well… Something funny happened while I was over there."

Daphne grabbed two cookies, set them aside, and then snapped the lid in place again. She took a bite out of one and leaned back on the couch with her wineglass. "What's that?"

"Do you remember Brie Berk?"

"Yuck. Of course," Daphne said, crinkling her nose like she'd just caught a whiff of bad smelling cheese.

"Well, she's back in town."

"Oh, boy. Be still my beating heart."

"That's not all. I, uh, may or may not have sort of accidentally invited her to hang out with us on Halloween."

Daphne almost spit out the cookie she was chewing. "You did what now, Jude?"

"Her mom's in the hospital. I felt bad," Judy said, shrinking in her seat.

To her relief, Daphne put her head back and laughed. "Oh, man. When we were in high school, did you ever think we'd be hanging out with Brie Berk?"

Judy blushed and shook her head.

"What's she like now? Still a huge bitch?"

"Yeah, kind of."

"Okay, so that means she's probably an even bigger one." Daphne smirked, knowing Judy was sugarcoating the truth. "Eh, it'll be fine. We'll have fun anyway."

"Yeah," Judy smiled.

"What're we doing for Halloween, anyway? Hitting the bars?"

"Sure. That sounds fun." Then, Judy's face flushed red with embarrassment. "I haven't gotten a costume yet, though."

"Uh-oh."

"I've been busy," Judy said, feeling like she was having an argument with the air.

"I know, Jude. It's all good. We'll find you something. Wait, wait, you did remember to take off work for Halloween, right?"

"Of course I did." She wasn't the biggest fan of drinking, but Halloween was different. She always enjoyed going out on that night—whether it was trick-or-treating as a kid or a house party in her teens or barhopping with her best friend.

"Alright, good," Daphne nodded. "What time are you done work tomorrow?"

"I'm done at six. Then I have the next five days off."

"Finally taking some time for yourself, huh?"

"Yeah. Working all of these shifts is kind of starting to catch up to me." As if on cue, a yawn escaped her. Judy picked up her wine and downed some more.

"Okay, well, let's go downtown tomorrow and hit the Halloween Store," Daphne suggested. "I need a certain shade of green lipstick for my costume anyway."

"You're being a witch, right?"

"Do you think I would go as anything else?"

Judy laughed. "Guess not."

"I'm doing a forest witch this year." Daphne winked and took another gulp of wine. "This cape better impress people. It took me all fucking month to sew."

Judy laughed, but she knew Daphne's Halloween costume was going to wow everyone. They always did.

"You didn't give me an answer, though, toots. Halloween Store tomorrow?" Daphne asked, then emptied the wineglass. She poured herself up some more.

"Oh, sorry. Yeah, Halloween store tomorrow sounds good," Judy said, another yawn coming out at the end of her answer.

"Great. It's a date then." Daphne said, grabbing the bong from the coffee table. She packed it up with some weed from a dime bag that was sitting on the table next to it. "You want a hit?"

"No thanks," Judy answered, as she always did. "Think I'm gonna go to sleep, if you don't mind."

"Nah, that's alright." Daphne glanced at the wineglass in Judy's hands. "I'll finish that off for you, if you want."

"Yup, please do." Judy laughed, getting up.

"By the way, tell Mama Olmos I said thanks for the food." Daph said, sitting back with the bong and pressing it to her lips.

"Will do."

Judy set the wineglass down on the table and let out a big yawn as she stretched her arms up to the ceiling.

They said goodnight and then Judy headed to her bedroom.

Judy had struggled with bouts of anxiety since she was a little girl. She wasn't sure where they came from.

Maybe it had something to do with growing up with a cop for a dad. She'd often overhear her father recounting stories to his buddies while they drank on the porch or played cards in the dining room when he thought she wasn't within earshot.

She didn't always grasp the whole story, especially since he used police terms that went over her head when she was really young. Terms like "premeditated homicide" and "aggravated assault," but it was the tone he used that haunted her mind.

Whatever the reason, Judy had episodes where it felt like something bad was about to happen.

And right now, as she was walking down the hall from the bathroom to her bedroom, she could feel the anxiety demon trying to dig its claws into her mind.

Down the hall, she could hear the faint score of the B-horror movie Daphne was watching in the living room. Her anxiety was stirring up, making her start to imagine worries around every corner. The living room was only a few paces behind her, but the anxiety was making it feel like Daphne and the TV were miles away.

Judy got to the bedroom door and rested her hand on the knob. She paused and took in a deep breath. Her mind was tricking her into expecting the worst possible things now. Maybe someone was behind the door with a knife. Maybe an endless abyss was gaping just beyond, ready to swallow her whole. Maybe spiders had hatched in the walls and now were swarming, hungry, in need of blood.

Or maybe there was a chainsaw wielding maniac waiting for her.

Okay, that's just silly. Judy thought, almost laughing to herself.

Even still, she clenched her teeth as she pushed open the door and flicked the light switch on.

Her bed was made. The books on the nightstand were in neat piles separated by fiction and nonfiction. The carpet still had lines on it from the vacuum. The windows were closed, and the latches locked.

It was exactly as she'd left it this morning before her run. There wasn't even a trace of Daphne's cat having been in here.

It was clear the only thing waiting for her was the anxiety in her head.

Judy breathed a little easier, but just to be sure, she went over to the window. She peered through it. From her bedroom, she could see the same strip of bushes as she could from the kitchen window. Parts of them were illuminated by the light fixture outside of the building, but mostly it was dark out there. Beyond the hedgerow, she could see light inside the houses behind the apartment building.

A woman appeared at the window of one of the houses on her left. She bent over a tall candle sitting by one of the windows and blew it out. With the flame extinguished, the woman disappeared into total darkness.

Judy took this as her cue to go sleep. She'd had her fingers on the blinder rod but let go of it now. She'd been trying to decide if she wanted to close them or not, but now that she saw there wasn't anything out of the ordinary out there, she settled on leaving them open. She liked seeing sunlight first thing in the morning when she opened her eyes.

Besides, closing them would mean she'd let the anxiety win tonight.

It's all just in my head, Judy told herself, turning away from the window and crawling under the sheets.

9

They met at a bar called Tough Annie's, a former tattoo parlor now turned dive bar. The place was named after the logo outside, a rip-off of the Wendy's logo except the girl had jet black hair, a backwards baseball cap, and black lipstick.

The funny thing was, the name "Tough Annie" was nowhere to be found on the sign. Someone had just started calling the girl on the logo "Annie" one night and the name stuck. The original name of the place was "Hilltown Tavern," but the name became so ubiquitous the owner just changed it one day.

The waitress came to their table with a plate of hot wings and another round of beers for them.

"Okay, we've been sitting here bullshitting for like twenty minutes now. You finally gonna tell us what this idea you have is?" Dan asked Tucker, who was sitting across from him at the booth.

"*We have*," Tucker corrected him, glancing over at Hudson. Hudson nodded.

"Yeah, yeah. Go on, Tuck," Dan said.

"Okay, so, you guys remember that abandoned house we found over the summer? When we were in the search party for that missing girl?"

"Madison Charleston," Dan said.

"Did they ever find her?" Hudson interjected. From across the table, he saw Tucker give him a dirty look.

Dan shook his head. "Nope."

"Jeez. That…that really sucks. You think she's still alive?"

"Fuck no," Tucker said. "Anyway, we were thinking about how badass it would be to host a Halloween party there."

"Eh, I dunno man," Dan said, shifting in his seat. "I don't know how the sheriff would react to that."

"He doesn't need to know. What the hell? Do you tell him everything?"

"No, shithead. I mean word travels quickly in Hilltown."

"So we'll keep it lowkey," Tucker said. "We won't invite a lot of people. None of the cops will know."

Dan looked over at Baxter.

Baxter shrugged.

"No cops allowed—except for you," Tucker said, then grinned as another thought flashed in his mind. "No one's even allowed to come dressed up as one."

Dan wasn't really listening to what he was saying, he was more weighing out the pros and cons in his head. Hudson and Tucker had taken him to the house a few days after they found it, and he hated to admit it to Tucker, but it *would* make a cool spot to host a Halloween party.

"Come on," Tucker said, looking at Baxter Miller who was sitting next to him. "You could invite people from college and shit."

Baxter considered this.

"Chicks, to be specific," Tucker added in quickly.

"Okay, but let's keep it lowkey, like we said," Dan said. "I can't have Sheriff Olmos finding out I'm attending this kind of stuff."

"What's lowkey?" Tucker asked.

"No more than fifteen people."

"Twenty."

Dan narrowed his eyes at him.

"Fine. No more than fifteen," Tucker said, caving. He knew if Dan went along with it, then Baxter would, too.

"Okay, well, let's figure out the logistics," Dan offered. "The place likely needs to be cleaned up, right?"

"Yeah, but we could just use like two or three rooms," Tucker said. "And I'll borrow one of my dad's work vehicles to move shit in and out."

Tucker's father owned a construction company based out of Hilltown. He would ask him to use one and keep the reason vague. It'd worked before.

"Alright," Dan said.

"It's probably going to be dirty as shit in there," Tucker admitted. "It's gonna take us a few hours to clean it up."

"Can everyone meet up tomorrow?" Dan asked, looking around the table.

"I can after like, four," Baxter said.

"I'm free all day."

"Same," Hudson echoed.

"Okay, let's meet there around six-thirty," Dan told them. "Does that work for everyone?"

A murmur of agreement went around the table.

An excitement passed through them that none needed to vocalize, because they all felt it. The four of them had been friends in high school, but early adulthood had wedged some distance between them. This Halloween, though, they hoped it would be like the old days.

Back when things were simpler.

The rest of the night they would spend laughing, making fun of each other, telling work stories, discussing costumes, and just in general having a good time. Just a night of the boys chopping it up, if you will.

10

IGNACIO SAT ON his bed, back against the wall. His knees were drawn up to his chest, his arms wrapped around them. He'd moved the wooden stake Mamá's head was on from behind the offrenda to the side of his bed, hoping it would bring him comfort.

"They are Barbies... My Barbies..." Ignacio muttered into the empty room, drumming his fingers against the side of his arms. "Ignacio's Barbies... Barbies for Ignacio..."

Veracruz, Mexico

Ignacio walked a few paces behind the neighbor girl. Her name was Selma, but Ignacio couldn't remember that. So, to him, she was just "the neighbor girl."

Ignacio wasn't very good at remembering names.

They were walking home from school. There was no one else with them. Not an adult or even another kid. It was just them two, walking along the dirt road, staying close to the trees for shade.

A six-year-old boy and an eight-year-old girl shouldn't have been doing this even in broad daylight. But things were different in this part of Mexico. It was pandemonium when school let out, and the teachers couldn't keep track of the hundreds of students leaving the premises even if they tried.

The neighbor girl had gotten a new bookbag. It was pink with purple butterflies and had the name BARBIE written on. The letters sparkled under the hot Mexican sun.

But Ignacio's attention wasn't on that. Or the bookbag itself, even.

No, his focus was on the neighbor girl's new doll. It was stashed in the side pocket, the one meant to store water bottles. The doll's arms hung over the mesh netting. Its hair, as gold as the corn Mamá used to make esquites on cold nights, bounced with each step the neighbor girl took.

Pelos de elote, Ignacio giggled.

The doll was new, so its hair was shiny. It looked soft. He wanted to touch it.

Ignacio walked faster to it, reaching out to run his fingers through the doll's hair.

As if feeling what he was doing, the neighbor girl whirled around, her long ponytail almost whipping him in the face. Ignacio pulled his hand back and stared at her.

They both stopped. Ignacio put his hand behind his back and looked down at the ground.

"Nachito, are you thirsty?" Selma said, smiling at him. "Is that why you're reaching for my bag?"

Ignacio looked up at her. He'd been expecting her to be mad at him. People at the school got mad at him all the time when he was acting "the way he wasn't supposed to," as the teachers called it.

The neighbor girl being nice to him surprised him. As always.

Selma set the bookbag down on the ground and opened the front pocket. She took out a plastic bottle of water with a bendy straw and a bag of Sabritas. Then she sat down on the grass at the side of the road, underneath a palm tree looming over the road from someone's backyard.

"Come," she said, patting the grass next to her. "We'll take a little break before we keep going."

Ignacio sat down next to her. Even though she was older, Ignacio was much bigger than her. He was much bigger than most of the kids at his school, which was the reason he seemed to draw so much attention there.

Selma handed him the water bottle. He took it and slurped on the straw. The water was lukewarm.

"We'll drink cold Cokes when we get back to the village," she said, laughing at the grimace on his face.

"Cokes," Ignacio repeated.

Selma opened the bag of chips. The loud pop sent an iguana hanging out on the branch above them scuttering away to the opposite side of the tree.

"Want one?" she asked, taking out a chip and tilting the bag toward him.

"Yes." Ignacio took two and munched on them. "Gracias. Mamá says I have to say that. When someone is nice."

"You're funny, Ignacio," Selma said, smiling at him again. "Pero, de nada."

Selma grabbed the water bottle from him and took a sip.

"Yuck! It is gross," she said, this time laughing at herself.

Ignacio grinned at her.

They sat quietly for a few minutes, munching on the potato chips and passing the water bottle between each other.

Somewhere in the distance, a rooster let out a loud crow, which roused a dog nearby to start barking and yapping.

They could hear the murmurs of a ranchero song playing from a stereo on a rooftop nearby, and every so often the men working on it laughing and hollering at one another.

"Barbie," Ignacio said.

"What?" Selma said, a confused laugh at the end of the question.

Ignacio pointed to her bookbag, which was on the ground in front of them.

"Oh. Yeah. Mi mamá *bought me the bag and the doll yesterday.*"

She grabbed the toy from the pocket, brushed its hair, and then held it up for Ignacio to get a good look at it.

"I like it," Ignacio said.

"You can touch her when we get home, and you wash your hands," she said, crinkling her nose.

Ignacio nodded.

A blue truck was coming down the road. It was going slow because of the rough and uneven terrain. The bottom of the vehicle clanked and clattered, sounding like it would fall apart if it went any faster.

The driver, an old man with glossy eyes and a white cowboy hat, saw the children and waved to them.

Selma had no idea who that was, but he looked drunk. This was their cue to get on out of here. She folded up the empty bag of chips and stashed it in her bookbag to discard when she got home. Then she got up, brushing the seat of her shorts.

"Come on, Ignacio," she said, strapping the bookbag on. "Let's go."

"Barbie."

"Yeah, it's my Barbie bookbag," Selma said, a bit confused again. Ignacio shook his head at her.

"The doll. I can play with it. You said that. Remember?"

"Yes," Selma said, forcing a smile onto her face. "Yes, I did. Once we're home."

"You won't forget?" Ignacio asked, getting up.

"I won't," Selma said, grabbing his hand. "I promise."

"Promise," he muttered.

Still holding onto his hand, Selma pulled him. They started walking alongside the road again.

"I don't mind sharing my chips or letting you play with my Barbie," she said, squeezing his hand. "We're friends. We're supposed to share."

"Friends," Ignacio repeated.

He never had a friend before, or after, the neighbor girl.

Ignacio remembered playing with the Barbie doll that day. The neighbor girl let him touch its hair. Comb it. Dress her up.

But she didn't let him take the doll home. The Barbie wasn't his.

The Barbies he'd collected over the years *were* his, though. It didn't matter what anyone said. It didn't matter that the Barbie in the attic was being bad and telling him they weren't his Barbies.

"They are!" he yelled up in the direction of the attic. "My Barbies… Mine, mine, mine!"

Ignacio jumped out of the bed and went over to the closet. He changed into a pair of black and gray camo pants and a black long-sleeve shirt. Then, he grabbed the wooden stake with Mamá's head and carried it back into the living room.

He set the stake down behind the offrenda. Even though he had her head, he couldn't feel Mamá's spirit the same way he had at the camp.

But Ignacio needed comfort right now. So, he was going to do something that always brought him comfort.

He was going to see Judy.

11

Sophie Benson was supposed to be asleep. Tina, her babysitter, had tucked her into bed over an hour ago. But as soon as Tina had closed the door, Sophie grabbed her tablet off the nightstand and had been reading Teenage Mutant Ninja Turtles comic books in the dark since.

Her eyes were starting to hurt, though, so she put the tablet down on her stomach, remembering her mother telling her she needed to "give her eyes a break" every once in a while.

Sophie stretched her arms out, yawned, and then looked out her window to see if there were any lightning bugs out there. Instead, she saw *him*.

Her bedroom was located on the second floor of the house. From here she could see over the plastic jungle gym her daddy had gotten her for her birthday, the one he'd built while saying the f-word and s-word a lot.

She could see over the hedgerow in the backyard, too.

The scary man was at one of the windows of the first-floor apartment over there. He stood sideways to Sophie. His hair was up in a ponytail that draped over his big back.

Sophie had only ever seen him twice before, once in the summer and once when school had just started again.

No one else had ever seen him. Only she had.

Her parents and Tina said it was just her imagination.

But tonight, she was going to prove he was real. She pushed the covers off herself and swung her legs out of bed. She found her bunny slippers on the floor, put them on, and raced out of the bedroom.

"Oh no. Hold on, Joey," Tina told her boyfriend, who she was FaceTiming with. "The little brat woke up."

She heard Sophie stomping down the stairwell from here in the kitchen. Her fuzzy slippers muffled the sound, but Tina could still tell she was coming down fast. She must've woken up from a nightmare or something.

"I'll call you back," Tina said, ending the call.

She downed the Iced Smirnoff she'd taken from the fridge and threw the glass bottle in the recycling bin just as Sophie appeared in the doorway.

"Tina! That scary guy is back!"

"Scary guy?" Tina said, leaning against the counter. "What are you talking about?"

The oven started beeping, letting her know the pizza rolls were done. Tina went over to shut it off.

"The big scary man with the long hair and the mask," Sophie said, trailing behind her. "Remember? I told you about him before. He shows up at the apartment behind the house and stares through the window."

Tina hit the button to silence the oven. With her back to Sophie, she rolled her eyes. She had no clue what Sophie was talking about. Sophie might've told her about this before, but Tina doubted she'd been listening. Most of what Sophie talked about went in one ear and out the other.

"It's just your imagination playing tricks on you," Tina said, turning to face her with her arms crossed.

Sophie stared at her for a second, eyes wide, urging Tina to believe her.

"Okay, fine. Look, we'll go up to your room together." Tina said, grabbing her hand. "If there's no big scary man out there, promise you'll go to sleep?"

Sophie nodded, her pigtails bouncing on her shoulders. "But if there is?"

"Then I'll go out there and karate chop him in the neck."

Sophie laughed, but she wasn't so sure Tina would actually do that. The man was *big*. Even bigger than her daddy's friend Fred—and Sophie once saw him eat six whole slices of pizza.

"Come on," Tina said, leading Sophie by the hand she was still holding onto. "Let's get you tucked into bed."

"I don't see anything," Tina said, scanning the view of the window.

She had to admit, there was plenty of darkness between the Bensons' yard and the apartment building where someone could be hiding. The jungle gym and hedgerow cast long shadows that covered most of the grass visible to her.

She scanned the area one more time just to make sure. Nothing. Tina untied the curtains on either side of the window and closed them. Then she sat down on the edge of Sophie's bed.

"You really didn't see him?" Sophie asked, tucked under the covers. Her eyes were big.

"I didn't, Soph."

"I swear I saw him, Tina. I swear."

"Maybe you were just having a nightmare and woke up from it and so you *thought* you saw a scary man."

Sophie blinked.

"Maybe you're just spooked because it's Halloween time, but I promise you, there's nothing out there," Tina said, rustling her hair. "Now, go to sleep before your parents get home and I get in trouble."

"I swear I saw someone standing at that window," Sophie said.

"Well, he's gone now. So go to sleep." Tina told her, getting off the bed.

"Fine," Sophie sighed.

"You want me to leave the hallway light on for you?" Tina asked, trying to not make it sound like she was mocking her. Even though she was.

Sophie pouted and shook her head.

"Good night, Soph," Tina said, flicking the light off and heading out of the bedroom.

The door was halfway closed behind her when she heard Sophie call her name. Tina hung her head low and let out a small groan.

"Yes?" she asked, popping her head into the room.

"Were you making pizza rolls?"

"I was."

"Next time you babysit, can you make me some? They're my favorite."

"Yeah, Sophie. I'll make you a whole bag if you want. Now, go to sleep."

Tina closed the door, glad that was over.

12

IGNACIO WATCHED THE lights go out in the window.

He focused his hearing inside the house, listening to the older girl going downstairs while hitting buttons on her cellphone. She was making a call.

Ignacio waited... If it was the police, he would have to get out of here, quick.

After the third ring, a guy answered the phone. Ignacio listened to them talking. The guy on the phone did not sound like a policeman. He sounded too young, and he sounded the way Papa had talked when he'd had too many beers.

Ignacio heard them laughing. Relief washed over him. She hadn't seen him, and she didn't believe the little girl.

But that was a close call, Varias Caras said. *You need to be more careful.*

Ignacio nodded. He rose from behind the bushes where he was hiding, and then went back to Judy's window.

Some nights, Judy would close the blinds and Ignacio couldn't watch her sleep.

Tonight was not one of those nights. Tonight, he would watch her sleep. Watch until the alarm on her phone went off in the morning.

The moonlight came into her bedroom through the slits between the blinds. The lustrous strips of light highlighted her beautiful facial features, making him want to reach out and touch her even more than usual.

Ignacio's hands itched, longing to run his hands through her hair. Longing to feel the softness of her skin on his own. Only an inch or two of glass separated them. And if the wall wasn't in the way, he would only need to take about six steps to be able to grab her and take her home.

But not yet. He had to wait until Varias Caras said it was okay. And tonight was not the time. Especially not with the two girls from the house almost seeing him.

Ignacio turned to the house, and saw the curtains were still closed and the lights were still off in the bedroom.

Good.

Ignacio didn't want to stop looking at Judy. Just being around her made him feel better after the horrible things the Barbie had said to him earlier in the night.

"They are my Barbies…" Ignacio muttered to himself, clenching his hands.

And in time, he wouldn't ever need another Barbie. No, because he would have her. He would have Judy. The Perfect Barbie.

En tiempo serra tuya, Varias Caras reassured him.

STALKING

1

HUDSON WOKE UP, feeling like he'd just been hit by a spacecraft going warp speed. After they left the bar, he and Tucker had come back to his house. They'd stayed up almost all night drinking the shitty beer Tucker had in the back of his truck while alternating between playing Xbox and watching horror movies on Netflix.

Hudson sat up in his bed. The candy wrappers he'd fallen asleep on top of crinkled around him. He grabbed his pillow and wedged it against the headboard, then leaned back on it, feeling the consequences of last night pounding in his head.

He closed his eyes and sat there for a second, motionless. He listened to the birds twittering outside the bedroom window. It was obviously daytime, but he had no idea if it was morning or afternoon. It could've been twilight for all he knew. He had no concept of time right now.

On the floor, he heard Tucker groaning. "Yo…you up?"

"Yeah," Hudson grumbled.

"Are you going back to sleep?"

"I don't know…maybe. You?"

"What time is it?"

Hudson opened his eyes and looked over at his phone sitting on the nightstand. It was within arm's length, but with his lack of desire to move, it may as well have been miles away. Then, next to it, he saw the black Sharpie. He turned his head, ignoring the soreness in his neck muscles, and looked at the Dragon Force calendar on his wall.

It was October 30th. Tomorrow was Halloween.

The realization that Halloween was less than twenty-four hours away was the cure for his hangover. Hudson bolted up in bed. He grabbed the marker off the nightstand, knocking a Reese's Cup candy wrapper off the bed in the process.

"Hud… What the hell are you—"

"Shhh," Hudson said, taking the cap off the marker and turning to the calendar. "This is sacred."

He drew a big X over the current date, feeling a wave of excitement course through him.

"What?" Tucker said, propping himself up on his elbow to see what his friend was doing.

"Tomorrow's Halloween, Tuck. The most magical time of the year," Hudson said, putting the marker back on the nightstand and checking the time.

"That's Christmas, you goof."

"Yeah, sure. That's what they want you to think."

"Who's 'they'?"

"Society."

Tucker groaned.

"No, no. Think about it, Tuck. Halloween is the only holiday you can celebrate no matter what age. Christmas loses its magic once you don't believe in Santa. The best part of Thanksgiving is the pumpkin pie. Easter is boring—even when you're a kid."

"Mashed potatoes," Tucker said, cutting him off.

"What?"

"The best part of Thanksgiving is the mashed potatoes, not the pie. We have this argument every year."

"Okay, sure," Hudson said. "But anyway, New Year's only really means anything when you're an adult. But Halloween… yeah. Halloween, everyone can partake in. From infants to adults, anyone can dress up. You can go trick or treating or get drunk in the woods or…go to a haunted hayride. It truly is the most magical time of the year."

Tucker laughed.

"Do you disagree?"

"No. I guess not." Tucker sat up, brushing his fingers through his hair. "You know what I do disagree with? This fuckin' headache. How are you feeling, Hud?"

"Great, now," Hudson smiled.

"That's good." Tucker reached into the pocket of his jeans for his keys and threw them on the bed. "That means you can drive us to Wawa. I need a Gatorade and a sandwich."

"Okay, but I need to brush my teeth first," Hudson said, peering at the keys.

"Yeah, yeah." Tucker said, taking his phone out. He saw it was only ten-thirty am. "We've got a while before meeting up with Dan and Bax, anyway."

2

DAPHNE WOKE UP on the couch, not having remembered falling asleep last night. She was underneath a flannel blanket she knew belonged to Judy. The TV was blacked out. The "are you still watching?" screen on Netflix had long winked out.

Daphne sat up, the room blurring with the motion.

"Oh shit," she gasped.

She paused to reorient herself, then looked at the coffee table. The wine and glasses were gone, replaced by a tumbler filled with orange juice and a tall glass of chilled water.

Next to the drinks was a bagel with chive cream cheese spread over it in a meticulous, even layer. Daphne couldn't help but snicker, knowing Judy had most likely made the bagel for her while rushing out this morning, but still managed to make it look like something out of a commercial.

Daphne guzzled down the water and then took a few bites of the bagel.

She sat there, grateful for the quietness of the upstairs and next-door neighbors. The building was so quiet right now that she could hear her cat snoring in one of the bedrooms. Judy must've fed him before leaving work, otherwise he would've been at her side screeching for food by now.

Thank God for that, she thought, feeling the back of her head throb.

She finished one half of the bagel, then started reaching for the bong and weed when she felt a vibration in her ass cheeks. At the same time, she heard her phone dinging between the couch cushions.

Daphne reached between them and fished her hand around until she found it. She pulled the phone out and looked at the text message alert on the screen.

Butthead: Yo, call me when you see this!

Daphne dialed her brother while she downed some of the orange juice. He picked up on the third ring. In the background, she could hear some shitty power metal playing through car speakers.

"Yo, turn that down," her brother said to whoever he was with. "Daph, you up?"

"How could I be calling you if I wasn't?"

"Damn, someone woke up on the wrong side of the bed."

Daphne didn't bother telling him she hadn't woken up on her bed at all. Instead, she said, "What do you want, Tuck?"

"I just missed your voice, sis."

"Shut up," Daphne said, touching the back of her head. "I'm hungover and don't have time for your shit."

"Okay, okay. My bad," Tucker laughed. "What, did you party last night or something?"

"Nah. Just had one too many glasses of wine."

"Ah. Well, speaking of partying…what're you doing for Halloween?"

"Just going downtown with Jude."

"Oh. How *is* my girl doing?" Daphne could practically hear her brother's smile behind the question.

Ever since they were little, Tucker had a thing for Judy. Of course, they both knew she would never go for someone like him. As much as Daphne loved her brother, he was way too much of a dirtbag for her.

"She's been working a lot, but I finally got her to take some time off for herself," Daphne told him. "Anyway, Tuck, why'd you want me to call you?"

"Okay, well, two things."

"Okay, I'm listening," Daphne said, getting up slowly. She headed into the bathroom.

"I'm throwing a Halloween party tomorrow. You and Judy are invited."

"Where?" Daphne said, looking at herself in the medicine cabinet. She had some hefty bags under her eyes and her hair was sticking out all over the place.

Yikes. She opened the medicine cabinet so she wouldn't have to see her reflection and started looking for the Tylenol in there.

"Wait, hold up. I guess there's technically three things." He cleared his throat. "Okay, so to answer your question, it's going to be at an abandoned house."

Daphne laughed. She found the bottle of Tylenol, took it out, and closed the medicine cabinet.

"And I kind of need to ask you for a favor."

"Uh-oh," Daphne said, leaning against the sink. It was never a good thing when her brother was trying to get her involved with his hair-brained ideas. "What favor?"

"You have to promise to say 'yes' before I tell you."

"No."

"Fuck," Tucker laughed. "I'm going to get you with that one day."

"No, you aren't," Daphne said, unscrewing the cap on the Tylenol bottle and dry swallowing two capsules. "Tuck, speed this up or I'll just hang up."

"Okay, okay," he said, cackling. "Okay, look. I need you to help me decorate the place."

"What? Why me?"

"I want the place to look cool and you've got the mind for this stuff. Please say yes. Pleeeease," he whined.

Daphne took in a deep breath.

Her brother really knew how to get what he wanted from her. They were twins, and technically Daphne was only fourteen minutes older than him, but she always felt like he was way younger.

Maybe it had something to do with how immature Tucker was, but either way, she'd always found it hard for her to say "no" to him when he asked for her help. Whether it was forging their mother's signature on his all F's report card, picking him up from county jail when he got his DUI a year ago, or something simple like being asked to help decorate for his party, an older sister instinct kicked in and she always agreed to help him.

Especially when he was being a kiss-ass the way he was now.

"Fine, Tuck," she sighed. "When do you want to do this?"

"Me and some of the guys are going to go there tonight. We're going to scope the place out and move shit out of there."

"Wait, you haven't even gone inside?"

"Nah, not yet."

"How do you know it's even safe to have a party there?"

"We don't. We'll find out tonight, I guess."

"Why am I not surprised you're doing this backwards?"

Tucker laughed. "Look, if the place is in shambles, we'll just cancel the party."

"Sure." Daphne doubted that. "Well, I don't know if I can tonight. Me and Judy had plans."

"Fine."

"Don't act like you're not just throwing this on me at the last minute."

"I'm not," Tucker argued. "If we have to wait until tomorrow, can we do it early?"

"I guess," Daphne said, then considered something. "Wait, are you not working?"

"Uhh… no. Dad kind of, uh, gave me some time off."

"What did you do?" Daphne said, her tone accusatory.

"I didn't do anything. I just wanted off for Halloween."

"Bullshit."

"Okay, fine," Tucker relented, breathing into the phone. Daphne was one of the few people Tucker had trouble lying to. "I got into a little spat with one of the clients. But that fucker was wrong, okay?"

Her brother was lucky their father had his own construction company. Otherwise, Daphne didn't think Tucker would be able to hold a job down. Any other employers would've canned his ass within weeks—maybe even days—because of his smart mouth or his knack for being tardy all the time.

"Alright, well, the earlier we get to the house tomorrow the better," Daphne said, getting the conversation back on track.

"I agree," Tucker said.

"Look, I got this fucking headache. Can I text you about this later?"

"Yeah, yeah. Sounds good," Tucker said. "Thanks sis. Love you."

"Love you, too, butthead. Talk to you later."

She put the Tylenol bottle back in the medicine cabinet, then went out into the living room to finish the rest of her bagel.

"Okay, so I tricked Daph into decorating the house," Tucker said, slipping the phone into his pocket.

They were still inside Tucker's truck, parked in front of the Wawa.

"Did you trick her, or did you beg her?" Hudson asked, smiling proudly at his quip.

"Shut up," Tucker said. Then quickly changed the subject. "You know what time the beer store opens?"

Hudson shrugged.

"Alright, whatever. I'll look it up while we're waiting on our sandwiches," Tucker said, opening the passenger door. The crisp October morning air filled the car. "Come on."

3

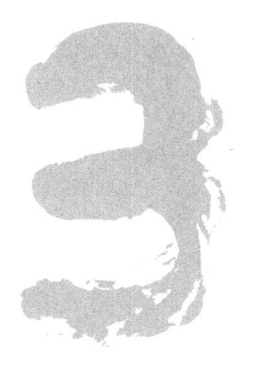

IGNACIO JUMPED UP onto the first level of the fire escape. Despite his heavy boots, he landed onto the metal platform with little noise.

He raced up the first set of stairs, going past a window looking into a young couple's apartment. The couple was in the middle of setting up for lunch. The man tossing a spinach salad at the kitchen counter, his back to the window. Meanwhile, the woman was slicing up some French bread at their kitchen table.

The woman saw a shadow cast over her and looked up, but she was too slow to see Ignacio. By the time she was looking out into the fire escape, there was nothing there. She chalked it up to a bird that had flown by and went back to cutting into the bread.

On the next floor, Ignacio went by a living room window where an old man was sitting on the couch. The lights were off in the room, the blinds half-closed, making the room almost as dark as it could be in the middle of the afternoon.

The television the old man was watching flashed with scenes from a cable-edited version of Wes Craven's *Nightmare on Elm Street*. He grabbed a Cheeto from the bowl on his belly and popped it into his mouth, munching on it, none the wiser to the cannibal that had just rushed passed his apartment.

The third window looked into someone's bathroom. The hairy man who lived there was currently unloading in his toilet. He'd opened the window to air the room out. The pink curtain swayed as Varias Caras ascended past it.

From the corner of his eye, the hairy man saw the motion. He glanced over, but just like the woman two stories below, he was too slow to see anything. Figuring it was the wind, he went back to watching Sixers' highlights on his phone.

Varias Caras made it to the rooftop. Undetected and unnoticed. As always. Ever since hunting in Hilltown, his stealth had become panther-like.

He made his way across the rooftop, over to one of the electrical units up here, hiding in its shadow.

Ignacio reached up and touched his face. The black mask he'd put on while going from his car to the fire escape was still on, but it was always better to be sure. There was no such thing as being too careful.

Sure that his face was concealed, Ignacio poked his head around the electrical unit.

The rooftop of the building he was on was across the street from the Hilltown Hospital, level with its third floor. From here, Ignacio could see part of the lobby, a few corridors, and three patient rooms through the large windows.

Ignacio flicked his eyes across the hospital floor, trying to find her, but he didn't see her. He watched the rooms.

And waited…waited to see where she would appear.

The door to the room directly in front of him opened. She came in, smiling at the middle-aged woman lying on the bed. Her hair was up in a messy ponytail. The sun glinting off it, turning it gold.

The same way the neighbor girl's doll's hair had.

"Judy…" Ignacio muttered under his breath. His hands flexed open and closed, itching to touch her.

En tiempo Ignacio, Varias Caras reminded him. *But for now, you can watch.*

"Hi Mrs. Berk," Judy said, coming into the room, carrying a tray with her lunch. "How are you feeling now?"

"Feeling much better," Leslie Berk said.

"I'm glad to hear that," Judy said, putting the tray down on the table and rolling it to the bed.

Seeing the food, Mrs. Berk repositioned herself on the bed, wincing against the pain.

"Whew," Mrs. Berk whistled.

"Are you sure you're okay? I could lower the table for you," Judy said, grabbing on the crank on the side of it.

"Okay, maybe just a little," she said, grinning.

Judy smiled and lowered the table a few inches. "How's that?"

"Perfect. Thank you, sweetheart," Mrs. Berk said, sinking down on to the bed until she was almost horizontal.

"Anything else I can do for you, Mrs. Berk?"

"No, I think I'm okay," she said, looking at the sandwich, bottle of water, and apple on the tray.

"Great. I'll be back in a bit to get this out of your way when you're done."

"Oh!" Mrs. Berk said as Judy was turning to leave.

"Hmm?"

"I spoke to Brie earlier," Mrs. Berk said, smiling. "She told me you two are going out for Halloween."

"Yeah," Judy said, returning the smile. "Should be fun."

"Just between us, you were the only friends of hers I liked." The woman crinkled her nose like someone had just opened up a sewer line. "I always thought she hung with the wrong crowd when she lived in Hilltown. Buncha airheads and knuckleheads."

"Well, Mrs. Berk, I'm glad you liked me." Judy said, laughing uncomfortably at the woman's naivety.

"Oh come on, Judy Olmos. Everyone likes you."

"That's very sweet of you to say." Judy blushed. She wasn't exactly the best with compliments.

"Anyway, I don't mean to keep you," Mrs. Berk said, picking up her turkey sandwich and waving it through the air. "I just wanted to say, I'm glad you and Brie are still friends after all these years."

Friends. Judy didn't have the heart to tell her they'd never been friends and she'd only accidentally invited her daughter to hangout on Halloween. Before the conversation could get anymore awkward, Judy started out of the room.

"Enjoy your lunch, Mrs. Berk," she said as she stepped out into the corridor.

She headed for the elevators, letting out a big yawn on her way. Staying up with Daph last night had been a bad call. Despite the smiles and cordial demeanor she'd been putting on for the patients all day, she was feeling sluggish.

It wasn't just the lack of hours of sleep, though.

No. Her anxiety hadn't gone away even when she finally went to sleep.

She'd had an intense nightmare in the middle of the night. A recurring, familiar one that was probably better described as a night terror. In the dream, Judy woke up to find a man standing at her window, watching her while she laid in bed. Presumably, he'd been watching her while she slept. Either way, it was the kind of nightmare where you were powerless to do anything. All she could do was move her eyes, and when she flicked them over to the window, the man would vanish from her sight.

The worst part of it was that her mind didn't seem to know if it was awake or not when she had these nightmares, so she'd usually wake up feeling like a sloth in the morning. Her mother said it was likely from the stress of working so many hours. If she was right about that, Judy hoped taking off the next few days would help them go away.

If not, she was going to start considering therapy of some sort.

While Judy had been thinking about this, she'd gotten to the end of the corridor and hit the down arrow and was waiting for one of the elevators. The one to her right chimed.

The door slid open. Inches from her, a face she didn't recognize was staring back at her. The eyes dark, endless…

Judy took a half step back, a gasp caught in her mouth as she realized what she was looking at was a plastic skeleton.

"Hey!" A woman poked her head around the decoration. "Hey, you okay?"

It was Tori, one of the older and veteran nurses at Hilltown.

"Yeah, sorry. I was just daydreaming and wasn't expecting *that*," she said to her, shaking her head and laughing out of nervousness.

"Oh, shoot. Sorry," Tori said. "Didn't mean to startle you."

"That's okay," Judy told her with a smile.

She stepped to the side to let her out of the elevator, eyeing up the skeleton. Now that she had her composure and got a better look at it, though life-size, it was obviously made of cheap plastic.

"He doesn't bite," Tori said as if reassuring her. She grabbed his jaw and snapped his teeth together. "Unless I make him."

Judy laughed but felt her face flush red with embarrassment. She could feel the heat all the way to her ears.

"You heading out now?" Tori asked, mercifully changing the subject.

"No, not yet," Judy glanced down at the thin watch on her wrist. "I still have a few hours before my shift is over. I was just going downstairs to grab some coffee."

"Ah, lucky you. I'm pulling a double."

"Yikes."

"Yikes is right," Tori said, laughing. "Anyway, sorry again for scaring you there."

"That's okay," Judy said, shaking her head. "Don't worry about it."

"Alright, alright. I'll try not to. Anyway, I'm gonna go set this guy up." Tori made the skeleton wave as she awkwardly carried him down the corridor.

"Okay. See ya around," Judy said, yawning as she stepped back into the elevator and hit the close button.

The metal doors shut in front of her. There was a certain comfort that came with the small, quiet space of the elevator that Judy liked. It was like for the few seconds the elevator made its descension, nothing beyond these four walls existed. It was just her and her thoughts.

Now that the embarrassment of the incident was going away, and she could feel her face returning to normal temperature, she could see the humor in it.

Thanks, man from my nightmares, Judy thought, smiling to herself.

4

Hours later, when Judy's shift was ending, Ignacio was crouched behind a row of bushes hugging the first floor of the hospital. The bushes were trimmed level and an inch below the window ledges so as to not block out the sun.

Only the top part of his head was exposed. The elevator at the end of the hallway he was staring into chimed. The doors slid open.

Judy came out of them. Handbag at her side, cellphone in hand. She let out a yawn as she started walking down the long corridor.

She went past the first window. Ignacio sidestepped along the bushes, repositioning himself in front of the next one. She was too busy looking down at her cellphone to notice him.

He moved along the building, continuing to track her down the stretch of the hallway. This was when he got one of his best looks at her. At the end of her workday.

He watched her let out another big yawn.

"Sleepy Judy...." he muttered to himself.

He wished he could tell her that he was going to take her away from all of this. That she wouldn't have to work anymore. That eventually they would just play all day.

But not yet. Now wasn't the time. There were too many people around. He had to wait.

Had to have patience. Had to wait for Varias Caras to tell him it was time.

It was warmer outside than she expected it to be. That was the trademark of an October in PA, though. Frigid mornings that hours of golden sunshine turned into hot afternoons.

Judy zipped her jacket all the way down as she crossed the parking lot. There'd been a lull at the hospital for the past hour or so, and the parking lot was a reflection of that. The only cars in the lot belonged to the staff and maybe one or two visitors.

There was a girl in one of the cars, a young nurse named Lisa. She was in the driver seat, arguing with her boyfriend on the phone, waving a soft pretzel covered in mustard through the air in frustration. She paused midsentence when she saw Judy passing her car. She waved and smiled at her.

Judy smiled and waved back, making a mental note to ask her if she was OK next time she ran into her.

Selfishly, she was glad Lisa was out here, yelling loud enough to be heard through her car windows. Without the murmurs of her argument, the lot would've been quieter—quieter and lonelier.

That was the last thing Judy wanted right now because her anxiety was gnawing at her mind. All shift long, she'd had this pervasive feeling of being watched. Watched and followed. It felt like someone had been breathing down her neck the whole workday. Of course, whenever she would turn around, there was no one there.

It's all in your head, Judy took in a deep breath, then continued to her car. Trying her hardest to keep calm.

But she lost out this time.

Judy reached into her jacket and hit the unlock button on her remote key, then hurried to her car.

The Sheriff

1

Sheriff Olmos was staring at the names on the corkboard, his gray eyebrows knitted close together, still trying to find a possible pattern or some clue from the list of missing people.

But nothing new was coming to him.

There was a knock at his office door. Without having to ask, he knew who it was.

"Come in," he said.

Lieutenant Rooney came into the office with two coffees from the breakroom. He set them down on the sheriff's desk, then joined his side by the corkboard, noticing the Baker Brothers' names remained pinned on it.

"We're officially considering them missing?"

"Not officially," Sheriff Olmos said. "I left them up only because I'm trying to look at the facts we have in front of us."

"Sheriff…" Lieutenant Rooney shifted his weight from one foot to the other. "Sheriff, the facts are that both Baker Brothers haven't been seen or heard from since a young lady went missing."

"Yeah, that's right," the sheriff agreed.

"Tell me if I'm missing something, but everything seems to be pointing to this being a Baker Crime. The brothers likely kidnapped Diana Santos somehow—maybe she broke down on the side of the road and—"

Sheriff Olmos turned to him, eyes wide.

"What's that look for, Sheriff?" Lieutenant Rooney asked.

"To answer your question, there's no evidence connecting the brothers and Diana Santos's disappearances, that's why it's hard for me to chalk it up as a Baker Crime—but what you just said. I hadn't considered that at all."

"What?"

"That Diana Santos's vehicle might've broken down."

"Yeah, she was driving a 2001 Elantra. Not exactly a new car." The Lieutenant shook his head out, trying to follow the line of reasoning that was so obvious to his superior. "What're you getting at, Sheriff?"

"If she broke down, she might've called one of the towing companies." Sheriff Olmos walked away from the corkboard and went behind his desk. "Miriam Santos hasn't sent Diana's phone records, has she?"

Lieutenant Rooney shook his head.

"Of course not. That would make things too easy."

The sheriff picked up the phone and said, "Have one of the officers make a list of all the towing companies within fifteen miles of us. Then, give them all a ring. See if they heard anything about a gold Hyundai recently."

"On it, sir," Lieutenant Rooney said, starting out of the office.

"Start with the ones furthest from us," Sheriff Olmos said, starting to punch in a phone number he was very familiar with. "I'll start with Harvey's."

2

Baxter Miller was just finishing up in the bathroom when he heard the phone going off. It rang five times before he realized Harvey wasn't in the office.

Ah, shit, he quickly dried his hands off, gave the bathroom a quick spray of the cheapo air freshener on the tank, and raced out.

In the office, the phone continued to ring, its old-school clanging noise loud and jarring. Baxter wiped his hands on his coveralls and scooped the phone up with the hand that felt driest.

"Harvey's Towing and Junk."

"Sheriff Olmos speaking. Who am I talking to?"

"Uhm, Baxter. Baxter Miller. How can I help you, Sheriff?"

"Baxter, is Harvey there?"

Baxter turned around to face the back windows that looked out into the junkyard in the off chance that his boss was walking by, but no such luck.

"He's out in the yard." Baxter said. "I think."

"Can you do me a favor and go get him for me, son?"

"Uhm, yeh. What's this about?"

"Just go get him for me. It's important."

"Okay. Give me a few minutes. Gotta hunt him down."

"Sure."

Baxter made his way through the yard, following the faint sound of a power drill going off in the distance. He found Harvey in the garage at the back of the junkyard, working on his latest project.

The 1990 Ford Bronco was raised up, and he was putting brand-new tires on it. Baxter took a second to admire his progress. When Harvey had first brought it to the junkyard at the beginning of summer, it'd been a rusted-out, dented piece of crap with a shattered windshield and two flat tires.

Currently, it wouldn't win any car shows or anything, but it at least looked drivable and had a new windshield.

Harvey stopped drilling when he saw Baxter out the corner of his eye.

"What's up, boy?" he said to him.

"Hey Harv, uh, the sheriff is on the phone."

"Who?" Harvey said, scrunching up his face.

"The Sheriff."

"What the hell's he want?"

Baxter shrugged. "Wouldn't tell me."

"Well, alright," Harvey said, letting out a big sigh and rolling his eyes. He set the power drill on a shelf behind him and then tapped the side of the Bronco. "Guess we're gonna have to wait to test drive your new shoes."

Harvey trudged past Baxter, mumbling under his breath at all the interruptions a man had to put up with in his life.

"Harvey's Towing and Junk, how can I help you?" Harvey said, trying to hide his annoyance.

He'd never been a fan of the police. Even as a teen who just wanted to smoke and drink at a kegger in the woods, he'd always disliked them. They'd always come into the woods to crash the fun, pointing their flashlights every which way and hollering about giving out citations while everyone ran through the trees.

In adulthood, and as a businessman, Harvey liked them even less. They were always sticking their nose in his business. Asking about if his employees had licenses for the machinery around the junkyard and if he had the proper permits and blah, blah, blah. From a young age, he'd learned to play it cool with any and all authority figures. He was always as respectful as possible, but he made sure to not say too much.

"Good afternoon, Harvey. It's Sheriff Olmos."

"Yeah," Harvey said. "How can I help you, Sheriff?"

"Well, we've got a missing person case on our hands. A girl to be exact."

"Aw, shucks," Harvey said, rolling his eyes toward Baxter, who was seated on a plastic chair on the other side of the desk. "That's unfortunate, Sheriff."

"I I was wondering if maybe you got a call about a gold car recently. A 2001 Hyundai Elantra."

Harvey gulped. "Uh, I think so. Let me check my records to make sure, Sheriff."

"Okay."

Harvey hit the hold button, then put the phone in its cradle.

"He's askin' about that gold Hyundai from the other day," Harvey said, opening the binder that had all the records of the calls and cars they'd towed within the last six months.

"The goner from yesterday?" Baxter asked. "The one you sent Ignacio to get?"

"Yeah." Harvey flipped through the pages until he found the sheet with the Hyundai's info.

At the top of the page, over the fancy header that had a graphic of a tow truck pulling a car and the company name on it, the word "GONER" was written in red pen. This indicated that the vehicle hadn't been there when the driver showed up. Harvey flipped back a few pages to make sure there wasn't another gold Hyundai in their records. He went as far back as two months and saw no such thing.

Harvey picked up the phone and unmuted the call. "Sheriff, you still there?"

"I am."

"You said the girl's missing?"

"What do you have for me, Harvey?"

"Well," Harvey said, clearing his throat. From across the room, he could see Baxter staring at him, slack jawed. Looking more confused than usual. "We had a call for a pickup that day, for the exact car you're askin' about. But the person wasn't there when my guy showed up."

"Where was the location?"

"Well, see. That's the thing, Sheriff. Poor little lady didn't know where she was. All I got in my notes was that she was on a paved road a few miles off the highway. My guy couldn't find her anywhere, though."

"I see," the sheriff sighed.

"Sorry I can't be more help, Sheriff." Harvey hoped that the little nuggets of information he'd provided were enough to end the call.

He should've known better.

"Who went to go look for the car? Baxter?"

"No, Sheriff. My other guy."

"Other guy?"

"Yeah. I hired another guy. I ain't getting any younger, so I figured I'd double my muscle 'round here," Harvey said, chuckling.

"I hear you on that, Harv," the sheriff said. "Let me ask you something, is your guy there now?"

"Sheriff, we don't know anythin' about the Hyundai," Harvey said, a little more forcible than he probably should have. "This happens in our line of business all the time. People need to be towed, they call us. Then get tired of waitin' around so they fix it themselves or someone else stops to help them."

"I understand that Harvey, but a girl is missing. I need to talk to your guy as soon as possible," the sheriff said.

"Her phone service was all out of whack, Sheriff," Harvey said, powering through and ignoring the sheriff's request again. "The call got dropped before she even told me what was wrong—could've been somethin' as simple as a flat and she put on the spare and drove on."

"She was driving into town according to her mother, but she never made it in, Harvey." The sheriff paused. "You're likely the last person she spoke to before disappearing."

Harvey picked up a pen and started digging it into the stack of sticky notes on his desk out of frustration.

"What about them darn Baker brothers?"

"They're at the top of the list of suspects."

"And what? Now my guy's a suspect? There's no way that makes any kind of sense, Sheriff. This guy wouldn't hurt a fly."

"No, nothing like that. I just need to talk to him. So, I'm going to ask again, is he there now?"

Harvey sighed, but he was ready to give in. As much as he didn't like it, the reality was that a girl was missing, and he'd been the last one to speak to her. Worst case scenario, the girl was dead. Buried in a ditch somewhere or at the bottom of a river with a rock tied to her corpse.

The least he could do for the poor thing was let the sheriff come talk to Ignacio. It wasn't like Ignacio was much of a talker, anyway.

Plus, as much as he didn't want to cooperate, the sheriff was still the big cheese around town. Things could get ugly if he got on his bad side.

"Okay, Sheriff. My guy's not here right now, but he will be in about an hour," Harvey finally said, rubbing at his eyes with his fingers.

"Will you be there?"

"Yeah, I'll stick around."

"Okay. I'll see you then, Harvey. Thank you."

"Yeah, Sheriff. No problem at all," Harvey said, hanging up the phone with a lot more force than was necessary.

3

SHERIFF OLMOS RAPPED his knuckles on the lieutenant's desk to get his attention. James Rooney was standing up, staring out into the October afternoon while on the phone with one of the towing companies.

"Nothing? Are you sure? Can you check again?" the lieutenant said into the receiver as he turned toward the Sheriff.

"She called Harvey's," the sheriff said to him.

The lieutenant's eyebrows arched up. Then to the person on the phone he said, "Hey, are you still there? Yeah, never mind that." He thanked them and hung up.

"Harvey has a new guy working for him," Sheriff Olmos started explaining, cutting to the chase. "The guy was sent out to pick up Diana Santos's vehicle."

"Oh, shit," Lieutenant Rooney said. "You thinkin' that's our guy?"

"I don't know." Thinking it through, the sheriff started to pace. "According to them, Diana Santos and her vehicle were gone by the time he showed up."

"What's the move then, Sheriff?"

"I'm going to go to the junkyard to have a chat with him later." He looked up at the clock on his wall. Time seemed to have slowed down now that he needed an hour to pass.

"Why not just go to his residence? Harvey has to know where he lives, right?"

"No way that old crow would give me that information without a warrant. You know how stubborn he is," Sheriff Olmos said, shaking his head. "Besides, it wouldn't exactly be neighborly."

One thing most people didn't consider was that being the head authority of a town skirted on the edge of being a political figure. Part of the responsibility of the title of Sheriff was having the residents' trust and respect. Sending police storming into a new resident's home would accomplish the opposite. Especially if the man had nothing to do with it. A casual chat with Harvey there acting as a buffer was the best way to go about this.

Time was of the essence in missing persons cases, but it wasn't like Diana Santos had been missing for all that long. The possibility that this was just a young woman not wanting her parents to know her whereabouts was still in play.

"I see where you're coming from, Sheriff," James started to argue, "but there's a girl missing—"

"And nothing but a paper-thin connection between the two," Sheriff Olmos said, a tinge of annoyance in his voice. James would understand these situations better when he retired in the coming years, and he took the title of Sheriff for himself.

"Okay, true," Lieutenant Rooney acquiesced. "Want me to come with you?"

"No, that won't be necessary. No one is in trouble, and we don't want it to look like someone is. I just want to have a quick talk with the guy. It'll be easier to get a read on him if he's relaxed."

"Understood."

"All right. So, what's the update on the press?"

"We sent the info over to the county station. They'll be running a story with a photo of Diana and her car. Some of the local papers have already posted about it online."

"Good," the Sheriff said, nodding in approval. "Has Miriam Santos called again?"

"Not that I know of."

"Alright." The sheriff started walking out of the office. "I'm heading downtown for some lunch. Give me a ring if anything else comes up."

"Will do, Sheriff."

4

THE SOUND OF the locks opening woke her. It wasn't the sudden light flooding the attic or his clambering up the staircase. No, it was the latter part of the pattern that had stirred her awake.

Something about that disturbed her. It was like she was getting used to being here. Like a pet getting acclimated to their new home.

Diana picked herself up as her captor came through the door. He wore a dark brown, tattered mask. There were several rows of stitches running along it, making Diana think of some sort of fucked up football. It was dry and looked hard to touch on certain spots. The eye holes on it were small and crudely cut, making his eyes hard to see behind the mask.

He was wearing coveralls with a piece of silver tape over where Diana presumed his name was stitched. A small satchel was slung over his shoulder. The strap was made of nylon, but the bag itself was made of a light-brown leather with a bumpy surface.

He started across the attic.

As he drew closer to the cage, Diana realized what gave the bag its "bumpiness." The satchel was made up of multiple peoples' faces sewn together. The rises and curves on the surface were noses, ears, and lips still attached to the leather.

"Good morning," he said, reaching into his back pocket for the set of keys to unlock the cage door. "Do not look afraid. El Monstro said you will not be punished."

Diana heard the shackle on the lock snap open.

"You ate your food." He nodded in approval. "Good."

After a few hours of wrestling with the idea of not eating the soup, she'd finally caved. The hunger had gotten the best of her.

The broth had been an odd, but good flavor. The taste was similar to something like red pozole. The meat, however, had an odd taste to it. Almost gamey. She'd only eaten three chunks before deciding to eat around it.

"We play for a little bit. Then I have to go," he said, coming into the cage."

Diana felt herself frozen to the mattress as he loomed over her. The space in the cage wasn't very big to begin with, and with him in it, it felt that much more cramped.

He unzipped the front pocket of the satchel. The movement made the noses on the bag look animated, like they were inhaling. He pulled out a cordless electrical razor with no guard from the bag.

"But first…I make you pretty."

Diana screamed, and out of pure instinct, kicked at him. He grabbed her foot and threw her leg to the side.

"NO!" he screamed. "No! No! Don't make him mad!"

She started to get up to attempt running around him, but he jumped on top of her and seized her against the mattress. She felt his mask, rough to the touch, press against her cheek.

"Don't… don't make him mad… He wants to hurt you… But I won't let him…" he whispered.

Diana whimpered and started to cry as he caressed her hair.

"But your hair…it is the wrong color." he said, taking some of his weight off her.

He still held the razor in one hand and hit the power button. In the confinements of the attic, the motor sounded like it belonged to a chainsaw. Diana writhed underneath him, but it was fruitless.

He was too damn heavy. Too damn strong.

All she could do was watch as he reached out and grabbed a fistful of her hair.

He pressed the razorblade to her scalp and started shaving her head.

Diana laid on the mattress, her face still buried in it, while he'd returned downstairs. Her eyes felt small from all the crying. For some inexplicable reason, this seemed like the worst thing he'd done to her yet. It wasn't even a vanity thing. It just felt dehumanizing and humiliating to have her head shaved against her will.

She heard him come back into the cage. Diana turned her head to look at him. The satchel with the faces was gone, but he was holding onto two bags. One black and one white. The white one was opaque, and Diana could see the contents inside were colorful.

He came inside the cage and walked over to the mattress. He tapped Diana's back with his fingertips. The gesture would've been tender if it wasn't coming from a masked killer keeping her captured inside of a musky attic.

"Come on. I make you pretty. Then we play," he said to her.

Diana remained laying on the mattress. He moved his hand to her arm and forced her into a sitting position. Diana stared at him, blinking. She felt herself in a catatonic state where she wasn't sure if she had the will to fight back—or even live—anymore.

The masked man spilled the contents of the white bag on the floor next to the mattress. Some plushies tumbled out and onto each other, forming a loose pile. He grabbed the two he'd already put in here with her from the corner of the cage, the monkey and the white tiger, and added them to the pile.

Diana recognized these stuffed animals as the ones that had been in the cage with Madison her first night here. There was the giraffe with only two legs, a red gecko with no eyes, an orca whale that had a ball of stuffing coming out of its stomach, and a dirty toucan.

The masked man moved the pile of plushies, and from the black bag, took out a blond wig. It looked cheap, like something a kid would wear on Halloween night for their princess costume or—

Barbie costume, Diana thought, realizing what he'd meant by "making her pretty."

Before Diana had time to process this, or even really know what was happening, he grabbed her by the back of the neck and put the wig on her. The elastic fit snug around Diana's head, like it was hugging her. There was almost a comfort to it.

Almost. But not quite.

"We play now." He picked up the monkey and giraffe to bring Diana's attention to the plushies. "We play zoo."

Diana nodded.

"Put them around."

"Around?" The command seemed simple enough, but Diana wasn't sure of anything right now.

"Around us," the masked man said, pointing to random spots between them. "Like we're at the zoo."

Right, Diana thought. *Of course.*

The plushies were covered in filth. Some of it was obviously dust and dirt, but there were dark stains on them, too. Dark, ambiguous stains with an indeterminable color because of the fabric. They could've come from any number of things. Grease, paint, anything. But Diana had her bets on it being dried-out blood.

"Go," he said, nodding to her, like a parent trying to encourage their child. "Make the zoo. Make the zoo!"

He clapped and let out an excited giggle. Diana's stomach turned sour.

She put them on a zigzag line and glanced up at the masked man to see if this was OK.

His eyes were glued on the plushies, swimming with fascination. It made her think of when her little brothers would play with action figures, and how their faces would light-up as they saw superheroes flying and crashing through buildings in their imaginations.

Play. When he'd said that, he really meant the word.

Diana's mind had conjured up the worst possible images when she'd first heard him use that word. She'd been thinking maybe it was code for something else, for torturing her in some twisted way, but no. That wasn't it at all.

"Make the monkey dance," the masked man commanded. "Mamá took me to the circus once. There was a monkey that danced. Make this one dance."

Diana swallowed. Her mouth was dry.

She picked up the monkey and grabbed each of its wrists with two fingers, then moved them side to side. The beans inside of the plushie rattled as the body jigged around.

"Make him spin. Monkeys like to spin," the masked man said.

Diana held its head and twirled the plushie through the air.

"Faster!" he said, clapping. "Faster! Faster!"

She spun the monkey a second time, faster. The plushie's limbs slapped against one another.

"Again! Again!" He was laughing now.

Diana did so, watching the plushie instead of looking at the man's eyes. There was something off-putting about this. In some fucked up, metaphorical way, *she* was the dancing monkey. These thoughts made her hesitate to spin the plushie again.

"I said, faster!" His voice came out deeper than usual.

Diana spun the plushie, making it a blur in the air. Meanwhile, the masked man watched on. Giggling. Clapping. Enjoying every second of it.

Twenty minutes later, he grew tired of it. He took the monkey from Diana and packed up all the plushies. As he was doing this, he kept his eyes on Diana.

"You… you did good." He nodded to her. "You made me happy."

Diana just stared back at him. She had no words.

He patted the piece of duct tape on the breast of his coveralls. "I cannot tell you my name…he says so…but for being good… I can tell you his name. El monstro's name…is Varias Caras."

Many Faces. She translated the words into English with a shiver. That explained the masks. For some inexplicable reason, knowing this made Diana feel worse about everything.

"I have work now… Bye-bye."

With that, he exited the cage, locked it up, and left the attic.

5

HARVEY MOON WAS waiting outside when the sheriff pulled up to the junkyard office. The dark blue coveralls identified him as the owner of the place—not that anyone needed that confirmation. Most people within fifty miles of the place knew Harvey.

Harvey's company wasn't the only towing service around, but he was the only one who was open 24/7. As such, a lot of townspeople, the police especially, had called Harvey to remove a vehicle at some point. Whether an illegally parked car at a business or someone breaking down and needing towing to the nearest repair shop.

Add to that the fact the man was seventy-five, and most people knew him by name and face. He was part of the trusted "old guard" in Hilltown, so to speak.

"Good afternoon, Sheriff," Harvey said, tipping his hat to him.

"Mornin' Harv," the sheriff responded, climbing out of the cruiser.

He stepped up onto the curb and shook hands with Harvey. "No one else with you?"

"Nope. Just me." Sheriff Olmos smiled. "Disappointed?"

Harvey didn't respond, he just returned the smile while thinking *one of you fools is more than enough.*

"Your guy here yet?"

"He is," Harvey said, then put his hands on his hips. "Hey, Sheriff, ain't no one in trouble, right? You're just here to ask questions is all?"

"Correct."

"Okay. Just making sure I'm not throwing my guy to the wolves, you know?" Harvey chuckled.

"You're not."

"One more thing, Sheriff."

"Yeah?"

Harvey rubbed the back of his neck with a hand, thinking how to put what he was about to say. "My guy…well, you see, he isn't exactly like other people."

"How do you mean?"

"He's, uh, quieter than most people."

"That's fine. I only have a few simple questions to ask him."

"He might come off a bit odd at first, Sheriff. Intimidating, even. But he's a real gentle giant if there ever was one. Heck of a worker, too. For whatever that's worth."

"I'll keep that all in mind," Sheriff Olmos said, then gestured inside the office. "Shall we go on and get it over with?"

"Yeah, yeah," Harvey said, opening the door.

The breakroom in the office building was small, with just enough room to walk past the small, round table to get to the fridge and counter up against the backwall.

The man waiting for Sheriff Olmos at the table was massive—Harvey hadn't been kidding when he called him a "giant"—making the room appear even smaller. He was wide, with thick arms and shoulders that looked strong enough to barge through a door with minimal effort.

"Sheriff, this is Ignacio," Harvey said, walking around the table to lean against the counter behind Ignacio. "Ignacio, Sheriff Olmos here just wants to ask you a few questions."

"Yes…" he responded. Then, under his breath he muttered, "Questions…Ignacio can answer questions."

"Hello, son," the Sheriff said, pulling a chair out and settling into it. Sitting across from the hulking man now, he'd never felt smaller.

"Hello," Varias Caras said, taking over the conversation.

Sheriff Olmos tried analyzing the man's face, but a tangle of long, curly hair obscured it. No matter. Just as he'd told Harvey, this was only preliminary work. A few questions, and he would be gone.

"Harvey tells me you were sent out to pick up a gold Hyundai on the 28th?"

"Yes."

"Do you remember what time this was?"

There was a pause, as if the huge man was adding up the hours in his head. "Eleven-fifteen. Maybe eleven-thirty."

"In the morning?"

"Yes. In the morning."

"Did you know where she was?"

Ignacio shook his head. "Boss told me to find her. We didn't know where. I looked and looked, but she was not anywhere."

"You checked all the roads in the area?"

Ignacio nodded.

"Just like I said, Sheriff," Harvey butted in. "Maybe someone helped her before Iggy got there."

"Of course, of course," Sheriff Olmos said, glancing over at Harvey. Then, to Ignacio said, "Did you happen to see or hear anything?"

"Nothing," Ignacio said. "No cars. No people around. Roads were quiet."

"As they usually are," Harvey interjected again.

"Yeah," Sheriff Olmos said, frustrated. "Kind of strange that you didn't see or hear anyone on the road, considering someone must've helped Diana with her car troubles."

"Whoa, whoa," Harvey said, leaning off the counter and taking a few paces toward the table. "Sheriff, if you're gonna start talking like that, we're gonna need a lawyer in here."

Sheriff Olmos leaned back in his chair. Harvey was right. He was going beyond a quick chat with the guy at this point, but he was irritated. His best lead—only lead, really—had nothing for him.

The man was odd, just as Harvey had described him. But that was the only thing he was able to read from him. If he was lying, there was no hint of it whatsoever.

"Sheriff, are we done here?" Harvey said. "Ignacio needs to get back to work."

"Yeah," Sheriff Olmos said, getting up. "Yeah. Thanks for your cooperation, Ignacio."

The Sheriff extended his arm over the table for a handshake. Ignacio regarded it for a few seconds, like maybe it might bite, then shook it. It was a gentle squeeze, but still the Sheriff winced from the pressure behind it.

"If you remember anything—anything at all—please call the police station and let us know," Sheriff Olmos said, trying to hide how uncomfortable the man's handshake was.

It felt like he'd just stuck his hand into an iron vice, and the worst part was that it didn't even seem like the man was trying.

"We will," Harvey said. "Are we done, Sheriff?"

Sheriff Olmos nodded. Ignacio let go of his hand.

"Nice to meet you, Ignacio," Sheriff Olmos said.

"Nice to meet you," Ignacio repeated, then gave him a polite bow.

As the man walked past him in the tiny room, Sheriff Olmos took one last glance into his eyes. Often times, at the end of an interrogation—even a small, quick chat like this one—the person in question would let their guard down. A flicker in their eye or a nervous tic of some sort would surface. And if he suspected anything like that, Sheriff Olmos would stop them and ask them one last question to try to trip them up.

Here, though, it seemed unnecessary. There was nothing in the man's eyes.

Ignacio pushed past the door, and let it swing closed behind him. A wooden decoration of a witch riding a broom hanging from it rattled as the door shut.

"Sorry we couldn't have been more help," Harvey said, stepping to the sheriff's side. "But I told ya, my guy knows nothin'."

"It's quite alright," Sheriff Olmos said.

They started out of the breakroom, this time Sheriff Olmos leading the way. The main room of the office was empty, Ignacio was nowhere in sight.

"Thanks for letting me do this, Harv," Sheriff Olmos said, stopping in front of the exit door. "It's never easy when an out-of-towner goes missing."

"We all know you're doing your best, Sheriff," Harvey said, giving him an encouraging pat on the back. "I'm thinkin' this smells like something them Baker boys would do, though."

"It wasn't them," Sheriff Olmos said.

"How you figure that? Them two knuckleheads always getting' themselfs into something."

"They haven't been seen since Diana Santos went missing. You haven't by any chance seen them around lately, have you?"

"Nope. Fortunately. Or I suppose unfortunately, dependin' on how you look at it," Harvey said, hand on his hip. "Maybe it was some other hillbillies then."

"Yeah, maybe," Sheriff Olmos said. "Thanks again for your time, Harvey. You have a good rest of your day."

Ignacio was outside, crouched by one of the windows, watching the Boss and the policeman with the big hat talking inside the office.

Varias Caras wanted to get a good look at the sheriff's face. He might need to know it…for later…

The Big Hat Policeman started out of the office. He had a look of frustration and sadness on his face. He was looking for Ignacio's Barbie. If only he knew how close he was to finding her, he maybe would not look so sad.

Ignacio stepped away from the window. He turned around and walked down one of the aisles, keeping to the shadow cast by one of the junkpiles.

When he was sure he was far away enough from the office, he started talking to Varias Caras.

"How did I do?" Ignacio asked.

You did good. Real good, Ignacio. He doesn't know about your Barbie.

"Good. He won't take her away?"

No. Not unless the Boss talks. Unless he tells him where you live.

"The Boss will not do that. Will he?"

Let's hope not.

"Hope not," Ignacio said, shaking his head.

Don't worry about that now.

"Okay."

You got him off your trail for now. Mamá would be proud.

"Mamá would be proud?"

Yes, Ignacio.

Ignacio's lips curled into a big smile at hearing that.

6

Sheriff Olmos was staring out of the back window of his office, looking out into the woods behind the police station. One hand on his hip, the other holding a mug filled with coffee.

There was a knock at his door, followed by it being opened.

"I'm guessing the visit to Harvey's brought us no new information." Lieutenant Rooney said, coming in and stopping in front of his desk.

"Nope," Sheriff Olmos said. "I don't think Harvey's guy is capable of such a thing. There was a certain…I don't know…innocence—for lack of a better word—to the guy."

"Is it possible he was lying?"

Sheriff Olmos chuckled and finally turned to look at the lieutenant. "I don't think so, James. Not unless the guy has a second personality he was hiding."

Lieutenant Rooney nodded, then changed the subject. "No one has seen or heard from the Bakers still."

"Figures," Sheriff Olmos said, turning back to the window, watching the wind sway the trees.

"Want me to file them as missing persons?"

"Yeah, sure. Why not?"

"You sound like you've given up on the case."

"No. On the contrary, James. I have this feeling that whoever is behind this is just getting started."

Outside, another gust blew by. Dead leaves shook off the trees. Sheriff Olmos took a sip of his coffee, watching the shades of autumn flitter past the window.

FROSTY HOLLOW MANOR

1

THE ABANDONED MANOR was like something right out of a Hollywood set. Three stories high with pointed rooftops that pierced the sky. Most of its arched windows had been boarded up, but from how worn the wood looked, that had been done long ago. The paint on it had gone from white to an ambiguous shade of gray. It was chipped and faded. A few large chunks hung from the side of the house like dried skin, exposing the brick underneath in various patches.

Tucker drove the work truck up the incline toward the iron-wrought fence in front of Frosty Hollow Manor where Dan and Baxter were waiting for them.

Dan was leaning against the fence, sipping on a can of Budweiser, when Tucker pulled up in front of them. Baxter was on the hood of his Mustang, digging into a bag of barbecue flavored chips.

"Did you fucks remember to bring flashlights?" Tucker asked, parking his dad's work truck next to Baxter's car.

"Yeah," Dan said, tapping his back pocket. He noticed the big machine in the bed of the truck. "Is that the generator?"

"Yeah," Tucker said, getting out of the car. "We're gonna need power aren't we?"

Hudson got out of the passenger side while Tucker went over to the bed of the truck and took out a cooler. "Brought some brews, too. Consider it payment."

"Crazy that no one's found this before us," Hudson said, admiring the manor from this distance. The mental image he had from when they found it this past summer didn't do the real thing justice.

"We live in the fuckin' sticks," Tucker said, carrying the cooler from the truck to where the others were standing. "No one finds shit around here."

"Including missing girls," Hudson pointed out, turning to Dan for affirmation.

"What?" Tucker asked, opening the cooler. He took four cans out and handed them to the others.

"Yeah, you guys heard about the other missing girl, right?" Dan asked them.

"No. What the fuck are you guys talking about?" Tucker said, putting his beer on the hood of the truck and fishing in his pockets for his carton of cigarettes.

"She was supposed to have an interview at the wildlife clinic, but she never made it, according to her mother."

"I told you about this." Hudson grumbled to Tucker.

Tucker rolled his eyes at him, realizing it'd probably been when he wasn't paying attention.

"And her car is missing, too," Baxter added.

"How do *you* know about this?" Tucker asked.

"She broke down and called Harvey's when she was near town," Baxter told him. "But she wasn't there when the tow truck showed up."

"Yeah, so there isn't really much of a lead to find her," Dan informed them.

"Sucks that a girl's missing," Tucker said, trying to light the cigarette dangling from his mouth against the sudden October breeze blowing by. "But can we stop talking about this shit? It's bringing the mood down."

"Fine, fine," Dan said, taking a sip of his beer and turning over to the mansion. "You guys wanna scope the place out before it gets too dark?"

"Yeah," Tucker answered for the others.

Baxter hopped off the hood of the car, letting the empty bag of chips fall by the wayside. Dan gulped down the rest of his beer, crushed the can, and set it down on the grass. Then, he led them to the gate a few paces from where they stood.

Hudson was the only one who stayed put. He looked over his shoulder at the bag of chips Baxter left on the hood of the car, thinking about how his dad would be disappointed in him for not telling him to pick it up. Then, it dawned on him that he could just pick it up himself. But before he could move to go get it, another breeze kicked up.

The wind sent the bag off the hood of the Mustang and carried it through the air toward the surrounding woods. Hudson watched the bag get lost somewhere in the foliage, serving as a reminder of how deep in the trees they were.

"Yo! Hurry up, slowpoke!" Tucker called out, standing in front of the open gate. The others had gone through it while Hudson had been watching the litter. "You bird watching or some shit?"

Hudson shook his head. Both to answer Tuck's question and to rid himself of the thoughts of how unsettling the area around here was.

"On my way, on my way," he said, powerwalking over to the gate.

2

Judy and Daphne stepped out of the coffeeshop with pumpkin spice lattes. Daphne had a small paper bag with two muffins for them to eat later when they got home.

When they'd first arrived downtown, the sun had been out, but now twilight was quickly approaching. The sky was a beautiful purple and orange fighting for dominance.

The streetlamps along the sidewalk had come on and the Halloween lights hanging from the front windows of the shops and restaurants were plugged in. The glow from the lights coalesced in a way that gave everything on the street a slight orange hue.

Every building was decorated in some way. Some of the places, such as the flower shop and the bakery, had gone more autumn with their adornments, opting to put pumpkins and gourds and beds of leaves on their window ledges. While other businesses, like the tattoo parlor and the bars, were decorated with skulls, spiders, bats, and ghosts and such.

Judy and Daphne were admiring the spirit of Halloween all around them as they walked from the coffeeshop to the Halloween Store.

"So, Jude," Daphne started. "My doofus brother called me this morning."

"Oh?"

"Yeah. He called to tell me about some Halloween party he's throwing tomorrow."

Judy knitted her eyebrows, confused because as far as she knew, Daphne's brother lived at home. "Are your parents away or something?"

"No. Him and his friends are throwing it at some abandoned house—a manor, or something."

"Is it in town?"

"Outside of town. He said it's only like forty-minutes away, though."

"Are you going?"

"That's what I wanted to talk to you about," Daphne said. "Do *you* want to go?"

Judy took a second to study Daphne's face. They weren't just roommates; they'd been best friends since freshman year of high school. They knew each other's tells well-enough, and right now Judy could tell Daphne wanted to go.

"Sure." Judy said, and then because she felt it wasn't enthusiastic enough, she added, "That sounds cool."

"Okay, great!" Daphne said. "He wants me to help him decorate the place…and can I tell you something?"

"Of course."

"Okay, you have to promise not to tell anyone I said this—especially not Tucker."

Judy laughed. "I won't. I swear. Cross my heart and hope to die."

"I'm excited to decorate it. Honestly, the whole idea sounds cool as shit. Tuck sent me some pics of the place."

"So, I guess I better tell Brie Berk about the change of plans?"

"Oof, yeah. Almost forgot she was coming."

"I wonder if she'll even want to do something like that," Judy said, thinking about the very expensive clothes she'd been wearing.

"Who knows?" Daphne shrugged. "Did you ever think she would have wanted to hang out with us, period?"

"Good point."

They were still laughing as they reached the Halloween Store's entrance.

3

TUCKER TWISTED THE front door lock, but it wouldn't budge.
"Fuck!" he screamed.
The front door was locked and the windows on the first floor had all been boarded up. He turned to the others to see if they had any suggestions.

"I told you it'd be locked, idiot," Dan laughed.

"Can't you get a key from the police station or something?"

"Yeah, I'm sure the sheriff will hand that right over to me," Dan retorted.

"Shit," Tucker spat. He grabbed the handle and twisted the knob harder, hoping by a stroke of luck the brass would break off the wood or something. But nothing like that happened, the knob just rattled.

"Now what?" Hudson asked.

They were huddled on the veranda at the front of the manor. Tucker and Dan by the door, Baxter and Hud hovering behind them.

"I just got an idea," Tucker answered, turning to Baxter Miller he said, "Why don't you put those athletic skills to test?"

"What're you suggesting, Tuck?" Dan asked, eyes narrowed.

"He's built like a fucking moose. This old ass door should be no trouble for him."

Baxter and Dan exchanged glances. Baxter grinned. He looked up for it, so Dan shrugged. Tucker had had worse ideas before.

"Alright. Let me show you guys why Tampa Bay was scouting me." Baxter said, walking down the veranda steps onto the grass.

The others moved about the veranda, clearing the way. Tucker was howling in laughter thinking about what was about to happen.

Baxter lowered his stance, and then charged at the door, picking up as much speed as he could in the short distance. He came stamping up the veranda stairs and used the last one as a launching point, flying through the air. His shoulder slammed into the door. The door cracked and splintered on impact, but it held strong. The resistance sent Baxter bouncing backward, spilling him onto his ass.

Off to the side, he could hear Tucker laughing like a hyena. But he paid him no mind. Baxter had tunnel vision. It was just him and the door.

With a grunt, he picked himself up and walked off the veranda. He lowered his stance again, clenched his teeth, and charged. Faster this time.

At the top of the steps, he jumped into the air again. Only this time, he landed short of the door, and using the momentum he had, took a second hop. His shoulder smashed a hole through the door. The sound of wood breaking filled the air as the door broke off the frame.

Baxter was still stuck in the door, so he crashed onto the floor as the door toppled inside the manor.

"Holy fuck!" Tucker cried out, laughing so hard he had to lean against the veranda banister to keep from falling to the ground.

Dan gave him a reproachful punch on the arm, and then ran over to check up on Baxter.

"You okay, man?"

"I'm good," Baxter said, sitting up on top of the fallen door. There was a dusting of wood remnants on his head and shoulder.

Dan clapped him on the back and checked his eyes to make sure there weren't any signs of a concussion. His eyes looked clear and alert. He was likely OK.

"I've felt worse on the field," Baxter said, grinning.

"You sure?"

"A hundred percent."

Dan nodded, then helped him up to his feet.

"That was…impressive," Hudson said, coming up beside them.

"How many braincells you think he lost on that one?" Tucker asked, composed now.

He came into the house, barging between Hudson and Dan to get a look at the interior of the house.

Dan said something to him, but Tucker didn't hear. His attention was elsewhere.

He turned his headlamp on and shone the beam through the foyer. The walls were damaged, but it mostly seemed cosmetic. Large rips in the wallpaper, a few spots of eroded plaster exposing the brick and wood underneath, and so on. Nothing stood out to him as particularly hazardous. At least, not in this room.

"Oh, man! This ain't that bad," Tucker exclaimed, stepping off the toppled door.

The other three all had their flashlights on and were shining their lights in different directions while staying bunched up in the foyer.

"It's really not," Hudson agreed. He swiped a finger along the closest wall and grimaced. "Could use some heavy-duty cleaning, though."

"I got a bunch of cleaning supplies in the truck," Tucker let him know.

"And we're sure the cops won't come here, right?" Hudson asked, turning to Dan.

"Nah, they won't," Dan reassured him. "It's way too far out from town."

This place was technically in the Hilltown Police Department's jurisdiction, but it was about forty-minutes out from downtown. No way the sheriff would care about a group of twenty-somethings partying all the way out here.

"We should probably see how the rest of it looks before we get too excited," Dan said, giving Tucker a sideways glance.

"I'm with Dan," Hudson agreed.

No one waited for Baxter's response because he always sided with Dan, anyway.

"Fine," Tucker sighed in frustration.

He was certain he knew what the rest of the interior would look like. Tucker had been remodeling houses with his father since he was in junior high. But just to put the three clowns at ease, he would go along with it.

"Alright," Dan said, pointing his flashlight toward a hallway. "We stick together, though. Just in case."

"Yeah, yeah," Tucker said. "Lead the way, Officer."

They went through the first floor in a matter of minutes. The kitchen, a den, a small guest bathroom, and the dining room were all on the first floor. Except for the long, wooden table in the dining room and a few chairs, the rooms were all empty.

Connecting the rooms were short corridors with old paintings and photos still hanging on some of the walls. They were going down one now, with Dan and Baxter leading the way into the last part of the first floor.

Tucker stopped to look at a black and white photograph framed on one of the walls. It was a picture of a family wearing what looked to be their Sunday best. The father and son had their hair slicked back and wore a suit and tie, while the daughter and the baby in her arms were wearing fancy dresses with bowties on them. All four of them were looking a little off center, like the family dog had just run by them seconds before the photo was snapped.

"Jesus. This picture looks older than Hud's mom," Tucker snickered.

"Hey!" Hudson said, brows furrowed. "Take that back."

"Come on, guys," Dan said, walking into the large living room.

The room was empty except for an old, stonewalled fireplace in the corner. Above the mantel was a gold-trimmed mirror that reached all the way up to the ceiling. Next to the fireplace was an iron rack with a fire poker, a pair of tongs, and a brush hanging from it. The tools had horse heads on the end of their handles, giving them an old-timey look.

Tucker went over to the rack and picked up the tongs, snapping them in the air like he was trying to catch flies with it.

"Don't touch that!" Hudson protested. "You might get tetanus or something."

"Oh, chill out," Tucker groaned, but he did put the tongs back.

He turned to Dan, who was on the opposite side of the room, shining his flashlight onto some ripped wallpaper dangling down from the ceiling.

"I don't think this place has any structural damage," Dan said, shining his light over at Tucker.

"Yeah, I agree," Tucker said, trying his best not to say *I told you so*. "Dude, can you not fucking shine that directly into my eyes?"

The others laughed, and Dan moved his flashlight a little off to the side but kept it concentrated on Tucker.

"I think maybe we should keep the party down here, though," Dan continued. "I think we shouldn't even bother going upstairs."

"Yeah, I agree with that too," Tucker said. "We could put some caution tape over the stairwell, so no fuckers get any bright ideas."

"Yeah," Dan echoed.

"I think that's all the rooms, right?" Hudson asked.

"Seems like it," Tucker said. "Alright. Well, let's start cleaning up."

Dan looked at the sports watch on his wrist. "Tuck, it's about to get dark out."

"I know, Danny-Boy. That's why I have the generator out in the car." He slapped himself sarcastically on the forehead. "Duh."

"Wait, why didn't you just drive over here in the first place?" Hudson asked.

"Because for all we knew, the floor might've crumpled underneath our feet the moment we stepped inside."

"True enough."

"Now, if that happens, at least we know we'll die getting our party on," Tucker grinned.

"Okay, then. Let's go. I don't want to spend all night here."

"Me neither," Hudson said.

4

THEIR SHOPPING CART was full of Halloween decorations and kitchenware. The standouts to Judy were the Ouija board serving tray and a candy bowl with a bloody animatronic hand that would drop down and touch whoever was reaching inside the bowl.

They'd made the transition from the party good aisles over to the costumes area and stopped in front of one of the costume display walls.

"Hanging ghosts, spooky punch bowl, fake blood, spiderwebs..." Daphne looked up from the note in her phone, laughing at the irony. "I wonder how many spiderwebs I'm gonna have to clear just to put up fake ones."

Judy chuckled.

"Oh, shit! I forgot to see if they had shot glasses," Daphne said, shaking her head. "You think they sell them here?"

"Not sure."

"I'm gonna go look. You mind if I leave you with the cart?"

"Nope," Judy said. "Go ahead. I'll start looking for a costume while you do that."

"Alright. Be back in a jiffy," Daphne said as she trotted away.

Judy pushed the cart through the costume section, looking at the different personas hanging up there on the wall.

The first section was the kids' costumes. Princesses, superheroes, cowboys, cartoon characters, and more. As she continued along the wall, the kids in the photos got older and the costumes became spookier and less childish. Zombies covered in blood, reaper costumes, Frankenstein, various vampires—the classic ones and the twinkling kind alike—and a whole slew of licensed characters from video games and TV shows Judy didn't recognize. But a few of them had big SOLDOUT signs slapped on them, so the kids obviously did.

The last quarter of the wall was dedicated to adult costumes. Half the section was for the scary costumes like werewolves, evil clowns, chainsaw-wielding madmen, and zombies.

The other half of the section had the more "fun" costumes, like sexy police and firefighter costumes. Judy liked these more than the ones that were supposed to be scary, so she stopped at this part of the wall. She glanced up and down the rows, reading the names of the costumes before really looking at the pictures.

Rockstar, sumo wrestler, dentist, sexy ladybug, sexy coffee cup—what?

Before she got a chance to study that one closer, someone tapped her on the shoulder. Judy spun around, expecting to see Daph, but instead found herself face-to-face with someone in a white mask. They were about arm's length from her. The person jumped a few inches toward her, slashing a knife through the air.

She stumbled backward, trying to get away from the weapon coming at her face. She crashed into the Halloween costume display wall, letting out a small grunt. At the same time, the knife swiped past her nose, missing by mere centimeters.

"Boo!" the kid in the clown mask yelled, then turned around and ran away.

A second, younger kid came running out from behind a coffin decoration, his face red with laughter as he joined his buddy in running down an aisle of masks.

Judy tried to calm herself, still pressed against the wall. Her heart was beating fast in her chest, but it was slowing down some now that she realized what had happened.

"Get out of here, you little shits!" Daphne yelled, coming over to Judy's side.

She'd been just a few seconds too late to stop the kid's stupid prank but had seen the whole thing from a distance. The kids were just at the end of the aisle they'd been running down. They both turned around.

The older one, who looked to be about twelve, took the mask off his face and gave them the middle finger with each hand. The boys laughed harder, cut to the right, and disappeared from sight.

"You alright?" Daphne said, turning to Judy.

"Yeah, he snuck up on me, is all," Judy said, blushing. She let out a small chuckle that was both from embarrassment and relief.

"If we see them out trick-or-treating on Halloween, I'm going to steal their candy," Daphne said, grinning, but also serious about it.

"Ah, they're just excited to be at the Halloween Store." Judy shrugged, trying to get past the stupid prank.

"Yeah, well, they're little shits," Daphne said. "Anyway, I had no luck with the shot glasses. You find a costume?"

"Not yet."

"Ohhh, how about this one?" Daphne said, pointing at a sexy nurse costume.

"No thanks," Judy laughed.

"Okay, okay," Daphne said, smiling. "Okay, let's find you one for real."

"It's too short," Judy said, coming out of the dressing room and tugging on the yellow skirt.

"Whew, mama!" Daphne said, looking her up and down. "Do those legs ever end?"

"Daph, seriously," Judy said, laughing while her face burned red with embarrassment. "Is it too short?"

"Shorter than anything I've ever seen you wear."

"I feel like even the shortest shorts will poke out underneath it and it won't look right," Judy said, stepping back into the dressing room to look at herself in the mirror.

"Oh, screw it. Who cares?" Daphne said, following her into the dressing room. She leaned on the doorframe. "It's essentially a party out in the woods. There'll probably be people on molly licking each other's faces, no one's going to care about a short skirt."

"Fine," Judy said, reaching into the plastic bag where the rest of the "sexy bumblebee" costume was. She put the antennae on her head and gave them a quick little tap to get the springs to bounce around. "I really do like this costume."

"It's cute," Daphne said. "The boys'll be crazy to try to get stung by you."

Judy laughed. "Bumblebees rarely sting."

"Only you, Jude. Only you would turn my innuendo into some geek shit," Daphne groaned.

"I'm just saying," Judy laughed. She took the antennae off her head and packed it in with the rest of the costume in the plastic bag.

"They'll want you to pollinate their flowers. How's that? Better?"

Judy threw her head back and laughed. "That sounds gross."

Daphne considered this for a second. "And a bit backwards, I suppose."

"Ew yuck!"

"Hurry it up, Judith," Daphne said, patting her on the butt before leaning out of the dressing room. "Let's pay for all this and go get some food. I'm starving."

They were on the rooftop of the ice cream parlor, looking down at Main Street in all of its seasonal glory. Mr. and Mrs. Mahoney, the owners, had closed shop for the season last week after their limited-edition pumpkin pie flavor ran out, but they were nice enough to leave the rooftop access open to the public year-round.

Cars whizzed through the streets, shoppers came in and out of places carrying bags filled with clothes, shoes, or food. Couples strolled down the sidewalk, holding hands or sharing a sweet treat with their sweet somebody—milkshakes, cinnamon sugar pretzels, and such.

It was that perfect hour where people of all ages intermingled. The younger crowd was just beginning their nights, going to a restaurant or to the movies before hitting the bars later on.

Families with young children, pushing strollers or carrying toddlers (some crying), were hitting their final stores and wrapping up their evening out.

Joggers in bright clothes wove in and out between the crowd, trying not to mow anyone down while at the same time keeping their momentum going. Dog owners walked their pups, letting them sniff each other in the brief moments that they crossed paths.

A few of the shop owners stood outside of their buildings, fixing the Halloween decorations the wind might've knocked around or rearranging the jack-o-lanterns and pumpkins on their porch.

Some of them were in costumes. Mrs. Florence from the bakery had a pair of cat ears on her head, a tail sticking out of her jeans, and cat whiskers drawn on her face with black greasepaint. Across the street from her, Andy Marrs was dressed up like a farmer, but it looked like all he did was put on a straw hat and his usual flannel and called it a costume.

Judy and Daphne were alone on the rooftop, sitting at one of the tables close to the edge. An umbrella stuck out from the center of the table that was meant to block out the sun but wasn't doing much of anything now because the sun was nearly set.

Daphne took the last bite of her pizza and leaned back in her chair, putting the top half of her body in the shadows of a tree neighboring the ice cream parlor. She pulled out a zippo and a carton of Marlboros from her leather jacket.

While Daphne took a cigarette out and started to light it, Judy inched her chair away from the table.

"You think you'll miss this place when we move?" Daphne asked. Underneath the cape of purple shadows, the ember at the end of the cigarette burned bright red.

"You know what?" Judy said, yawning. "I think I will."

"We could always come back to visit," Daphne said, taking a puff on her cigarette. "Or maybe we'll pull a Brie Berk and not show up for six years."

Judy laughed. "I almost forgot about her."

"You saw her mom today?"

"I did."

"How is she doing?"

"She's doing OK."

"Okay, great. So, you can uninvite her daughter now, right?"

"Mean," Judy said, laughing. At the end of it, she yawned again.

"What about you, Jude?" Daphne asked, looking at her.

"Me?"

"How are *you* doing? You've been working so much, feels like forever since we've gotten to really talk."

Judy thought about this for a few seconds, and realized Daphne was right. They lived together, so naturally they ran into each other at the apartment. But they hardly had time to sit down and really spend time together the way they used to. Back when they were younger. Back when things seemed simpler.

"I've been okay, I guess."

"You guess?" Daphne said. "Come on, tell me what's really going on."

"I've been having those dreams again…" Judy stopped herself and looked down at the toe of her boots.

"No, no, toots. No being bashful. What dreams?"

"The ones…the ones of the guy at my window." Judy shook her head. "Mind if we talk about this later?"

Daphne took a drag of her cigarette and nodded. Then, she looked at Judy's paper plate and saw there were at least two more bites of the slice of pizza on it. She knew Judy's squirrel-like eating habits well-enough to know she likely wasn't going to finish it, though.

"Are you done with that?"

Judy nodded.

Daphne reached across the table and shoved it in her mouth. Then, she sat back and smoked the rest of her cigarette. When that was done, she mashed it out against the floor and stood up.

"You wanna head home and watch shitty horror movies?" she suggested.

"That sounds good to me." Judy smiled, getting up.

5

TUCKER'S PLAN TO get electricity into the place had worked, and by some miracle the mice and rats hadn't chewed through the wiring. They placed the halogen lamps Tucker had brought throughout the manor and put in new bulbs where there were any light fixtures, including around the perimeter outside.

The rooms weren't dark, but there was a certain eeriness and quietness to the manor. The kind that was shared by all abandoned places, as if you might be able to hear the whispers of the life and activity that was one present within the walls.

They were gathered on the living room floor, drinking beers after spending the last hours cleaning the place up. They'd swept, dusted, and scrubbed all the floors and walls in the rooms they were going to use.

Tucker finished the beer in his hand, crushed the can, and reached into the cooler for another. "Anyone else want one?"

Baxter put his hand up. Tucker threw one across the room at him. The big lug caught it in one of his bearpaws.

"You want one?" Tucker asked Hudson, who was sitting next to him.

Hudson had his head pressed up against the wall, his eyes were half closed. His forehead was shiny with beads of sweat.

Hudson shook his head slowly. "Nah…I think I'm already drunk."

"You had like two," Tucker criticized.

"Lay off him, man," Dan said, but he was laughing. "You know, Tuck. I'm impressed you actually planned any of this stuff."

"Oh, wow. That means the world to me, Dannyboy." He said it in a sarcastic tone, but deep down he was glad to get his approval. "But if it weren't for Bax's muscle, all my planning would've been for nothing."

"This isn't the first door I've busted through," Baxter said.

"What?" It was Tucker who asked.

"Yeah, what?" Dan echoed.

"I didn't tell you guys the real reason I got kicked out of Bloomsburg."

Tucker and Dan exchanged a look. Tucker grinned like the Cheshire cat, knowing there was something juicy coming.

"You mean you didn't just flunk out?" Tucker asked.

Baxter shook his head.

Across from him, Hudson had been following the conversation with his eyes closed. But since he didn't hear a response to Tucker's question, he opened them to look at Baxter.

"Naw, man. I played D-1 football." Baxter took a nervous sip of his beer. "They protect us like crazy."

"Okay, so then what did you do?" Dan asked.

"Got into a fight at a party. I was talking to this girl, telling her how I played football, but my passion was always comedy and acting. But I'm a natural athlete, ya know?"

"Yeah," Tucker said, biting the inside of his cheek to keep from laughing.

"So, this big guy overhears this." Baxter paused to drink some more of his beer. "And he says to me, 'I bet I'm funnier than you.' And I try to ignore him, but I think he had a chip on his shoulder because I was wearing a Bloomsburg football shirt. So, he just keeps interrupting and saying it."

"What did you say back?" Dan asked him.

"So, I finally said to him, 'if you were in movies they'd be on Tubi. Mine would be on Netflix.' And I dunno why, but that set him off. So, the guy puts his beer down and takes a swing at me."

"Oh shit," Tucker said, unable to contain himself. He started laughing his head off.

"Then what?" Hudson asked, sitting up.

"My football instincts kicked in when I saw the fist coming my way, I guess. Cuz I just went. I ducked under it and slammed my shoulder into his stomach. We were near a closet, and we smashed right through the door." Baxter drank some more beer.

"Holy fuck," Tucker said, wiping tears from his eyes. "Did you beat him up on the ground?"

"Naw," Baxter said, shaking his head. "Some other guys came over and pulled me off him. Guy didn't seem to want to fight after that, anyway. I think he was concussed or somethin'."

"How are you not telling everyone in Hilltown this story?" Tucker said.

Baxter shrugged. "I dunno. I'm embarrassed that I got kicked out of Bloomsburg for it, I guess."

"Fuck," Tucker said, clutching his stomach from laughing so hard.

"One of his buddies ended up driving him to the hospital. Word got back to my coach somehow. A week later I got a letter in the mail telling me it was my last semester due to 'misconduct' and blah blah blah."

"Jesus," Dan said. He was laughing, but a part of him felt bad about the whole situation. "You're lucky you didn't get arrested."

"Of course you say the most cop shit possible," Tucker said, rolling his eyes.

Dan gave him a sideways glance. It was meant to intimidate Tucker, but instead made him laugh.

"Is the other guy alright?" Hudson asked. Realizing that was the end of the story, he closed his eyes and rested his head against the wall again.

"Yeah. Last I heard, he's still playing football."

"How pissed are you gonna be when he has a comedy special out on Netflix?" Tucker couldn't help himself from poking that bear a little more.

Baxter just smiled, shrugged, and took a sip of his beer. Then he thought of something. "Do we need furniture here?"

"Yeah, but I hadn't really thought of what to do about that. I was just gonna bring chairs or something."

"I got my furniture from my apartment in Bloomsburg at my parents'. It's sitting in the garage, wrapped up in plastic. We could use that."

"Fuck yeah," Tucker said. "I'll swing by with the truck tomorrow so we can bring it."

"Alright, well. We're done here, right boys?" Dan said, but the question was more rhetorical than anything. He started picking up the empty cans around him and Baxter and gathering them in one arm.

"Yeah," Tucker said, looking around at the room.

The place looked brand-new in comparison to how it'd been when they first got here. Getting the layers of dust and dirt off the walls and floors had really done wonders for the place. They couldn't do much about the holes throughout the place, or about the large rips in the wallpaper, but that was okay, it would add to the effect of partying in a spooky house.

"Yo, we're leaving, Hud," Tucker said, nudging his shoulder as he got off the floor. "Get your ass up."

Hudson's eyes fluttered open. He'd been on the verge of falling into a deep slumber. "Whoa! We're still here?"

The others laughed.

"Yeah, we're still here," Dan reassured him. "But if you help us clean up, we won't be for much longer."

Hudson got the message. Using the wall to stabilize himself, he stood up on his feet. They gathered up the brooms, mops, cleaning sprays, rags, sponges, dusters, and beer cans and took it out to Tucker's truck.

They put everything in the back, and then Tucker and Hudson climbed inside. Dan and Baxter hopped in the back with the supplies. Tucker drove them over to where Baxter's Mustang was still parked outside the gate.

Dan and Baxter hopped out of the truck and went into the Mustang with Dan taking the driver seat.

"Follow me out," Tucker said to Dan.

"Yeah, yeah," Dan said, giving him a dismissive wave.

They drove across the grass and onto a paved road in front of the manor. With Tucker leading the way, the two vehicles disappeared into the woods, leaving Frosty Hollow Manor abandoned in the middle of nowhere for yet another night.

6

Judy was in the kitchen, pouring wine into glasses for them. Behind her, the microwave beeped to let her know the popcorn was done. She recorked the wine bottle and then carried the wineglasses into the living room.

Daphne had the mood set in the room for their horror movie night. The lights were off. The candles on the center table were lit. The fragrance from the teak-scented candle was already filling the air. The two plastic, battery-powered jack-o-lanterns were turned on—one decorated the bookshelf, the other was on the window ledge. The blinds were closed.

Daphne herself was snuggled up on the couch, wrapped around with the candy corn and spiderweb throw blanket. She was scrolling through the streaming services, trying to find a movie. The glow of the television turned her face different colors as she went through the catalog.

"What are you feeling tonight? Evil twin or insect horror? Or something else?" Daphne asked as Judy set the wineglasses down.

Judy shrugged.

"Ugh, so many choices," Daphne sighed.

Judy smiled to try to encourage her, and then went back into the kitchen. She took the popcorn bag out of the microwave. A few kernels were still popping inside, and a nice puff of steam came out when she opened the bag. Judy poured some of the popcorn into a bowl and headed back into the living room.

Daphne had set up a corner of the couch with some throw pillows and a blanket for her. The cozy spot seemed to be waiting to give her a big hug. Judy nestled into the spot as she set the bowl of popcorn on the coffee table. She grabbed the throw blanket underneath her and wrapped it around her lap.

"I still haven't picked anything," Daphne said, her voice flat and full of disappointment.

Daphne narrowed her eyes at the TV, clutched the remote, and clicked the buttons to scroll back to the beginning of the catalog. She did this with the gravity of someone working the controls of a space shuttle. But after a few minutes, she still hadn't put a movie on.

"Jude, help me out!" she whined.

"That one." Judy pointed to a movie that had a picture of a giant spider on the front, one with a human face and a bunch of tiny spiders crawling over it.

"*Arachnid Mutation Part V: House of a Thousand Hatchlings.* What the fuck?" Daphne turned to her with an incredulous look on her face. "You've seen the other four?"

"I have." Judy blushed. "I watched them between studying for exams when I was in nursing school."

"I didn't know you liked sick shit like that," Daphne teased.

Judy shrugged and sunk back into her seat.

"I'm just messin' with you," Daphne said, taking a big drink of her wine. "I haven't seen any of the others, so you're gonna have to fill me in on what's happening.

Judy smiled and nodded. It wasn't like there was much to them in terms of plot, anyway, but they were great fun for an evening.

Daphne hit play on the movie, then sat back in the couch with her wine and a handful of popcorn. Judy did the same, except she opted for a peanut butter cup from the candy dish next to the candles.

The movie title appeared on a black screen covered with spiderwebs and splatters of blood. The intro score rumbled through the surround sound. A breeze came in through one of the cracked windows, wafting the smell of teak in their direction.

Judy picked up her glass and took her first sip of wine. Daphne had taken the bottle out of the fridge when they first got home, so the wine was perfect. Chilled, but on the verge of being room temperature.

Judy sat back with her wine and a handful of warm popcorn, ready to end a night of fun with some relaxations. No anxiety. No dreams of men stalking her.

Nothing to worry about. Just letting her mind disconnect and relax.

7

"Alright, fine," Neil said, throwing the rag he'd been using to clean a counter down in frustration.

Tom, his coworker, was supposed to close with him tonight, but he'd been begging Neil all shift long to close the pizza shop by himself tonight so he could go to some Halloween party. After six hours, Neil finally caved.

"You the man," Tom said. "I owe you. I owe you big time."

"What time's the party, anyway?" Neil asked him.

As if to answer his question, a beat-up two-door Scion pulled up in front of the building. The driver, a kid in a half-assed Elvis costume, honked the horn and flicked the high beams on and off multiple times to announce his arrival.

"Hurry the fuck up!" a kid in the passenger seat, dressed in a hotdog costume, yelled out at Tom.

Tom had planned to ditch Neil no matter what his answer had been.

Fuckin' dick, Neil thought to himself.

Tom flipped his friends off, which elicited a laugh from them. Then he turned to Neil and answered his question. "Party already started like an hour ago."

"Oh. Well, in that case you should head out then," Neil said, waving him away.

"Seriously, man. Any time you need me to cover a shift just let me know—"

"Bro, just go," Neil said, too pissed to say anything else.

Tom took his hat and apron off and headed into the back. Five minutes later he came out dressed in a black hoodie with a ghoulish mask clinging to the top of his head. And here Neil thought the driver's Elvis costume was as shitty as Halloween costumes got.

"Alright, man. Thanks again," Tom said as he raced past Neil and headed out of the pizza shop.

From behind the counter, Neil watched as the passenger of the Scion tried getting out of the car to let Tom in. The problem was the bulky foam of his hotdog costume wouldn't let him through the frame. The driver started pushing him from inside, while Tom grabbed one end of the hotdog and pulled on him, but the foam still wouldn't give. They tried moving the hotdog kid in several angles, the whole time yelling and cursing at one another.

After a few minutes, they finally managed to force him out. The kid stumbled out of the car, almost losing his balance. Tom moved the passenger seat and hopped into the back of the Scion. Then, the kid in the hotdog costume tried getting back in the car only to run into the same problem in reverse—the costume was just too bulky.

Neil shook his head, wondering how long it would take those three dummies to figure out he could just take the hotdog costume off to get in and out of the vehicle.

He wasn't going to tell them. *Figure it out yourselves, assholes.*

Ignacio was stopped at a red light, two streets away from the pizza shop. He watched the Scion pull out of the parking lot. The driver didn't even bother to look both ways as he pushed down on the accelerator and sped out into the street, going the opposite way of Ignacio.

Ignacio looked over at the lot in front of the pizza shop. There was only one car there. A blue Honda Civic sitting underneath the single streetlamp. He drove by here every night he went to go see Judy at her apartment. Every time, there were at least two cars, making it too risky for him to try anything.

Tonight, though, there was only one.

The neon pizza pie hanging at the shop's front window winked out. At the same time, the lights inside the shop dimmed.

The pizza shop wasn't exactly isolated. There was a drugstore across the street and a small neighborhood about a quarter of a mile away. But the drugstore had closed hours ago, and a bunch of trees separate the shop from the nearest house.

Varias Caras had an idea… Seeing Judy would have to wait.

Opportunities to hunt for fresh meat were few and far between. He had to take any that presented themselves, and here was an obvious one.

Ignacio licked his lips.

The traffic light he was waiting at turned green.

Ignacio stood outside the pizza shop, looking through one of the large windows. The dining area was dark and empty. Only every other ceiling light was on. The tables and parts of the floor underneath the fluorescent bulbs glistened, still damp from the cleaning agents used on them.

He could hear the murmurs of voices in the back area, but it didn't sound like people who were there. No, the voices had a certain robotic ting to them that told him they were coming from a speaker.

In the same area, he could hear a sink running. Water was sprayed out of a hose and blasted onto some metal. The activity sounded like the movements of only one person—two at the most.

Either way, it was a manageable situation.

Ignacio went over to the front door. If it was locked, he would have to abandon the hunt. He didn't see a camera anywhere outside the building, but he wasn't going to take the risk of his ambush being caught on footage. The person or people inside would get to live another day if they'd remembered to lock the door.

Ignacio pulled on the door. It swung open. The bell above it jangled.

Varias Caras slipped inside. It was killing time.

Neil was in the dishwashing room, listening to the Halloween episode of his favorite podcast on the Bluetooth speaker they had back here, spraying a pizza pan down with a hose. He rinsed the clumps of dried-up cheese off the pan and loaded it into the dishwasher with all the other stuff he'd given the same treatment.

He pulled a lever on the side of the machine, closing its doors.

Neil was about to hit the button to get the dishwasher started when he noticed the reflection of someone else in the machine's silver door. Someone was standing behind him, by the doorway.

Tom and his friends…

Just as the thought passed through his mind, the person moved to the right in a blur. Gone from the reflection's view.

Neil whirled around.

"This isn't funny you, assho—"

Before he could finish the insult, a hand seized him by the throat, and then Neil was thrown backward. He hit the dishwasher, headfirst. Lightning cracked in his vision.

His legs turned to spaghetti, and he felt himself about to crumple to the ground. No such thing happened, though.

Varias Caras grabbed him by the front of the shirt and slammed him into the dishwasher. He moved his hands up and wrapped them around Neil's throat and squeezed.

Neil stared at his assailant. The pockmarked mask on his face made him freeze for a second, making him feel like a deer caught in headlights. Then, the instinct to survive took over. Neil reached for the side of the dishwasher, found the lever on the side of the machine and pulled it upward.

The doors flung open. Neil fell backward onto the dishrack, crashing on top of the dishes. Pizza pans, pots, utensils, and cutting boards clattered as they went flying every which way.

Neil reached for the back of the dishrack, for the cubby where the utensils were and felt the handle of a pizza cutter. He brought it over his head, meaning to use it to slice his assailant.

But Varias Caras saw it coming and stepped back.

Neil felt the end of the cutter slice through the air, missing the masked assailant by mere inches, before the man grabbed his arm. The clamp on his fingers was like nothing Neil had ever felt, like the man was superhuman.

Once again, he froze with terror.

The masked man stared at him, head cocked to the side, as if asking him *what else do you have?*

The answer to the question was nothing.

Neil felt his bladder empty itself into the front of his pants.

The masked man used both hands to force Neil's arm back inside the dishwasher, bending it so the elbow was pointed upward. Neil tried to fight it, but the man was pulling so hard it felt like his shoulder was going to rip out of the socket.

Once his arm was in place, the masked man pulled on the lever, bringing the metal door down on his arm. Neil screamed in agonizing pain as the door shattered his elbow. He lost his grip on the pizza cutter and fell to his knees, holding onto his broken arm.

The masked man grabbed him by the top of his hair and forced his head back.

"NO! PLEASE! PLEASE!" Neil begged, seeing the masked man was holding the pizza cutter now.

Varias Caras pressed the cutter into the kid's neck and rolled it across his throat, splitting the skin open. The boy's eyes rolled into the back of his head, but he was still alive. Varias Caras forced his index finger and thumb into the wound, enjoying the warmth and stickiness of the blood flowing onto his hand. He pinched the kid's larynx, and then with a quick pull, ripped it out of his throat. Blood sprinkled out of the wound and got onto his mask.

The kid's lifeless body started falling backward. Ignacio hooked him by the armpits and then hauled the corpse up. He took it over to a counter next to the dishwasher, the counter that the pizza shop employees used to prep food. He laid the corpse face up on it, then grabbed a bunch of dish rags sitting on a shelf in the back of the room. He used these like makeshift bandages and wrapped up the wound in his throat.

The kill had been messier than he'd hope it would've been, but Varias Caras had decided to have fun with this one. There was no telling when the next opportunity for a kill would be.

He raced out of the room and to the janitor's closet he'd seen as he was coming to kill the kid. Inside he found the bucket Neil had been using to clean the dining room earlier tonight. There were still suds from the cleaning agent at the bottom of it, but it needed to be refilled.

Ignacio put it in the slop sink and ran the water. While the bucket was filling, he looked for the floor cleaner on the shelf at the back of the closet.

8

JUDY REACHED FOR the popcorn on the coffee table. As she sat back, the room blurred by in her peripherals. It was like she'd moved too fast for her eyes.

She blinked. Once, twice.

The movie on the TV was suddenly fuzzy. It looked like just a bunch of hazy light flashing on the screen.

It was happening again. Another panic attack. Or anxiety attack. Whatever it was, the sensation that she was being watched was beginning to overwhelm her. The room started to feel smaller, like the walls were closing in on her.

Judy set her wineglass down on the end table and tried to compose herself.

It wasn't the alcohol. She'd had two glasses, so she wasn't exactly sober, but she was positive she wasn't drunk.

"You alright, Jude?" Daphne asked, sensing something was wrong.

Judy looked over at her. The color from the TV flashed across her pale, worried face.

Judy nodded. She relaxed the hand that didn't have the popcorn, realizing she'd been digging her nails into the couch's armrest. "The wine's just sneaking up on me."

"You want me to get you some water or something?"

"No, that's okay," Judy said, getting up, trying to act normal. "I can get it."

Judy heard Daphne say something encouraging as she went into the kitchen, but she wasn't sure what it was. Her mind was on getting out of the dimness of the living room.

She came into the kitchen, grabbed a glass from the cupboard, and filled it with water from the Arrowhead jug in the corner. She downed the whole glass in one gulp, then leaned against the counter, wiping her mouth with the sleeve of her sweatshirt.

Despite the fact the lights were on in the kitchen the feeling was getting worse. It felt like at any moment someone might break into the apartment. Maybe knock down the front door or smash through one of the windows behind her.

The thought made her whirl around and look out the window above the sink. The hedgerow across the yard swayed, their shadows dancing on the lawn. But other than that, the October night was still.

Judy filled her glass with more water. She drank this cup a little slower while staring out the window, then finally returned to the living room.

Ignacio ducked under the window ledge just as Judy had turned around. He'd gotten here about ten minutes ago. He'd been staring at Judy through the kitchen window as she'd been watching television in the living room.

Close call, Varias Caras said.

"Close call... Bad, bad, bad," Ignacio said, shaking his head.

Judy couldn't know he was watching her. She would get scared. If she got scared, she would call the cops. That would be bad.

He didn't want the cops to come looking for him. Cops had guns.

Instinctively, he reached up and touched the two spots where he'd been shot months ago at the camp. The bullets had missed hitting him in any vital spots, and the wounds had healed within weeks, but the skin had grown back pale and disfigured.

Ignacio shook his head to get rid of the bad memories. He shifted his focus to what was happening inside the apartment. Judy was walking back into the living room. The noises on the television cut out, and he heard her talking to the *bruja*.

The *bruja* asked her if she was OK. Judy said she was. But Ignacio could tell from the slight tremble in her voice that she was not.

He wished he could tell her that he would take her away from all of this soon.

9

DAPHNE SAT THERE, listening to the TV but no longer paying attention to *Arachnid Mutation Part V*. The human-spider monster was currently wreaking havoc inside of a laboratory, tearing some poor scientists to pieces and throwing their limbs around, but not even that caught her attention.

Judy said she had a headache, and the wine was making her feel shitty, so she'd gone to bed. But Daphne knew she was just being modest about what was bothering her. There was something else going on with her.

And it wasn't something that was exclusive to tonight, either. Daphne had taken note of how many times Judy said she "didn't sleep well" last night. Sure, it was possible she was just overworking and stressing herself out, but Judy wasn't a stranger to that.

Back when Judy was still in school, she'd stay up at all sorts of hours of the night to review for an exam. Daphne knew this because she would see Judy's bedroom light on while she was in the living room smoking weed and watching TV. Sometimes Judy wouldn't go to bed until three in the morning or later if she had a big test that week.

This was something else. Or at least, from an outsider's perspective, there *seemed* to be something else. Because, really, as much as she might know Judy Olmos, it wasn't like she was inside of her head. And really, that's what sometimes made watching a loved one suffer—you could only do so much as an external force.

Daphne sighed.

She and Judy weren't just roommates, they were best friends. They'd been best friends since ninth grade. Both had been in the after-school book club, which Judy had founded their freshman year. As such, she'd been the inaugural president of the club.

Jude had approached Daphne after one of their first meetings and asked her to be the unofficial PR person. She'd asked the question without a stutter or a stumble, even though she'd been shaking nervously the whole time. Knowing what she knew about Judy Olmos now, Daphne assumed she'd been rehearsing the question in front of the mirror for days.

Judy explained to her that part of the role involved picking books that would be on the ballot each month. Daphne accepted with almost no hesitation. Not because she was trying to advance in the club or anything like that, but because she wanted to see how a bunch of nerds would react to the fucked-up novels she was going to sneak in on them.

The first title she got them to read was a space horror/erotica novel Daphne knew about from her mother's secret stash of books. She'd sold it to the book club as *Star Wars* meets *Fifty Shades of Gray*. Which hadn't been the most inaccurate description, but none of them had been prepared for what they were about to read.

There was a scene in the first few chapters where a woman found an alien instrument in a remote Nevada valley. The instrument was phallic shaped, enticing the nymphomaniacal character to please herself with it later that night—until she accidentally hit a hidden button on the side of the instrument and a laser came shooting out of it while it was still inside of her, splitting the woman in half. It happened so quickly the woman didn't get a chance to realize she'd been masturbating with a ray gun.

Daphne had laughed so hard when she read that and thought some of the others would get a kick out of it. Instead, the members came into the meeting with confused and embarrassed looks on their faces, full of questions.

Judy had been furious with her. She didn't even look at or acknowledge Daphne during the whole meeting. The following days in school, she ignored her in the hallway and at lunch too. It wasn't until a week later that Judy came up to her at her locker and apologized to Daphne for being mad at her.

She admitted the book was funny and said she wanted to treat her to pizza to make up for overreacting. At the time, Daphne didn't really care, but free pizza was free pizza. They'd gone out to DeLorenzo's that night and became friends.

Since then, they'd only gotten closer and closer until one day Daphne realized she was best friends with Miss Goodie-Two-Shoes and future valedictorian of their graduating class.

But it seemed that even someone like Judy, who had everything together, could struggle with their mental health.

Daphne paused the movie. She got up and went over to the coatrack by the front door and felt inside the pocket of her leather jacket. The joint was still in there. She'd meant to smoke it while they'd been downtown but forgot about it.

It was a good thing, too. This was her last joint, and the wine had her feeling way too lazy to roll another one. Daphne put her jacket on, went into her bedroom to slip on a pair of Doc Martins, and then headed out of the apartment.

Ignacio was crouched down next to Judy's bedroom window. After the close call in the kitchen, he decided to play it safe and not watch her until she was asleep. Instead, he just listened to her getting ready for bed.

The dresser drawers rolled open and closed. Jewelry was unfastened. A pair of earrings and a necklace. He heard her put them away in a box, and then heard the lid snap shut.

Finally, she laid down on the bed. The wooden slats made a slight squeak that would've been inaudible to anyone besides Ignacio. He heard her click the lamp on the nightstand off and saw the light in the windows go out.

Ignacio stayed pressed against the wall, listening to her breath and heartbeat. Waiting to hear them fall into a tempo that told him she was asleep.

While he waited, he heard the TV silenced in the living room, followed by footsteps going back and forth through the apartment. It was the *bruja*. She was still awake, but it sounded like she was heading outside.

On the other side of the building, the front door opened and closed. Meaning the *bruja* was out here alone.

Ignacio looked over at the houses past the hedgerow. There were a few lights on in them, mostly in the bedrooms upstairs. The faintness of the lights suggested they came from either a nightlight or a bedside table.

He could see a few silhouettes of people propped up in their bed reading, watching television, eating a late-night snack.

But for the most part, the houses were still. The streets, as far as Ignacio's extraordinary hearing could pick up on, were quiet as well.

He moved, keeping to the shadows, making his way to the front of the building.

He went around the first bend that put him near the kitchen window again. He looked up at the apartment building above Judy's. The lights were on in one of the windows, and Ignacio could see the outlines of two people who seemed to be wrestling in bed. Whatever the man was doing to the woman, he was using his hips and making her moan a lot.

Ignacio ignored them for now and poked his head around the next bend to look at the front of the building. The *bruja* was sitting on the front steps of the building, smoking something stinky that looked like a long, skinny cigarette. The lights hanging outside the building turned her skin paler than usual, making her look like a ghost. She was staring up at the star-dotted sky, blowing a cloud of smoke into the air.

Varias Caras assessed the situation. She hadn't noticed him, but if he came around the wall, he would be putting himself just outside the light fixture's radiance. If she noticed him, she would scream, alerting the people all around that something was wrong.

There was no way he would be able to get upstairs to kill those people before they called the cops. If he got Judy and just ran, they might see him from one of the windows. Even worse, if enough noise was made, maybe people in the houses behind the apartment building would see him, too.

No, it was all too risky. He already had the kid he'd killed at the pizza shop in his trunk. He shouldn't get greedy.

Tonight, we just watch, Varias Caras said.

"Just watch," Ignacio muttered, bringing his head behind the wall.

He made his way back to Judy's bedroom window.

Daphne took one last drag of the joint. She let the smoke fill her lungs for a few seconds before blowing it out into the October air.

She put the joint out against the side of the steps and stood up.

Judy'll be alright, she thought to herself, brushing dirt off the seat of her pants. *We'll both be alright.*

She headed back inside, unaware that only a few feet away from her was the source of her friend's anxiety. Unaware of the danger she'd narrowly missed.

10

They'd wound up at Tough Annie's after coming back to town. The place was dead most of the night because Halloween Eve was more of a house party night in Hilltown. Dan, Tucker, Hudson, and Baxter had been the only ones left in the bar by last call.

They walked across the parking lot to where they left their vehicles. Hudson was so drunk he was using Dan and Baxter as crutches to walk straight.

Besides the sound of their feet stamping across the black top and the buzzing of an overhead powerline, the night and streets were quiet.

"Jesus Christ, man," Tucker said, noticing a missing person flyer stapled onto a streetlamp in the lot. He'd seen a few of them in the bar too. In the bathroom and the bulletin boards where they had miscellaneous local company's ads on them. "Did you guys put these fucking things everywhere?"

"Yeah," Dan said. "That's kind of the point of them, so everyone in town knows, dummy."

Although, he himself hadn't put any up. This must've been a thing the Sheriff had the other officers do after he'd been done work today.

"It's just a buzzkill, man," Tucker said, shaking his head.

They got to their vehicles. Tucker and Hudson hopped in the back of the Mustang. Dan got into the driver seat, and Baxter slumped into the passenger seat.

Tucker had gotten the OK to leave his work truck here from the bar owner. And since Dan was the only one who wasn't drunk, he was the designated driver tonight.

"Well, sorry a girl went missing and it's fucking up Halloween for you," Dan said as he put his seatbelt on.

"I don't mean it like that. I mean you cop fuckheads had to put one near a fun spot in town—you know what, never mind, fuck you," he laughed.

Baxter and Dan laughed, too. Hudson couldn't laugh because he'd already dozed off against the window, a string of drool coming out of his mouth.

"We dropping the load off first?" Tucker asked, giving Hud a sideways glance.

"Yeah," Dan said, putting the Mustang in drive and starting out of Tough Annie's parking lot.

None of them said a word as they drove to Hudson's neighborhood. Baxter and Tucker just watched their humble town roll by the window as they tried to fight off sleep.

Meanwhile, Dan sat back in the driver's seat, listening to the classic rock songs playing on the radio. Maybe it had something to do with the music, or that it was past two in the morning, or the four beers he'd drank tonight, but he was feeling particularly emotional at the moment.

He looked over at Baxter, who was sitting there like the world's largest child with his hands laced across his lap, watching the Halloween decorations and lights on Main Street whizz by the Mustang.

In the rearview mirror, he saw Hudson was sound asleep. Eyes closed tight, his posture as rigid as a scarecrow.

Tucker was leaned back against the car door, his feet up on the car seat, not caring that he was putting his dirty shoes on the upholstery. He was clicking around on his phone, the screen casting a ghastly glow over his face. Tucker noticed Dan looking at him and looked up from his phone and quickly flipped him off.

Dan laughed.

As annoying as Tucker could be, he really did love these three knuckleheads. And ever since they'd graduated out of college, they didn't really get many chances to hang out the way they had tonight.

It seemed the older you got, the less time you got to spend with those important to you. Perhaps in some way, that was a good thing. Because it meant you cherished those moments with them more.

Dan blinked and brought his focus back to driving them home safe. He grinned, thinking how Tucker would call him a pussy if he could read his mind.

They dropped Hudson off. Tucker had gone inside to make sure he made it to the bedroom safely and came back to the car eating some cookies he'd taken from the Crosley's kitchen.

They were back on the road now, driving to Tucker's neighborhood next.

Baxter was asleep on the passenger seat, his head cocked in what looked like an uncomfortable position and one of his nostrils kept whistling. Tucker was sprawled out on the backseat, munching on the macadamia cookies. Slow classic rock songs continued to play through the speakers.

But other than these sounds, the car ride had been quiet.

"Yo, Dan," Tucker said, breaking the silence. He leaned forward, poking his head between the two front seats. "You think you guys will find her?"

"What?" Dan asked, taken aback by the sudden question.

"The girl that went missing. On the posters. You think the police—you guys—will find her? Or she'll show up, eventually?"

"That's what you're thinking about?"

"Yeah," Tucker said, swallowing the bite of cookie he'd been working on. "Honestly, it's all I've been thinking about since you guys brought it up earlier tonight."

"Why?"

Tucker shrugged. "I dunno. According to that poster, she was our age."

"Yeah, and?"

"Well, it would just suck for life to end now, you know? When there's so much to see and do in the world."

"Jesus, Tuck. Did you and Hudson smoke a joint at his house or something?"

Tucker laughed. "Nah. I'm just contemplative is all… Must be the full moon."

He laid back down in the passenger seat, his hands laced behind his head as he stared out the window at the trees rushing overhead of the car.

Another stretch of silence fell between them before Dan spoke.

"Maybe we'll find her. Maybe we won't. Either way, I don't think she'll be the last person to ever go missing in or around Hilltown. Unfortunately."

"Yeah," Tucker said, yawning.

Dan turned into Tucker's neighborhood.

Considering the time, the houses were mostly dark. Some Halloween lights hanging from the awnings, railings, and fences had been left on, but most of them had been unplugged. The jack-o-lanterns' candles had long been blown out. Lawn decorations that had been animated hours ago were powered off and frozen midmotion. The cornstalks, scarecrows and countless pumpkins lining the walkways and decorating the porches were obscured by the blanket of darkness covering the sleeping neighborhood.

Dan stopped the Mustang in front of Tucker's house, which was one of the few houses on the street that had its porchlights on.

"Alright, man," Tucker said, sitting up and reaching out to slap five with Dan.

"You're good, right?" Dan asked.

Tucker scoffed. "Yeah, I'm good."

"Alright," Dan said.

They slapped five. Then Tuck nudged Baxter on the shoulder.

"Yo, I'm out," Tucker said.

Baxter shrugged his shoulder and then, still half asleep, mumbled something that sounded like, "Be nice, man."

"Okay, well. Thanks for driving us," Tucker said, opening the door. "And, uh, Happy Halloween, I guess."

Before Dan could respond, a group of teenagers came running down the sidewalk. They came underneath a streetlamp, which rendered their all-black attires useless. One of the kids, the one wearing an alien mask on his face, was carrying an orange bucket with a jack-o-lantern face painted on it—but they weren't out here to trick-or-treat.

They stopped in front of Tucker's house, somehow not noticing the Mustang with its lights on. The two other kids, who weren't wearing masks but had the hoods of their sweatshirts up, reached into the bucket. They each pulled out two eggs.

"Yo!" Tucker screamed, jumping out of the car.

The kids jumped in surprise and all three simultaneously turned around. The kid closest to him screamed "oh shit!" as he lost his grip on the eggs. They slipped out of his hand and splattered on the pavement. He and the kid with the alien mask started sprinting down the sidewalk, laughing their heads off. Meanwhile, the third kid launched his eggs at the house in rapid succession. One egg splatted against the front steps; the other smashed into the railing.

Tucker managed about three steps toward the kid before he took off running behind his buddies.

"I'm gonna beat your fucking asses!" Tucker called out to them. He was way too drunk and tired to chase them down, so an empty threat would have to do.

The kids roared in laughter as they got to the end of the street. Then, the one with the alien mask turned around and gave Tucker the finger.

Tucker answered back with two of his own.

"Little shitheads," Tucker muttered.

"Don't act like you didn't do stuff like that at their age," Dan said through the open passenger window.

"Yeah, and you were right there with me," Tucker said.

"A hundred percent," a half-asleep Baxter said.

Tucker turned, seeing the egg all over the house he'd have to clean up. "Fuck!"

"Alright, we're heading out," Dan said, yawning. "I gotta go drop Bax off and get my car."

"Okay," Tucker said. He reached through the window to fist bump both. "See ya guys tomorrow. And you better fucking wear costumes or I'm not letting you into the party."

"Yeah, yeah," Dan said, rolling up the passenger window.

"I'm serious!" Tucker screamed, not caring that it was in the middle of the night and he might wake some of the neighbors.

Dan waved at him, and then drove off. They went down four houses and saw a tree with orange string lights wrapped around it that had been TP'd.

"You think those same kids that just hit Tuck's house did that?" Baxter asked, coming fully awake as he laughed.

"Probably," Dan chuckled.

11

DIANA COULDN'T SLEEP. No, not with the constant sounds of the sewing machine from downstairs. The whirring. The tick-tick of the needle striking.

The masked man—Varias Caras—as she was thinking of him now, was down there… making something…

She closed her eyes, trying to will the sounds into becoming white noise to her. But it wasn't working. Her imagination wasn't letting her.

It kept flooding her with grotesque images of what he might be sewing.

Maybe another satchel of people's faces…

Maybe a mask…

Maybe he's turning someone's skin into a pair of gloves… Winter is right around the corner…

Diana shuddered.

Downstairs, the sounds from the sewing machine continued. *Whirr, whirr, tick, tick, tick…*

Ignacio held the mask up to the lamp on the desk.

The base layer of the mask was leather from Madison Charleston's back. This was the part that would be touching Ignacio's own skin, and for the most part he liked using women's skin for that. Their skin usually made for a softer leather. It also had a subtle, sweet aromatic scent to it that men's skin didn't seem to have. Ignacio enjoyed that.

The second layer was made from Timothy Baker's belly to give the mask some flexibility.

The final and outside layer was Dale Henderson's face. It'd dried out nice and tough under the sun. Perfect for protection from branches whipping him in the face when he was out hunting in the woods.

Ignacio rubbed his thumbs over the mask, admiring what his victims' bodies had become. He'd fashioned this one into something that looked like a luchador mask. The holes cut into the mask were big and wide, meant to make breathing and seeing easier.

The first part of the mask was done. Now, it was onto the second half.

Ignacio got up from behind the sewing machine. He crossed the room and went over to a desk streaked with paint and littered with art supplies. Brushes, tubes of paint, stencils, scraps of leather, and more.

Ignacio moved some stuff around, making space in the center, and laid the mask down on the desk. Using both hands, he flattened it out neatly. Done with this, he pulled the chair that was pushed under the desk out and settled into it.

Then, from a drawer in the desk, he pulled out a photo.

It was a photo of him and Mamá from their first Halloween here in the United States. They were standing in front of the apartment building they lived in at the time. Mamá had her arm around Ignacio, who was only ten-years old in the picture, but almost as tall as her. Ignacio was bunched up against her, dressed up like a luchador and holding onto a bucket filled with candy with both hands.

Ignacio didn't like pictures then and he didn't like pictures now.

But the important thing to him was the mask. Mamá had made it for him the night before Halloween.

He'd watched over her shoulder as she cut and sewed the fabric together, memorizing every step. After the mask was all sewn together, Ignacio watched her paint a sugar skull design on it. The mask had a set of teeth around the mouth hole, dark blue circles around the eyeholes, green and yellow dots here and there, and a rose in the middle of the forehead.

Ignacio was going to attempt to recreate it. He was not as good as Mamá at painting, so he didn't think it would come out looking the same. But he was still going to try.

In honor of Mamá.

He opened a bucket of red paint, grabbed a paintbrush, and began painting his Halloween mask.

HALLOWEEN

1

HUDSON WOKE UP to the smell of pancakes, bacon, and coffee filling his nose. He sat up in bed, yawning, stretching his arms out. One of his knuckles hit the calendar hanging on the wall, almost knocking it off. He turned to straighten it up, and as his eyes fell over all the X's on the days of October, it dawned on him.

Halloween. The best damn day of the year.

Hudson threw the covers off himself and jumped out of bed, almost screaming *hallelujah* in the process. He did a little jig in the middle of his bedroom, something akin to an Elvis Presley move with his arms flailing about and his legs shaking. He finished the dance by pointing at the closet where his Bigfoot costume was hanging, waiting to be worn on this magical day.

Done with the dance, he glanced over at his bedroom window, hoping Tucker hadn't been there the whole time. Confirming that he wasn't, Hudson flopped onto the bed and marked an X over October 31st.

He was about to jump out of bed and dance some more when there was a knock at his door.

"Hey, champ. You up?" It was his father.

"Yeah, Dad. What's up?"

"Well, two things. Your friend is here. And also, your mom made breakfast."

"Wait, which friend?"

"Tucker," his dad said.

"Oh." Hudson said, surprised Tuck had opted for the front door instead of their usual routine.

He picked his phone up and looked at the time. It was 10:30am.

"Okay. I'll be right out, Dad," Hudson said, heading over to the closet to get dressed.

Tucker was sitting at the kitchen table with his father. He was wearing a light gray hoodie and his hair was combed better than he'd seen it in years, but despite that, Hudson could tell he was battling a hangover.

"Good morning, sunshine," Hudson's mother said, carrying a plate of bacon through the kitchen. She set the plate down in the middle of the table, and then sat down next to his father.

Hudson took the chair next to Tucker.

"Yo," Tuck said to him, trying to sound energized.

"Hey, man," Hudson said. "Thanks for last night."

"Last night?" his father asked, narrowing his eyes at them.

"Yeah, we were playing Xbox last night," Tucker answered before Hudson got himself into trouble. "I jumped in and saved Hud's sorry hide—that's what friends are for, after all, you know, Mr. Crosley?"

Hudson's dad nodded. "I don't know anything about those video games, but I once won a doubles ping pong tournament with my best friend in middle school. Makes me glad to know the youth of today still understands the importance of teamwork."

"You know it," Tucker grinned.

They shared a small laugh at this, then started putting pancakes and bacon onto their plates and passing around the butter and maple syrup.

"Tucker, do you want to say grace for us?" Hudson's dad asked.

Tucker cleared his throat and was about to answer when Mr. Crosley pointed at him and laughed.

"Gotcha!" he said, a smile breaking out on his face. "We're agonistic, but spiritual in this household."

"Ha! Good one, Mr. Crosley, you almost got me there." Tucker feigned a smile.

"Stephen," Hudson's mom chastised. "So, you boys have any plans tonight?"

Tucker answered for them. "Yeah, we're just going to chill at my house with some friends. Maybe help my parents hand out candy to the trick-or-treaters. But nothing too exciting."

Hudson squirmed uncomfortably in his seat. For one, he didn't like lying to his parents. And two, the "good boy" voice Tucker was using made him cringe. He stuck a piece of bacon in his mouth and tried to act cool.

"Oh. You boys aren't going out?" Mr. Crosley asked.

"We might go out downtown to see some Halloween costumes if the movies get boring," Hudson said, trying to at least tell a half-truth.

"Well, if you do end up going out, be safe out there," Hudson's mom said.

"We will, Mrs. Crosley," Tucker said, shoveling a piece of pancake into his mouth.

"Oh, come on, Meredith," Hudson's dad interjected, grabbing the maple syrup and drenching his pancakes with it. "It's Halloween night. Don't you remember being their age?"

"When we were their age, we were already engaged and living together. Our Halloween nights consisted of handing out candy to trick-or-treaters and trying not to fall asleep before ten."

Mr. Crosley opened his mouth to say something, but whatever he meant to argue never came out. Instead, he fixed the glasses on his face and just said, "…You're right."

"I know I am," Mrs. Crosley said, smiling at him.

"However!" he said, putting his finger up in the air. "It's a different time than when we were young! Let them—as the kids say these days—get as lit as they want this Halloween night."

Hudson groaned.

"Stephen, quit embarrassing him in front of his friend," Mrs. Crosley said, a lot sterner this time.

Tucker couldn't help it. He threw his head back and cackled, eliciting Hudson's dad to smile proudly, not realizing Tucker was laughing at him.

"I'll make sure me and Hud have a great time tonight," Tucker said, putting his arm around Hudson's shoulder. "It'll be the littest of Halloweens, ain't that right, Hud?"

Hudson nodded, and then took a big gulp of orange juice.

"The littest of Halloweens, Tuck?" Hudson said, shaking his head.

After breakfast, they were sitting in the Crosley's sunroom. The light coming in through the glass was bright and on a slant that put it eyelevel with Hudson as he sat in the wicker chair, forcing him to shield his eyes with a hand to look at Tucker.

"Your dad seemed proud of using that word," Tucker laughed, as he paced back and forth in the room.

"Why are you pacing?"

Feeling called out, Tucker settled into the loveseat across from where Hudson was sitting.

"I'm feeling like I fucked up."

"How so?"

"By agreeing with Dan to keep tonight lowkey."

"How is that messing up?"

"Because I could've made a post about it on social media. I could've told Bax to invite a bunch of his friends from college. We could've had a sick Halloween party tonight."

"Oh." Hudson considered that. "Since when are you all into Halloween, anyway?"

"It's not about Halloween. It's deeper than that."

"What do you mean?"

"Well, last night I was thinkin' about shit," Tucker said, looking out of the sunroom to the house across the street where one of Hudson's neighbors was mowing their lawn.

"Like what?"

"Like how life can just end for people, you know? Like that chick who went missing, for example. She was coming up here for a job interview and ended up disappearing before making it to Hilltown."

"She could still be alive."

"Yeah, sure, but let's assume not for the sake of what I'm going to say."

"Okay."

"And we're getting to that age where we're no longer gonna be considered the "youth", you know? Daph is talking about moving away next year. Dan is a fucking cop. My parents are probably gonna kick me out soon."

"Kick you out, why?"

"Not in a like *fuck off* kind of way, but more like, *hey we want to be empty nesters so get your own place* kind of way."

"Oh, right." Hudson nodded. "Right."

"And other people we know are engaged and getting pregnant and shit." Tucker turned to look at Hudson. "In like two or three years, I think our Halloweens will look a lot different. I think they'll be a lot less exciting. And also, lonelier."

"Jeez." Hudson said, his eyes dropping down to his shoes. "That's… depressing to think about."

"But, oh well." Tucker said, digging in his jeans pocket for his carton of cigarettes. "I guess there's always next year."

"Yeah," Hudson muttered. "We'll still have fun tonight, though, right?"

"Yeah." Tucker said, sticking a cigarette in his mouth and then putting the carton back in his pocket.

Silence fell between them. The wind moved some chimes hanging outside the sunroom. Their melancholy tunes seemed to reflect their own thoughts.

Tucker got up and went over to the nearest window. He opened it, screen and all, and leaned out of it.

"Anyway," Tucker said, lighting the cigarette in his mouth. "Didn't mean to be a buzzkill."

"It's alright." Hudson said, then chuckled. "Not even you can ruin Halloween for me."

Tucker laughed, blowing the cloud of smoke in his mouth he meant to inhale out into the crisp air.

"Of course not." He said, taking another drag of the cigarette.

"What're you dressing up as, anyway?"

"A cult leader."

"A cult leader?"

"Yeah," Tucker said, smoking some more. "Why do you sound confused?"

"Is anyone else going as a cult member?"

"Not that I know of."

"Then how can you be a cult leader?"

"Hud, what the fuck are you going on about?"

"I mean, how can you be a 'cult leader' without other cult members? By definition, a cult is a group of people—and a 'leader' is the person they follow. So, without cult members, there's no group. So, you, as a solo person, can't possibly be a 'leader' since there's no other people following you. It makes no sense."

"Hud..." Tucker turned to look at him to see how serious he was. He was very serious, judging by the look on his face. "Shut up."

"I'm right, aren't I?"

"You are." Tucker said, rolling his eyes.

Hudson nodded in approval. "So, we agree you're not going as a cult leader, then?"

"Right." Tucker said, putting the cigarette in his mouth. "I'm going as a guy in a black robe with a skeleton mask. Happy?"

"So, the grim reaper?"

"Yeah, let's go with that, Hud."

"Do you have a scythe?"

Tucker sighed. "No, I don't have a scythe, man."

"I have one somewhere in my room." Hudson said. "It's plastic but it looks badass. You want to borrow it?"

"Yeah," Tucker said. "Yeah, I'll borrow it, man."

"Cool." Hudson said, standing up. "We'll go inside once you're done with your cigarette."

"I'm done now." Tucker said. He put the cigarette out against the outside wall. "Come on, show me this thing and then I gotta bounce."

2

"**H**OLY SHIT," DAPHNE said, as they pulled up to Frosty Hollow Manor. "It looks like something out of—"

"*Scooby Doo,*" Tucker said.

Daphne turned to him with an eyebrow cocked up.

"Read your mind, huh? It's a twin thing," Tucker grinned.

"Tucker, don't ever say that again."

Tucker threw his head back, laughing hysterically.

"That's not even what I was going to say, anyway, dumbass," Daphne spat.

"A Stephen King novel, yeah, yeah," Tucker said, sobering up and opening the truck door. "Wait until you see the inside."

He drove the truck through the gate and parked on the cul-de-sac in front of the manor.

"How'd you guys find this place, anyway?" Daphne asked as they walked up the stone-cobbled walkway on the overgrown lawn leading to the veranda.

"Me and Hud found it over the summer. Remember we were in the search party? For that chick who went missing back in May?"

"Yeah."

"We found it while riding around. I had the idea to throw a Halloween party kicking around since."

"Not your worst idea." Daphne stopped before entering the manor, noticing the front door was on the ground, off to the side, and had a hole about the size of a watermelon in it. "What the hell happened to that?"

Tucker shrugged. "Baxter knocked on it. Really hard."

Daphne wasn't entirely sure what he meant by this, but she didn't care to ask him to clarify. She followed him into the manor. Tucker took out a flashlight from his back pocket and turned it on. He pointed the beam around the foyer, letting Daphne take in the sight of the place.

"We're going to keep the party downstairs," Tucker told her, seeing her take notice of the crisscrossed caution tape blocking entry to the staircase. "And also keep it to a few rooms. Here, I'll show you what we mean."

He led her to the right, taking her into the dining room.

"We can use this for beer pong," Tucker said as they walked past the wooden table they'd left in there.

The dining room led into the kitchen, which was empty. From here, they cut to the right and went down the corridor with the paintings and the old photo of the family hanging on it.

"What's the story behind this place, anyway?" Daphne asked.

"I don't know. Who cares?"

"Me. That's why I asked."

"Well, look it up then."

Daphne reached for her cell phone but quickly noticed there was no service. This deep in the woods and away from town it wasn't surprising. She made a mental note to look this place up later and put the phone back in her jacket.

The corridor ended and they were in a spacious room with a fireplace in the corner.

"Me and Baxter are coming back later to put some furniture in this room, and we'll use it as the main spot for the party," Tucker said, then he pointed to a smaller room off to the left. "That one we can use for extra shit."

"Extra shit?"

"Yeah, like to smoke weed or whatever." Tucker thought of something, a sly grin forming on his face. "Your roommate is looking cute these days. Maybe she'll make out with—"

"Shut up, Tucker. Just shut up," Daphne said, turning away from him.

He burst out laughing in that high-pitched way that annoyed her to no end.

She ignored him and instead brought her focus to trying to visualize how to decorate the place. Tucker was right—though, she would never admit this to him—in saying that this manor was like something out of Scooby Doo.

"What do you think?" Tucker said, stepping next to her.

"I think this is the first time in a long while you had a good idea." Daphne said, refusing to give her brother the satisfaction of knowing she was excited about one of his plans.

Tucker crossed his arms and leaned against the nearest wall, a shit-eating grin on his face.

"It wouldn't hurt to be nice to me for once, you know."

"You're right," Daphne said, walking past him and hitting him on the shoulder. "It'd probably kill me."

Tucker laughed. "So, you wanna get started on decorating?"

"Yes," Daphne said. "Yes, I do."

3

Downstairs, she heard Varias Caras coming up into the attic, heard the familiar sound of his clomping up the stairs.

The locks were thrown off. The door hinges squeaked as they swung open.

Diana felt Varias Caras' shadow over her. The shape was unusual, like something that only appeared vaguely human.

A thought entered Diana's mind. Maybe he wasn't exactly human. Maybe he was a literal monster and could shapeshift into some sort of beast. That would explain his unnatural strength and speed.

A split-second after the thought came to her, she realized how absurd the thought was. Then again, everything about what was happening was absurd.

Diana turned to look at him and saw why his shadow looked different. He was carrying a naked person over his shoulder. A man, from what she could tell.

Varias Caras stood staring at her through the small eyeholes of the leather mask on his face. Today's mask was a brown, bumpy one that looked like a piece of bark.

"He cannot scream," Varias Caras said, as if she'd asked him.

He strode through the attic, going over to the wooden table.

From this angle, Diana could see the boy's head. It lolled and bounced around erratically with the movement. Some dish towels had been tied together and wrapped around the neck like a makeshift bandage.

Varias Caras set the body down on the table, then went over to where the cabinets were.

With him out of the way, Diana got her best look at the corpse. The kid's pale, graying skin was a direct contrast to the brown table he laid on. His face was frozen in a combination of surprise and anguish—a look that made Diana think of the skinny man in the woods.

Varias Caras returned to the table, carrying a rolled-up tarp under his armpit, a hacksaw in one hand, and a white bucket in the other. He stopped in front of the dead body, blocking most of her view of it again and set the bucket down on the ground by his feet.

All she could see now was the top of the guy's hair and his legs from the shins down.

Varias Caras turned to face her. He'd put on an apron and a pair of long, purple rubber gloves. The apron was yellow, with dark brown stains on it that could've been confused with a pattern at a quick glance, the silhouettes of some birds or a bunch of flowers, maybe. But once she got a good look at them, it was obvious they were bloodstains that hadn't washed out.

"You don't have to watch…if you don't want," he said to her, then turned back to the corpse.

Diana gulped. Her throat felt as rough as sandpaper.

She didn't want to watch, but she couldn't bring herself to look away, either. Maybe it was some morbid curiosity. Or maybe it was because she felt like she was about to watch her own fate unfold before her eyes.

Varias Caras set the hacksaw down on the table, then knelt down to spread the tarp out on the floor.

Done with that, he stood up and returned his focus to the corpse.

He grabbed its limbs and straightened them out, making sure they were parallel to one another. Then he put the kid's palms facedown and spread the digits out as far as they would go.

Satisfied with this repositioning, Varias Caras picked up the hacksaw and readied it. He pressed it against the arm closest to him, then used his free hand to press down on the kid's torso, and started sawing through the arm, an inch above the bicep.

Diana couldn't see it happening, but she could hear the hacksaw going through the body. Could hear the wet sounds as the teeth tore through skin and muscle. After a few seconds of this, there was a small clink as the hacksaw struck bone. She saw Varias Caras's arm flex as he put more muscle into the sawing.

Diana saw blood starting to drip off the edge of the table, and that was enough for her. She closed her eyes.

But it wasn't enough.

She could still hear the teeth grinding against the bone. Could still hear the pitter-patter of blood dripping down onto the tarp.

But worse, she could hear Varias Caras's small giggles of excitement.

Several minutes later, the attic went quiet. The butchering replaced by Varias Caras walking through the room.

Diana opened her eyes in time to see him standing by the door, turning the knob with a blood covered glove. His other hand was holding onto the bucket, which was now filled with chunks of flesh.

He glanced over at her as he exited through the door and went downstairs.

Diana looked over at the corpse, almost involuntarily. The limbs had been stripped of most of their meat and were now mostly bones attached to hands and feet. The lower torso had been sliced open, and the organs had all been pulled out, and was nothing more than a cavernous hole now.

The head had been cut off the body and set to the side.

Whatever blood was left in the veins seeped out from the mutilated body parts. A small stream oozed over one side of the table in a long, sticky stream, plopping down onto the tarp.

Despite the mess, the corpse was still discernible as having once been human because the limbs—or what was left of them—were laid along the torso.

And that made the sight worse. So much worse.

Tears rolled down the side of Diana's face. She closed her eyes, but the horrific image of the carnage was burned into her mind's eye.

4

Tucker plugged the outdoor lights into the power surge connected to the generator.

"And then God said, let there be light."

All five of the projector lights came on, their bright color washing over the façade of the manor. Parts of it turned green, other parts were dark blue. One of the lights had a piece of cardboard over it that Daphne had cut into the outline of a witch. This specific light oscillated, making it look like the shadow of a witch riding her broom was passing over the house.

The front yard was decorated with plastic tombstones, gourds, and jack-o-lanterns. On the veranda, there were more pumpkins and jack-o-lanterns strewn about. The overgrown bushes in front of the house had spiderwebs and tiny plastic spiders on it.

While Daphne had been decorating both the inside and outside, Tucker had put up a new front door. The new door had an "X" made of caution tape over it, and some red handprints on it that looked like smeared blood.

"We make a pretty good team, huh, sis?" Tucker said, stepping back to admire their work.

"I guess we do," Daphne let out a big yawn. "What time is it?"

"About to be three PM," Tucker said.

"You're buying me tacos, right?"

"I guess," Tucker said. "You wanna head out now?"

Daphne nodded.

"Alright. I'll just shut the generator off, and we can head out," he said, jogging to the side of the house.

A few seconds after he disappeared from her view, the generator started to shut off. The loud, mechanical buzzing replaced by deafening silence. The lights both inside and outside the manor went off.

Shadows and silence surrounded Daphne, almost engulfing her. She wasn't one to scare easily, but there was a certain eeriness to being out here alone.

She waited for Tucker, tapping her foot to rustle the grass just for some added noise. Her brother seemed to be taking his sweat old time.

"Yo, Tuck! Hurry up, I'm starving," she called out into the shadows, trying to keep the edge out of her voice.

Inside the manor, she saw some movement. *How long have they been in there?* she wondered.

The front door opened. Tucker came out, his mouth bleeding. He held his hand out, covered in blood.

"Daph..." he croaked, taking a few steps out onto the veranda. She looked at his stomach, his wifebeater was streaked with blood.

"Tuck, stop fucking around!" Daphne said, moving closer to him, her heart beating so hard she could feel it in her throat.

Tucker fell to his knees. The blood continued to flow from his mouth, pouring down his chin. "I... I'm not."

Daphne took a few steps toward him, her heart threatening to come shooting out of her chest.

Then, without warning, Tucker hopped up to his feet, laughing.

"Okay, okay, I'm done," he said, wiping the fake blood off his face with a rag from his back pocket. "I'm sorry, I'm sorry. I found a packet of blood in my jeans, and I had to."

"You're a fucking asshole."

"Yeah, yeah. Look, I'll buy you nachos to make up for it," he said, grinning as he walked past her toward the truck.

"I'll take the nachos, but that doesn't make up for shit," Daphne called after him. Under her breath she added, "Prick."

Daphne was in the bathroom when Judy came back from her daily run. She popped her head out, her hair bunched up into four big sections on her head, wearing a pair of plastic gloves and holding a paintbrush with black dye on its bristles.

"Hey, stranger," Daphne said.

They hadn't seen each other this morning because Daphne had left to Frosty Hollow Manor with Tucker before Judy had even woken up. Usually, Judy was up hours before her, but this morning had been a rare instance of the opposite.

"How'd decorating go?" Judy asked her, going into the kitchen for a glass of water.

"Awesome," Daphne said, continuing to apply dye to a section of her hair as they spoke. "The place looks really fucking cool."

"That's exciting!"

"Yeah, this place is in the middle of the woods," Daphne said, shaking her head. "Like, way deeper than I thought it would be—you know how my brother exaggerates shit?"

"Yeah," Judy said, coming back to the end of the hallway. The ice cubes in the glass clinked as she drank some water from it.

"Well, he wasn't this time."

Judy laughed again. "What time does the party start?"

"Ten," Daphne said. "By the way, did you let Brie Berk know about Tucker's party?"

"Yeah, I texted her last night."

"What did she say?"

"She just said 'OK' with the hand painting the fingernails emoji," Judy said.

It was Daphne's turn to laugh. "What the fuck does that mean?"

"I'm not entirely sure," Judy chuckled. "I guess it means she's in, though?"

"Yeah, probably," Daphne said.

"I'm gonna go text her. See what time she wants me to pick her up."

"Alright. I'm gonna finish up with this."

"Why are you dying your hair, anyway? It looked pretty dark to me already."

"The roots were starting to come in brown…" Daphne said, looking at herself in the mirror. "I saw way too much resemblance between me and Tuck today."

"You're something else, you know that, Daph?" Judy laughed. "I'm gonna make cookies. Any preferences?"

"Those peanut butter ones your momma gave you were bomb!"

"Okay, I'll make those. She gave me her recipe a while ago," Judy informed her, walking away.

"You the best, Judy!" Daphne called out to her and went back to finishing up dying her hair.

5

He put the tray of food down on the floor by the feed door and looked through the cage at Diana. The smell of spices and herbs filled her nostrils. She rose on the mattress to take a peek at the food he'd brought.

It was two plates with meat, rice, and green beans. The plates had different meats on them; one looked like pork chops, the other looked like maybe pork floating in a reddish-brown sauce.

Varias Caras' hair was up in a ponytail, and he was wearing a mask that was made up of leather lattice going across his face. Even though she could see more of his face than usual, the gaps between the straps were small enough that she still wouldn't be able to pick him out of a lineup.

He crouched down, eyelevel with her and worked the lock off the feed door. He talked while he did this.

"Meat today," he told her. "Pork or special mole for the Barbie?"

It took her a split second to realize he was asking her a question.

"Pork," she said, barely recognizing her own voice.

Talking, and especially talking to him, was strange. It was unsettling how quickly she'd gotten used to not using her voice.

He opened the feed door and put the plate with the pork chops on her side.

Diana looked over at the dish, her stomach growling. The idea of eating more of this guy's food—food he likely cooked and handled with the same hands that he'd used to murder Madison and butcher that guy—made her sick.

At the same time, though, she could feel her body craving calories. Could feel it craving sustenance.

Diana crawled off the mattress and got closer to the plate.

The dish looked like something you might get served at a restaurant. The pork chops had been seared in a pan and had dark and crispy edges. The mound of rice was perfectly portioned. The string beans all parallel to one another. If he had indeed cooked these, then this man knew what he was doing in the kitchen.

"I need a fork," she said.

The masked man had started eating his own food and stopped to listen to her with a forkful of meat halfway to his mouth. He cocked his head to the right, as if listening to someone debate the idea with him, then shook his head.

"No. You use hands," he said, setting his own fork down on the ground.

He must think I'm going to try something funny with it, she thought, an idea starting to form in her head.

Diana picked up one of the chops. It smelled like garlic and oregano. She took one bite. It was delicious. Crispy on the outside, juicy on the inside.

The second bite she took was bigger. Meat never tasted so good. Diana ate the meat until she was down to the bone, then started plucking tiny bits out of it, the whole time feeling like a ravenous beast trapped in a cage, but she couldn't stop.

She hadn't had a real meal in days, the broth and vegetables from the soup had been nothing.

Diana ate the second pork chop just as fast, then used her fingers to shovel string beans and rice into her mouth. All in all, it took her less than five minutes to finish off all the food.

"It was good?" Varias Caras asked after he saw her plate was cleared.

Diana looked up at him. He had a big smile on his face.

Diana nodded. Now that the initial rush of eating real food was over and her stomach was full, she felt defeated. Feeling like she'd just given up the last shreds of her humanity by eating his food like she was his pet.

"Good," he replied.

Diana sat there with her head low, listening to him slurp up his food.

As shameful as she felt about it, it wasn't all bad. She could feel the carbs from the rice, the vegetables, the meat, and all of the calories giving her energy already. The fog that her mind had been put under from hunger started to clear up.

The pork chop bones started to look different now. They started to look like tools.

She glanced over at Varias Caras. He was mixing the last of his rice and mystery meat around the mole sauce with his fork. The light from the bulb hanging on the ceiling reflected off the fork handle, but Diana realized she didn't need it.

She grabbed one of the pork chop bones and stuck it in the pocket of her jeans. The other one she carefully, quietly snapped in two while she pretended to bite at the last scraps of meat on it.

"All gone," he said, setting the fork down on the plate.

He stared into her eyes as he reached through the feed door for her empty plate. For a terrifying moment, she thought he knew what she was up to, that perhaps he'd notice how small the two bones were on the plate, and how they couldn't possibly have been all he gave her...

But then he set the plate down on the other side of the cage and started locking the feed door back up.

Diana tried her best to hide the sigh of relief.

He finished locking the cage and stood up with the plates in his hand.

"I will see you later," he said, and exited the attic.

Diana waited for the door to close behind him before taking the porkchop bone out of her jeans. She went over to the cage wall, then started sawing the bone against the steel mesh. She prayed to a God she wasn't sure existed that this would work.

6

AROUND AN HOUR later, Judy popped into her parent's house to give them some of the freshly baked peanut butter cookies. To her surprise, her father was home. She said hello and goodbye to them, and then headed next door to get Brie.

"Hey, neighbor!" Brie said, opening the door. She was wearing a cashmere sweater, skintight jeans, and a pair of bedazzled high-heeled boots.

She'd told Judy through text that she'd be ready when she got there. Unless she was going as herself, she wasn't.

"Hey Brie," Judy said to her. "You ready?"

"Yeah!" Brie reached inside the house for a big canvas bag. "You mind if I get dressed at your place?"

Ah. Well, that explained it. "No, I don't mind. Not at all."

By the time they were leaving the neighborhood, the sidewalks were crawling with kids in costumes. Judy was driving slower than usual because kids were excitedly running across streets without looking before crossing. Not just that, but some of them were dressed in dark costumes—reapers, ninjas, spooky nuns—that made them difficult to see even if they had light-up bracelets and necklaces on.

"Remember when we were that age?" Brie said in the passenger seat. "Feels like such a long time ago—yet like yesterday. I think they call that ying-yang."

Judy opened her mouth to correct her pronunciation, then thought better of it and didn't.

"Do you remember the first costume you ever picked out for yourself?" Brie asked her as she reached into the breast pocket of her peacoat for a vape pen. She cracked the window, then took a hit of it without bothering to ask Judy if it was OK to do so.

"I was a cat," Judy said, answering her question. "Nothing fancy. I just wore all black with some ears and a tail and my mom painted my nose and drew some—"

"Mine was a beauty pageant queen. I even wore a sash with the word 'winner' on it," Brie said proudly. "That was my dream when I was a girl. But alas, as I grew up, I realized my real passion was in writing about fashion."

"Is that what you're doing in New York?" Judy asked, stopping at a stop sign and signaling to a woman with a group of trick-or-treaters to cross the street.

The woman at the curb looked both ways before bringing her arms down, which she was using to keep the band of six little kids back from running past her. At the go ahead to cross the street, the kids jetted across, screaming and laughing and chasing one another. One kid in a karate uniform kicked at the air and did spins as he crossed.

The woman waved her thanks to Judy when they crossed safely to the other side. The kids, on the other hand, took crossing to mean they could run as fast and hard as possible as long as they stayed on that side of the street. They all started gunning it for the nearest house to knock on its door.

"Sort of," Brie said. "I'm more of a curator for a fashion magazine. Subscribers send in questions for the stylists the magazine works with, and I pick the ones that get asked and written about."

"I see," Judy said. "That sounds like something you would enjoy."

Brie hit her vape pen again, blew the cloud out toward the window before saying, "Why do you say that? Because you think I'm some judgmental, shallow bitch?"

Judy looked over at Brie, feeling like she'd just had her thoughts invaded.

"I'm just kidding, neighbor," Brie said, letting out a small laugh. "It's because you know I've always been into fashion, right?"

"Right," Judy sighed.

They drove through the neighborhood, looking at the trick-or-treaters. Occasionally, they would point out a particularly good one—like the kid in the inflatable sumo costume or the group of kids dressed up like the Ninja Turtles—but other than that, their drive back was mostly silent.

7

DAPHNE CAME OUT of her room when she heard Judy and Brie Berk coming into the apartment.

"Oh my god!" Brie shrieked. She ran across the living room and gave her a big hug. "Oh my god. It's been so long since I've seen you."

"Hi, Brie," Daphne said. She didn't return the hug, instead, she just patted her on the back.

Brie took a step back, eyeing her up and down. Daphne's hair was still damp from having just gotten out of the shower, and she was wearing an oversized black Hellraiser t-shirt and a pair of purple leggings.

"Is that…is that your costume?" Brie asked, genuinely confused. "I don't know what it is."

"Yeah. I'm going as a girl who just dyed her hair and is lounging around the house."

It took Brie a moment to realize she was being messed with, but when it hit her, she broke out in a phony smile.

"Oh. I forgot. You're a jokester!" Brie said, then looked out into the kitchen. "I'm going to go fix myself a drink. You gals want something?"

"I'll take a beer, please," Daphne said.

"Jude?" Brie asked as she walked past her.

Judy shook her head. "No, thanks."

Brie went into the kitchen, leaving Judy and Daphne in the living room.

"It only took about three seconds to remember why I didn't like her," Daphne whispered.

Judy laughed and put her index finger up to her lips. "*Shhh.*"

"Wish someone would *shh* her for the whole night."

"Daph…be nice."

"I know, I know," Daphne smirked. Then she looked up at the bird clock they had hanging over the television. "I should probably go get ready after Miss Sunshine comes back with my beer."

Brie came back from the kitchen with drinks in hand. A yellow mixed drink for herself, a Budweiser for Daphne, and a glass of water for Judy. She handed them out and then noticed the Bluetooth speaker under the television.

"This thing work?"

"Yeah," Daphne said. "You just gotta connect your Bluetooth."

"Got it!" Brie said, putting on an upbeat pop song. "To Halloween!"

Judy and Daphne exchanged a look. Daphne shrugged at her, leaned in close to her, and said, "Hey, at least she's got good taste in music."

They laughed, then toasted with Brie and all three girls started dancing in the middle of the living room. Pre-Halloween had officially begun.

Ignacio stood at one of the living room windows. It was chilly out, so he could see his breath. That was good. He knew how far to stand so he wouldn't fog it up.

He watched Judy and the *bruja* and a third girl he'd never seen before dancing in the living room. The music playing in the apartment was loud. He could barely hear Judy when she laughed or said something. But seeing her was exciting enough.

Her cheeks were rosy from dancing around. Her blue eyes were shiny and happy. She was enjoying herself. Ignacio couldn't wait to make her look like that when they would eventually play together.

The song they were dancing to ended. The girls started moving in different directions. The one he'd never seen before, a girl with hair the color of an acorn, went into the kitchen. The *bruja* and Judy went to their bedrooms.

This was Ignacio's cue to move. He sidled up closer to the wall and went around to the kitchen. He wanted to see what the New Girl was up to.

Ignacio got to the windows over the sink and popped his head up. The new girl was standing at one of the counters, facing him, but looking down as she filled a cup with orange juice.

He could hear her whistling through the window. The tune sounded a lot like the song they'd just been dancing to and not the one playing in the empty living room now.

Once her glass was filled to the top, Ignacio saw her hand move and grab the glass that was out of his sight. Then, her eyes flicked upward, toward the sink, almost seeing him.

Ignacio ducked down and waited. If he heard her scream, it meant she'd seen him.

No such thing happened. Instead, he heard the sink running.

There was nothing of interest in the kitchen.

Ignacio moved down the building, crouched over and keeping to the shadows as much as he could.

He made it to Judy's bedroom. The blinds were open. Good.

He peeked into the window, mindful of his distance.

Judy was sitting at her dresser, putting make up on. The room was well lit. Even the parlor lights dotting the mirror and a desk lamp on her nightstand were on.

Ignacio watched her gracefully apply blush onto her face. The soft brush leaving behind a light-pink dusting, turning her cheeks rosier than usual.

Ignacio flexed his hands in and out, wishing he was putting the makeup on her.

The New Girl appeared at the doorway, holding the two glasses. Just like in the kitchen, she was facing the window, but didn't see Ignacio because her focus was elsewhere.

"Got you some water," she said, coming into the room. She set a glass down in front of Judy.

"Thank you," Judy said.

The New Girl grabbed Judy by the jaw and turned her head, making her face her. She narrowed her eyes as she examined Judy's face.

"You know, Jude, you'd look pretty if you used my makeup."

"Uhh, thanks I guess."

"*Prettier*, I meant to say," the New Girl said, laughing.

Ignacio didn't get what was funny. To him, Judy always looked perfect.

Brie walked over to her canvas bag and started taking things out of it, including a box of makeup she had in there. She stripped out of her clothes until she was just in her lacey white underwear, then took the makeup over to Judy. She set it next to the glass of water.

"There's a yellow shade in there that'll look cute on you, if you want to use it," Brie said.

"Thanks," Judy said.

"You ever catch any perverts watching you get changed?" Brie asked, crossing the room to the windows.

"Hm?" Judy said, not sure what she was getting at until she saw Brie twisting the blinds closed. "Oh, uhm, nope. It's all a bunch of families that live in those houses. Older couples or newer couples with young kids."

"Most of the guys who hit on me at bars in NYC are married men," Brie said, moving away from the windows. "You'd be surprised how desperate they can be. Do you get hit on a lot, Jude?"

"Not really. Tonight's the first night I've actually gone out in a while. I'm usually working—"

"Ah, consider yourself lucky," Brie cut her off. "I know the grass might seem greener on this side, but trust me, it's not always."

Judy wasn't thinking that at all. Not even a little bit.

"Does my butt look good in this?" Brie said, walking up next to her.

The bottom portion of her costume was what looked like red athletic shorts with strawberry seeds on them. The shorts hugged her curves and lifted her booty up. The top half of her costume was a crop top with the same pattern as the shorts that showed off her belly button piercing.

"Aren't you going to be freezing in that?"

"Eh, the party's inside, right?"

"Yeah."

"So, how's it look? Would you pick me out of all the strawberries in a patch?"

"It looks great," Judy said, managing an uncertain smile for her.

"Okay, great. Now, help me pick my shoes."

Judy turned in the chair to follow her walking back over to the bed. She held up two pairs of shoes for Judy to pick from. One was a pair of white wedges, and the other were open-toed, short heels.

"I'm going to say the white ones."

Brie nodded in satisfaction, then sat down on the bed and put them on. She walked over to the full-length mirror hanging on the bedroom door to check her costume out. She turned, getting several views of herself and making different expressions like she was at a photoshoot.

"Okay, they look good. Good choice, Jude," Brie said, returning to the bed. She sat down on it and took the shoes off. "But if I keep them on, they might kill me."

Judy cringed, wishing Brie could be less like the girl she remembered from high school.

BEHIND THE APARTMENT, at the Benson house, Sophie was watching *Hocus Pocus*. It was a movie she only knew of because of her mother. Usually, these really old movies bored her, but this one was a lot of fun.

The only thing that would make it better was some pizza rolls. Sophie got off the couch to go find her babysitter.

She walked down the darkened hallway, still wearing the circus clown costume she'd gone trick-or-treating in earlier in the night. Tina had made her wash the makeup off, but she still had the red nose on. The big shoes on her feet click-clacked as she made her way to her father's study where she could hear Tina giggling.

"I'm hungry," Sophie said, coming into the room.

Tina was sitting in the reading chair, one of her legs thrown over the arm, her eyes glued to the phone. A cocktail she'd made using rum from Mr. Benson's liquor cabinet dangled from one of her hands.

The Bensons never gave her permission to drink while babysitting Sophie, but tonight she didn't care. She was pissed at them. It was Halloween, and they were supposed to be home an hour ago. And now their little brat was interrupting her Facetime call with her boyfriend.

"What?" Tina said, lowering the phone and all but rolling her eyes at the little girl.

"You said you were going to make me pizza rolls when we came back from trick-or-treating."

"Hold on, Joey," she said to her boyfriend. "Look, Sophie, why don't you just eat candy or something?"

"I don't like candy. It makes my teeth hurt. I want pizza rolls."

"There's some pizza flavored Pringles in the pantry, aren't there? Just eat those. I'm busy." Tina put her phone in front of her face, hoping Sophie would get the message and go away.

"That's not the same," Sophie protested. "Pringles are gross."

"Well, it's too late for me to turn the oven on," Tina said. "So just go find something in the kitchen. Make yourself a sandwich or something."

"Fine," Sophie said, crossing her arms and marching out of the room.

Sophie walked back through the living room, picking up her bucket of candy from the couch. She took it into the kitchen, sifting through it. Sophie had been telling the truth when she told Tina she didn't like candy. The only exception to this were Reese's Cups.

And she'd just gotten her best idea ever. She was going to make the most delicious sandwich of her entire life; a PB&J, but instead of regular old peanut butter she was going to use Reese's Cups.

Sophie plucked four out and looked up from the bucket as she came into the kitchen. Through the sliding door, and through the hedgerows in the backyard, she saw the masked man standing at the apartment window. He was difficult to see because he was partially hidden in the shadows.

But there was no mistaking it. That was him. The same masked man she'd seen before.

Still standing in the shadows, he turned to look at her. His gaze met hers, the moonlight reflecting off his dark eyes.

Sophie felt her heart skip a beat.

She dropped everything in her hands. The bucket crashed onto the kitchen floor, spilling candy everywhere.

Screaming, Sophie turned and ran through the house to go find her babysitter once again.

The scream rang through the house, piercing Tina's ears like a needle.

"Oh, my god!" Tina jumped out of the seat, dropping her phone, and spilling what was left of her cocktail.

"*Yo, you alright? What's going on over there?*" Joey asked through the phone speaker.

"Nothing. I'm good," Tina said, finding the phone under the reading chair and picking it up. "It's just the little twerp. She probably spilled something in the kitchen."

Tina looked at her own spillage. The reading chair and floor were drenched with cola and rum with a twist of lime.

"*What if she cut a finger off with a knife?*" He asked, ending it with a laugh people often described as a "pothead" laugh.

"Shut up, Joey," Tina said, blotting some tissues from a box sitting on the end table. "You're not making things better."

"*I'm just saying,*" he said, laughing at nothing.

Throwing a clump of tissues onto the bigger parts of the stains, she turned her attention to the phone and said, "I'll call you back after I see what's going on."

"*Alright, babe. Don't keep me waiting. Love you.*"

"Love you too," Tina said, ending the FaceTime call.

She looked at the mess and let out a loud groan before starting out of the room.

They met in the darkened living room, with Sophie stopping short of running right into her thighs.

"Tina! Tina! I saw him again! I know you don't believe me, but I swear." Sophie wrapped her arms around Tina's legs. "He's coming this way. He's coming this way!"

"Wait, wait. Slow down, Soph. What? What're you talking about?" Tina asked, pushing her away gently.

"The guy with the mask. The one I told you shows up at the apartment behind the house." Sophie stopped to take in a breath. "I think he saw me this time, Tina. He was looking through the sliding door. He saw me and I think he's coming here!"

"That's why you screamed? Cuz you think you saw this ghost guy or whatever?" Tina chuckled in relief.

"Tina, I'm not kidding!" Sophie looked over her shoulder, as if she were terrified this mysterious ghost man might be lurking in the house by now. "What if he got inside the house somehow?"

Tina shook her head, then crouched down to be eyelevel with her. "I think maybe you're watching too many spooky movies tonight. Let's call it quits on that, okay?"

She could tell by the look on Sophie's face that wasn't going to be the end of it, though. Sighing again, she caved. Tina grabbed the remote from the couch and changed the channel from *Hocus Pocus* to the first non-Halloween related thing, which just so happened to be an episode of Hell's Kitchen. Then she went over to turn on one of the floor lamps in the living room.

"Stay here," she said to Sophie. "I'm going to make sure no creepy guy is out there, and then I'll make you some pizza rolls. Okay?"

"Okay…" Sophie said, settling into the couch with a long face, arms folded.

"I'll be back in five," Tina said, pinching her on the cheek.

The night was darker than Tina remembered. Then again, she was looking out behind the houses instead of the front street, where streetlamps and porchlights provided plenty of lighting through the neighborhood.

A fixture hung outside of the Benson's house, right over the sliding door that took you out to the backyard, but it only reached so far. There was still a good stretch of darkness between the deck and the bushes at the end of the yard.

Tina crossed the kitchen to where the counters were, avoiding stepping on the candy littering the floor. She grabbed a flashlight from one of the drawers, then went over to the sliding door.

She opened it and stepped out into the yard. The crisp October air penetrated through her hoodie, raising her skin into gooseflesh. Maybe it wasn't actually darker, but it was certainly chillier. There was no denying that.

For a second, she thought about running back in to grab her jacket, then decided against it. The sooner she checked the yard and proved this was nothing but nonsense, the sooner she could get back inside.

The only house that had their back light on was the neighbor to the left. The other yards were dark. A slight breeze stirred the bushes and plants in them, making them waver ominously in the shadows.

Tina clicked on the flashlight. She shined it across the yard. The beam only reached to the jungle gym and didn't let her see into the hedgerow. But there was a light fixture hanging near the apartment window where Sophie claimed to have seen the masked man. It was possible the little twerp had seen something over there.

More than likely Sophie had just seen an animal—if wasn't outright lying to try to spook her for not making pizza rolls earlier.

Just in case, Tina punched in 9-1-1 into her phone, ready to hit the call button if anything funny happened.

She started across the yard. After about ten steps, the end of her beam reached the hedgerow. Tina stopped, standing about halfway through the yard and a foot from the jungle gym now.

She shined the light into the hedgerow, flicking her wrist left and right, trying to find anything that might explain what Sophie saw. She even angled the beam downward and moved it along the mulch.

But there was nothing. No weird guy. Not even a raccoon or a possum.

Tina breathed a sigh of relief, and started to turn, when something whizzed past her ear. The rock struck the top of the wooden fence to her left.

Out of instinct, Tina turned her attention there—then, realizing how stupid that was—quickly turned back.

From behind the jungle gym's rock-climbing panel, a gargantuan man popped out. He lunged at her with unbelievable speed, so fast she almost didn't have time to process what was happening. He reached out with one arm as he came toward her, hand open, big fingers splayed out.

Tina opened her mouth to scream, but before she could make a noise, his massive hand was clamped over the bottom half of her face. The next second, she was thrown to the ground.

The cell phone and flashlight went flying out of her grip, both now useless as she felt the man's weight crash on top of her.

Ignacio could feel her breath against his palm as he cupped her mouth and held her down with his knee on her stomach. With his free hand, he took the hunting knife out of his back pocket. He drove it through the middle of her chest.

He did it so fast and hard, giving her no time to react whatsoever. The knife went through her chest like she was made of clay. The tip of the blade pierced through her heart, rupturing it. The knife made wet sounds as Ignacio pulled it out of her body. He rose and stood over her corpse. Blood dripped off the blade, splattering down on the front of the dead girl's sweatshirt in thick drops.

Her arms had fallen out to her side horizontally, so that she looked like Jesus on the cross. The word VARSITY stitched onto her hoodie was ripped in half from where the knife had gone into her body. Underneath it, a dark stain was blossoming as blood continued pumping out of the wound.

Ignacio cleaned the knife against the side of his pants, then put it back in his back pocket. He bent down and picked up the corpse.

He wouldn't have time to clean up the mess. The little girl inside the house was likely calling the cops by now, but he had to at least hide this body.

Sophie sat in the living room, staring at the television without really watching it, trying to distract herself, but it wasn't working. She looked at the time on the cable box in the middle of the entertainment stand. Four minutes had passed, and Tina still wasn't back.

She said she'd be back in five.

Sophie gulped and waited for the digital number to change. Without taking her eyes off the clock, she reached across the couch for the remote and muted the TV.

She waited, listening for any signs of Tina.

But the only thing she could hear was her heartbeat.

The time on the digital clock changed from 7:54 to 7:55.

Sophie hopped off the couch, went down the hall, and stopped at the kitchen doorway. She looked out into the backyard. Tina was nowhere to be seen.

"Tina!" She called out, stepping halfway into the kitchen.

Nothing.

"TINA!" Sophie called out louder, hoping to see her babysitter emerge from the shadows.

But still no response.

Sophie stepped deeper into the kitchen, not caring that she was stepping on the spilled candy. The wrappers crinkled and the chocolates smooshed under her clown shoes as she walked over to the sliding door.

Before she knew she was doing it, Sophie opened the door and stepped out onto the patio.

"TIIIINAAA!" Sophie called. "Tina! Are you—"

The words got caught in her mouth as her eyes fell on Tina's Ugg boots. They were sticking out from underneath the plastic covering over the jungle gym's slide.

"Tina!" Sophie yelled out, almost laughing in relief as she raced across the backyard. "Tina! I see you!"

The lack of response made her uneasiness return, and she slowed down as she came up to the slide.

"Quit messing around, or I'll tell my mom," Sophie said, her voice lower than ever now.

She climbed up on the slide to get a better view of Tina, but it was too dark for her to see anything past her feet. Sophie reached out and swatted the toe of her boot.

Tina came sliding down, hurtling toward her. Sophie jumped off the slide, and watched her babysitter go flying right off the end of it. The momentum sent her gliding through the air for a few seconds before crashing to the ground with a heavy thud.

It took Sophie a moment to process what she was looking at. It was her babysitter, alright. Except there was a hole in her chest with lots and lots of blood coming out of it.

Tina lay there on the grass like one of Sophie's dolls. Eyes wide and staring at nothing. Bloody mouth open like she wanted to scream.

But she couldn't.

Because she's dead, Sophie thought, and then screamed. She screamed so loud her neighbors came running out to see what was happening.

But by now, Ignacio was gone.

9

INSIDE THE APARTMENT, none of the girls heard the screams over the music they were dancing to. The neighbors would probably complain and get angry, but that would be a tomorrow problem.

Tonight was Halloween. Tonight was about fun.

Daphne was standing in front of her full-length parlor mirror, looking at the costume that was a culmination of a month-long process of sewing and finding the right parts.

She was wearing a dark green dress with a teal floral pattern she found at the thrift-store downtown. The maroon cape that she had sewed herself flowed behind her, almost draping down to the floor. The black, knee-high boots she had on looked hefty enough to stomp goblin heads with.

The forest witch costume was complete…almost.

She reached into the top drawer of the dresser and took out two important pieces. The first one was practical, and something she usually carried with her when she was venturing out at night. She stuck the switchblade in one of the pockets of her dress.

Next, she picked up the final accessory for the Halloween costume, but she didn't put it on. Not yet. She needed an audience to witness the completion of the forest witch costume.

The door to Judy's room was slightly ajar, and she could see her and Brie moving in there as they finished up getting ready. Daphne knocked on the door.

"Come in," Judy said, loud enough to be heard over the music.

"I don't know if you're ready for this," Daphne said, feeling giddy with excitement.

"Let's see it." Judy giggled.

Daphne threw the door open and stepped inside, feeling like she was about to walk down the runway at any huge show full of models and bright lights and paparazzi. The cape flowed behind her as she strutted into the middle of the room.

"Oh my god," Judy said. She'd been sitting down on the chair in front of the dresser but stood up to get a better view of the costume. "You look amazing, Daph."

"Thank you, thank you," Daphne said, giving a slight curtsy. "This damn cape was a bitch to make."

"Is this real silk?" Brie asked, touching the cape to appreciate the softness.

"More like discount satin, but it looks real, doesn't it?" Daphne smirked.

"You really do go all-out for Halloween, huh?" Brie's tone suggested she was genuinely impressed. It was probably the most genuine thing either girl had ever heard from Brie Berk.

"Yeah, and there's still one more thing," Daphne said, moving her right hand from behind her back.

She held the tiara up in the air for the other two to get a good look at it. It was made of plastic bones, with five spires sticking up from the top like fingertips. In the middle of it was a big, green emerald that matched the one she was wearing on her ring finger.

"Made from the bones of those who've crossed me," Daphne said with a mock-serious expression, placing the accessory on her head.

All three girls laughed.

It started to feel like despite their differences in high school, and a few annoying things Brie Berk had said, they might be able to put that all aside and have a good night partying together tonight.

"You girls look great, too," Daphne said, reaching out and tapping one of the antennae on Judy's head.

Judy sat down in the chair to put her flats on. Brie went over to the mirror on the closet door and put a green beret on her head, trying several angles and slants to figure out which looked best.

"We should start heading out," Judy said, checking the time on her watch. "We don't want to miss the start of the party."

"I'm ready whenever you girls are," Brie said, settling on leaving the beret slanted to the left.

"Whoa, what's going on over there?" Brie said, stopping them on the front patio.

They turned to look at the blue and red police lights flashing over by the houses across the way.

"Who knows?" Daphne said, going down the steps. "Probably some rednecks causing trouble."

"I'll be back," Judy said, opening the apartment building door.

"What? Where you going?" Daphne called after her.

"Just making sure the windows are locked in the apartment."

Before Daphne could protest, Judy was inside the building and jogging down the hall.

In the apartment, she checked all the windows, including the bathroom and Daphne's room.

The last room she went into was her own.

Brie had reopened the blinds and cracked one of the windows after she'd gotten dressed. The curtain swayed from the draft coming in like a ghost. Judy went over and closed it, then secured the lock.

She stared out the window for a moment, looking at the police lights. She felt her mind—with the aid of her anxiety—trying to come up with the worst things that could've possibly happened there.

Judy closed her eyes, took in a deep breath, and tried to expel the bad thoughts on the exhale.

She opened her eyes and checked the window locks one more time. They were still secured, of course, but doublechecking made her feel better.

The place was empty. Nothing to worry about. Anxiety was still trying to wrap its dirty, cold fingers around her mind, but she wasn't going to let it win.

Tonight, she was going to allow herself to have a good time with her friends regardless of anything.

SLAUGHTER

1

OFFICER DiLossi AND Officer Roos were outside with the Bensons and their daughter, asking them questions and gathering as much info as they could about what happened. Meanwhile the lieutenant and Officer Gordon were out back, where the body of a dead girl lay prostrate on the grass.

Lieutenant Rooney inched toward the body, scanning the backyard to make sure there was no trouble as dozens of people from the surrounding homes looked on. This was a show for them. For the dead girl in the grass, the night was all about tragedy.

He had his hand on his holstered gun, just in case. The little girl had told dispatch that she saw a man in a mask lurking around the area, so they were on high alert.

There was a nasty gash in the middle of the dead girl's chest. Whatever had been used to stab her had torn right into her heart, causing her shirt to be soaked with blood.

The lieutenant put the collar of his shirt up to his nose. He wasn't exactly squeamish, but the smell of blood wasn't on the list of his favorite scents, either.

"One stab. Right through the heart," Lieutenant Rooney said, almost in fascination.

"Killed her instantly, huh?"

"And expertly."

"Yeah," Officer Gordon acknowledged. "Sheesh."

Whoever had killed this girl knew what they were doing. This wasn't the work of a loon, or a home invasion gone wrong. In those cases, the victims were usually stabbed multiple times and died from blood loss. This was a precision kill from a skilled hand.

Lieutenant Rooney thought back to the conversation with the sheriff. About the possibility of a new threat in Hilltown they hadn't been aware of. With the Baker Brothers still missing, and from what was in front of him, it seemed the sheriff's instincts might've been correct.

There was a new threat in Hilltown. Except now, they were very much aware of it.

"Come on," Lieutenant Rooney said, waving Officer Gordon to follow him back to the front of the house.

Because the Hilltown Police Department was too small and lacked the resources to do a proper crime scene investigation, they would let the County police take over from here.

2

IGNACIO PARKED IN a wooded area off the side of a road that was about a mile away from Judy's apartment. The headlights on his Saturn were off, making the black vehicle virtually invisible underneath the cover of shadows.

This was the perfect location. He was far enough away from where he'd killed the girl, but he was right where he knew Judy would have to drive past to get into the main parts of town.

Almost as if on cue, he heard a vehicle coming down the road. Music played inside of it. The same kind Judy and her friends had been dancing to in the apartment.

The Honda Fit drove underneath a streetlamp at the same time it passed by Ignacio. Judy was in the driver seat. Smiling. Laughing.

And then they were out of sight, but he could still track the car with his hearing. He listened until the car got to an intersection three blocks away and turned left.

Ignacio thought this was strange. The main part of town was to the right. Where could they be going in that direction?

Not like it mattered. He was going to follow Judy, anyway.

Ignacio turned the key in the ignition, firing the engine on. The headlights cut through the dark like a saber as he drove out onto the road.

"You don't mind, do you Jude?" Brie Berk asked from the backseat.

Judy looked in the rearview mirror. Brie had her compact on her lap, with a line of coke across it. She was holding an inch long piece of a plastic straw near her nose.

Judy shook her head.

Brie was already bringing the compact closer to her face and lowering her head before getting an answer, though. She snorted the cocaine. Then sat back, reveling in the sudden rush to her brain.

"Anyone else want a bump?" Brie asked, leaning between the two front seats.

"Nah. I'm more of a pot kind of gal," Daphne said. "And Jude is more of a not-do-any-of-that-shit kind of gal."

They laughed.

"Hey, I drink!" Judy protested. "Sometimes…"

"More like *rarely*."

More laughter.

Even though Judy was sober, she was feeling just as good as the other two. A Bruno Mars song came up on the playlist, the bass making the speaker jump. Daphne turned it up and all three started bopping around in their seats.

3

TUCKER FINISHED LOADING the cooler with beer. He took two from the top of it and handed one to Hudson, who was finishing loading up the second cooler with spiked seltzers. They were in the dining room, waiting for everyone else to show up.

"Those assholes were supposed to be here to help us," Tucker complained, popping the tab on the beer. He took a big swig of it.

"I mean, maybe they got lost?"

"They've been here before."

"True, but… I don't know. It's dark out. That has to make it harder to find this place, right?"

"I guess," Tucker said, leading them out of the kitchen.

They went into the living area. Tucker sat on the big sofa and Hudson in the loveseat.

Hudson looked around, admiring the decorations. There was a wall where they'd hung rubber hands that looked like demon hands, complete with yellow claws at the end of the fingers.

Yards of string lights were strewn on the walls. Some in the shapes of jack-o-lanterns and others in the shape of ghosts. Hanging from the ceiling were some bats. A draft was coming in from one of the windows Tucker had taken the wooden boards off, making them sway, giving the illusion that the bats were in motion.

On the mantel were bowls of candy. One was clear and was filled with Halloween colored M&Ms. The other one was a basket shaped like a skull with a variety of fun-size chocolates in it.

Next to the bowls there was a disco lamp and the Bluetooth speaker Tucker always brought with him when they went to the beach during the summer.

Then, there was the natural wornness of the house itself that added an authentic spookiness to the place. The tattered wallpaper, the holes in the windows, the permanent undeterminable stains on the walls and floor.

"You guys did a bang-up job, if I do say so myself," Hudson said.

"Huh?" Tucker said, then realized Hud was talking about the Halloween decorations. "Oh. Thanks. It was mostly Daph, though, if I'm being honest."

"Well, I'll tell her she did a good job when I see her then," Hudson smiled. Then he got up. "I'm gonna go put my costume on."

"I should get mine on, too," Tucker set his beer on the floor and got up, belching in the process.

They went into the side room where their bags were, both looking forward to an epic night.

Tucker's costume consisted of slipping a black robe over his regular clothes. He was done and back on the couch drinking his beer in less than a minute. About ten minutes later, Hudson came strutting out and stopped in front of him.

"Does this look bad?"

Tucker looked up from his phone and turned his head so as to not spit the beer in his mouth all over Hudson. The beer shot out in a jet stream over the couch's armrest instead.

"What…what the fuck…is that?" Tucker said, then started howling with laughter.

Hudson's costume looked about two-sizes too big. The fabric sagged and folded in on itself every which way. He frowned, trying not to be disappointed. "It really looks that bad or are you just being a dick?"

"Hud, you look like a hairy piece of dogshit." Tucker laughed harder. "I don't mean it looks bad. I mean literally, you look like you're a turd covered in fur."

"Well, damn," Hudson said, looking down at himself.

"I'm surprised you didn't try it on before you bought it." Tucker had finally found his composure, but he made sure to look away from Hudson as he said it.

"I sent the guy I bought it from my measurements. He said it was gonna fit me," Hudson whined. "Maybe he measured wrong…or was lying. Dammit."

Tucker looked over at him and started laughing again. He laughed so hard he fell back onto the couch and kicked his legs up in the air.

"Whatever, man," Hudson said, shaking his head.

"Look, if it makes you feel any better, it'll be the funniest costume here."

Hudson didn't respond. Instead, he just stormed across the room to pick his beer up off the floor.

"Do you have any service here?" Tucker asked him.

Hudson checked his cellphone, which was sitting on the loveseat's armrest.

"Not in here. I did outside, though."

"Alright. Let's go out there," Tucker said, grabbing his jacket off the back of the couch. "I need a smoke after that laugh, and let's find out where the fuck everyone else is."

Tucker was just lighting up his cigarette and leaning against the veranda railing when they saw a pair of headlights coming toward them. The area outside the manor's glow was dark enough that they couldn't see the vehicle's black body, so it just looked like a red racing stripe was floating toward them.

Baxter was flying up the street, easily going over forty miles an hour. As he blasted past the gates, he slammed on the brakes. The tires screeched against the pavement as the Mustang stopped inches short of colliding with Tucker's truck.

"Yo, what the fuck!" Tucker complained, hopping off the veranda. He walked around to the back of the truck to make sure nothing happened to it.

Meanwhile, Baxter and Dan climbed out of the vehicle, unloading bags filled with snacks.

"You guys need any help carrying stuff?" Hudson asked, hurrying over to them.

"Nah, we're good," Dan said, then noticing Tucker was still looking over the truck's bumper said, "We didn't hit it. Chillout."

"Jesus, man," Tucker said to Baxter. "Can you drive anymore reckless?"

He finished looking over the truck. The first thing Tucker noticed when he turned to look at the others was Baxter's costume. He wore a Phillies jacket over a 76ers jersey, a bright green old school Eagles hat, and a hockey mask on his face.

"What the hell is that costume supposed to be?" Tucker sneered.

"He's a sports fanatic," Dan answered, deadpan serious.

"Oh, I thought he was being every douchebag in Philly at once."

They laughed and when they stopped, Baxter shrugged. "I just grabbed a bunch of stuff from my closet."

"Yeah, you didn't have to tell us," Tucker chided.

"And what are you supposed to be?" Dan asked Tucker.

"A cult leader—or a guy in a black robe, since Hud says I can't call myself a cult leader without any followers."

"I mean, he's right," Dan grinned.

"Yeah, yeah," Tucker said. "Well, what are you? James Bond?"

Dan nodded. "You have something to say about it, I'm guessing?"

"Nope. Can't hate on it," Tucker shrugged. "Hey, what do you guys think Hud is supposed to be?"

Baxter and Dan looked over his costume, puzzled looks on their faces.

"Bigfoot," Hudson finally told them in a small voice.

"You guys were thinking pube monster, right?" Tucker threw his head back, laughing.

"Shut up," Hudson said, trying not to laugh at himself now. "Let's go inside."

He started toward the manor. The others followed, Tucker still laughing the entire time.

4

"TURN LEFT AT the tree that looks like it's holding onto its cock—oh, Jesus Christ. Of course, my dumbass brother would write something like that in his directions." Daphne said, rolling her eyes. He wasn't even here in the car and still, somehow he managed to be annoying.

"Wait, what?" Judy said.

Up ahead, all three girls saw the tree Tucker was talking about. The tree had an erratic branch sticking out of it. Growing from the bigger branch was a series of smaller ones vaguely shaped like hands.

From the backseat, Brie snickered.

Judy made the left at the tree, giggling. In the distance, about a quarter of a mile up an incline, they saw the multicolored projector lights on the façade of the manor. Some of the pumpkin trail leading to the veranda was lit as well.

"That's where the party is?" Brie asked

"It is indeed."

"It looks old." Brie Berk said. "And rundown."

"Jude didn't tell you it was an abandoned manor?"

Brie shrugged. "Yeah, but I was imagining something more elegant, I guess."

They came up to the top of the incline and went through the gate. Judy parked her car behind the Mustang, and they got out.

It was quiet out here except for the murmur of bass coming from somewhere inside the house.

They walked past the cars and onto the lawn. Judy admired the gourds and pumpkins lining the walkway as they walked toward the manor.

"You like my handiwork?" Daphne asked her, lighting up a cigarette.

"It looks great," Judy reassured her.

"Tucker picked out all of the pumpkins, but this little walkway was my idea."

"Oh, is that a twin thing?" Brie asked. "Like, having good teamwork?"

Brie was trailing behind the two other girls, so she didn't see Daphne clamp down on her cigarette for a moment before pulling it out of her mouth and turning to Brie.

"For better or for worse, everything we do together is a twin thing," she said, trying to keep the edge out of her voice.

"Must be nice, though, you know? Having someone your age who looks like you. It's like a built-in friend," Brie said, sounding sincere.

"Unless one of you is evil and practices the dark arts," Daphne said, giving Brie a grin.

Brie was uncertain if it was a joke or not. She looked up and down at Daphne's elaborate witch costume, only adding to her confusion.

They got to the front door and went inside.

"Wait, you're allowed to smoke in here?" Brie asked.

Now that they were in the house, they had to talk louder to be heard over the music. It was so loud that the walls were visibly shaking.

"What? It's not like the owners are going to complain." Daphne said, blowing out a cloud of smoke into the foyer.

"Oh yeah…good point," Brie said.

She looked around the foyer. When they told her they were partying at an abandoned manor, this wasn't what she pictured at all. For some reason she'd been picturing a Victorian house like in one of those ghost movies. But this was more like a pricey suburban home with extra rooms. It was the house of someone who'd wanted the isolation of being in the sticks while still living luxuriously.

"The party's back there," Daphne said, pointing down an entry to one of the hallways. "In case you can't hear it."

Judy laughed. The girls made their way down the hall and into the living room where the guys were hanging out.

A song by The Weeknd was making the Bluetooth speaker bump. The disco lamp was spinning around, sending rays of light throughout the room.

"Thought you girls would never show up," Tucker said. He was sitting on the armrest of the couch, feet up on the cushion, and rolling a joint.

"We're not the only ones coming, are we?" Brie asked, a slight panic in her voice.

Tucker gave her a dirty glance. "Maybe more will show up. Maybe not. Small-town people tend to be boring as shit."

"Well, we're here." Daphne interrupted. "Now, where's the alcohol?"

Noticing that Tucker was distracted, Hudson took this opportunity to lower the volume of the Bluetooth speaker. It was still loud, but it was at a volume that didn't require everyone to shout to be heard anymore.

"Hold on," Tucker said, then licked the edges of the paper and sealed the joint up. He wedged it behind the tweed rope around his waist and then hopped off the couch. "Alright, follow me."

In the kitchen, Tucker showed them the coolers pushed up against one of the walls. There were six of them in total, all filled with different types of beers, spiked seltzers, and wines. On the counters were a few bottles of hard liquor; tequila, mezcal, vodka, and rum.

"And over there is a ton of food," Tucker said, pointing into the dining room.

The wooden table was covered with all sorts of snacks, chips, bowls of peanuts, candies, a hoagie tray, cookies, and dips.

"Holy shit. That looks like the table for the Last Supper," Daphne teased.

"Ha-ha," Tucker mocked. He sat down on top of one of the coolers. "The food was all Hud's idea. Yo, any of you got a lighter?"

Daphne took hers from her pocket and handed it to him. Then she started rummaging through the cooler next to the one he was sitting on. She pulled out three seltzers and handed them to the girls.

"Anyone wanna smoke?" Tucker asked, taking the joint from his rope belt and lighting it up.

"Yeah," Daphne said immediately, opening her seltzer.

"Me too!" Brie chimed in, hopping over to him so that the three of them were forming a loose triangle.

Judy and Daphne exchanged a look and a smile. Both were thinking the same thing, Brie really didn't want to be sober tonight.

"What about you, Jude?" Tucker asked, taking a hit and passing the joint to Brie.

"No thanks," Judy said. "I think I'll go grab some food, though."

"Yeah, help yourself."

"What's your costume supposed to be anyway?" Brie was asking Tucker. "Are you like, a magician or something?"

"No. I'm a cult leader," Tucker said. "What about you? Are you Strawberry Short Cake?"

"Just a strawberry," Brie Berk said, spinning around. Smoke from the joint furling around her. "You like it?"

"Yeah, sure," Tucker said. "Now hurry up. Take a hit and pass."

Dan was walking through the kitchen to the snack table in the dining room. The three beers he'd slung back were already hitting him and making him want to munch on some snacks. His eyes were set on the bowl of chips and assortment of dips next to it.

"Dan Sigler!" Brie said, breaking away from the smoke circle to jump in front of him. She put her hands on his chest, stopping him from going into the dining room. "My God. You're really going to walk by me without stopping to talk to me?"

"Oh, hey. Yeah, sorry," Dan said. "You look nice, though."

Brie Berk was one of the girls he used to hang out with in high school. He didn't particularly like her, they just had mutual friends and got invited to the same places in their teens.

"That's it? After like six years of not seeing me? All you have to say is I look nice?" She tossed her hair back, her eyes annoyed. "How you been?"

"Been great," Dan told her. He grabbed her wrists and gently moved her hands off him. "I'm hungry, though. Mind if we catch up later?"

She pouted, then shook her head. "Nah, that's fine. But you better not avoid me all night, mister."

"I won't. I promise." He gave her a weak smile before walking past her to go into the dining room.

He grabbed a paper plate and walked over to a bowl of tortilla chips, which put him across the table from Judy.

"Hey, Judy," Dan said to her.

Judy looked up from pouring peanuts into a bowl for herself. It took her a second to recognize Dan in a tuxedo instead of his cop uniform.

"Hey," she said back with a polite smile. "Almost didn't recognize you."

"Do you know what I'm supposed to be?"

"Um, are you like, an FBI agent or something?"

"Close. That's better than if you would've said a guy going to prom."

Judy laughed. "Okay, but what are you, actually?"

"I'm James Bond." He leaned over the table. "Can I tell you a secret?"

"I like secrets," Judy giggled, getting into the game.

"This isn't even really a Halloween costume. It's just what I wore to some formal last year."

Judy laughed.

A silence fell between them. They both munched on some of their snacks.

In the living room, an upbeat Dua Lipa song came on.

"Hey, you wanna go dance?" Dan asked her.

"I would love that." Judy smiled.

"Great," Dan said, returning her smile.

They started walking out of the dining room, shoulder-to-shoulder.

Brie Berk had taken a fourth hit of the joint before heading back into the living room, leaving just Tucker and Daphne by themselves. Daphne was sitting on the kitchen counter next to the coolers now.

They watched Dan and Judy walking together, too busy making googly eyes and smiling at each other to really notice the twins were still hanging out in the kitchen.

"That crazy fuck is actually doing it," Tucker said.

"What?" Daphne asked, blowing out a cloud of smoke.

"Going after his boss's daughter," Tucker laughed.

"Oh." Daphne glanced over at them as Dan and Judy entered the living room. She shrugged. "Eh, Judy's chill."

"Yeah, true," Tucker said, holding his hand out for the joint. "By the way, who the fuck was that annoying chick smoking with us?"

"Brie Berk," Daphne said, as if that explained everything. "You don't recognize her?"

"Not really."

"She's from Hilltown. She was like two grades above us."

"Oh," Tucker said. He hit the joint, holding the smoke in his lungs for a few seconds while he tried to recall who Brie Berk was. He blew the cloud of smoke out and said, "Wait, wait. Is that the chick who cried when she didn't win Prom Queen?"

"Holy shit. I forgot about that—but yes, that's her."

"Oh man."

"How do you remember that?"

Tucker threw the roach on the floor and stomped it out. He stood up, flipped the top off the cooler he'd been sitting on, and took out a can of Busch Light from it.

"I like to remember embarrassing shit about people to use it against them," Tucker said, popping the tab on the beer can.

"Oh yeah? What do you remember about me?"

"Way too much."

"Fuck off." Daphne said, trying not to laugh. "We heading back over there?"

"Yeah," Tucker said, drinking some of his beer. "I gotta yell at Hud for turning the music down."

5

HE COULDN'T BELIEVE Judy had led him here. Ignacio stared at the lonesome manor surrounded by wilderness and darkness.

Somewhere behind the house, he could hear a generator interfering with his acute hearing. That was OK, though. He would take care of that.

On the road in front of the manor, he saw only three vehicles. Judy's. A black vehicle. And a work truck with a lot of stuff in the back. He would have to search the area to make sure there weren't more cars parked elsewhere, but so far, this was looking like the perfect moment.

Ignacio drove past the gate and veered off to the right. He found a clearing in the trees and drove about fifteen feet into the woods, making sure the Saturn was properly hidden, before parking the vehicle.

He tied his hair back in a ponytail, then took his luchador mask out from the duffle bag on the passenger seat.

Ignacio slipped it over his head, pulled his ponytail out from a hole he'd made in the back of it, and then pulled the laces to secure the mask on his head.

Next, he took the machete and hunting knife from the gym bag.

He slipped out of the car. It was cold out, and would only get colder as the night progressed, but Ignacio was properly dressed. He was wearing a black and dark green camo jacket. Dark brown pants. Heavy black boots.

The off-white mask with the crude flower painted on the forehead was the only thing he wore that would make him easy to see. But if Varias Caras' plan worked, it wouldn't matter.

Before he could do anything else, though, he had to go scope out the scene.

Ignacio slung the sheathed machete onto his back, put the hunting knife in his back pocket, and then sprinted out of the trees toward the manor.

6

I F Dan Sigler wasn't going to give her any attention, then one of these other guys would have to. The chubby nerd kid standing by the fireplace was out of the question. Daphne's brother wasn't her type—he was kind of cute but that mop top was really off-putting. So, by process of elimination, it was the big oaf's lucky night.

Brie Berk grabbed her purse from the couch where she'd left it. She took out a lipstick and a compact mirror and quickly touched up her lips. She smiled at her reflection, practicing her best flirting skills.

Satisfied with what she saw—and sure that Baxter Miller would be, too—she put everything back in her purse and went over to the loveseat where he was sitting. Baxter had pulled his hockey mask down around his neck so he could pound down the beer he was holding.

"Long time no see, Bax," Brie said, standing over him.

He looked up, the brim of his Eagles hat casting a shadow over his face. A combination of the alcohol making him sluggish and not having seen the girl since high school made him take a second before he realized who he was looking at.

"Oh hey, uh, Brie. You look…different than I remember."

"Yeah, I'm all grown up." She reached out and caressed one of his shoulders. "Looks like we both are."

He smiled but didn't say anything.

"How you been?" Brie asked.

"Been alright." Baxter grinned. "How about you? Didn't you move to San Fran or something?

Brie shook her head. "New York City. Depending on how things go, I might be moving to the West Coast in a year or two, though."

"That's funny. The Forty-Niners and the New York Giants both were scouting me when I was playing college football." Baxter knew it was a white lie, but he hoped it would impress her.

"Ohh, that's so cool." Brie had no idea what relevance that had with the conversation, but she was getting bored of whatever he was talking about, so she didn't bother to ask. She took a big gulp of her seltzer, then told her own lie. "My legs are getting tired from standing. You wanna go sit and talk over there?"

She motioned for the couch. It took Baxter a few seconds to get the hint. As they relocated over to the couch, Baxter continued yammering on.

"Yeah, but my passion has always been in acting." He said, settling into the couch.

"Oh, acting, huh?" Brie said, settling close to him on the couch. "Wow."

"Yeah, I might go and take some acting classes when I get enough money—"

"Look, man. I don't really care," Brie said, finally unable to keep up the charade any longer. "I just want to make out with someone, so just kiss me already."

"Oh…" Baxter blinked. "Okay."

He put his beer on the floor and leaned in to kiss her. When they finally broke apart, Brie smiled at him, then threw her seltzer on the floor, and jumped onto his lap.

"Jesus Christ," Tucker said, noticing Baxter and Brie making out on the couch from across the room. "I hope your friend still has a face left after this."

"Friend?" Daphne said, turning an eyebrow up at him.

"I mean, you brought her."

"Technically, Jude brought her."

"Fair."

Tucker turned to look over at Hudson, who was only a few feet away from them. He was crouched inside the fireplace, pointing his cellphone flashlight up into it.

"Hud, what're you doing?"

Hudson crawled out from the fireplace, soot smeared on his nose. "I was checking to see how dirty it was. No one cleaned it, right?"

"Of course not. Why the hell would we clean the fireplace?"

"You think it'll be alright if I get a fire going?"

Tucker shrugged.

"I saw some wood out back when we were setting up the generator."

"Yeah. I saw it, too," Tucker said. "It might not be any good. Probably infested with snakes or whatever, too."

"I'll go see," Hudson said gleefully.

"You want me to go with you?"

"No, that's okay. I gotta go number two, anyway."

"Ew, TMI," Daphne interjected.

"Hey, it's a normal bodily function," Hudson said, throwing his hands up in the air. Seeing that Daphne wasn't amused he said, "Sorry, though."

"I'm just messing with you." Daphne said, punching him on the arm.

Hudson laughed like he was in on the joke, then excused himself and jetted out of the living room.

Tucker kicked one of his legs back and leaned against the wall. "Sorry I wasted your time."

"What?" Daphne asked.

"With decorating this place. This party sucks," Tucker sighed, then drank some of his beer.

"Oh, come on. Don't be a grouch," Daphne chided. "Everyone else seems to be having fun."

She gestured to the others in the living room.

Brie and Baxter's make-out session was even more intense than when they first noticed them. Their hands were all over each other and parts of Baxter's costume were being systematically removed.

Judy and Dan were in front of the fireplace, dancing to the pop song filling the room, drinks in hand. Judy's antennae were bouncing all around her head, and Daphne recognized the natural blush on her face underneath the makeup. It warmed Daphne's heart to see Judy having a genuinely good time.

She nudged Tucker in the ribs with her elbow. "Come on, Tuck. Let's dance."

"Dancing's for suckers—"

Daphne grabbed him by the arm and pulled him as hard as she could. He rolled his eyes but went along with it as she dragged him over to where Dan and Judy were, so that now a little dance floor had been formed.

Just to appease his sister, Tucker started moving his feet and shoulders.

"Loosen up," she told him. "You're dancing like Frankenstein."

Daphne grabbed him by the shoulders and shook him to get him limber.

"If Hud were here, he would correct you that it's actually Frankenstein's Monster," Tucker grinned.

Daphne flipped him off, making the gesture a part of her dance move. Tucker laughed, took a big drink of his beer, and then tried to move his body more fluidly as the song's tempo picked up. Daphne got closer to Judy and checked her hip into hers, getting her attention.

"Selfie!" Daphne yelled out, taking her phone out of her pocket.

Judy leaned in close to her, their cheeks touching. She didn't realize it until she looked into the phone screen, but she was already smiling as much as she could. Daphne made an exaggerated snarl and snapped a picture.

"Let's switch," Daphne said, taking her tiara off.

They exchanged head accessories, then took another picture, both of them smiling this time.

"That's a good one!" Daphne cheered, taking an admiring glance at the picture.

Judy nodded in agreement.

"I'll send it to you later." Daphne put the phone back in her pocket.

They switched headgear again, and then went back to dancing with the boys.

Neither of them realizing that if they'd looked a little harder at the background in the photo, they would've seen a masked cannibal staring at them through one of the broken windows.

7

IGNACIO HAD FINISHED walking around to make sure there were no more vehicles around. He was standing at the back of the house now, looking into the window where the party was happening. Watching Judy dance with the guy in the tuxedo.

She was smiling. Excited. Her eyes were brighter than ever. He could see her blushing under the makeup.

Envy exploded in him like a grenade. His hands twitched. He wanted to take the machete out, go in there, and chop the man to bits. Judy was his to play with. His Barbie!

Mine, mine, mine!

Tranquilo, Ignacio, Varias Caras said, reining him in. *You can get Judy. If you do this the right way.*

"The right way," Ignacio echoed. He shook his head out like a dog with an ear infection. The envy and anger subsiding, his mind refocusing.

There were only six people in the house besides Judy. Six people. He could go through six people with ease. And as the drive to this place had proven, they were in an isolated part of the woods. The nearest town was miles away.

Still. The problem was they had three vehicles parked out front. An easy escape. He couldn't just burst through the window and try to kill them right now. He had to think this through.

If even just one got away from him, it would be big trouble.

Ideally, he would pick them off one-by-one. But he didn't like the odds of that happening given the type of gathering they were having. He would have to keep staking the place out and wait for an opportunity to strike.

Hopefully no one else would show up while he waited. If more people started to show up, Varias Caras would have no choice. He would just have to storm into the place and go on a killing rampage and take Judy. Then hope for the best.

This was the first opportunity to grab her. The first time she'd been away from the town since they saw her. There was no telling when—or if—he would ever get another chance like this. He had to take it.

8

HUDSON WAS WADDLING to the port-a-potty behind the house, his butt cheeks clenched on a turtling turd.

Tucker had put it in the worst spot possible, making everyone go out through the front of the house, then all the way to the back to use it. But he'd insisted putting it on the front lawn would make it look like a white trash party instead of a Halloween party.

He was right, even though Hudson would've put it in different terms.

Either way, he was really regretting that big burrito he'd had for dinner because each step felt like it might dislodge the poop right into the pants of this stupid, oversized, ragamuffin costume that he'd been so excited to get. *Well. Live and learn.*

He made it to the back of the house. Hudson saw the blue port-a-potty and charged ahead with tunnel vision. One hand reached for the plastic handle as he drew in closer to it, the other unzipped the back of his costume.

He threw the door open and took his arms out of the sleeves to pull the onesie down below his waist. Hudson didn't even bother to lock the door behind him, he just hopped right onto the toilet seat. The plastic was cool from the late-night autumn air, and he sighed in relief as he unloaded into the toilet.

It was almost as if God was on his side. Out the corner of his eye, Ignacio saw the chubby kid blur past him. He'd been too focused on getting to the port-a-potty to notice Ignacio standing at the window only a few feet away.

Varias Caras was sure of this because the boy would have stopped to at least ask questions—if not flat-out scream. But he'd just rushed past, unaware of his surroundings.

Perfect, Varias Caras thought, unsheathing the machete as he made his way over to the port-a-potty.

As he approached, the door flew open. The chubby kid stood on the other side. He'd been slipping on the costume over himself but stopped when he saw Ignacio standing there.

Before he could even so much as scream, Varias Caras hacked the machete at the kid's right leg.

"OWWWWW!" The pain caused Hudson to lose his balance and fall back against the toilet seat.

He looked down at the gash on his leg, dizzy and beginning to hyperventilate. Blood was squirting out where an artery had been severed.

Varias Caras grabbed him by the front of his shirt and slammed him up against the plastic wall. The chemicals and water inside of the toilet swished around from the vibrations.

"NO, please. Stop. Please!" Hudson begged as he stared at the grotesque face.

The huge man crouched down to fit inside the portable toilet. A second look made Hudson realize it wasn't the man's face that was grotesque… No, it was some sort of strange mask he was looking at.

His attacker sheathed the machete, but he knew he wasn't safe yet. That look in his eyes told Hudson everything. He was going to die tonight. His only wish was that he could warn the others.

That thought evaporated as the huge man changed tactics. He grabbed the side of Hudson's head with both hands, right around the temples, and then shoved him face first into the tank under the toilet seat.

Hudson screamed—which was the worst thing possible to do—as his head dunked below the water. His lungs filled with water and chemicals. He could feel the chemicals burn everything from his tongue down to his esophagus as he swallowed at least a cup's worth.

Ignacio held him in place by putting pressure on his shoulders. Hudson kicked with his good leg and thrashed his arms, but he wasn't strong enough to budge the guy. Not even an inch.

Varias Caras continued to hold him there, feeling him getting wilder and more desperate the closer he got to drowning. Reveling in his victim's fear.

About thirty-seconds later, the boy's movements slowed. His thrashing turned to taps. With each passing second, they became weaker and weaker.

A few more beats, and then he was still.

Just for good measure, Varias Caras counted an extra twenty seconds before taking his weight off him.

One down. Five more to go, Varias Caras thought, barging out of the port-a-potty, leaving Hudson Crosley's corpse dunked inside his own filth.

He strode past the generator giving the house electricity. He would cut that off later. Hopefully, it would stop the music and he would be able to use his super hearing to hunt down the others.

First, though, he needed to go deal with the vehicles.

Killing time had officially begun.

"**H**EY, YOU WANNA go to my car?" Baxter asked as he pulled away from Brie.

Brie brushed strands of hair out of her face. The hair she'd spent so much time straightening out was wild and messy from Baxter having ran his fingers through it. The beret had long since fallen off and was stuck somewhere between the cushions.

She grinned and looked down at him. Partly because she knew what he was trying to get at, and partly because he looked like a bigger oaf than usual with lipstick smeared all over his face.

"Oh, you're *really* trying to get lucky tonight, huh?" she said to him. She hopped off his lap, not waiting for his answer, and grabbed him by the hand. "Come on. Show me how much horsepower that Mustang has."

Holding hands, they walked out of the house together.

Judy felt the cold, icy touch of anxiety. That same pervasive feeling like doom was just outside, watching. She could see the others dancing around her. Bopping around to the rhythm of an upbeat song.

Smiling, drinking. Having fun.

She was having fun, too, but it was more like her mind was split into two. One part of her was here "in the moment," enjoying dancing with her friends in the spiraling disco lights.

The other part was worried about what was going to happen after this moment of pure fun was over. Not just her own future, but everyone's. Dan's. Tucker's. Hudson's. Daphne's especially. Even Brie Berk and Baxter Miller were somewhere in the back of her mind.

And it wasn't just the immediate future she was worried about. She wondered what everyone would look like in their old age. Would they still be in contact with one another? She and Daphne definitely would be, they were going to be best friends for the rest of their lives. But what about the others? Would they still be friends? Would they all one day come back to Frosty Hollow Manor to recreate this night to catch up, and talk about retirement, and show each other pictures of their kids and grandkids—maybe even their great grandkids?

Or maybe they would take a moment to mourn the ones who'd died by then?

Judy felt these kinds of thoughts creeping into her mind and closed her eyes for a second. The dance lights flashed behind her eyelids as zooming red dots. She took a big swig of her seltzer as she tried to get back into the moment. Back into the fun.

"Hey, you okay, Jude?" Dan said, leaning in close to her ear.

Judy smelled the mixture of peppermint and beer in his breath. She opened her eyes and nodded.

"If you want to take a break, we can," he said, seeing her eyes swimming with deep emotions.

"No, I'm fine," she said, forcing out a chuckle.

"Alright." He nodded and then smiled at her.

Judy wasn't sure what possessed her to do this next thing she did. She'd never done anything remotely close to it. She reached up and put her arms around his neck, then got up on her tiptoes and pecked him on the lips.

For a second, Dan wasn't sure what had just happened. A look of confusion flashed across his face but then was replaced by a big smile.

"That was nice," he said, leaning in for a second kiss. This one they both took their time with. They held it for a few seconds before breaking contact.

Judy giggled, and felt her face get as hot as a stovetop. To the side of Dan, she saw Daphne wiggling her eyebrows to let her know she saw what had happened. Judy glanced at her and laughed.

"To Halloween!" Daphne cheered, holding up her beer can.

All four toasted along with her and took a sip of their drink. As they finished drinking, the song playing switched to a faster one. They danced harder, really feeling the alcohol and the beat of the music flow through them now.

In Judy's mind, she could still feel the cold fingers of anxiety wrapping itself around her mind. But it was getting easier and easier to ignore. She would be fine, she told herself.

Everything would be fine.

10

As Ignacio watched two of the five remaining people coming out of the house, he thought back to one of the days Papa had taken him to the casino. Ignacio didn't like the casino. There were too many lights and noises. And if Papa had a bad day there, he would be mad at everyone—including Ignacio and Mamá.

But there were also times when Papa would have good times at the casino. It was one of these days Ignacio was thinking about right now. Papa was rolling a small, white ball between his hands. Sweat was formed at his hairline. He'd been throwing this ball inside of a spinning wheel with red and black squares painted on it.

Ignacio didn't know the name of the game. He just knew it was one of Papa's favorites to play.

"Listen, Ignacio," Papa said, turning to him with a big smile on his face. "There will be times in life when it feels like the Devil is cursing you. When it seems like he's around every corner, waiting to foil everything you try to do."

Papa stopped rolling the ball and cupped it in one of his hands before continuing.

"But there will also be moments when God smiles down on you from the heavens. And even the Devil isn't strong enough to stop His will—never take God's blessings for granted, *mijo*."

Ignacio didn't really know what most of that meant, then or now, but he knew God was good, and smiling was a good thing.

And right now, watching the two people coming out of the house, separating themselves from the group, he could feel God smiling down at him.

Ignacio took two steps back, putting himself in the shadow cast by the manor, and watched.

"It's freakin' cold," Brie said, giggling as they walked to the Mustang.

"I'll turn the heat on when we get there," Baxter promised, leading the way.

He clicked the unlock button on his key fob. The alarm system chirped as the doors unlocked, echoing all the way into the trees. They both climbed into the backseat.

Before the doors were even closed all the way their lips were locked. The music from inside the house was just a murmur out here. The loudest sound to them now was their lips smacking.

Baxter took his hat and jacket off and threw them into the driver seat, then leaned away from Brie. He tried taking the hockey mask off, but the straps got all tangled up around his neck.

"Who cares? Leave it," Brie said, watching him struggle.

He nodded, then reached down for the zipper on his jeans instead.

"Whoa, big guy. What are you doing?" Brie asked.

"Isn't this why we came out here?"

"You go down on me first." Brie said, sliding her shorts off. "Then maybe I'll do the same. If you're good. And lucky."

"Come on. Just a kiss on the tip. Please?" he said, unzipping his pants.

He reached inside with his hand to pull his throbbing dick out but stopped when he noticed someone approaching the car. For a second, he thought it was one of the guys—maybe Tucker coming out to try to pull a prank on them—but as the person got closer and Baxter got a better view of them, he realized how big he was.

"Who's that?" Baxter said, pointing over Brie's shoulder.

"Who's who—?" Brie saw the masked man as he came into the glow of the string lights outside the manor.

The man marched toward them, moving fast despite the fact he was about the size of a refrigerator.

"I have no idea," Brie said, reaching down and pulling her panties and shorts back up around her waist. "Must be someone here for the party."

"Yeah, he looks like he's in costume."

"Go out and say something to him," Brie said.

He unlocked the door. "What should I say to him?"

"Tell him to go the fuck away, dummy!"

The man stopped at the passenger window on Brie's side, crouched over.

Brie got a better look at the mask on his face. It had teeth painted along the mouth hole and sloppily painted floral patterns on it. His eyes flicked left and right, sweeping through the interior of the car like he was searching for something.

"Okay, he's weirding me out," Brie said, shifting uncomfortably in her seat. "Hey, bud! The party's in there!"

She pointed toward the manor. The man's eyes stopped moving, locking gazes with her. Then, before any tension could build up, he stood up straight and took a few steps away from the vehicle.

It seemed like that did the trick. Baxter took his hand off the doorhandle, deciding that getting out wasn't going to be necessary.

Just as they started to relax, the man swung something at the car.

The handle of the machete smashed into window, breaking it into tiny little pieces. Glass rained down on top of Brie as she screamed. She went to scramble into the front of the car and tried to get out from one of those doors, but the masked man was faster.

He grabbed her by the arm and yanked her toward him. Brie threw her free arm out toward Baxter, hoping he would grab it, but he was too busy getting out of the car to notice it.

"HELP! HELP!" Brie screamed, feeling jagged pieces of glass still stuck to the window slash through her skin as she was pulled out of the car.

Varias Caras slammed her onto the ground, then stomped on her chest, pinning her down.

The air was blown out of her as his weight crushed into her sternum. He raised the machete over his head as high as he could. For a second, the moonlight shimmered off it, turning it silver, then he dropped it down onto her face as hard as he could. The blade split her face open from her forehead down to her lips like it was a cantaloupe.

Varias Caras pulled on his weapon. It'd gone in deep, so there was some resistance as he slid the blade out of the gash.

As much as he wanted to admire the kill, he shifted his focus to the guy. He'd seen him running away while he'd been dealing with the girl, but for some reason now he was coming back to the car.

Baxter had remembered Dan's gun was in his glove compartment. Running away was the smarter thing. He should leave. He should save himself. Something inside him told him to go back, though. Go back, save everyone.

Perhaps too late, considering Brie's screams had already stopped, but maybe he could save himself—and the others—if he got to it.

He made it to the driver's side door and thanked God it was unlocked. He dove across the interior of the car, reaching for the glove compartment. He got it open and looked out the window as he fumbled for the gun, but the masked man was no longer at the passenger side.

Oh fuck.

Looking over his shoulder, he found the enormous man standing behind him. He'd sheathed the machete and instead had a knife in his hands.

Baxter reached for the gun again inside the glove compartment, keeping his eyes on the masked man.

The man grabbed him by the belt, and then pulled him out of the car like he was a bag of leaves. Never in his life did Baxter think he could be handled this way. The strength was inhuman.

Baxter hit the ground outside the car, landing on his knees. He refused to go down without a fight, though. That was the difference between a regular person and an elite athlete like him—he had no quit in him. He didn't have the gun, but he wasn't a small guy, either.

He saw the man standing in front of him and exploded forward, slamming his shoulders into the man's knees.

The giant murderer stumbled backward, the knife flying out of his hands, but he kept his balance. He leaned forward to stabilize himself, and then dropped all his weight down on Baxter, trapping him under him.

Baxter felt like someone had just dropped a piano onto his back. Arms like tree trunks wrapped around his waist and he was picked up off the ground, lifted into the air. He found himself dangling upside down with his head five feet off the ground.

He kicked his legs in the air, trying to budge himself out of it, but it was useless. The man's hold was too strong.

He should have run. He should have saved himself…

Ignacio dropped down to his knees, slamming the guy headfirst into the ground as hard as he could. A series of pops and cracks thundered through the night as Baxter's spine collapsed into itself.

Ignacio felt him go limp in his arms, the feeling of a human becoming a corpse all too familiar to him. He let the body flop to the ground and stood up.

One of the neckbones snapping had been what killed him upon impact. The broken bone jutted out of the side of Baxter's neck, ripping through the skin like a demon claw slicked with blood.

Varias Caras searched the ground for his hunting knife. As he was doing this, his eyes fell on the discarded hockey mask a few inches from the corpse. It had come off the guy's neck at some point in their scuffle and now it lay there, faceup.

Ignacio walked over to it. There were a few droplets of blood sprinkled on it. Ignacio bent down and tapped it with one of his knuckles. It wasn't a Halloween mask. No, this was an actual piece of equipment meant to protect a goalie from sticks and pucks.

For a second, Ignacio considered wearing it, but then threw it off to the side. He didn't need it. He had his own masks.

11

"**I** FEEL LIKE HUD'S been gone a while," Tucker said.
   Him and Daphne had gotten tired of dancing and relocated to the kitchen to smoke another joint. They were sitting on the floor by the coolers, a plate filled with cheese and crackers between them.

"Isn't he taking a shit?"

"Yeah," Tucker said, then for once remembered Hudson was lactose intolerant. Maybe he'd had some cheese or something that was keeping him on the toilet.

"Should someone go check on him?"

Tucker passed the joint to her, raising his eyebrows. "I like how you said 'someone,' but you actually mean me."

"Whatever. He's your friend," Daphne laughed. She took a hit of the joint, then tried passing it back to him.

"Nah, I'm good," Tucker said, getting up. He straightened his robe out and then grabbed his headlamp from the kitchen counter. "I'm already high as fuck. Anyway, I'm gonna go find Hud."

Ignacio plunged the hunting knife into the work truck's tire and dragged it across the rubber, slashing it open.

He was taking the knife out of the tire when he heard the front door open. Someone else was coming out here. They were almost making this too easy.

Ignacio was crouched on the passenger side of the truck, hidden from view. He took the knife out of the tire and poked his head up above it to see who it was.

It was the guy in the black robe with the shaggy hair. The one who looked like the *bruja*. He'd seen the slashed tires on his vehicle and the other vehicles and was coming this way.

Ignacio got down on his stomach and crawled underneath the truck, just barely fitting underneath.

"What the fuck?" Tucker screamed, fixing the headlamp onto his head.

The work truck was listing to the side, the tires closest to him flat from slashes in the rubber. His vehicle was the only one completely in the glow of the outside lights, but something told him the other cars had been fucked with, too.

"Yo, who the fuck did this!" Tucker hollered into the night, as he made his way over to the truck.

He took the headlamp off his head as he crouched down to inspect the damage. He shined the light directly over the gash, realizing this hadn't been done by an animal. Couldn't have been. An animal claw wouldn't have left a single, clean slice like that.

Tucker felt the hairs on the back of his neck stand up. This wasn't a prank from Baxter or Hudson, neither of them would do something this extreme. He was sure of that.

Someone else had done it. Someone else was here with them.

Maybe someone he'd pissed off? Or some random redneck assholes? Maybe it was those Baker Brother assholes, even. Who knew? Either way, he wanted to kick someone's ass.

Tucker stood up and walked around to the other side of the vehicles to see if all the tires had been slashed. He saw all four of his had been, then pointed the headlamp toward the Mustang.

He shined the light through the windshield, trying to see if Brie and Baxter were in there and had seen anything. But the car was empty.

Then, he noticed the Mustang's broken side window.

"What the fuck…?" he thought, shining the light on the ground next to the vehicle.

He saw Brie Berk lying on the ground, surrounded by countless shards of glass twinkling underneath the light. Her face was split open like a sausage someone was about to stuff with cheese. A steady stream of blood oozed out from the wound.

"OH FUCK!" Tucker turned to run, knowing he was in danger, but felt someone grabbing onto his robe.

He looked down and saw the massive hand gripping the bottom of it from under the truck. Tucker kicked at the hand and jumped backward at the same time. He felt the toe of his shoe hit the hand, noting how it felt like a damn brick. At the same time, the cheap material his robe was made of tore away, freeing him from the person's grip.

The surprise of this made Tucker stumble. He fell back on his ass.

A giant wearing a fucked-up looking mask crawled out from underneath the truck using one hand. With his other hand, he held a big hunting knife.

Tucker was halfway up to his feet and turning when he felt the knife cut the back of his thigh. The sudden pain made him lose his balance again, making him spill forward.

"FUCK!" Tucker screamed. He threw his hands up to keep himself from faceplanting and used his arms to launch his momentum forward.

He started running, despite the explosion of pain in his leg. But there was no doubt, he was moving slower because of it. He looked over his shoulder, and saw the masked man was coming after him, knife readied.

Seeing him hurt, the monster of a man came more quickly.

Halfway to the veranda, Tucker bent down and grabbed a pumpkin from the walkway. He turned around and launched it through the air. The attacker saw it coming and blocked it with his forearm. The pumpkin splattered into several heavy pieces, showering him with its guts and juices.

Tucker bent down to pick up another, but by now the humongous man was within arm's length. He slashed the knife at Tucker, catching him in the arm grabbing a jack-o-lantern by the stem, cutting his forearm open.

Tucker let out a bloodcurdling scream, and then abandoned the idea of offense. He turned and started gunning it for the house, knowing deep down inside that he had no chance of getting away.

The only thing he could hope for now was that the others would hear his screams over the music and start running to save themselves.

He craned his neck to see where his attacker was. The motion made him dizzy, his vision wobbled left and right like he was on a boat in unsteady waters, but he could still make out what he was seeing. The masked man was coming after him, and he'd switched weapons.

The knife in his hands was now a machete with a blade about four times longer.

"Oh shit, oh fuck. Oh fuck, fuck, fuck!" Tucker screamed, trying to move faster, trying to ignore the pain in his injured leg.

It did him no good.

Varias Caras swung the machete at him, hacking him right under the ribs. Blood spurted out from the boy's side. The pain was too much. His wobbly legs gave out underneath him. He crashed onto the lawn, so close to the house now that one of his outstretched arms landed on the first step of the veranda.

Ignacio stood over top of him, raised the machete in the air, and hacked down at his arm. The blade struck the humerus and got stuck. Varias Caras pulled it out, and then drove the machete into the arm again. This time faster and harder. The blade went through the bone like it was a branch being bushwhacked, severing the limb off the body.

His latest victim yowled in pain, watching the open wound where his arm used to be spray blood all over the staircase. The music from inside was still too loud, and no one could hear him scream. Inches away from him, he saw the fingers on his severed arm twitching. It was an out-of-body experience, impossible for him to process that that was the same arm and hand he'd once used on a daily basis.

Varias Caras didn't give him much time to think about this, though, as he continued his onslaught.

He slashed the machete down wildly, not caring about where he struck. Each new cut speckling his hands and arms with fresh, hot blood. So much blood that the machete's handle was getting too slippery to hold onto.

He stopped and looked down at the kid's remains. His robe was shredded. There were at least twenty gaping cuts in his body, most of them concentrated on his back, crisscrossing every which way. Blood flowed out of them in dark red rivulets.

It had been an overkill. A beautiful overkill.

Varias Caras would've admired it longer, but there was more work to be done.

Two people remained. Two more kills, and then he could take Judy home with him.

12

"I HOPE YOU LOVEBIRDS don't mind me joining you," Daphne said, coming into the living area. Dan and Judy were sitting on the couch, drinking.

Since no one was dancing, Daphne took the liberty to turn down the music before settling into the loveseat. She put her head back and stared up at the cracks in the ceiling, high out of her mind.

"We don't mind at all," Judy said. It's not like they'd been doing anything except talking. Nothing had progressed between them beyond the kissing on the dancefloor. No reason not to have some company.

"Tuck's pissed no one else showed up," Daphne laughed.

"The plan was to keep it lowkey," Dan said.

"Yeah, but you know how Tuck is. This is too lowkey for him." Daphne wiggled her eyebrows at them. "But we're still having a good time, though, right.

"Oh stop." Judy laughed, blushing. Then she changed the subject. "Where'd everyone go anyway?"

"Brie and Baxter probably went to go bang somewhere," Daphne said, counting off on her fingers. "Hud went to go use the bathroom. And Tuck went to go check up on him to make sure he didn't fall into the toilet—"

Before she could finish the sentence, the lights went out in the house. On the mantel, the Bluetooth speaker made a series of quirky beeping sounds before powering off.

In a matter of seconds, the entire vibe in the manor changed. It went from a party spot back to feeling like an abandoned building in the middle of nowhere.

The only lighting in the living room was coming from the disco ball because it was battery powered. The whirring of it gyrating on its stand was the loudest sound in the place.

"What the fuck?" Daphne said.

"Something must've tripped," Dan said, setting his beer on the floor and standing up. "I fucking told Tucker this would happen."

"Sounds like the generator's still running, though?"

"Yeah." Dan said, walking over to the nearest window. He lifted it up. The dry, old wood squeaked as the window slid up the frame. He stepped back and waited for some of the dust that puffed out to clear before leaning through the window. He could see part of the port-a-potty behind a tree in the backyard, but no sign of either Hudson or Tucker.

"YO! Hud! Tucker! Can you guys hear me?" Dan called out, waiting for a response or any sign of them, really.

But nothing.

"YO! You guys out there!"

He waited again, but there was still no response.

He ducked back inside the house and turned to face the girls, who'd moved closer to him.

"You can't see them?" Judy asked.

"Nah. The generator's on the side of the house," Dan said, pointing toward the kitchen. "I'm gonna go see what's going on."

He reached into his pocket and pulled out his keys. There was a small flashlight attached to the ring.

"The hell is that thing going to do?" Daphne asked him.

"Hey, it's better than nothing." Dan shrugged, laughing.

"You want us to come with you?" Judy asked.

"Nah, that's alright," Dan said, shaking his head. "I'm going to take a shortcut."

He took his jacket off, folded it in half, and then put it over on the mantel next to the disco ball. Then he came back to the window and swung one of his legs out over the ledge.

"Guess you really are the brains of the group," Daphne scoffed.

Dan chuckled as he brought his other leg over the window and dropped outside. "Honestly, we weren't even sure these windows would open."

"Yeah, yeah," Daphne said. "Hurry up and get the power back on. I feel like dancing."

"Okay, okay! Be back in a bit!"

Inside the house, Daphne and Judy heard him calling out to the others as he made his way to the generator.

13

AS HE RACED past the port-a-potty, a thought crossed his mind. He should probably check to see if Hudson was there first. Dan pivoted on the soles of his shoes and went back to it.

Dan rapped his knuckles on the door. "Hud, you in there?"

No response.

He knocked on the door again, this time harder.

"Yo, you in there, man?" Dan said, leaning in toward the opening.

He kept his eyes low, just in case the door opened some more. If Hudson was in there, he didn't want to pop in on him while he was doing his thing.

Dan knocked on the door a third time—*third time's the charm, as they say.* The door smacked against the opening and bounced back, opening wide.

Wide enough that Dan could see inside of it.

"What the hell—?"

Hudson was kneeling on the ground with his head inside the toilet. A pool of blood had formed around his knees and was running down toward the door like fingers.

"Oh shit! Hud! Fuck, man!" Dan rushed inside, knowing his friend was dead but still feeling the need to try and help.

He was just bending down to grab Hud's shoulder and pull him out of the toilet, when he felt something hit him in the back of the head.

A web of lightning flashed behind his eyelids. He felt his legs go woozy, and then he was falling forward. The last thing he felt before losing consciousness was his face hitting Hudson's hairy costume.

Dan was going in and out of consciousness. Above him, the dark sky and all of its stars scrolled by. It was an odd thought given the predicament, but he realized how much brighter the stars looked out here than they did from Hilltown.

He was only vaguely aware of what was happening. The grass rustled underneath him. Someone was holding onto the back of his shirt...*and dragging me...*

Every now and again he felt a rock scraping against his skin. His head was pounding, and he could feel a knot beginning to form at the back of his skull. To make matters worse, something in the distance was roaring.

No. Not something. It was the generator. He could hear the subtle, mechanical ringing behind the roar now that his bearing seemed to be coming back. And it wasn't in the distance, either.

The person stopped dragging him, letting his upper body crash to the floor. Dan moved to get up. His body was weak, and sluggish, and wouldn't obey him.

"Stay!" the person shouted, and then stomped on his chest.

Dan fell back to the ground with a whuff of air, feeling like someone had just dropped a cement block on him. He grabbed at the boot flattening him on the ground and tried to move it, but it was useless. Not only was he still groggy and hurt, but it felt like the person's leg was bolted in place. There wasn't even the slightest give.

Varias Caras squatted down to pick up the cord that had been connecting the generator to the manor's electrical box. He'd used the machete to cut it in half, but since the generator was still running, the exposed wires at the end of it were very much alive.

He took the cord and wrapped it around the man's neck. The guy threw up limp hands, trying to claw his grip away, trying to fight him off.

"No, no!" Varias Caras said, swatting his hands away like he was disciplining a child.

He gave the cord a good yank, making it snug around his throat, but careful not to be choking him. It was only meant to serve as a leash and keep him in place if he managed to slip out from underneath him at some point.

Varias Caras grabbed the cord near the top with one hand, then with the other he pushed up on Dan's nose. Forcing his mouth open. Ignacio stepped off him and shoved the end of the cord into his mouth.

Electricity scattered in little feathery sparks inside the man's mouth. The smell of burning flesh followed, and smoke mixed with saliva. He watched in fascination as the tongue swelled. Ignacio shoved the cord deeper into his mouth. Steam started coming out of every orifice, ears, nose, even the corners of the eyes. His entire body was convulsing now, his limbs thrashing wildly.

The heat in his mouth built up so high, his cheeks started to expand from the pressure. The left one swelled up to about a three-inch bubble, then burst open. Blood shout out everywhere as the skin tore apart.

Ignacio held the cord in there for another five seconds and then pulled it out. A few sparks licked at the air as Ignacio let the cord fall to the wayside.

Besides the teeth, nothing in Dan's Sigler's mouth was distinguishable anymore. It was all just one charred mess in a gaping cavity. His eyeballs were rolled to the back of his skull.

The skin on his face and neck was burned bright red, with a few boils here and there, but most of the damage had been internal.

Varias Caras watched the body spasm for a few more seconds before going still. Just to be on the safe side, he kicked the corpse. There was no response.

There's still one more to go, Varias Caras said, shifting his focus.

"Then we get Judy..." Ignacio muttered, feeling how close he was.

He took a single step that brought him over to the generator. There was a big red switch on the side of it. Ignacio was told his whole life he was stupid, but even he understood what a switch like that meant. He toggled it from "ON" to "OFF."

The generator started powering off, quieting.

Now that there was silence, Ignacio could adjust his hearing to locate where Judy and the *bruja* were. He heard them talking... in that same room where they'd been dancing. He headed in that direction.

One more to go.

14

"**A**RE YOU GUYS like a thing now?" Daphne said, lounging close to Judy on the couch in the dark.

"No!" Judy said, blushing. "We just had one little kiss."

"I counted more than one," Daphne teased.

"We're not a 'thing,'" Judy argued, but she was smiling.

"Never took you for the jock-type, to be honest."

"He hasn't been a jock for like five years," Judy laughed.

"Oh, right." Daphne tucked her feet up under her. "Just like I haven't been a goth chick since high school."

Judy chuckled, then stood up. Their cellphones were lighting the way now.

"I wonder what's going on?" she said as she went over to the same window Dan had left open. She stuck her head out of it and listened for the others. Instead, what she heard was the generator slowing down.

"Huh…sounds like the generator is powering off."

Daphne was at her side, leaning against the wall with a newly lit cigarette in her hands. The end glowed bright in the gloom. "What in God's name are those dummies doing? We should probably go out there to make sure everything is okay."

"Probably," Judy said, bringing herself back into the house. "You wanna take Dan's shortcut?"

"Sure." Daphne said, sticking the cigarette in her mouth. She took her cape off and draped it over the ledge. And then, even though Judy was in front of the window, she took the initiative by grabbing onto the ledge. Judy moved back to give her space as she hopped out.

"Ta-da!" Daphne said dramatically, landing outside. She took a puff of her cigarette with one hand and pulled down on her dress with the other. "Did that look as finesse as it felt?"

Judy opened her mouth to answer her question, and then stopped.

There was someone standing in the shadows behind Daphne. The person was broad-shouldered, and Judy's first thought was that it was Baxter. But…no. This was someone else…

Then, the person took two steps closer to Daphne, emerging out of the shadows and into the moonlight. Judy saw he was wearing a mask that was rough and crudely painted. It was even white like Baxter's, but it was a completely different kind of mask.

This was a stranger. A huge, hulking stranger.

"Jude, you alright?" Daphne asked, seeing the odd look on her friend's face.

Judy felt her senses overloaded, her mind going haywire as it tried to figure out what was happening. She was too stunned to speak. Too scared to move. To wired to do anything but stare and hope that Daphne would turn around and see for herself and tell her this was someone she knew, nothing to worry about, nothing to be scared of.

But then her eyes darted down to the man's hands. They were slicked with blood. Some of it was fresh and bright. Most of it, however, was drying into a sticky crust on his skin. The effect much too realistic to be a Halloween stunt.

Judy pointed a shaking finger over Daphne's shoulder, and finally screamed.

Daphne looked, and saw the giant man standing behind her. She shrieked, and lunged for the window, scrambling to get back inside.

The monster of a man was faster, though. He wrapped one of his arms around her waist before she could get a good grip and pulled her back. Daphne screamed as her hands were ripped away from the window ledge, feeling the rough wood cutting into her hands.

Ignoring that pain, she twisted in his hold, and threw her fingers out at his face. She intended to rake his eyes out, but the mask defeated her attempt. Her fingernails just scratched along the leather instead.

Ignacio didn't let her get another attack in. He squeezed her harder, feeling her spine start to bend. At the same time, he took the knife out from his back pocket and stabbed her in the abdomen. The *bruja* had been bringing her arms back to try another series of scratches at him, but at feeling the knife slide into her flesh she dropped her hands down, grasping the knife handle.

Varias Caras dragged the knife inside of her, feeling the blade slicing through her guts as a torrent of blood poured out from the incision he was making. He watched her eyes roll to the back of her head and felt her crumple in his hold.

But unlike the other ones, there was no thrill to this kill. Nothing to revel in. Killing the *bruja* was just going through the last obstacle to get to Judy.

Ignacio pulled the knife out of her and threw her to the ground.

Judy was still at the window, staring at him. Her beautiful, blue eyes were wide open. Her pink lips twitched. He wasn't sure if it was because of the moonlight or not, but her skin was as pale as he'd ever seen it.

Ignacio stared back at her, thinking that even with a horrified expression on her face, she looked perfect.

She wanted to stay. She wanted to jump out of the window and go see if her friend was okay. But her mind and body weren't on the same page—raw, unadulterated fear the likes of which she'd never experienced took over. This was worse than her anxiety. This was real.

Judy pivoted on her heels and sprinted through the living room. The manor was so dark, she could hardly see where she was going. She was going to need a lot of luck if she was going to get out of here.

Halfway through the living room, she crashed into the loveseat. Her thighs hit the armrest. Judy yelled as she flipped over it. On the other side, she landed hard on her legs.

As awkward as the position was, she managed to push off and spring up to her feet.

Behind her, the monster who'd just killed her friend dropped inside the house. His heavy boots thudded against the wooden floor like someone had just dropped a set of dumbbells.

"Judy! JUDY!" he yelled out after her.

He knew her name. Somehow this damn maniac knew her name.

Judy continued running through the living room, getting lost down a stretch of darkness. From what she could remember of the layout of the place, that was where the hallway was.

She pumped her legs, going in that direction. Her arms outstretched in front of her like a zombie, feeling for anything that might be in her way. She didn't remember there being anything else that would trip her up but better safe than sorry.

Safe. The word seemed to have lost all meaning.

She entered the hallway and picked up the pace.

"Judy! Judy! Juddddddyyyy!" She heard him call after her.

Her name bounced off the walls and followed her through the hallway almost as if it, too, was chasing her.

15

There was a certain calmness to dying. A certain calmness in not having to worry about anything anymore, in knowing that nothing from this point forward mattered.

A certain peacefulness in accepting that the end was near.

Daphne heard Judy's name being called out. It was faint. Distant. May as well have been on another planet with how far away it sounded, but it was the name of her best friend. No doubt about it.

"Judy!"

There it was again. That unfamiliar, distant voice shouting. This time, it stirred something in her.

Daphne didn't realize it until she opened them, but her eyes had been closed this whole time. Ever since that masked man had attacked her.

Slashed my stomach open. That's where all this blood is coming from. Fuck.

She was holding her hands to her stomach, feeling the blood seeping through her fingers and spilling onto the grass. The pain from the slash was hot and throbbing, yet there was a certain coolness to where the autumn air was touching her insides.

The masked man had left her for dead. And she could feel herself close to it. She could feel herself knocking on death's door.

But he hadn't quite finished the job.

Daphne took one of her hands off her stomach, wiped it off as best as she could on a clean part of her dress, then unzipped her right-side dress pocket.

She pulled her cellphone out and unlocked the screen. Relief washed over her as she saw she had one bar of service. Daphne laid the phone down on the grass. Using one finger, she punched in 9-1-1.

"Hilltown Police Department. Office Gordon speaking, how can I help you?"

"Frosty Hollow Manor… Big guy with mask…attacked us. Need help…fuck, I think I'm dying."

"I'm sorry—what?"

"Send help…. Frosty Hollow Manor… I think he killed everyone here…" Daphne took the time to take a slow, stuttering breath. "I'm going… to try to go help… my friend. Before I… die."

Daphne hoped that would be enough to get her message across because she could hardly manage to string a sentence together. Her mind was using all its resources to fight against the pain in her abdomen.

Daphne planted her hand on the ground and pushed herself up to her feet. The wound exploded in pain. With the pain came lightheadedness and nausea. Daphne paused for a few seconds, taking the night air deep in her lungs.

Then she started trudging over to the window.

The dry grass hissed underneath her feet as she shuffled through it. She was trying to pick them up as little as possible, because she could feel parts of her intestines trying to come out from the gash. They slipped between the edges of it like eels. Daphne kept pushing them back inside of her, hoping she had enough life left in her to find Judy.

She had to get inside the house. Judy was still in there last she remembered. She needed her help.

Besides that, though, there was something she needed to get inside the manor. The switchblade in her dress pocket was serviceable as a weapon against a normal person, but from what she remembered of the guy who'd just attacked her, he was humongous.

She would need something bigger if she was going to have a fighting chance against him.

Daphne got to the ledge and paused again. It was going to take a lot of strength to get back inside, a lot of strength she wasn't quite sure she had, but she had to try.

Even if it meant dying, at least she would die knowing she tried her best.

Her cape was just barely still dangling on the ledge. Daphne grabbed it now and tied it around her stomach. She took in a deep breath, and then cinched it right around the wound. Her flesh squished. The bleeding slowed.

And it *hurt*.

"Fuck, fuck, fuck," she muttered as she exhaled slowly.

Here comes the hard part.

The cape was long enough that she could stick part of the knot into her mouth. She bit down on it, and then placed both hands on the ledge. She hauled herself up over the ledge and threw one of her legs over it. The splinters that were lodged in her palms went in deeper, but the pain was nothing in comparison to the wound in her abdomen. The fabric she was clamping down on muffled her yowls of pain as blood soaked into her makeshift bandage.

Daphne allowed herself another breather while the flash of pain eased but didn't go away, then continued. The second leg was easier. She planted the foot inside the house on the floor, and let it bear most of the weight as she brought the outside leg over the ledge.

Daphne leaned against the nearest wall, closing her eyes. The world felt like it was spinning around her. She wasn't sure she was going to be able to help Judy, but she knew the longer she just stood here doing nothing, the worse it would be.

She opened her eyes, waiting for her vision to adjust to the darkness of the house. Then Daphne started toward the fireplace set, which was only a few feet away from the window.

She grabbed the poker from the rack. It was made of solid metal and couldn't have weighed more than about three pounds, but in her condition it felt like it weighed a ton.

She was going to have to dig deep and muster the strength to bring it with her. The man who'd attacked her had been a giant sonofabitch, her switchblade was likely going to be as useful as a butter knife against him. She liked her odds with this weapon better.

Daphne held onto the fire poker with two hands, and let it drag across the floor behind her as she went after Judy, and her would-be killer.

If there was a God, she hoped he would answer her dying wish to make it in time.

16

"Hey, Lieutenant," Officer Gordon said, stepping into his office. "Does Frosty Hollow Manor mean anything to you?"

Lieutenant Rooney was in the middle of chowing down on some instant ramen. He put the fork with the noodles curled around it back into the cup and set it on the desk.

"Yeah. It's that abandoned house out on the west side of town. Why?"

"We just got a call from some girl," Officer Gordon explained. "Said some guy out there attacked her and her friends."

A pause, as the lieutenant considered things.

"You think it's just some prank?" Officer Gordon asked. "Bored kids on Halloween messing around?"

"Maybe, but with the way things have been going lately, it's probably best we go take a look," Lieutenant Rooney said, getting up. "Who's on?"

"DiLossi, Roos, Michaels, and Sanchez."

"Okay, grab Michaels. I'll take Sanchez. Get either Roos or DiLossi to work the phone." Lieutenant Rooney grabbed his uniform jacket off the back of the chair and put it on. Until they confirmed anything, he was going to treat this like an emergency.

17

THE VOICE. THERE was something strange about it, like it was too high-pitched to belong to a person that size.

Yet…at the same time, there was something familiar about it.

Judy reached the end of the hallway and came out into the foyer. The front door was open, letting some pale moonlight into the manor. If she could get to the car, she might be able to get out of here.

Except, she didn't have the keys on her. They were in her jacket, which she'd left on the back of the couch.

The realization hit her with a sense of dread, but she didn't break her stride. She continued running toward the door.

Once outside, she would have a better chance of escaping.

Judy made it to the veranda. Maybe it was all in her head, but the first inhale of fresh, October air filling her lungs seemed to give her a burst of energy.

She dared a look over her shoulder and saw that it didn't matter.

The masked man had caught up to her somehow. He leaped through the air at her like a jaguar pouncing on prey. His body stretched out, almost completely horizontal as he hurled through the air at her.

Judy screamed, and then she was in his hold.

His momentum sent them crashing into the railing and busting through the wooden spindles. They went flying off the edge and landed on the grass together.

Varias Caras continued to hold onto her as they tumbled on the ground. Dirt and clumps of grass flew through the air with each of their revolutions, until they stopped, with him on top.

He sat up, staring down at her. His dark eyes accentuated by the colorfulness of the strange mask on his face. Judy squirmed underneath him, but there was no space for her to move.

"You said…a while ago…that it was nice to take care of me…" Ignacio reached behind his mask and started undoing the laces, loosening up the mask. "Now, I want to take care of you…"

What are you doing? Varias Caras came awake. *You can't show her your face.*

"I can!" Ignacio screamed back.

Underneath him, Judy flinched. Confused as to what was going on even more.

"I can! I can!" he screamed again. "She can see! She can see! She *has* to see!"

Ignacio pulled the mask off his head, and let his hands drop to his side. He watched Judy's eyes swimming back and forth over his features. A ripple of excitement went through his body, raising gooseflesh on his arm.

She was looking at him. After all this time of having to hide from her, she was finally looking at him again. Looking at his face. Not Varias Caras, but Ignacio's face.

"You remember…?" Ignacio said, letting the mask fall out of his grip. "When you took care of me?"

The most horrifying part of the question was that she did.

There was no way she could've ever forgotten him.

The size of him. The wild, curly hair. The childlike demeanor of a man three times her size. She felt like a fool for failing to connect the dots before—maybe things had been happening too fast, and fear and adrenaline were clouding her judgment, but that wasn't the whole of it. Part of it was that she hadn't thought of this man in months, not since he was at the hospital.

All at once, everything made sense.

The man at the window hadn't been a nightmare. The feelings of being watched and followed hadn't just been in her head.

Her anxious mind had been trying to warn her. The nightmare was real.

Now here it was, pinning her to the ground, her friend's blood still fresh on his hands.

"You do remember." He smiled, nodded. Then he reached down and wrapped his hands around her throat. "Now, I take you to Ignacio's home."

18

DAPHNE STEPPED OUT of the house, leaning on the doorframe for support. The first thing she noticed was Tucker's dead body at the foot of the stairs. He was face down. His right arm was resting on the first two steps, severed from the rest of the body. His torso was hacked up, covered with gashes that made the wound in her stomach look like a papercut. And even though the robe he wore was black, it was obvious it was drenched with blood.

There was a point when she'd been walking through the house that she'd accepted the others were likely dead. That the masked man had killed them all, but actually seeing her brother's body like this was something she wasn't prepared for.

Her blood boiled with rage. She climbed down the veranda steps and crouched over her dead brother's body. Tears rolled down her eyes. She wiped at them with the back of her hand, smearing blood on her face in the process.

"Guess your idea was shit after all, huh, butthead?" she said to his corpse, crying harder.

There was a deep sadness swelling in her, but this was no time to mourn. Besides, she was sure she was going to join him soon, anyway.

Daphne stood up, wincing against the pain the movement caused, and cut her eyes over to the lawn.

She saw the masked man sitting on top of Judy just outside the outside lights.

Daphne dug deep and found a burst of energy—a reserve that seemed to have been stored for a situation like this very one.

Daphne clutched the fire poker in her hands. She didn't care about the bite of splinters in her palms. She didn't care that it stretched the edges of the grievous wound in her belly.

All she could see was her friend in danger, through a haze of red that colored her vision.

She stumbled across the lawn, readying to stab this fucking guy right through the heart.

Ignacio heard the footsteps from behind. Boots stomping on the dirt and brushing through the grass. The movement wasn't very fast, but the person was close. Ignacio had been too focused on Judy to notice the person approaching sooner.

He looked over his shoulder and saw the *bruja* thrusting the fire poker toward his chest.

In one quick motion, he let go of Judy's neck and jumped off to the side. The fire poker whizzed past him, missing him by only a few inches.

Realizing she missed, Daphne changed the trajectory of the poker, and swung it at him like a baseball bat as he was trying to get up to his feet. The iron clanged against the side of Ignacio's skull, sending him falling back on his ass.

"Come on!" Daphne said, hurrying over to Judy, who was already halfway up to her feet.

Judy turned, trying to figure out what was going on, and saw a blood-covered Daphne standing over her like a wounded angel. A short distance behind her, the massive man—Ignacio—was on the ground holding onto the side of his head.

Daphne came up to her side and grabbed her by the arm and started pulling her toward the trees. The man choking her had nearly put her out, but now that the grogginess was subsiding, she remembered what happened to Daphne and knew she had to do something to help them both.

As they trudged away, she took Daphne's arm and put it over her shoulder, so she could put her weight on her like a crutch and they could move faster.

"Are...are you okay to run?" Judy asked.

"Not fucking really," Daphne said, forcing a weak smile on her face. She looked over her shoulder.

"Hey, Jude." Daphne reached into the pocket of her dress. It was difficult to do because they were in the middle of running and everything agitated her wound, but she managed to take the switchblade out.

"Here," Daphne said, putting the switchblade in the waistband of Judy's skirt.

"What's this?"

"A last present from me—consider it payback for the bagel the other morning."

"Daph, save your energy—"

"Shut up," Daphne said. "Listen, Judy. I didn't tell you this enough, but I love you."

"I...I love you too, Daph." Judy said, perplexed.

"I want you to run," Daphne told her, cutting through her confusion. "Run as fast and as hard as you can, Judy."

"That's what we're doing," Judy said, feeling ridiculous for arguing.

"Pretty sure...I'm going to hell, so...we won't see each other in any afterlife."

"Daph, what are you—?"

"But I want you to know...you were my best friend in this life. Take care...of yourself, Jude." Daphne slipped her arm off Judy's shoulders, then twisted out of the one Judy had around her waist.. "If you try to come back for me, I'll never forgive you."

Judy stopped, wanting to argue, wanting to ask her friend what she was doing, but Daphne shoved her weakly, wanting her to go. Wanting her to save herself.

Before Judy could argue, it was too late.

The gargantuan man had recovered and was only a few paces behind them. Daphne turned and threw herself straight at him, fire poker in her hand like a spear.

Judy turned her head, feeling a fresh stream of tears coming to her eyes. She couldn't bear to watch whatever was about to happen. And she knew if she tried to help her, they would both die, making Daph's sacrifice vain.

Even at the very end, Daphne had used her stubbornness as a weapon. Or rather, more like a shield to help Judy get out of this alive. There was something almost cosmically funny about it.

She picked up the pace as she ran into the woods.

Deep down inside, Daphne knew she wasn't going to win. She was no match for this mammoth of a man. But if she could buy Judy enough time to escape, it would be worth it.

Her battle cry filled the night air as she came within range of the masked man and thrust the fire poker at him.

This time, though, he wasn't taken by surprise. He sidestepped the attack, moving a lot more cumbersome than usual because of the blow to his head, but he was still faster than the *bruja*.

He caught the fire poker in one of his hands and ripped it out of her grip. Daphne jumped at him, ringing her arms around his neck, and bit him in the face. She clenched her teeth down on his cheek.

He screamed as he pushed her back. Daphne spit the chunk of flesh between her teeth into his face.

Take that, fucker, she thought, tasting his blood in her mouth.

Then, before she had a chance to really react, he was thrusting the poker at her. The end of the poker pierced right through the wound already in her stomach.

Daphne dropped down to her knees. Her hands wrapped feebly around the iron rod, but the gesture was useless. It was in deep, and she didn't have anywhere near enough strength to get it out.

Ignacio reached down and pulled the fire poker out of her stomach. Then, he grabbed her by the hair. Her face was covered with blood—his blood—and she had something like a trace of a smile on her face.

Ignacio stabbed the poker into the middle of her forehead, driving it hard enough to go through the skull and pierce the front of her brain.

Sure that the job was done this time, Ignacio let gravity drop her corpse to the side.

He was furious that the *bruja* had delayed him getting to Judy. He cocked his head to the side, listening…and found her running through the trees, her steps frantic. He would have to rely on his hearing and what little moonlight there was to hunt her down, but that was okay.

Ignacio had more than enough experience hunting in the woods.

Stepping over the *bruja's* corpse, he sprinted into the trees.

19

JUDY FELT BRANCHES whipping at her, felt the terrain underneath her constantly change without warning, felt like her lungs had been replaced by fireballs in her chest.

Despite all that, she thought she was doing a good job running through these woods with what little light there was. She had no idea where she was running to. Her only plan was to put as much distance between herself and where she'd left Daphne.

The thought of Daphne came with a pang of guilt that would be more than that once this was all settled.

She would run until she couldn't run anymore. Or until she came out on the road and found a car or someone—anyone—that could help her.

Then, out of nowhere, she heard branches clattering. The sound of someone running through them. She couldn't pinpoint where it was coming from because sounds bounced off the trees and echoed with eerie intensity.

Judy looked over her shoulder. No one there.

To her left. Nothing.

On her right…

She saw the silhouette of someone running through the woods with her. The shape way too large to be Daphne. She felt a tug on her heart and swallowed against the golf ball of emotions forming in her throat.

"JUDY!" the monster called out.

Involuntarily, she turned her head to look at Ignacio just as a rock came hurtling out of the darkness. Judy screamed as it hit her in the ribs, knocking her off balance.

The assault wasn't over, though.

Another fist-sized rock came flying out from the trees. This time, it hit her closer to the hip, causing her to stumble. Her foot struck a root that was sticking up several inches from the ground. From the momentum, her ankle rolled underneath her. Lightning shot through the joint as she fell backward, crashing to the ground.

The particular spot she fell was populated by trees with very little leaves on them. Judy kicked her legs out, to try to get up to her feet, but her ankle kept giving out underneath her. Her flailing hands found an overhead branch and grabbed onto it to pull herself up.

Under the moonlight, she saw Ignacio striding out of the trees.

"Wh—why are you doing this?" she demanded in a quavering voice. "What do you want from me?"

She was up on her feet, but she knew there was no way she was going to be able to outrun him. She couldn't before, and now that her ankle was hurt, the chances were even slimmer.

"I just want to play," Ignacio said in a small voice, stepping closer.

This is a mistake, Ignacio! Varias Caras screamed in his head. He didn't care what el Monstro had to say. He'd promised Ignacio that Judy would be his as long as he fed him while they were in town. He'd done his part, now Varias Caras had to play nice.

Judy watched his massive hand reach out for her, going for her throat again. Without taking her eyes off his face she reached for the switchblade still clipped onto her skirt and pulled it out. In one fluid, seamless motion, she hit the release button and slashed it through the air.

Ignacio screamed as the switchblade sliced the top of his wrist open.

"No! No! Bad Barbie!" he yelled, hunching over, holding onto his fresh wound as it dripped blood all over the grass.

With shaking hands, Judy slashed at him again, this time cutting him on the shoulder.

Ignacio didn't just scream this time.

"NO!" he roared. Throwing his arms wide he came for her, intending to bearhug and tackle her to the ground.

Judy remained unflinching. She took a step forward and plunged the switchblade into his stomach, pushing it all the way until the blade was lost inside of him.

He didn't look hurt, but he stopped coming at her to look at what she had done.

Judy took this opportunity to try to pull the blade out, but it was harder than she thought it would be. She only managed a few centimeters before blood poured out from the wound all over her hand, making the handle slippery.

Judy was used to bodily fluids, given her profession, but not quite like this. She screamed and stepped back, leaving the knife where it was.

Ignacio stumbled, looking down at the switchblade stuck in his abdomen.

"No, no, no…" he muttered. This wasn't how it was supposed to happen.

I'm ending this, Varias Caras said, trying to wrest control…

"NO!" Ignacio screamed, louder this time. Louder because he could feel el Monstro start to take over his body.

There was nothing he could do to stop Varias Caras now. El Monstro was too angry. Too hungry.

One of his hands reached into his back pocket and took out his luchador mask. He slipped it over his head, leaving the ties loose.

It was loose, but just the same, Varias Caras took over.

He pulled the blade out of his stomach. Dropped it to the ground.

The machete rang as he unsheathed it from his back. Judy had taken the opportunity of him arguing with Ignacio to run. She was a few paces ahead now.

Not far enough to save herself.

Varias Caras chased after her. In only five strides, he was within reach of her. He grabbed her by the shoulder and spun her around.

Ignacio saw her blues eyes fill up with fear, moonlight reflecting in them. Her mouth turned into a perfect "O" but before she could scream, and before she could plead for her life, Varias Caras stabbed the machete through her stomach. The blade punctured through Judy's torso and came out of her back.

El Monstro gave Ignacio control back, so he could feel what he'd done.

He let go of the machete handle, horrified, and stepped back. Judy dropped down to her knees, reaching out into the air. Then, she fell forward.

There was a soft thud as the end of the machete's handle struck the ground and got stuck in the dirt. The machete propped her body up on a slant, but gravity started pushing her down the length of the blade. Blood blossomed out of her mouth, speckling the dead leaves on the ground.

Ignacio watched as she collapsed, dead.

"Why? Why? Why?" Ignacio screamed, crumpling to the ground.

She was making you weak, Ignacio. Look how she hurt you. Look how you bleed because you let your defenses down. Look what happened when you didn't let me protect you.

Ignacio picked his Barbie up and cradled her in his arms. She was still warm. The scent of the shampoo in her hair filled his nostrils—the smell of strawberries and cream. He rocked back and forth, squeezing her tight.

"I'm sorry...I'm sorry..." he said, putting his lips close to her ear. "I'm sorry... I could not control him... I'm sorry..."

Somewhere in the distance, far away still, Ignacio heard sirens.

He couldn't stay here much longer. The police were coming. He didn't know how they knew what had happened out here, but it didn't matter.

It felt like nothing mattered. Judy was dead.

Vamonos, Ignacio! Varias Caras urged.

He grabbed the handle of the machete and pulled it out of Judy's stomach. The sticky and wet sound it made as it slid out of her body disturbed Ignacio. Sent chills up his spine, even.

"I will still take care of you…" Ignacio said. "And we will see each other again… I promise."

He laid her faceup on the grass, then grabbed a fistful of her hair. It felt even better than he imagined it would.

But he couldn't waste any more time. He needed to get out of here. He would have plenty of time to appreciate her hair later.

He bunched the hair in his hand like he was trying to tie it in a ponytail and pulled up on her head, stretching her neck out. Raising the machete, bringing it down again, he severed her head at the neck.

Ignacio sheathed the machete to free his hands. Then, he grabbed her head by the temples and pulled on it. The sound of the last bits of skin and tendons ripping apart as he pulled the head completely off the body filled the night air.

Ignacio held the head up in the air, blood dripped out from the wound in the neck, drenching the ground. He could still feel her warmth, but he knew it wouldn't last forever.

The realization stung, but he had an idea on how to get close to her.

Ignacio tucked the severed head under his armpit and started moving. It was time to get far away from here.

AFTERMATH

1

AS SOON AS they arrived at the abandoned house, they knew this was no Halloween prank. The four dead bodies in front of the manor told them at least that much.

Lieutenant Rooney parked the cruiser next to the work truck. Officer Gordon pulled up next to him. The spinning red and blue lights from both cruisers joined the Halloween lights decorating the façade of Frosty Hollow Manor, giving the place some extra lightning.

The four police officers got out of the vehicles. Sanchez and Michaels had their guns drawn and the flashlights on.

"Jesus." Officer Gordon said, staring at the girl closest to them who'd had her face chopped in half. "Was this guy using a sword or some shit?"

"Sanchez, radio County. Tell them we have an emergency out here," Lieutenant Rooney ordered.

"Right. On it, sir." Officer Sanchez said, climbing back into the cruiser to do as instructed.

"Hey, Lieutenant…" Officer Gordon said, stepping closer to him and speaking in a whisper. As if he didn't want the others to overhear. "Does that vehicle belong to who I think it does…?"

James Rooney didn't have to look to know he was referring to the Honda Fit, and he didn't need Officer Gordon to tell

345

him who he thought it belonged to. They were both thinking the same thing.

"Let's not get ahead of ourselves, Gordon," he told the other officer.

Officer Gordon nodded. "You want us to start inspecting the area?"

"Yeah, you two search the perimeters. Me and Sanchez will go through the house once he gets back."

The officers acknowledged the order, then moved out with their guns drawn.

"Keep your eyes sharp!" he shouted after them.

The vibe in the air out here reminded him of how a street felt after a parade went through, or a music venue after the headlining band played their last song and left the stage. There was a certain calmness out here in Frosty Hollow Manor, the kind that was only perceptible in the aftermath of a noisy, chaotic event.

In this case, though, the calm was tainted with a hint of death.

2

DIANA'S HANDS WERE cramping up from grinding the porkchop bone against the steel wire. Sweat poured down her forehead. She reached up and wiped it off her brow before it could get in her eyes, then looked the bone over. The end of it was shaved down to a fine point like a sharpened pencil, thin enough to be inserted into the padlock.

A part of her wanted to celebrate, but she knew she wasn't quite out of the woods yet. She still had to pick the lock.

Diana moved along the cage over to the door. She stuck her arms through the wire, with the sawed down pork chop bone in her right hand. The bone went in easily, and Diana started jigging it around. Up, down, left, right, circular motions.

After a few minutes of this, her hands started to get clammy. She brought them back inside the cage, set the bone down on the floor and wiped her hands on the side of her pants, getting them as dry as she could.

Let's try this again. She grabbed the bone off the ground and put it inside the lock, this time with a little more vigor to try to get it deeper. But she was careful about it, because she knew if the bone snapped while inserted, it was over. There would be no getting out.

She wasn't sure if it was just in her head or not, but it felt like the bone went in a few extra centimeters than before. She moved it around, listening and feeling for any sign of something inside giving.

Come on, come on, she thought, gritting her teeth. *Just fucking open already.*

And then, almost as if her frustration had manifested it, she heard a clink inside. The shackle loosened, causing the padlock to shift ever so slightly in her grasp.

No way.

Diana tugged on the lock, dislodging the shackle from the body. She unhooked the lock from the door and then threw it at the ground as fast as she could—as if it might become sentient at any second and decide to relock itself. The lock clattered and bounced across the floor several feet away from the cage as Diana pushed the door open.

She stepped out of the enclosure, overwhelmed with a surreal joy. She'd been trapped here for days or weeks or maybe even months, fantasizing about this moment. And now here it was. The air almost felt fresher out here beyond the steel wire.

She took another moment to savor this small taste of freedom before bringing herself back to the reality of the situation. This was only the first step. Now, she had to find something to help her escape out of this hellhole.

3

HARVEY WAS SITTING at his desk, watching his favorite YouTube channel on the computer. It was a channel where a guy rebuilt totaled cars and made them drivable again, a lot like the project he had going on with the Bronco out in the garage.

A yawn escaped him. As he let it out and stretched, he glanced down at the time at the bottom of the monitor. It was past midnight and Ignacio hadn't come in for his shift yet.

Strange.

In the months he'd known the guy, he was always at least five-minutes early.

Oh, well. Everyone gets at least one, he thought, turning his attention back to the video.

Several minutes later, the Youtuber finished installing the doors on the '67 Corvette Stingray he was working on, and Ignacio still wasn't in.

This was getting stranger.

Harvey logged out of his YouTube account, clicked over onto the second tab that was open, and logged out of his email, too. He didn't know if this was necessary or not, but he always did this for security measures. He didn't want to get hacked—not that he really knew how that happened, but still.

He turned the monitor off, stood up, and went over to the coat rack by the front door. Harvey put his hat and jacket on, and then went outside.

His Buick was the only vehicle in the parking lot. No sign of Ignacio whatsoever.

Harvey got in his car, fired it up, and started driving down to his old home. This wasn't like Iggy. He probably just overslept his alarm or something, but just in case, Harvey wanted to swing by and make sure the big man was alright.

The only thing Diana found as she rummaged through the cabinets in the attic was a can opener, a roll of duct tape with an ambiguously colored fingerprint on it, a few folded-up tarps tucked into a dark corner, some gauze, and two plastic bowls. The hacksaw he'd used earlier, and any other tools that might've been here before, were nowhere to be found. He must only have kept them here temporarily or something.

Dismayed, Diana stepped back from the cabinets and surveyed the rest of her surroundings. There really wasn't much else up here besides the wooden table and the shelf with the canned goods.

Maybe the cans might help? Maybe I can use them like some sort of hammer to break the wood off the window?

Diana went over to the shelf. She grabbed the biggest can of diced tomatoes on the shelf and carried it over to the boarded-up window, measuring its weight in her hand.

It was hefty and wide. She just hoped it would be enough to break the wood.

Diana got to the window. She set her aim on the plank at the bottom, then cocked her arm back and swung it through the air, thinking of the tomato can as the head of a sledgehammer. The can struck the wood, leaving a deep dent in it, but it was nowhere near breaking it.

Diana inhaled, then loaded up to strike at the wood again. This was going to be a lot harder than she thought.

Harvey hadn't been to the house since Ignacio moved into it at the beginning of summer. The first thing that caught his eye was the brightness from the outside lights. He must've cleaned the light fixtures and replaced all the bulbs. A few moths and gnats danced in the pale glow surrounding the house.

The next thing Harvey noticed was that Ignacio's car wasn't in the driveway.

What in God's name?

Sure, it was Halloween, but Iggy didn't seem like the type of person to go out even on a night like this one.

He parked the Buick in the driveway, in the spot he'd once parked the family van—when he had a family—and got out. The tranquility of the isolation, the slight buzzing of the light fixtures, the crickets cheeping from their hiding places in the foliage, the trees in the yards rustling the last of their leaves together, it all came together and blasted Harvey with a melancholic nostalgia.

Before he could get too deep on these thoughts, a quick but heavy sound disturbed the night. It sounded like it'd come from up high somewhere. Harvey looked up at the single attic window, noticing for the first time that it was boarded up. The oddest thing was that the crisscrossing wooden planks were *inside* the house.

The sound came again.

Bang.

This time, he heard it clearer since he'd been expecting it. Something was definitely going on up there.

"Hey, uh, Iggy!" Harvey called out toward the window, feeling like his voice was swallowed by the night. "Ignacio! That you up there?"

Bangbangbang

Ignacio must've been working on the house—fixing up the window frame or something—and lost track of time. He'd probably just realized he was supposed to be at the junkyard in the middle of his task and was boarding up the window as a quick fix.

Makes sense.

It was October, after all, and Iggy wouldn't be home from work until morning. By then, the inside of the house would feel like a popsicle if the window wasn't sealed right and too much air was coming in.

Harvey went up on the porch. Ignacio couldn't hear him calling his name, but maybe he would hear him knock. He rapped his knuckles on the door, his knocking joining the continued bangs from upstairs.

"Hey, Iggy! It's Harvey!" he said.

The banging stopped. And then, it was replaced with a shrill scream. The scream was muffled, but it still made the hair on the back of Harvey's neck stand up. That wasn't Iggy. That sounded like a woman's voice.

"What in the..." Harvey muttered, stepping back on the porch.

He climbed down the stairs backward and brought his gaze up to the attic window.

The scream came again, joined by a rapid succession of bangs. Bangs that were frantic and meant to get attention. There was no confusing these sounds as someone doing carpentry this time.

Now that he wasn't under the awning, he could just make out the words that were being screamed. "UP HERE! HELP! HELP!"

Harvey felt frozen to the ground, barely able to process what was going on. The screaming and banging continued above him as he stared into the window. Then, a girl's face appeared near the bottom of the "X" the wooden planks were forming.

Seeing her made him snap out of his trance.

"HELP! HELP!" she screamed, louder now.

Harvey raced up the porch steps. He fidgeted in his pockets for his keys. Despite the fact that Ignacio had been living here the last few months, this was still his property, and Harvey always carried a spare key with him.

Harvey got to the front door. He unlocked it and pushed it open. The smell of death hit him, making him gag. He brought the collar of his jacket over his nose and took a few seconds to compose himself, swallowing against the urge to vomit several times.

Then, he found the light switch on the wall to his right and flicked them on. Illumination flooded the house, and Harvey saw that things were only going to get worse.

4

From the doorway, Harvey stared at the severed head of a woman, desiccated and withered, impaled onto a long wooden stake. It was set up on a cement base and sitting behind two tv trays fashioned into some sort of haphazard altar. There was a slew of candies, cookies, fake and real flowers, candles, and even a gaudy Jesus statue in one corner.

The expression on the dead woman's face was one of surprise and fear. Her mouth was agape, the skin on the forehead was wrinkled where it wasn't pockmarked, and the eyes were opened wide. It was an expression that suggested her death had been unexpected and brutal.

I wonder if this is how Dorothy felt when she peeked behind the wizard's curtain. The thought was as ridiculous as he felt, because he couldn't believe how wrong he'd been about Ignacio. It was like these last few months had been one big lie that was sitting right under his nose the whole time.

The screams from upstairs snapped him out of his thoughts. More bangs, only now the girl was hitting the door instead of the window.

"I'M IN THE ATTIC! THE DOOR IS RIGHT HERE!" she screamed, knocking harder.

"I'm coming!" Harvey shouted back to her.

But first, he needed to call the police and tell them what was going on. And to tell the sheriff how wrong he'd been. How very, very wrong he'd been.

As he ran for the attic stairs, he took his cellphone out of his pocket and dialed 9-1-1. The call connected as he came to the foot of the staircase. Harvey paused to catch his breath. He'd been moving faster than he realized, and it felt like all his old bones were rattling inside of him. His knees and his hips ached something fierce.

"Hilltown Police Department, DiLossi speaking."

"Officer DiLossi it's Harvey… have an emergency…" Harvey leaned against the wall.

"Okay, Harv. What's going on?"

"There's a girl…trapped…in the attic…"

"Okay, Harvey. Slow down. What attic? Your home?"

"My old home…you know the one?"

"No."

"It's…behind the junkyard. A half mile east…" Harvey told him.

"Okay, and this girl. Is she still alive?"

"Yes. I can hear her…trying to get out." Harvey held the phone up toward the door. Then, to the person on the other side he called, "I'm comin', just hang tight. Just talkin' to the police right now."

Harvey put the phone back on his ear.

"Don't do that," Officer DiLossi ordered. "Get out of the house and wait for the police."

"Like hell I'm doin' that. I think she's been up there for a while." His breath had come back to him by now. "He's the one who been kidnapping all them people."

"Who?"

"Ignacio. Tell the sheriff I was wronger than someone donating a three-dollar bill to a charity fund."

On the other line, Office DiLossi wasn't entirely sure what he was trying to say, but he wrote this down in a notepad to relay to the others.

"I'm gonna hang up and go get 'er now." Harvey announced, loud enough for the girl in the attic to hear. "If you ain't here yet, I'm driving her to the police station."

"I really wish you'd listen and—"

Harvey ended the call, stuck the phone in his pocket and hauled ass up the stairs.

Diana took a step back as the door swung open. A small, older man sweating underneath his little hat stood in front of her. The coverall he wore told her everything. It was the same kind Varias Caras wore.

The man looked shocked and horrified as he glanced past Diana and into the rest of the attic. His eyes fell on the bloodstained wooden table—the butcher's table, the cages, the boarded-up window, and of course, Ignacio's Barbie herself. Covered in filth, head shaved, clothes disheveled.

The awe disappeared from his face and twisted into panic.

"L-let's get…get you out…of here…little lady," he said, his lips quivering. He looked like he was ready to pass out from climbing up the stairs. So frail, so old, yet she looked at him like the savior that he was.

"Thank you, thank you, thank you," Diana said, grabbing onto his arm. She could have kissed this old man on the cheek if they had time to spare.

They didn't, so she went down the stairs with him as fast as he could manage.

"Left," the old man said behind her as they stepped off the staircase.

Diana could see the open front door down the hall, past the kitchen and a relatively empty living space. Beyond the porch, she could see the starry night sky, part of it obscured by tall trees out in front of the house. Underneath the funk of death, she caught the scent of the fresh autumn air.

But then a pair of headlights approaching through the darkness changed everything. Her stomach dropped.

Varias Caras was coming home.

5

CLOUDS HAD ROLLED over the moon, turning the woods darker than they had been even just a few minutes ago.

Officer Gordon shuffled forward through the trees. Despite the lieutenant's orders, he and Officer Michaels had let some distance gather between them to cover more ground. They were still close enough that each of them could hear dead leaves crunching underneath the other's boots.

Officer Gordon shone his flashlight into a clearing of trees and saw a pair of legs in black stockings. The stockings led up to a yellow, ruffled skirt. The front of the skirt had a long trail of blood running down it, and as he moved the light up toward the torso, he found the source.

The girl was lying on her back. She wore a black and yellow striped shirt that had a wide bloodstain on it, framed around a vertical slit in the middle of her chest that was easily six inches long.

Swallowing, his throat suddenly hot and sticky, he moved the light beam up some more, and his stomach turned to knots. She'd been decapitated, the end of her neck now just one massive gash. Severed tendons hung out of the wound like snapped cables. The skin around the opening was peeled back from the muscle. He hadn't seen anything like this since the last time he'd watched a buddy skin a deer.

A shallow pool of blood was soaking into the dirt, around the spot where her head would've been. Officer Gordon shined the light a few feet ahead, trying to locate the rest of her. He swept it left and right in the general area but didn't see anything except disturbed earth and more blood.

Conceding that he wasn't going to find the head, he brought the light back to the body. He swept the flashlight across the torso and saw the girl's hands were covered in blood. It was difficult to tell if it was from when her head had been severed or from something else, but it wasn't like it mattered much.

Officer Gordon grabbed the walkie clipped to his shirt, still keeping the light concentrated on the corpse.

"Hey Lieutenant? I found another body out in the woods. God, it's bad." He cleared his throat, trying to compose himself. "Someone killed these kids while they were in their Halloween costumes. They must've been having some kind of party out here."

"*I think killed is putting it lightly.*"

"Yeah…" Officer Gordon said, putting the flashlight up to the bloody stump of a neck again. "I think you're right about that. This was more like…a slaughter."

Officer Sanchez was huddled over the trunk of the cruiser. With rubber gloves on, he was going through the wallets they'd found with the people to try to identify the bodies.

He got to the last ID in the stack, and almost spit his gum out. Except for this one, he put the cards down on the vehicle. He looked up and past the cruiser, where Lieutenant Rooney was pacing back and forth talking on his walkie with the other two officers.

"Hey, Lieutenant," Officer Sanchez called out, but he didn't hear. He walked around to the front of the car and as he got to the lieutenant's side he said, "Sir, you need to see this."

"Okay, Gordon. Rendezvous back here." Lieutenant Rooney finished up his radio conversation with the guys in the woods and turned to Officer Sanchez. "What's up?"

"Look," Officer Sanchez said, shining his flashlight over the face on the card.

He saw the lieutenant read the name, then look at the picture, and it was like a ghost had just appeared in front of him.

No, more like a demon.

Lieutenant Rooney took the ID from him but kept it within the light. He stared at it, eyebrows knitted close, as if he could change the information if he concentrated enough. Officer Sanchez watched the lieutenant's Adam's apple bob up and down.

He stared at the picture some more, then glanced over at the name. He did this, over and over for a stretch of a few seconds, but the name on the ID stayed the same:

Judith Marie Olmos.

The sheriff's daughter.

"I don't think we found her body yet," Officer Sanchez offered. "I've been trying to match up the pictures with the corpses we found—despite the carnage, it's clear who's who. She's not here at the house, sir."

"They might've just found her," Lieutenant Rooney all but whispered, seemingly snapped out of the trance he'd been in. "There's another body. Out in the woods. Gordon and Michaels are coming back with pictures…but that might not be enough to say if it's her."

"Why do you say that?"

"Because…"The lieutenant's voice came out flat and somber as he spoke the next few words, the tone of someone trying to keep their emotions together. "Because the corpse they found in the woods has no head."

6

DIANA AND THE old man got to the porch as the Saturn pulled up in front of it, blocking them from escaping.

She was ready to climb over the side of the railing, and run, and never stop running, but the old man stopped at the top of the stairs.

"STOP! Ignacio, stop!" the old man was yelling, his face bright red, almost wheezing the words out. "I called the cops already! It's over!"

Varias Caras climbed out of the car. He stood next to the vehicle for a few seconds, staring up at Harvey, as if contemplating those words.

Stop…it's over…

"Come on!" Diana said, tugging on the old man's jacket.

He pulled his arm away from her, then reached into his jacket pocket for a set of keys. Without taking his eyes off Ignacio, he handed them over to Diana.

"Go on…get on out of here," he said. "I'm gonna make sure this bastard stays put until the cops come."

"Bad Boss! Bad Boss!" Ignacio suddenly shouted, reaching back into the Saturn. When he stood up again, he had the machete in his hand. He lifted it high and ran straight for the Buick.

Diana had started climbing over the porch railing to escape to the car, but now that she saw him wielding the weapon and going toward the vehicle, she stopped. She didn't want to be in the way of his wrath.

She stepped back again as she saw him hack at one of the back tires with the machete. Air rushed out of the gash in the rubber. The tire went flat almost immediately, making the car useless as an escape vehicle.

"Stop this!" Harvey yelled, trying to sound stern.

It didn't do anything to stop the huge hulking man with the blade in his hand.

Ignacio walked slowly back to the front of the porch and started coming up the steps.

"Stay where you are, Ignacio!" Harvey hollered. He reached into his jacket and pulled out a boxcutter. He popped the blade out a few inches and held it out in front of him. "Don't come any closer or I'll cut ya! I will! I promise!"

Harvey bounced on the balls of his feet. His heart felt like it was going three hundred beats a minute. The boxcutter was nothing compared to what his employee was carrying.

"Ignacio…is…not here," Varias Caras said to him, and then lunged forward.

Harvey swiped the knife at him, meaning only to keep him at bay.

Varias Caras sidestepped the cut and wrapped his arms around Harvey, restricting his arms from moving. Then, in a quick fluid motion, he turned around and tossed Harvey off the porch like a ragdoll.

Harvey went through the Saturn's windshield headfirst. Inside the vehicle, he landed on the backseat, in the fetal position, nearly unconscious, only half aware of what was going on.

Diana didn't need to see anymore. She sprinted over the railing and ran. Varias Caras saw her, but he wasn't worried. She didn't know this area. She didn't know she was running toward a narrow road that only led to more wilderness.

Still, there was a certain urgency to the situation, given that the cops had been called. His old Barbie was getting away. His new Barbie's head was on the front seat of his car. This was not good. He had to do something.

Varias Caras descended the porch steps. The interior of the Saturn was covered in tiny, sticky shards of glass. He took the machete out and used it to sweep most of them off the driver's seat before sliding in.

The windshield had a hole in the middle of it where Harvey had launched through it. The edges of it were still crumbling in tiny bits. The rest of the glass was a web of cracks that were going to make visibility difficult.

"I'm...sorry..." the Boss moaned from the backseat. "I'm sorry...I ever helped you..."

As much as Ignacio didn't want to kill the Boss, he knew he had to. He had betrayed him by calling the cops. Now, Varias Caras was going to make him pay.

He reached into the backseat and grabbed him by the hair.

"You'll...burn in Hell, Ignacio!" Harvey tried to yell, his voice hoarse. Ignacio's eyes were dark and blank. They were wild, like he'd never seen them before, almost like they didn't belong to the man he'd once considered his star employee. Like he was looking at someone else entirely.

Varias Caras pulled him to the front of the vehicle, and then slammed his face into the dashboard. A sound like someone had just stomped on a cardboard box filled the interior of the car as Harvey's nose smashed into his face.

Varias Caras slammed him into the dashboard a second time. This time the impact knocked two teeth out of Harvey's mouth. He spit them out as Varias Caras slammed him into the dashboard a third time, the blood spilling out of his mouth leaving behind an imprint.

He slammed his Boss's face a fourth time. A fifth time. Sixth. Seventh.

After the eighth time, the junkyard owner's face was a caved-in bloody mess to the point of unrecognizability. The dashboard was smeared with blood.

Varias Caras let him drop onto the center console, dead.

"I'm sorry, Boss," Ignacio said, patting him in the center of the back. He made a mental note to light a candle for him one night.

Then he put the car in drive and went after his Barbie.

He caught up to her on the lonely, narrow road to the side of the house. She was still running fast, but he could tell she was beginning to slow.

What he was about to do was going to be tricky. He didn't want to kill her. Varias Caras owed Ignacio a Barbie after killing Judy.

He needed to get her quickly.

At hearing the engine, Diana looked over her shoulder. She saw the Saturn coming up behind her. Screaming, she picked up the pace, but she couldn't outrun a car.

She screamed, and told herself to move faster, move faster, but then she felt the car clip her, taking her legs out from under her. She went tumbling over its hood, thrashing her hands at the air as if there would be anything to grab onto.

She crashed onto the ground with a heavy thud. Her shoulder and back took most of the impact, saving her from cracking open her skull. Even still, she was dizzy, and the wind had been knocked out of her. She was down, and she needed to run.

Get up! Get up! Come on! she told herself, trying to get her body to cooperate with her.

Get up!

Varias Caras parked the Saturn next to her. She was trying to get up, but he could tell she was hurt. He stood over her and put his boot on her chest and knocked her flat to the ground.

Diana grunted.

"You are…very lucky…" he said, as he dropped his knee down onto her stomach. With his weight pinning her, he wrapped both hands around her throat.

Diana reached up to grab at his arms, remembering how useless it'd been in the woods the first time she encountered this monster, and realizing how useless it was now.

She struggled and writhed underneath him, hoping that by some miracle she would be able to buck him off before the dark curtain in her peripherals closed all the way.

No such luck. Diana went unconscious.

7

"**Hey, Lieutenant? We just got a weird call from Harvey.**" Officer DiLossi's voice came through the speaker on James Rooney's walkie.

"Weird, how?"

"*He said he found a girl locked up in a house by the junkyard. His old home or something?*"

"Oh shit."

"*I told him to stay out of the house, but he insisted he was going in.*"

"Of course." Lieutenant Rooney had unhooked the walkie from his shirt pocket and was holding it in his hands. His grip tightened around it.

"*Here's the weird part.*"

"That's not it?"

"*He said a guy named Ignacio was behind it—and he said to tell the sheriff he was wrong about him. What's that mean?*"

James felt the wheels in his mind spinning. "Ignacio's one of Harvey's employees. The sheriff spoke to him the other day and…well, it doesn't matter right now."

He shifted his weight to his other leg and let out a small, deep sigh. It was all coming together. It felt like a jigsaw puzzle when it was almost complete—there were a few parts missing, but the bigger picture was becoming clearer.

"*What do you want us to do, Lieutenant?*"

"Take Roos with you and head over to the house to meet Harvey and the girl," the lieutenant said. "I'm guessing Harvey doesn't know where this Ignacio guy is, or he would've told us."

"*Yeah.*"

"We'll be heading back into town as soon as County shows up to hold the scene for us. Until then, keep me updated."

"*Will do.*"

"Lieutenant! Everything alright?" It was Officer Gordon asking from a few feet away.

The other policemen had gathered by one of the cruisers to look at the pictures of the crime scene after Gordon and Michaels returned from the woods. They were going over them, trying to matchup the bodies with the IDs. Michaels was sitting on the hood of the vehicle, scribbling down notes.

"We've got trouble back in town," Lieutenant Rooney said. "I'm going to call the sheriff. I'll brief you guys in a moment."

Lieutenant Rooney stepped away further from the group as he hooked the walkie back onto his shirt. He reached into his jacket pocket and took out his cellphone. His personal one, not his HPD issued phone.

Swallowing back his anger and mounting grief, he hit 2 on his speed dial. The screen read: **Calling Greg Olmos.**

8

GNACIO ONLY GRABBED what he needed from the house. A few masks, a box of sewing supplies, a first-aid kit, some clothes, and a blanket in case it got cold. And of course, Mamá's head.

As he was coming out of the house, with a bag slung over his shoulder and Mamá's head tucked under his armpit, he heard police sirens in the distance.

"Have to hurry…have to hurry!" He took the porch steps two at a time to get to his car.

The stake wasn't going to fit in the backseat, it was far too long. He could tell just by looking at it, but it would fit in the trunk. Ignacio went to the front of the car, hit the button to pop the trunk, and then went back to lift up the lid. The Barbie was lying inside in the fetal position, asleep. Near her feet, he had placed Judy's head.

"Sleepy, sleepy Barbie," he muttered, lying the stake with Mamá's head next to the two of them.

There was something nice about the thought that his Barbie was going to keep his two favorite women company.

He'd wanted to tie her up, but there just wasn't any time. Once he got far away enough from this place, he would pull over and restrain her somehow, just to be safe. But for right now, since she was still sleeping, he trusted it would be okay.

He closed the trunk, and went to get behind the wheel, but then he remembered one more thing he'd forgotten. It was inside, in his closet, hidden at the back.

Ignacio ran back into the house, to his bedroom, throwing open the closet and grabbing the steel case for his chainsaw. Couldn't forget this.

He had to go, go, go. There was still one more stop to make before he could leave this town behind.

9

"**I**'M SORRY, SHERIFF," Lieutenant Rooney said through the receiver, finishing telling him about the body they found in the woods, about the possibility that it was his daughter.

"I-I need a moment. I'll talk to you in a bit," Sheriff Olmos said, hanging up the cell phone.

He was outside of the bedroom, but could hear his wife stirring awake, the sheets rustling as she got out of bed. It must've been his wife's intuition or something, because she'd been asleep the whole time he'd been on the phone, until now. Until the biggest moment of distress.

Sharon came out of the room, fixing her robe. The lights were off in the hallway, but she didn't really need to see her husband to know something was wrong.

"Greg? What's going on?" she asked.

"There's an emergency," he said, brushing past her and going through the open bedroom door. Sharon shadowed him as he went over to his closet. "I have to go."

"Where?"

"Somewhere."

"What do you mean *somewhere*?" More alarmed than before, she moved closer to him and put a hand on his shoulder.

"It's policework, Sharon," he told her, trying to sound stern to hide the shakiness in his voice.

"Greg…" Sharon took her hand off his shoulder and put it up to her chest. It took her a second to find her composure. She knew he was hiding something, and she had a feeling she knew what it was about. "Greg, did something happen to Judy?"

He turned to her. Their eyes met, and he found he couldn't bring himself to lie. Couldn't even talk. Instead, he slumped to the floor with his face buried in his hands.

Sharon watched her husband cry harder than she'd ever seen in their twenty-five years of being together.

The sheriff of Hilltown, the utmost authority, the one who carried the safety of the public on his shoulders, the bedrock of their family, the one who always kept it together when she couldn't, had broken into pieces. Sitting on the floor, with his pants half on, his shirt off, he cried so hard that his entire body trembled.

That was answer enough for her. Something had happened to their daughter. She didn't know what, but she knew her mind was going to the worst place.

Still. She had to stay strong. For now.

For him.

Sharon sat down on the floor next to Greg and buried her face in his shoulder. His skin was warm. She put her arms around him and squeezed him close.

A few minutes later, Greg Olmos found his composure. He took his hands off his face, found Sharon's hands and held them, then turned to face his wife.

She deserved to know the truth.

"Someone killed a bunch of people tonight. Out in an abandoned house. About forty-minutes from town." A pause. "Judy's car and ID were at the crime scene. But they're not sure if she's one of the victims…."

Sharon's eyes dropped down to the ground as tears started to flow out of them, but she still had some semblance of composure. She nodded, acknowledging that she understood what he was saying.

"I have to go, Sharon," he said, standing up.

"Where?"

"To the crime scene. The lieutenant is taking care of everything, but I need to see if it's her for myself."

She stood up with him, shaking her head. "I'm not understanding, Greg. How are they not sure if it's her?"

"I think you might not want the answer to that question."

"We're in this together," Sharon said, reaching out and grabbing his shoulders. "You tell me right now what he told you."

"The body…" Greg licked his lips. They were dry as cotton, and he looked away from her before he said, "It was found without a head."

Sharon let out a small gasp, and Greg was sure for a moment she was going to faint, but somehow, she held strong.

"There's a possibility it's not her," he promised, wanting it to be true. "It's possible it's just someone who looks like her and Judy is out there hiding in the woods."

"Yes," Sharon said, but she didn't sound convinced whatsoever.

She let go of his shoulders and let her hands drop to the side. "Did you call her yet?"

"No," Greg said. "I hung up with James and, well…"

"I'll call her," Sharon said. "Y-you finish getting dressed."

Greg nodded, and they kissed. It was a prolonged kiss. Maybe one that was a little too long given the situation, but it felt good. It felt like it would be the last time they ever felt any sort of affection, like the world was going to be a different place once this was all said and done.

Because deep down inside, they both knew it was their daughter that had been murdered out there.

10

"SHE DIDN'T PICK up." Sharon said from the kitchen table. She kept picking up the phone and putting it down, her hands trembling.

She kept hoping the phone would ring back and her daughter would tell her she was okay. It was awful, on some level, to wish that it were another young girl who'd been murdered out there. Because that meant wishing bad on another family, but Sharon didn't have the mental wherewithal to see it that way at the moment.

"I figured as much," Greg said, walking through the living room to the front door. He was in full uniform now, sheriff hat in hand. "I'll be back home as soon as I can. I'll let you know if I…if I find out anything."

"Greg," Sharon called out to him.

"Yeah?"

"B-be careful, okay?"

"I will," Greg said, putting his hand on the knob. He looked over his shoulder and looked into those blue eyes he'd fallen in love with the first time he saw them thirty years ago. "I promise. I love you. I'll…I'll see you soon."

"I love you too, Greg," Sharon said.

He twisted the doorknob, pushed the door open, and stepped out into the night. The door slammed closed behind him. He knew that as soon as he was gone, when she didn't have to be strong for him, Sharon would begin to cry uncontrollably.

But he couldn't let that thought shake him. Duty called. The mental transformation from Greg Olmos to the sheriff of Hilltown was already happening.

For the next few hours, he would have to keep it together. The whole town would be counting on him to figure out what was going on. And there were family members of the other victims he would need answers for. Family members who deserved the same closure he wanted for himself.

It started to drizzle as he strode down the driveway toward his cruiser, so he put the sheriff hat on his head. He couldn't help but notice how much heavier the uniform felt tonight.

Inside the police car, Sheriff Olmos took his cell phone out and called the lieutenant. James had told him there was more to this, but he hadn't been ready to hear it yet.

Well, he wasn't sure if he was ready or not, but he couldn't think of anything worse than the possibility that Judy was dead. And until he saw her body in person, that was how he was going to think of it—that his daughter was still alive. It was the only way he was going to be able to function properly.

The phone rang three times before the lieutenant answered.

"Sheriff?" Lieutenant Rooney answered. He sounded thrown off, like he wasn't expecting to hear back so soon. "How are you holding up?"

"I've had better nights," Sheriff Olmos said, fidgeting in his seat. "Now. What was the other stuff you had to tell me?"

"Are you sure you're good for this, Sheriff?"

"Don't make me ask again."

"Right. Harvey called the station. He said he found a girl trapped in an attic at his old home. I've got Roos and DiLossi heading over there now," Lieutenant Rooney informed him.

"Where is Harvey now?"

"Last we heard from him he was going inside to let the girl out. He had a message for you, Sheriff."

"What's that?"

"You know that guy you interviewed at the junkyard?"

"Yeah."

"Harvey said to tell you he was wrong about him."

"Fuckin' A," Sheriff Olmos swore, slamming his fist against the side of the steering wheel.

"It's all connected, isn't it Sheriff? The Baker Brothers' disappearances, the kidnappings, the massacre here at the manor…"

"Most likely, James," He felt his skin turn cold at the lieutenant's choice of words.

The massacre.

"Sheriff, the County's units just showed up. I'm going to go brief them on what happened."

"Okay, James. Keep me posted."

"Where will you be?"

"I'm going to meet up with Officer DiLossi and Officer Roos." Sheriff Olmos said. This new information had changed his M.O. entirely. If there was a chance to catch this bastard, he was going to take it. Thoughts of revenge were fueling him now. "I'll…I'll identify Judy's body when it's at the morgue."

"Okay, Sheriff. Just…be safe, okay? Remember, Sharon is still waiting for you back home."

"Yeah," he said, looking over at his house through the rain, unsure if it would ever feel like a home again. "I will, James."

"See you soon, Greg."

11

Varias Caras stopped the Saturn in front of the garage. He climbed out of the vehicle and went over to open it.

The Boss's white Bronco, his "fixer-upper" as he'd been calling it, was in there, ready to be driven. Ready to help Ignacio escape out of this place.

The key was in the ignition where the Boss always left it, shining silver from the light from a nearby lamppost. Ignacio slid into the driver seat and turned the key.

Dark smoke came out of the exhaust as the engine sputtered on. Ignacio put the headlights on, then drove the truck out of the garage over to the Saturn. He left the Bronco running and got out.

He opened the back passenger door closest to the truck and loaded everything in the Saturn into the Bronco. With that done, all he needed was to get the stuff out of the trunk.

He heard the sirens getting close, and closer still, and then two patrol cars rushed past the junkyard on the way to Harvey's house. Ignacio paused.

We have to hurry, Ignacio, Varias Caras urged.

"Si, si!" Ignacio responded.

375

The darkness that Diana had experienced in the attic was nothing compared to the pitch-black space she woke up in.

The smell of rotting flesh hit her nostrils.

For a second, she thought she was dead. She was sure what she was smelling was her own body turning into a corpse, and the conscious entity thinking these thoughts was her spirit or something like that.

It made no sense, but nothing was making any sense. The last thing she remembered was running down an empty street… *and then what?*

Varias Caras ran his car into me…

Then…he choked me…

As her mind started to clear up, her senses came back to her.

Above her, only a few inches from where she was lying, she heard the consistent, light drumming of raindrops splashing against a hard surface.

Yeah, there was no way this was some sort of afterlife.

Now that she was more aware, she felt something touching her elbow. Something cold to the touch and rubberlike. She wasn't sure what this was, but something told her this was the source of the awful smell in here. Diana moved away from it, and hit the end of the space she was confined in.

Her back touched metal. She was in a trunk. He'd put her in the trunk of the car.

That explained everything. The total darkness. The little amount of room. The vehicle wasn't moving, though. They were parked.

They must've reached their destination, meaning he would open the trunk to get her out eventually.

Sometime soon, probably. No, more than probably—most likely. It didn't make sense for him to keep her alive only to let her suffocate in here.

With these thoughts in mind, Diana started slapping her hands around the trunk, searching for anything she could use as a weapon. It was so dark she couldn't see anything at all, but she tried her best to avoid where the strange thing that had been touching her elbow was.

In the corner closest to her, she felt a bunch of rags piled up on top of each other. They were crumpled up. Parts of them felt crusty. *Blood*, she thought.

As much as she didn't want to touch them, she moved them to the side and felt around to see if anything was underneath them. A screwdriver, a wrench, anything of the sort.

Nothing.

Just as she was about to move and start exploring the other side of the trunk, she heard the latches disengage.

He was coming to get her.

She had to think quick.

She had no weapon, but the element of surprise was on her side. Diana moved herself over to where she thought the center of the truck was and curled herself up into a ball, bringing her knees as close to her chest as she could.

She was going to have to do this the old-fashioned way.

It would either work, or it would get her killed.

Varias Caras threw the trunk open, and before he could realize what was happening, Diana uncoiled her body like a spring suddenly released from pressure. She kicked him in the stomach with both legs as hard as she could, throwing her entire weight into the attack.

Taken by surprise, Ignacio grunted and stumbled backward.

Diana hopped out of the trunk before he could recover. As soon as she felt the ground under her shoes, she started sprinting.

It took Diana a second to figure out where she was, but the more she ran past the piles of old tires, scrap metal, and car parts, the more obvious it became that she was in a junkyard.

A maze-like junkyard, surrounded by chain-link fence that had barbed wire running over top of it. Climbing over it wasn't a viable plan unless she wanted to shred herself up in the process.

No, that wasn't an escape, but there had to be an exit in the fence somewhere…

Diana pumped her legs as fast as she could, wanting to peek over her shoulder to see if Varias Caras was on her ass already, but she didn't dare. The rain was coming down heavy now and turning the dirt on the ground into slippery, wet mud she was sure would take her feet out from under her if she stepped on it the wrong way.

She cut to the right, and nearly stopped when a few feet ahead she came to the heart of this labyrinth-like place. The piles of junk were even bigger and wider here and placed all about without any apparent rhyme or reason. She couldn't follow the fence anymore. It was blocked from her so now she had to go around and hope that it would come back into view.

Not like it mattered. There was no time to think. Diana picked an aisle between two junk walls at random and ran into it, hoping it would lead her out of here.

There was too much going on tonight. Between the rain, the sirens, the cuts to his body, and el Monstro trying to take full control, Ignacio hadn't thought to listen for the Barbie's heartbeat before opening the trunk.

You're being sloppy, Ignacio, Varias Caras scolded him.

Ignacio picked himself up off the ground.

He shook his head out, while at the same time pulling the rubber band out of his ponytail, letting loose his wild, curly hair.

Varias Caras used his super hearing to locate the Barbie. He heard her running through the junkyard, but she wasn't anywhere near the exits.

She was lost. Everyone got lost their first time through the junkyard.

It's as sure as the sun rising in the morning. He remembered the Boss saying that to him the first day on the job.

Ignacio had never gotten lost, though. Going through the junkyard had been easier than the woods back at the camp, and Ignacio had never gotten lost in those.

He could catch up to her, easy.

He went over to the trunk of the car, where the two heads were. The wind had pushed some rain inside the trunk, wetting them some. Ignacio had to protect them.

First, he brought the wooden stake with Mamá's head into the Bronco. Then, he put Judy's head on the floor in the back.

Varias Caras shifted his focus.

The urge to kill was growing with each second. Even though he'd already slaughtered numerous people tonight, it wasn't enough.

It never was.

El monstro's hunger was insatiable.

Varias Caras climbed into the Bronco, put it in drive, and headed for the Barbie.

Diana felt her lungs exhale the last of the breath she had. She couldn't run anymore, she had to stop. She leaned forward, resting against her knees and sucking in as much air as she could. Raindrops rolled into her mouth. It felt good, but she really wished she had a jug of water.

A few seconds passed. Her breath was returning to her, but she wasn't ready to run. Not yet.

Something told her she only had one more burst of energy. Once that ran out, that would be it for her. She would collapse to the ground, and she'd rather be out of this junkyard when that happened.

Diana scanned a few feet ahead of her. There was a small crevice in one of the walls of junk. The garbage just happened to be arranged in a way that the hood of a car protruded out over this gap like a makeshift awning. Diana shuffled over there and crawled into the space. Out of the rain, and out of the light.

Hopefully, this was a good enough spot to buy her some time.

She sat back against the wall. The jumble of junk wasn't comfortable in the slightest, but it felt good to have something supporting her weight. Diana closed her eyes.

She listened to the rain slowing down to a light drizzle. The drops barely making any noise as they plopped against the hood of the car hanging above her.

The growing quietness helped her to play all the events that led her here through her mind. One moment she'd been driving up for a job interview, the next some creepy brothers were trying to rape her, and then a huge guy had killed them and taken her into his nightmare toy attic. But the craziness hadn't stopped there, because now *this* was happening.

She was curled up inside a pile of junk that could come tumbling down and crush her to death at any moment, hiding from a crazed killer.

Diana opened her eyes. The lighting of this place was what she'd always imagined hell would look like. The orange glow from the lampposts were bright, but in a ghoulish way. In a way that made it seem like something in the vicinity was perpetually on fire.

She was starting to cool off, almost to the point of shivering. Her breath was coming back to her. The strength in her muscles returning. Diana took in a deep breath, ready to get moving, when she heard a car engine nearby.

The SUV drove past her hiding spot, its tires splashing water into the crevice. It was an old vehicle that looked like it'd been recently painted and had its tires replaced. A dark cloud of smoke escaped out from its rattling exhaust pipe.

She watched it, holding her breath, praying it would pass her by.

When it did, she breathed out, and thanked God that she would be safe here…

Then the truck stopped.

The driver side door opened. Someone stepped out of it, water splashing underneath the person's weight.

Diana knew it was Varias Caras without having to see him.

"Bad Barbies get broken… Bad Barbies get broken…" she heard him muttering as he marched over toward her.

Mud squished under his boots as he got closer to her.

"Bad Barbies get broken… Bad Barbies get broken…" he said again, repeating it like a mantra.

His shadow appeared in front of Diana, only a foot away from her hiding spot.

"Bad Barbies get broken…" he said, then he stopped walking. "*Hoy, te mueres.*"

12

INSIDE THE HOUSE, they split up. Officer DiLossi went to investigate the corner of the living area where there were some TV trays littered with a bunch of crap.

Meanwhile, Officer Roos went to the small kitchen on the opposite side.

Everything here seemed normal. A pot on the stovetop, a few wooden utensils in the sink, a wall with a set of different sized cutting boards, salt and pepper shakers in the shape of roosters, a wooden napkin holder on the counter.

Officer Roos walked through the kitchen, parallel to the small counter, until she got to the refrigerator. She pulled the door open.

The fridge was stuffed with packages of meat. It was so full she was surprised nothing had sprung out and hit her when she'd opened the door.

At a quick glance, the packages looked like what you'd find at a grocery store, just an assortment of meat on Styrofoam trays wrapped with cellophane. Some of the cuts looked like porkchops or tenderloins. A few of the packages had a dark pink, ground meat in them.

But then, what she saw at the bottom of the fridge changed everything. Taking up all the space was a human leg. It was bent at the knee so it could fit in the space, and in case there was any doubt that it came from a human, the foot was still attached and intact. Chunks of the thigh had been butchered off to the point where the bone was exposed.

Officer Roos took a step back, feeling her stomach lurching. She forced herself to take a second look through the fridge, though. It was like seeing the human leg opened her mind up to see the details in the other packages, because now she noticed the other human parts.

A package contained a tongue, another one some human ears. There were a few fingers from various different hands packaged together. A liver. A heart. She saw a package stuffed with eyeballs, and that was enough for her.

"Take a look at this." she said to Officer DiLossi, who was leaning close to the gaudy Jesus statue sitting on one of the TV trays. "I think we just found a bunch of the missing people."

Officer DiLossi looked across the house, confused. Officer Roos stepped to the side, holding the fridge door open so he could get a look at what was inside. He didn't really need to see the human parts to know what she meant. Seeing the meat packages was enough for it to click.

"Damn. This is some Hannibal Lecter type shit," he said, walking over to her.

"Yup. That's exactly what I was thinking." Officer Roos let the fridge door close, glad to have that hidden from view again.

"*Roos. DiLossi, it's Sheriff Olmos,*" the Sheriff's voice came through their walkies.

"Sheriff?" Officer Roos said into the walkie clipped to her shirt. "I thought you were taking the night off."

"*Things changed,*" he said. "*What's the update, did you make it to the house?*"

"We did," Roos informed him. "Uh. You know all those missing people, Sheriff?"

"*Yeah?*"

"I think they're in this guy's fridge."

Silence for a few beats. "*No signs of Harvey?*"

"His car's out front. One of the tires is slashed."

"*But no sign of him inside?*"

"We haven't checked the other rooms or upstairs."

"Okay, you do that. I'm heading to the junkyard to see if he's there. Keep me updated once you've swept the house, then come meet me there."

"Yes, sir," Officer Roos said.

13

Diana saw Varias Caras crouch down in front of her hiding spot.

"Found you!" he chirped.

Thrusting a hand into the space, he snatched the front of her shirt and dragged her out of the crevice in the junk.

Diana dug her heels into the mud, trying to keep her balance as she squirmed in his hold, but struggling was as useless as it always was with this guy.

Varias Caras lifted her up into the air, pivoted on his boots, and then slammed her into the hood of the Bronco. Diana kicked her legs, trying to hit him in the groin, but in the heat of the moment her aim was off.

He moved his hands to her throat and began squeezing.

It was different this time. There was something in his eyes. They weren't blank like usual. There was something behind them now. Something that hadn't been there even when he was killing those two guys in the woods. No, there was an intense rage in his eyes now.

This time, he meant to kill her.

Diana felt him squeeze her throat harder, his fingers getting tighter, and tighter. Her limbs started to go numb.

Just like before…only this time, she knew she wouldn't be waking up.

It was all over for her.

Unless I do something, she thought dimly, as black curtains began to close in on her vision.

Then, as if the universe was giving her a hint, the rain picked back up again. A few drops splashed against her forearm.

The windshield.

The moment the word entered her mind, she reached out with her right hand. She grabbed one of the windshield wipers, pulled it up vertically, then twisted it left and right. The plastic clip holding it in place on the arm snapped off.

With the wiper firm in her grasp, Diana arced her arm through the air and brought it toward Varias Caras' face. He saw it coming from the corner of his eye, and turned his head, but he was too slow.

The end of the wiper blade jabbed right into his eye. Diana pushed it in as hard as she could, feeling the eyeball pressing up into the back of the skull. Blood started to flow out from the socket. Varias Caras screamed in pain and took one hand off her throat.

Diana jammed the wiper blade in deeper, blood and ichor from the burst eyeball mixing with the rain flowing down her arm, and then all the pressure around her throat ceased.

Varias Caras fell back, shrieks of excruciating pain filling the night.

Diana took in a deep, gasping breath, feeling the cold October air rush oxygen up into her brain. She rolled over and fell off the side of the SUV.

She laid there, panting. Letting the blood flow back into her brain.

After a few seconds, she lifted her head up and looked around. Varias Caras was face down on the ground, holding a hand over his eye. The sound of his screams was loud in the driving rain.

A few feet away, Diana saw a chain hanging from the nearest junk wall. Part of the chain was looped around a car bumper. The other end dangled down almost to the ground. The chain was old and rusty, but still looked sturdy enough to her.

Diana planted her hands in front of her and crawled toward the chain. She didn't feel strong enough to stand yet. Grunting as she swam through nuts and bolts and glass and other bits of junk on the ground, she finally got to the wall.

The chain was slicked wet from the rain, and hard to grip, but she had an idea. Wrapping the end of the chain around her wrist several times she pulled on it as hard as she could, letting it bear all her weight until she could get her feet underneath her.

The chain came loose from the spot it was stuck in just as she got up to her feet. Diana leaned against the junk wall, the chain still wrapped around her wrist, so tight it felt like it was cutting her circulation off. But she took a moment to fill her lungs with air. The strength returning to her body with each breath.

Behind her, Varias Caras continued to shriek in pain, twisting around and beating the air with a fist, but she knew it wasn't over yet.

She still had to get as far away from him as possible. She began to unwind the chain, but then an idea came to her. It came from a dark part of her mind, a part she didn't know she had in her until now. Maybe she always had it.

Or maybe being trapped in that attic had changed her. Either way, the idea was taking hold of all her thoughts and emotions.

She held the chain in her hand, staring at it, thinking about the terror this monster with his skin masks had put her through. The dead guy he chopped up in front of her. The people he ate. The girl he'd kept before her, Madison Charleston.

If she ran, he might get up in the next ten minutes and kill some more people.

Unless she killed him first.

No one would ever be kept in a cage or chopped up and eaten by that monster again. It would be over. All she had to do was walk over a few feet and she could finish it…

Or she could run for her life.

Diana looked over at Varias Caras. He was on the ground still, writhing and yowling. Seeing him weakened like this gave her a sudden second burst of energy. She could do it.

Holding the chain with both hands, she slowly walked over to him.

Even in this vulnerable state, he was intimidating. His back and shoulders were enormous, he looked like a downed bull that might get up at any moment and gore her to death.

She pushed these thoughts away and took in a deep breath. Then she spread her legs and straddled his back.

He moved underneath her, but he was too hurt to do much of anything. Diana squeezed her knees against his sides to secure herself, then leaned forward.

His hands were still up on his face, so she fed the chain over his right arm. Then, she shifted her weight to the other side, reached over his left arm for the chain, and pulled it out the other side.

Varias Caras realized what she was doing and grabbed at the chain with one hand. But his focus was still on the agonizing pain of his injured eye, and keeping pressure there meant using one of his hands. He flailed and grabbed with his other.

Diana pinched her knees tighter and quickly tied the chain in front of her to secure it around his neck. Then she yanked both ends of the chain in opposite directions.

Ignacio felt the cold chain wrap around his throat. He felt his neck being pulled back as the Barbie tightened it around his neck. The links started to cut into his skin.

No te dejes Ignacio… No te dejes! Varias Caras hollered at him.

He kept trying to pull the chain away from his neck, to make space so he could keep breathing., but it was no use. The Barbie had sunk the chain in first. He couldn't scrabble his fingers into the links. It cut into his flesh, and crunched his windpipe…

I am going to die, he thought, as his weakening fingers slipped away from the chain.

Diana pulled on the chain so hard her knuckles were turning bright red. She'd felt him try to pry the chain loose, but then give up. She was winning. She was going to do it. She was going to avenge all of those that he'd killed and kidnapped before her.

Most of all, though, she wanted revenge for herself.

Throwing her head back, she let out a guttural war cry and pulled on the chain harder.

Underneath her, she felt him getting weaker and weaker with each second, but she knew if she let him breathe for even a second, that might be enough for him to get the best of her.

She mustered all the strength she had to continue to choke him.

Until finally, he went still.

She continued to hold onto the chain, feeling the links cutting into her palms. And then, a few seconds later, she felt him stop breathing.

Diana let go of the chain, and fell sideways, flopping into the dirt next to him. Fat, cold rain drops splashed against her face.

Her arms were sapped of energy, but she managed to get up to her feet. She stared down at Varias Caras. He laid there, a useless, gargantuan clump of meat.

It was done. It was finally over.

"Rest in peace, *maldito*."

Diana spat and turned away.

She started walking through the junkyard again. Somewhere in the distance, far away enough that she wasn't even sure if they were real or if she was hallucinating them, she saw red and blue lights flashing through the junkyard.

Somehow, someway, the cops were here. All she had to do now was follow the lights, and she would be free from this hell.

14

"STOP! HOLD IT right there!" Sheriff Olmos screamed out at the person. They were walking out of the junkyard toward the parking lot, obscured by shadows.

He aimed his gun, but then lowered it, realizing the person's frame was much too small to be Ignacio.

The woman put her hands up in the air, muttered something inaudible, and then dared two more steps that put her in the glow of the nearest lamppost. The iridescent light revealed a Hispanic girl with a shaved head and torn clothing.

Her face was covered in mud and nicks and scratches that were still bleeding. There were more cuts along her arms and legs. She stood there, staring at him, swaying back and forth, as if she were on a rocking boat. Her eyelids fluttered and closed.

Sheriff Olmos holstered his gun, and then moved in toward her. He swooped down and put his arms around her just as she started to fall.

"I've got you, sweetheart," he said, squeezing her close to him. "I've got you."

"He's dead," she whispered to him. "I killed him."

"Okay, okay. Just…just relax, sweetheart. You're okay now. Everything's okay." Sheriff Olmos tried to sound soothing, because he could hear the panic in her voice.

"No one has to worry about him anymore," she muttered as the sheriff walked her to his car.

"That's right, sweetheart. Including you." He said to her. Then into the walkie he said, "DiLossi, Roos, where are you?"

"We're still at the house… We found something in the attic, Sheriff," DiLossi responded. *"You need to see this."*

"I need you two over here quick," Sheriff Olmos told them, still walking with the girl. "There's trouble here at Harvey's junkyard. Hurry."

Diana Santos wasn't in as bad a shape as Sheriff Olmos thought. After a few sips of water, she was ready to talk. He felt too nerve-wracked by everything happening to sit down, so he was standing outside the cruiser. Diana was sitting, safe and comfortable, in the passenger seat.

She'd recounted everything to him, starting from when she'd gotten kidnapped and up until she choked Varias Caras—or Ignacio—with the chain.

Just as she was finishing, DiLossi and Roos arrived. DiLossi parked the cruiser next to the sheriff's vehicle and both officers hopped out at the same time.

"What's going on, bossman?" Officer DiLossi asked as they came up to his side.

Both officers glanced at the girl sitting in the car, and both assumed this was the girl Harvey had found trapped in the attic.

"Diana says she just killed our man—Ignacio," Sheriff Olmos told them. "But she doesn't know where it happened."

"I just followed the police lights to find my way out of the junkyard," Diana explained. "I had no idea where I was going at any point."

The sheriff nodded to her, then turned back to the officers. "I need you two to go in there and find the body. Radio back once you've located it."

"On it, sir," Officer Roos said.

"Keep your weapons drawn!" Sheriff Olmos called after them. "Just in case."

He watched them hurrying into the junkyard. Once they were out of earshot, he turned to Diana.

"You did good tonight, kid." Swallowing back a golf ball forming in his throat, he added, "Your mother will be…real proud of you. And incredibly happy to see you're alive."

"Thank you, Sheriff," Diana told him, putting her feet up on the seat. She hugged her knees close to her chest. "I-I can't wait to see her."

"I called an ambulance to get you to the hospital. You can call her from there, okay? Once we know everything is good. I don't think your mother needs any bad news along with the good news."

"Okay," Diana said, leaning back in the seat. She looked up at the night sky. The lights on the cruiser gave it an alternating blue and red hue, but even still, the stars never looked prettier.

For the first time since being kidnapped, Diana Santos allowed herself to be overcome with emotions. She buried her head between her knees and cried. Cried from joy, cried from the trauma, cried because she'd survived, cried because others hadn't survived.

But mostly, she cried because it felt good to finally let it out. Felt right, even.

15

THE CLOUDS ABOVE the junkyard got darker. Fat raindrops came down in rapid succession, plopping down and washing all over everything.

The water ran down Ignacio Calderon's still body in small rivulets.

His right arm twitched. Then his left arm stretched out and slapped the ground. Muddy water splashed up from the impact.

Ignacio turned his head, getting his face out of the ground. He could only see through one eye. The other eye was gone.. An endless void.

In the distance, thunder roared. Lightning cracked, turning everything in his monocular vision white for a few seconds.

Then, as it cleared, he saw a figure standing a few feet away from him.

The figure was bright. The same color as the flash from the lightning that had just passed. Ignacio could see the details of the clothes the person was wearing. Cowboy boots. Pressed slacks. Everything a monotonous white color.

Un fantasma, Ignacio thought. A *fantasma* that seemed… oddly familiar.

The figure came walking toward him, its feet moving with carefully paced strides, but the boots didn't quite touch the ground. The figure stopped, crouching over Ignacio, revealing its face to him.

"Pa…pa…?"

He had a pair of shades on his face—bright white like the rest—but Ignacio recognized him still. One hand was in the pocket of his pants.

"I know you're stronger than this, *mijo*," Papa said, taking the shades off. He hung them by an arm in the neckline of his shirt, and then looked into Ignacio's good eye.

"Papa…" Ignacio said. "I'm dying…"

"You know how to survive this," Arturo Calderon reached out and put his hand on Ignacio's head.

The cold rain running over Ignacio's head turned into the icy touch of his father's ghost.

"I do?"

"Yes, Ignacio. You just have to give him full control," Papa said, nodding. "You just have to let him out."

"Let him… out…" Ignacio moved his head in a way that was supposed to be a shake. "I do not understand…"

"El Monstro, Ignacio."

"Let out el Monstro?"

Papa's ghost nodded. "He will get you out of this."

Ignacio stirred. In his head, he could hear Varias Caras screaming.

Let me out! Let me out! LET ME OUT IGNACIO!

"He is screaming, Papa," Ignacio said.

Papa took his hand out of his pocket, holding onto a zippo lighter. Then, he reached into his shirt pocket and pulled out a loose cigarette.

"I told you one day you would have to do this," Papa said, lighting the cigarette and sticking it in his mouth. "Today is that day, *mijo. Hoy, te vuelves el monstro.*"

"El Monstro."

"See? I knew you'd understand, Ignacio," Papa said, ruffling his wet, dirty hair. "Mamá and I will be waiting for you."

"Waiting for… me…?"

"You know where." Papa took his hand off his head and stood up. He sucked on the cigarette, let smoke out into the air. "We will see you soon."

Another flash of lightning, and Papa's ghost was gone.

The pain, Ignacio… The pain… I can end it if you let me out, El Monstro said in his head.

"Bad things…bad things happen when I let you out…" Ignacio argued. "You killed Judy."

If you don't let me out, you will die here. And then you will never see her again. Don't you want to see her again? And Mamá?

"Yes!" Ignacio said. "I do."

Then let me out, and I will get us out of this. Let me out! Let me out! LET ME OUT!

Ignacio struck the ground with both palms, and for the first time in a very long time, he let el Monstro take full control.

Varias Caras pushed himself up to his feet. Ignacio's legs were wobbly. The Barbie had left him for dead, but she'd fallen short of killing him. She'd gotten closer than anyone ever had, though.

He took a second to find his center of gravity and then focused his hearing. Somewhere in the distance, he could hear two sets of feet walking through the junkyard, coming toward him. Further away, he could see the faint glow of police lights spinning in the night sky.

Now that the stronger of the two personalities had control, the night was going to be different.

Varias Caras trudged over to the Bronco where his weapons were.

16

OFFICER DiLossi AND Officer Roos had decided to split up. The junkyard was a lot bigger when you were in it than it seemed from the outside. Neither of them had ever been in here amongst all of the junk.

The rain was coming down heavy, making visibility even more difficult in the pockets of shadows between the glow from the lampposts. Not like there were many in the junkyard, or that these stretches were particularly long, but they were enough to make splitting up even more trepidatious than it felt.

"Britt, you find anything?" Officer DiLossi asked into his walkie.

Mud squished underneath his boots with each step. The rain drummed against the jumbles of junk surrounding him, making all sorts of sounds against the various materials.

"*No, nothing,*" Officer Roos radioed back. "*You?*"

Just as he was about to answer her question, he found a set of fresh footprints in the mud a few feet ahead of him. The trail started at the intersection where the aisle he was walking down crossed with another.

"Just found something," DiLossi told her, stepping closer to the intersection.

"*What?*"

"Footprints," DiLossi said. "I'm gonna shine my flashlight. Tell me if you can see it."

He pointed his flashlight straight up into the air and waved it around.

"*I see you,*" Officer Roos said. "*I'm heading your way.*"

"Okay. I'm going to follow the footprints."

Following the footprints, he turned down another aisle. At the end of his flashlight beam, he saw a white Bronco a few feet away, headlights facing toward him.

"Found something else," DiLossi radioed, stepping down the aisle, closer to the vehicle.

"*What now?*"

"An SUV. An old Bronco, I think," Officer DiLossi told her. He held his flashlight up in the air again. "How far are you from me?"

"*Not that far,*" Roos responded. "*As long as I don't get lost.*"

"Okay. I'm gonna get closer. Maybe it's nothing." He said, tightening his grip on the pistol. "Maybe it's just a car Harvey left out here or something."

"*Maybe.*"

Officer DiLossi stepped closer to the vehicle. He'd been a cop for fifteen years and been in some dangerous situations throughout his career, but given everything that'd been happening around Hilltown, he approached the vehicle with caution. He kept a firm grip on his pistol, finger on the trigger.

Closer now, he peeked through the Bronco's windshield. The front seats were empty. He shined his light, sweeping the beam across the floor. There was nothing there.

He shimmied down the side of the Bronco, keeping his light and gun concentrated inside. In the backseat closest to him, he saw an overstuffed knapsack, a duffle bag, and a medical kit. Just as he was thinking he wouldn't find anything here either, he pointed the flashlight beam downward and saw the severed head. Its blond hair turning silver in the light. The eyes stared back at him, begging for help that would never come.

"Oh fuck!" Officer DiLossi reached for the button to talk into the walkie and took a step back.

Unexpectedly, he felt himself smack into something. Something that felt solid and sturdy but had too much give to be a wall or a post.

Before he had a chance to properly process what it was or turn around, he felt someone grabbing onto his hand with the gun. Officer DiLossi turned on his heels to face the person and pulled on the trigger out of instinct. The bullet fired up into the air, nowhere near hitting his attacker.

Varias Caras wrenched his arm inward, rotating the shoulder until it broke. Officer DiLossi screamed and dropped the gun.

Still holding him by the arm, Varias Caras raised the hunting knife and stabbed it into the side of the policeman's neck. Officer DiLossi tried screaming, but he couldn't get the sound past the gout of blood that coughed out of his mouth.

Varias Caras pulled the knife out and drove it into the other side of Officer DiLossi's neck. He felt the policeman going limp in his hold and tossed him to the ground.

Officer DiLossi's legs kicked and twitched as his hands grabbed at the wounds in his neck. The blood squirting out squished through his fingers. He knew he would bleed out in a matter of seconds.

From the walkie clipped to the cop's shirt, Varias Caras could hear someone screaming.

Not too far from where he stood, he could hear footsteps approaching. It was the same person on the walkie. He knew this because the screams were the same.

Another cop.

It was time to get into position for the next victim.

"OH MY GOD! FUCK!" Officer Roos yelled, making her way to the downed officer. She hit the talk button on her walkie as she sprinted. "Sheriff! Officer down! Officer down!"

"What's going on, Roos?" The sheriff's voice crackled through the speaker.

She was close enough now to see that it was way too late to help Officer DiLossi. He was already a corpse. The wounds in his neck were deep, and there was a grotesque pool of blood mixing with the mud and rainwater forming around his head.

"He's still alive, Sheriff," Officer Roos said, shaking her head. "The suspect, I mean. The girl didn't kill him…. Oh my god… Cosmo is dead, Sheriff…"

"I'm heading your way now, Brittany. Shine your flashlight into the air so I can find you," Sheriff Olmos said, the panic and fear in his voice reflecting Officer Roos's own.

Officer Roos felt a shadow fall over her. She pivoted on her heels, ready to shoot whoever was standing behind her, but as she whirled around, she felt a blade go into her stomach.

The shock of the pain caused her to drop the gun. Officer Roos stared up at the huge man who had stabbed her—and was killing her.

Behind the mask, she saw he had only one eye. The other socket was filled with a gelatinous, bloody lump. Blood seeped out of it, streaking the right side of his mask, making it look like he was crying blood.

She noticed the rusted chain around his neck, and then the world turned black, and she felt herself falling, falling, falling…

Varias Caras caught her as she fell forward and took the knife out of her abdomen. He could hear her heart beating. It was faint. She would die from the blood loss soon. He would have to hurry if he wanted his plan to work out.

Varias Caras hoisted her up onto his shoulder and carried Officer Roos to the Bronco.

17

"Roos? ROOS!" Sheriff Olmos was grabbing onto the walkie so hard he felt he would shatter it. He knew it didn't matter how hard he jabbed the button to talk. Neither of the officers he sent in were going to respond.

"James!" he called to his lieutenant instead. "Where are you?"

"*We're ten minutes out,*" Lieutenant Rooney responded back.

"I've got an officer down—possibly two."

"*Yeah, I heard, Greg.*"

"I'm going in," the Sheriff said to him. "I'm leaving Diana Santos in my car. The doors are locked, you get to her fast as you can."

"*Greg, don't! We're almost there. Hold on a few.*"

The sheriff gritted his teeth. If he could find Roos…if he could save just one person tonight…

He clipped the walkie back onto his shirt, then banged on the window to get Diana Santos' attention. He'd been sitting in the cruiser with her, out of the rain, but had gotten out when Roos had radioed a few minutes ago. He didn't need her to hear how the nightmare wasn't over, even after everything she'd been through.

Diana looked at him through the glass, her eyes wide and glossy, dark thoughts swimming in them.

"I'm going into the junkyard," he said, talking over the rain pattering against the window. Just in case, he pointed to demonstrate where he was going.

Her expression changed, obviously terrified to be left alone. He understood, but there was no way around it. He was the only police officer here still standing, as far as he knew, and his people needed help. For now, Diana was safe. Other people needed him more.

"My lieutenant and another officer will be here soon," he told her. "Keep the window up and the doors locked at all times, okay?"

Diana nodded, huddling into herself as she reached out to press the lock button. The mechanism in all four doors clunked.

The sheriff nodded back to her.

Then, with his gun drawn and his mind set on murder, he headed into the junkyard.

Officer Roos awoke to the sound of her boots bouncing off a set of metal stairs. She was being dragged by the back of her shirt. The movement made the wound in her stomach flare with pain.

She reached up for the hand holding onto the back of her collar to try to pry the fingers off, but the grip was too strong. It was like the hand was fucking glued to her shirt or something. Even if she wasn't hurt, none of the strength from all the deadlifts and squats she did would have helped her here—this guy's strength was unmatched.

Superhuman, even.

Varias Caras reached the platform overlooking the feed port of the shredder. Dragging the policewoman behind him still, he went over to the control box and flipped the switch to "ON."

The shredder's engine came alive. The metal teeth in the feed port rotated, clinking and clanking.

Varias Caras dragged Officer Roos across the platform. He switched his grip from her collar to her throat, and then lifted her up into the air and over the railing.

Officer Roos kicked her legs and fidgeted with her hips to try to break loose. It was an exercise in futility.

"Bye-bye," Varias Caras said, and then threw her down the shaft.

She flipped through the air and landed inside the machine headfirst. The teeth grabbed at her ponytail and pulled her in.

Officer Roos screamed as her scalp was ripped off her head. The next second, the teeth clamped onto the top of her head, shattering her skull like it was an eggshell and grinding up her brain. At the same time the rest of her body had hit the feed port and the other sets of teeth latched onto her torso and tore through her flesh.

Varias Caras watched with fascination. He'd been fantasizing about what the machine would do to a human body ever since the Boss had shown him how to use it. And now, here it was.

It was even more beautiful than he could have imagined.

The metal teeth shredded through the policewoman's skin, sending sprays of blood and bits of flesh and other gore up into the air the way it had sent the shredded rubber when he'd destroyed the tires. He could hear her bones and cartilage snapping as the teeth latched onto those. The sounds were like music to his ears, and he wished he had time to watch the shredder destroy the whole body.

But he didn't. He'd only taken the time to do this because there was an exit out of the junkyard near the machine.

Varias Caras stared down at the torn-up body in the feed port for a few more seconds. The limbs had all been broken off from the torso at this point. Most of the policewoman's clothes and skin was ripped to shreds, nothing more than tattered scraps.

He walked over to the control box and shut the machine off. Over the sound of the motor slowing down and coming to a halt, he could hear more sirens somewhere in the distance.

More people were coming. A definite sign that he needed to get going.

Varias Caras descended the metal stairs two at a time.

Sheriff Olmos weaved in and out through the junk aisles. He was following the roaring of a machine somewhere inside the maze. The rain had subsided to a light drizzle, making it easier to hear exactly where it was located.

His heartrate was elevated by adrenaline as well as by the physical exertion of the pace he was running. This was as fast as he'd pushed his heart in years. He was hoping he wouldn't get a damn coronary before reaching the source of the noise.

He ran past Officer DiLossi's dead body. Out the corner of his eye, he saw all the blood, saw the lifelessness in a man he had called a friend, and knew he'd died an agonizing death.

Sheriff Olmos made a note to say a prayer for him if he made it out of here alive tonight. For now, though, he didn't let the sight slow him down.

Even though he could tell he was getting closer to where the machine was, the sounds were getting fainter. The machine was shutting down. Someone had turned it off.

Coming down the end of the aisle, he made a turn around the junk wall, putting himself in the open area where the machines were.

A few yards away, he saw an enormous man running. He was halfway to an old Bronco parked off to the left of him, by the big, blue machine.

The man turned to face him as Sheriff Olmos raised his gun to take aim. In the split second before he pulled the trigger, he noticed the blood-streaked mask on his face, saw the wet curly mane of hair on his head, the huge frame of his body, and had no doubt this was the man he'd questioned inside the breakroom.

Sheriff Olmos took the shot. The bullet whizzed by the top of the monstrous man's head, but missed. It struck the side of the tire shredder, instead.

He fired the gun again, aiming for another headshot. His hands were shaking in time to the beating of his heart.

Another miss.

Despite his size, the man was moving like a damn cat. He shot at him again, this time lower. All that body mass…he couldn't miss if he aimed for the body!

The bullet hit him this time, but it didn't do anything more than make the hulking brute stumble, just as he got to the Bronco, and slipped behind the car.

The sheriff shot at the windshield, hoping one of the rounds would hit the bastard and kill him by sheer luck.

Varias Caras appeared on the other side of the car, undamaged—and ran for the driver's door. It was a risky move because for a second or two he would be at a standstill, vulnerable. An easy target.

The sheriff shot at him two more times, emptying his clip. One of the bullets hit the top of the monster's shoulder, sending a spray of blood into the air. The other bullet missed him completely.

The sheriff dislodged the clip from his gun, threw it to the side, and began reloading with an extra clip from his belt.

This gave Varias Caras enough time to get inside the SUV. He started the Bronco, flicked the headlights on and then hit the accelerator.

The sheriff finished reloading the gun and looked up in time to see the vehicle moving away from him. He took aim at one of its back wheels and fired off three shots, but his trembling hands made him miss again.

Then, the Bronco suddenly stopped.

Bewildered, the sheriff froze.

What the hell…?

The Bronco came barreling toward him in reverse.

It was happening so fast, Sheriff Olmos barely had time to react, but he managed to pull himself together in time to jump to the side, while at the same time shooting the gun into the vehicle, hoping to get lucky and kill the guy.

Two of his shots hit the back window frame. The third one hit the passenger door, getting stuck in the metal.

Sheriff Olmos hit the ground. The Bronco tore past him, missing him by mere inches. Then crashed into the junk wall, the impact hard enough to crumple the vehicle's back bumper in on itself and dislodge a bunch of debris from the wall. The junk rained down on the vehicle, the metal making loud clinks as it thumped against it.

Sheriff Olmos started up to his feet, taking aim with the gun.

But before he could even take a shooting stance, something hit him in back of the head, right at the base of his skull. Stars exploded in his vision, and then he felt himself falling forward, going unconscious.

In the Bronco, Varias Caras was thrown forward. He was dizzy, but aware enough to put the vehicle in drive.

He needed to get out of here. Even though el monstro was in control now, and he was stronger than Ignacio, the body he possessed was still human.

He couldn't let it die.

Varias Caras hit the accelerator and sped through the junkyard. As he neared the fence he stomped even harder on the gas. The Bronco smashed through the exit gate in the chain-link fence.

He looked in the rearview mirror and saw the policeman lying on the ground. Unmoving. He'd missed him with the vehicle, but something had happened to him after. Varias Caras didn't know if he was dead or not and for a second considered turning around and finishing him off, but then decided against it.

It made no difference whether he was dead or alive.

Varias Caras was going to be long gone from this place either way.

18

"Sheriff... Sheriff, take it easy." the person crouching over him said.

With his eyes still closed, Sheriff Olmos threw his arms up to shove the person away.

"He's...getting away..." he said, opening his eyes to see the lieutenant in front of him.

Lieutenant Rooney had caught his arms and was holding them to Sheriff Olmos' side. "Glad to see your strength is coming back."

"Did you guys get him?" Sheriff Olmos asked frantically, trying to pick himself up.

"Easy, Sheriff," the lieutenant said, gently easing him back down to the ground. "We'll get you up, but we gotta do it slowly. You might've suffered a concussion."

Sheriff Olmos craned his neck to see what was going on around him. EMTs and police officers were walking through the junkyard. Some putting up caution tape, others marking specific spots and taking pictures. A pair of them caught his eye in particular because they were carrying a stretcher with a lumpy body bag.

Even in this groggy state, he figured the bag contained the remains of Officer Roos. The pit of his stomach turned cold as he remembered how poorly he'd failed them tonight.

"Tell me you got him," he all but begged the lieutenant.

"On three, Sheriff, and we'll get you up," James said, ignoring his question. "One… Two… Three…"

Sheriff Olmos felt himself being lifted, and he went along with it. Slow and with deliberation, they got him up to his feet. Officer Gordon appeared at his side, taking one arm and putting it around his shoulders to help stabilize him.

He didn't realize until now, when he was standing, how dizzy and lightheaded he was.

"Think you got cracked by that," Officer Gordon said, pointing to an unidentifiable engine part with a few specks of blood on it.

"You didn't catch him, did you? He got away, that bastard got away…" The sheriff heard his voice cracking, but he couldn't help it.

"We'll figure everything out eventually, Sheriff," Lieutenant Rooney told him, hoping that would be enough for now. "Let's just be glad tonight's over."

Greg Olmos shook his head, ignoring the pain it caused him. The lieutenant was wrong. Tonight wasn't over. It would never be over for him.

He'd failed everyone. His officers. Hilltown. Sharon. Himself. Most of all, he'd failed Judy.

For him, this nightmare on Halloween would never end.

EPILOGUE

They exited the Hilltown Diner with to-go coffees. It was a chilly afternoon in PA, so the warmth of the cups felt good against their hands.

"Thanks for lunch," James Rooney said. "It was nice getting together with you again, Greg."

They hadn't seen each other in weeks. Not since Judy's funeral.

"Nice seeing you, too," Greg Olmos replied, smiling at him. It was the first smile since Halloween that had felt real to him.

"Next time, it's my treat."

"I'll hold you to that."

A silence fell between them. They listened to a tree nearby swaying in the wind, the cool rush of air reminding them that winter was right around the corner.

"Hey, uh, I hope things get easier for you," James finally said.

All lunch long, they'd avoided talking about Judy's death, but Greg Olmos knew what he was referring to without him having to say it.

Easier? No. He knew it would never get easier. He knew the pain of his daughter having been murdered would last forever. That for as long as he lived, he would be wondering what that sick fuck did with her head. But he also knew if he said anything about that to James, he wouldn't be able to hold together the fragile bit of peace that he'd found for himself.

So instead, he took a sip of his coffee and then said, "Me too, James. Me too."

"I'll see you soon?"

"Hopefully."

"Looking forward to it."

"By the way, the badge looks good on you, Sheriff," Greg said, pointing with the hand holding the coffee cup, and giving him another smile.

"Thanks," Sheriff Rooney beamed. He looked down at the gleaming gold badge on his uniform. "I have big shoes to fill. Many great men wore it before me."

They chatted for maybe another minute, and then there were no more words. Sheriff James Rooney headed toward his cruiser.

Greg Olmos made his way to the Hilltown Cemetery.

As Greg came out of the flower shop, a thin girl jogged past him on the sidewalk. She was wearing a purple track suit and had her blond hair up in a bun. Something upbeat, a pop song of sorts, played loud enough through her earbuds that he could hear it.

The girl made him think of Judy.

She didn't really look much like his daughter, but nowadays, everything made him think of Judy. God, he missed her so much.

He got to the cemetery and walked down to where Judy's gravestone was. There was a pile of fresh flowers lying by it. People from the hospital, old high school friends, nursing school friends, high school teachers, maybe others, had all come into Hilltown over the weeks to bring her flowers when the news of her death began to spread.

Greg Olmos placed his bouquet of lilacs and baby's breath on top of the pile. He still couldn't really believe that she was dead. A part of him felt like she would come up from behind him at any moment, touch his shoulder, and ask why he was standing in front of a headstone with her name on it. She would wipe his tears away, then he would kiss her and hug her and never let go of her.

But of course, he knew that was silly.

He patted the dirt that his sweet, baby girl was buried underneath. It was late November now, so the dirt was cold and wet from the previous night's rain. Some of the surrounding grass even had frost on it this morning but he didn't care. This was as close as he could get to his daughter now.

He put a hand up to his face and wiped the tears from his eyes, then stood up straight. As he did that, he heard someone walking through the cemetery behind him, their steps rustling the grass.

Another poor soul coming to visit their dead relative or friend, he assumed—or maybe even someone who was here to visit Judy.

"Are you the sheriff of Hilltown?" the person asked, standing a few feet behind him.

"Not anymore," he answered, then pointed his thumb eastward. "The man you're looking for is likely at the police station."

"You're Greg Olmos, though, right?"

"Yeah, who's asking?" He turned around now and saw a girl in a black rainslicker standing behind him.

She had the hood up, hands in her pockets. Underneath the hood, he could see some locks of hair that were the color of moonlight, but most of her face was obscured.

"If you're Greg Olmos, then you're who I'm looking for," she stated.

"What are you? A journalist or something?"

The girl shifted on her feet. "Not quite."

"Then?"

"I'm someone who might be able to help you avenge your daughter's death," the girl said, gesturing toward Judy's grave.

He felt his walls coming up. He didn't need this. He didn't need crackpots making things worse, feeding off his grief. "Lady, I don't know what you're talking about."

"You guys never caught the guy who killed all those people on Halloween," the girl said. "Am I right?"

Greg Olmos didn't respond, he just stared back at her.

"My name is Noelle," she said, pulling her hood down. "A few months ago, that same cannibal attacked me and my friends out in the woods. He killed most of us. I'm one of the few survivors."

"Well, I'm certainly glad to hear you survived. I still think you want to tell this to the sheriff. Don't know what you think this has to do with me."

"I want you to help me kill him," she said, taking a step closer to him. "I think I might know where to find him. Mr. Olmos, have you ever heard of a place called Camp Slaughter?"

All Roads Lead Back to the Camp...

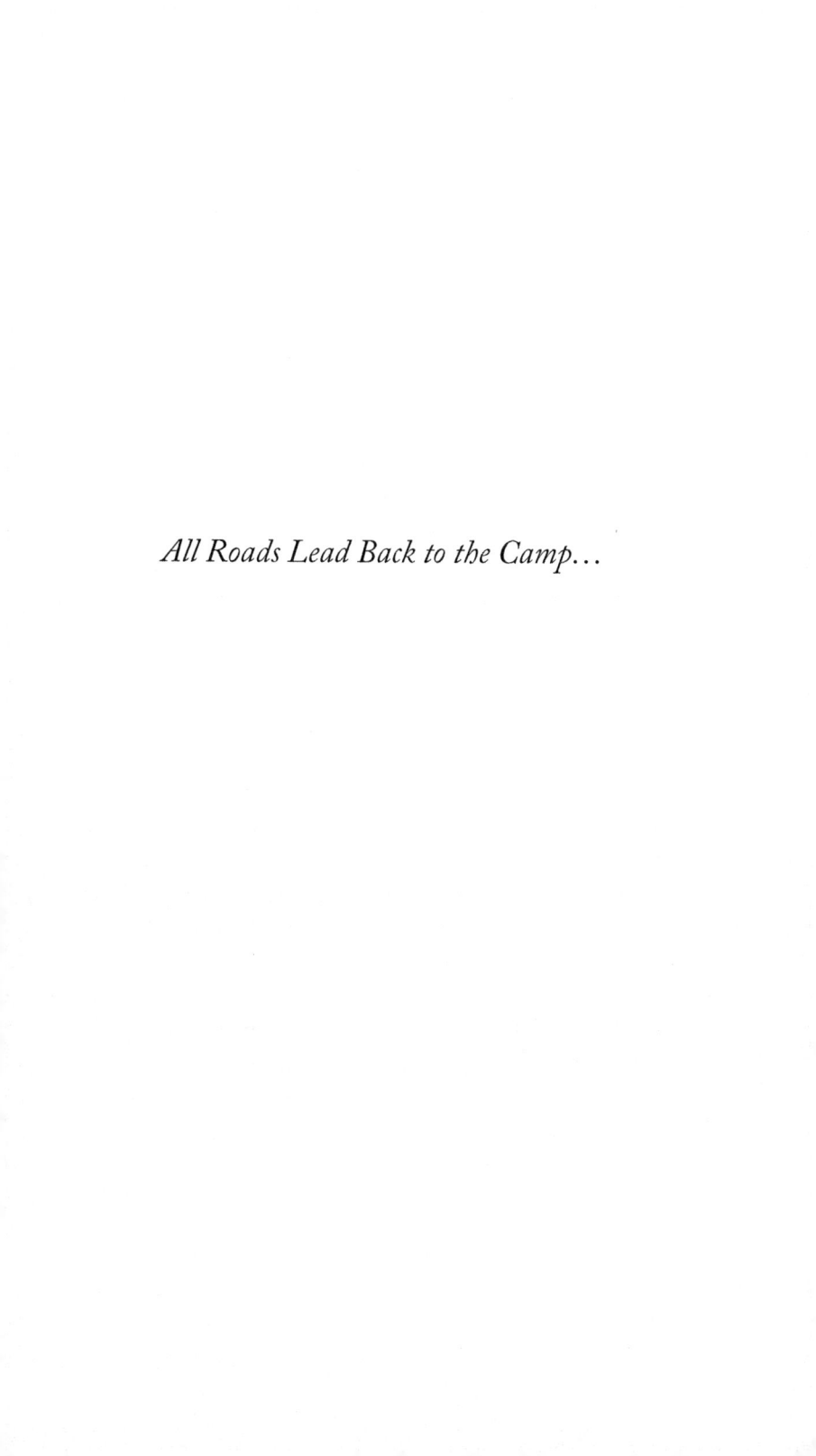

AFTERWORD

I know this book didn't end wrapped with a pretty bow. I hope if you expected that, you can see Diana's arc as the proper ending to this particular novel, and everything with the sheriff (including Judy's death) as a setup for the continuation of the series.

From the onset, this was always supposed to be a trilogy. So, with that said, this next book will be the ending you're looking for.

Just one more…and the legend will end.

You might even want to call this next one…

THE FINAL SLAUGHTER

Varias Caras will see you soon…

7/10/2022
S. Gomez

ACKNOWLEDGMENTS

Thanks to Cosmo and Brittany for letting me use you as characters and "slaughter" you in this book. I hope your characters' death scenes were as fun to read as they were to write!

Thanks to Jordaline and Ron, too. You guys know why, haha! Also, a very warm thank you to Heidi. Your help means the world to me.

And last but certainly not least, thanks to everyone who has read *Camp Slaughter* and this book. It truly means the world to me that people out there care enough to spend time with my stories. We have one more go with the monster Varias Caras, and I hope you're all coming along with me for the last one.